BLOOM

BLOOM

WIL McCARTHY

THE BALLANTINE PUBLISHING GROUP

NEW YORK

A Del Rey® Book
Published by The Ballantine Publishing Group

Copyright © 1998 by Wil McCarthy

http://www.randomhouse.com/delrey/

LIBRARY OF CONGRESS CATALOGING-IN-PUBLICATION DATA
McCarthy, Wil.
  Bloom / Wil McCarthy.—1st ed.
    p.   cm.
  "A Del Rey book"—T.p. verso.
  ISBN 0-345-40857-8 (alk. paper)
  I. Title.
PS3563.C337338B58   1998
813'.54—dc21   98-15435
                                                                   CIP

Manufactured in the United States of America
Book design by Mary A. Wirth

First Edition: September 1998

10   9   8   7   6   5   4   3   2   1

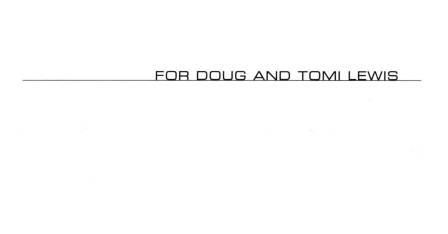

FOR DOUG AND TOMI LEWIS

ACKNOWLEDGMENTS

This book would never have existed without the influence of my agent, Shawna McCarthy, who doggedly persisted in mining my head on the theory that there must be gold in there somewhere; Stan Schmidt, who planted the nugget in a 1995 letter on nanotechnology; and Charles C. Ryan, who purchased the novelette from which this (quite different) story eventually grew.

I also owe a debt of thanks to Shelly Shapiro for being more editor than executive; to Kuo-Yu Liang, Tim Kochuba, Eleanor Lang, and the rest of the staff at Del Rey, who've gone well out of their way to make me feel at home; to Vernor Vinge, Greg Bear, Walter Jon Williams, and countless others for literary and conceptual influence; John Conway for his Game of Life; NCWW and the Edge Club for critical and moral support; Kathleen Ann Goonan and Linda Nagata for not pulling punches; and of course my wife, Cathy, who believed in me even when she shouldn't have.

BLOOM

SOMETIMES
THEY GET IN

This much we know: that the Innensburg bloom began with a single spore; that Immune response was sluggish and ineffective; that the first witness on the scene, one Holger Sanchez Mach, broke the nearest emergency glass, dropped two magnums and a witch's tit, and died. Did he suffer? Did it hurt? Conversion must have taken at least four seconds, and we can probably assume it started with the feet. These things usually do.

By the time the Response teams began arriving, the bloom was some ten meters across, and two meters high at the center—a

*fractal-jagged bubble of rainbow fog, class two threaded struc-
ture almost certainly visible to those unfortunate enough to be
standing within fecund radius when the fruiting bodies swelled
and popped. Twenty deaths followed almost immediately, and
another hundred in the minutes that followed.*

*There were cameras and instruments on the scene by this
time, windows on what can only seem to be separate events, each
holograph showing a different fleeing mob or collapsing building,
each soundtrack recording a different cacophony of whimpers and
death screams and jarringly irrelevant conversation. I personally
have collaged these scenes a dozen times or more, arranging the
panic this way and that way, over and over again in the hope
that some sense will emerge. But there is no sense in those first
few minutes, just the pettiness and blind, stamping fear of the
human animal stripped bare. And the heroism, yes; for me the
central image is that of Enrico Giselle, Tech Two, pushing his
smudged helmet and visor back on his forehead and shouting into
a voice phone, while the walls behind him froth and shimmer
and disintegrate.*

*"Class five! Class five! Drop two hundred and flush on my
command!"*

*At this point, finally, the city began to awaken. The Immu-
nity isolated samples of the invading mycorum, sequenced them,
added them to the catalog of known pathogens. Better late than
never, one supposes, but by this time the bloom outmassed the
city's Immune system by a factor of several million, and though
submicroscopic phages gathered at its sizzling interface, now
ropy with tendrils that sputtered outward in Escheresque whorls,
the growth was not visibly affected.*

*Fortunately, like all living things, technogenic organisms re-
quire energy to survive, and where the witch's tits had fallen or*

been hurled, pools of bitter cold had arrested the replication process. Not unusual, as any Response officer will tell you. And like organic lebenforms, mycora are also vulnerable to excess energy. Backpack UV lasers were proving effective weapons against the bloom, and soon the streets clanged with discarded chem spritzers and paraphage guns as bloomfighters concentrated on the things that worked.

High above the city, the cavern roof came alive with UV turrets of its own. Machine-guided and wary of the soft humans below, the beams swept back and forth, charring trenches through the rainbow mist, the living dust, the bloom of submicroscopic mycora still eating everything in their reach and converting it to more of themselves. And to other things, as well, a trillion microscopic construction projects all running in parallel, following whatever meaningless program the mycogene codes called out. By now the fecund zone was half a kilometer across, riddled with gaps and voids in the outer regions but much denser at its core, a thickening haze which already blocked the view from one side to the other. Up to four stories tall in places, higher than most of the surrounding buildings, and it had begun to take on structure as well—picks and urchins, mostly, standing out visibly in the haze, their prismatic spines lengthening more than fast enough for the human eye to see.

Some mycora eat lightly, sucking up building blocks like carbon and hydrogen while leaving the heavier elements alone, but this one was pulling the gold right off the streets, the steel right off the shingled walls, the zirconium right out of the window-panes. You've seen the pictures: a giant bite out of Innensburg's south side, gingerbread houses dissolving like a dream.

The UV lasers, while no doubt satisfying for those employing them, were if anything adding to the problem by throwing waste heat into the bloom, giving it that much more energy to work with, to feed on.

Finally, Innensburg's central processor sought permission from the mayor and city council to move to Final Alert. Permission was granted, the overhead lights and household power grid were shut off, the ladderdown reactors stopped, and the air system reconfigured to pipe through cooling radiators closer to the surface. The cold, the dark. How we humans hate these things, and how very much we need them!

Like all Jupiter's moons, like all the moons of the outer system, Ganymede's surface is cold enough to liquefy both oxygen and nitrogen, and while the spore-fouled air was not cooled quite that far, Innensburg's ground temperature quickly dropped below the freezing point of water, and then below that of carbon dioxide. A seconds-brief rain fell and froze. Mycoric replication slowed to a crawl. A sigh of mingled fear and relief went up all over the city, visible as columns of white steam in the flashlight beams of the Response. The emergency far from over, but now survivable, now something that could be dealt with in a reasoned, methodical manner.

Some thirty-one deaths were later attributed to the cold, to the darkness, to the lack of domestic power and computing, and though some of the families did attempt to bring suit against the authorities responsible, public and judicial outrage squashed the move before it had gotten very far. One hundred and eighty-seven deaths preceded the chilldown, after all, and most of Innensburg's fifty thousand residents came out of it with only minor injuries.

Throughout the Immunity, our problems are the same: so far from the places of our birth, so far from the sun's warm rays, so far from the lives we once expected to lead. Eaten by the My-

cosystem, those lives, and billions of others as well. And yet out here in the cold and dark we hang on, even thrive, because we're brave enough to believe we can. If the space around us is lousy with mycoric spores blown upward by solar wind, well, at least we can do what's necessary to keep them outside.

    I think the Honorable Klaus Pensbruck, in closing the book on Glazer v. Cholm, *speaks for us all with his immortal words, "Shut up, lady. We don't want to end up like the Earth."*

From *Innensburg and the Fear of Failure*
© 2101 by John Strasheim

DESTINATION WHERE?

That my first meeting with Vaclav Lottick went poorly goes without saying. The most powerful man in the solar system, yes, you can believe he had better things to do than exchange small talk with me. And yet, certain business can be conducted in no other way.

He looked up and smiled when his secretary, a quiet, efficient man, ushered me inside the office. Everything beige and cream and shiny, not quite sterile in appearance but compact, and clean. Very clean. The windows' light was from behind Lottick, highlighting every stray hair, and the desk lamp seemed designed to show off the lines in his face. A pale man, nearly bald, his rumpled smock no longer white. Even his zee-spec was an older model, blocky, folding his ears back, weighing on the bridge of his nose, leaving his features to sag that much more.

"John Strasheim, hi," he said, rising from his chair and extending a hand. "Thanks for coming on such short notice. You're a few minutes early, actually."

Shaking the proffered appendage, I shrugged. "Just eager to oblige, I guess. What can I—"

"Take a seat, then. Set to receive a flash?"

"Sure." Who wasn't?

His thick fingers danced in the space between us. My RECEIVING light went on, and the air before me came alive with information, image windows and text windows and schematic windows rastering in and then shrinking to icons as my spec compressed them in working memory. Too quick to see much in the way of detail. Pictures of blooms, I thought. Pictures of mycora. Well, what to expect from the Immunity's head of research?

I sat.

"I've seen your work," he said to me, his voice vaguely approving. "And read it. Funny, how nobody seems to be doing that sort of thing anymore."

"You're talking about *Innensburg*?"

He nodded. Behind the zee-spec, his eyes were bright green. "Yes, *Innensburg*. I survey your net channels from time to time, but it was that piece that really caught my eye. About as close as we have to a regional history, and plaintext was a . . . curiously appropriate choice of medium. Very astute. I stayed up all night reading it."

"Thank you," I said, nodding once to accept the compliment. Then I smiled politely, waiting. Whatever he'd invited me here to discuss, this wasn't it.

He studied me for a moment, then relaxed, turning off the charm like a lamp he no longer needed. "All right, then."

His fingers stroked the air, manipulating symbols and menus I couldn't see. One of my image icons began to flicker. I touched and expanded it, moved the resulting window to the lower right corner of my vision. It was a video loop, false-color, depicting a complex mycorum which replicated itself in slow motion, over and over again. Not quite crablike, not quite urchinlike, not quite organic in appearance. A tiny machine, like a digger/constructor but smaller than the smallest bacterium, putting copies of itself together with cool precision, building them up out of nothing, out of pieces too small for the micrograph to capture. In short, a pretty typical piece of technogenic life. At the bottom of the window scrolled a horizontal code ribbon showing, in a series of brightly colored blocks, what was presumably the data gene sequence which dictated both the mycorum's structure and behavior.

"This," Lottick said, "is Io Sengen 3a, a sulfurated mycorum with unknown environmental tolerance. Gave us a scare a while back when we thought it could replicate in the volcanic flows on Io, but that turned out to be a false alarm. Now we're concerned again, for different reasons."

"Okay." I nodded, waiting for more, not yet sure why he was telling me this.

Another image icon flickered. Summoned, expanded, and formatted, it depicted a macrophage of some sort, immediately recognizable to any Immunity citizen as one of the good guys, though the configuration was not a familiar one. Rather like a mechanized coral polyp, I'll say, though close inspection revealed details inconsistent with that tag. At any rate, it was the same apparent size as the mycorum, though of course the scale must have been ten or twenty times less fine. Indeed, the yellow tick marks along the top and side of the image probably marked out a grid of one-tenth-micrometer squares. Again, a data gene sequence scrolled by underneath.

"The Philusburg Optima phage," Lottick said. "Release one-point-four. Thermal IR power coupler, has to be within six meters of a mini-lad or other major heat source to function. Note the gene sequences, please. This may duplicate some of the information you've already got, but I wanted to impress upon you the potential significance of this finding."

"Finding?" I paused, blinked. "Doctor, I'm afraid we're speaking different languages. Why, exactly, am I here?"

Lottick seemed surprised at that, looking up, his brow furrowing. "You didn't get the information packet," he said. Not a question.

"I don't think so, no. I got a message with a meeting date and time, that's all."

He was out of his chair, grumbling. "My apologies, Mr. Strasheim. In their current task loading my staff may have . . . overlooked it. There was no intention of wasting your time."

"You people have a lot on your minds," I said, diplomatically. In fact, my trip here had been rather a welcome break from the factory, and if I had to linger a little longer than expected, well, that was more job time I could justify missing.

"I have a few things to attend to," Lottick said, ignoring my attempt at mollification. He gestured at the sliding glass door behind his desk. "If you'd like to wait out on the balcony, I'll come join you in a few minutes. Right now there's an ear that needs twisting before it goes off shift. Several ears, actually."

"Oh," I said, rising, "sure. By all means." I wanted to get involved in that about as much as I wanted to go back to work at the factory, which was not very much. But Lottick's balcony would afford fresher air, a view of the city, a rare moment of quiet. "Take as long as you need; it's really no trouble."

Cursing softly, he brushed past me, went out the door. Behind his desk, the sliding glass door did indeed appear to have a balcony behind it. I moved to it, touched the handle. It slid open, powered but silent, looking heavy. Glass? It was zirconium, of course—much stronger and heavier and, in these ladderdown days, just as free for the taking. But in language, as in life, the old habits linger.

Lottick's office was on the top floor of the tallest building in Ansharton, ten stories high and right up against the side of the cavern, so that essentially every part of the city was visible, a pool of tiny, picturesque houses and factories spilling out across the broad cavern floor. A magnificent view, but it probably owed as much to logic as to politics. Even here there were blooms, probably a few small ones every week, and Research certainly needed to keep an eye out. Vaclav Lottick was no prince, no president, no corporate bureaucrat from times gone by, but simply a harried worker like everyone else, the contents of his head and the work of his hands outvaluing all the golden streets of Ganymede.

He even had a small telescope mounted on the railing, pointing down at the city. I peered through it, saw only a street corner, not particularly busy. Whisper-quiet, the zirconium door slid closed behind me.

There were no chairs out here, no furniture of any sort; the balcony was really only large enough for standing, large enough for maybe four or five people at the very most. I put my elbows on the railing, leaned out. I'd long ago lost my fear of heights; we cling to architectural styles meant for ten times the gravity we actually experience, deep in the mantles of the Jovian moons. In fact, there was no height from which I could fall that was likely to injure me, except possibly the cavern roof itself.

But neither was I going to jump—for some reason, we don't do that, either. So I simply waited, looking down on the cars and trucks rolling along on their eggbeater wheels, at the fat-tired bicycles and occasional pedestrians that hurried through the Ansharton streets. Looking up at the cavern roof, stony but clotted densely with light sources that simulated, on this day, a diffuse sun shining through streaky clouds, with hints of blue breaking through here and there. And the cranes and work gantries and laser turrets poking down from this ersatz sky, completely ruining the effect. I sometimes wonder who we think we're fooling.

At least there was wind, which I stood there and enjoyed for what seemed like a long time. Ten minutes? Twenty? Longer than I usually have, to stand around doing nothing. Eventually, the sliding door opened and closed, and Vaclav Lottick was there beside me, leaning on the railing, looking out on the cityscape with me.

"I don't need the whole song and dance," I told him softly. "If it's easier, you can just give me the highlights."

"It's easier," he agreed, then paused, taking breath a few times. He was calmer now than before. "And I'm sorry for the delay. You know that mycora mutate quickly, right? Everyone knows that. A key strength, a key factor. The whole Mycosystem probably depends on this, or it would have died out long ago."

"So I've heard."

"Yes, well, what you probably *haven't* heard is that they're stealing data gene sequences from our own phages. Nothing major, nothing all that important, but the mechanism and its potential limitations are not known at this time."

"Stealing gene sequences?" I repeated stupidly. My skin had

gone cold and crawly. Mycora were not intelligent, not even alive, really. How could they steal?

"It's probably nothing," Lottick said. "Statistically, the chance that they'll steal something important and actually be able to use it to their advantage is ... Well, it's zero, basically. But we don't understand the mechanism, and that has a lot of people upset, and bringing pressure to bear. What if the Mycosystem gets hold of some of our environmental adaptations? What happens if they stumble on nuclear fission, or cascade fusion, or God help us all, they manage to copy some of our ladderdown designs?"

"I don't know," I said, still cold. "What?"

He shrugged. "They eat the solar system, I guess. They eat the universe. It's not going to happen, Strasheim, but that's the worst-case scenario we've got to dance around. Hence the mission."

"The starship?" I asked, puzzled but optimistic. Whatever the problem was, these people seemed to be on top of it. Sort of.

"The starship, yeah, right." He chuckled, sounding tired. "We get it built, we fuel it up, we go on our merry way, every single person that wants to. That's not going to happen either. I know it's the party line, and maybe that's best for the time being, but the real goal of the program is to get *our* spores out to the neighboring stars before the Mycosystem beats us to it. Immune system fully established, deny the mycora a toehold even in the warm, bright spaces. But we've probably got a thousand years to worry about it, and a lot to keep us busy until then."

"So what are we talking about?"

"The *Louis Pasteur*," he said. "You may have heard about it here and there; the program is being accelerated in a big way. Ship is designed for inner system operation; high-temperature, high-radiation, also the t-balance hull—theoretically bloomproof. But of course, ha ha, we're not going to test that here on Ganymede. The only way to test it is to fly it down there, into the Mycosystem, and see if anything eats it. We hope to do that soon, and if the testing goes well, we'll fly it all the way down to Earth and Mars and Luna. The thinking goes: Even in the inner system, there are places too cold, dark, barren for mycora to bloom. If any serious cold-weather adaptations start appearing, the first signs of it will probably be there. So we drop a few detectors on some polar caps, and suddenly nobody's bothering us about this problem anymore. Not unless the detectors start screaming at us, which I don't think is going to happen."

"Are these state secrets?" I asked, turning to look at his face. "Can I talk about this stuff?"

His look was disapproving. "There are no secrets, Mr. Strasheim. There's barely any state, and I didn't invite you up here to waste your time. If we didn't want you to talk about this, what would we want you for? To make shoes? You have skills which nobody else in the Immunity seems to possess. You're a commentator, an historian; you record simple facts in a way that's accessible to the public, even entertaining. That ability could be very useful for this project, if you're willing to lend it to us for a while."

"It sounds fascinating," I said sincerely. "I take it you want me to write an article?"

Lottick looked at me like I was somewhat stupider than he'd been expecting. "No, son. I thought we understood each other. I want you to go on the mission."

Wombs

Weightless in the solitude of a ballista car, I pondered. Thought of tunnels arching through the planet, of the cars being fired through them like signals through an optic-fiber network. Of cavern cities and macroimmune systems and the nearly million people who comprised the only society I'd ever really known. I was eleven when we left the Earth.

I keep the lights off when I'm cannonballing, at least when I'm doing it alone, so there was nothing around me but the sound-absorbing padding of the walls, neither seen nor felt. The iconified images on my zee-spec might well have been the only light in the universe. I studied them.

Lottick had indeed hit the highlights in his brief speech. Under some unknown set of conditions, mycora could absorb (scan? hack?) immunophages by an unknown process, and transcribe and adopt data gene sequences despite the supposed incompatibility of same. So little was understood about the phenomenon that the info packet, despite its reams of supporting data, occupied me for only about twenty minutes. Anyway, I was no doctor, and most of the jargon went right past me, leaving little more information than Lottick had given me verbally. Of more interest was the data on the ship itself; *Louis Pasteur* was at heart a light cargo ship, ladder-down-powered and capable of extended voyage at interplanetary velocities, though the mass of the "t-balance" hull coatings did cut into performance a bit. Normally crewed by four to five people, these ships, though *Pasteur* herself would carry six. Or seven, if I agreed to join them.

And that was the question, now, wasn't it? Could I do that, leave Ganymede behind, leave the whole Immunity behind to dive back into the warmth of the inner system? Protected from the mycora only by an experimental technology, protected from my crew-mates only by a curtain-thin cabin wall? The ship's interior was slightly smaller than my tiny house in Philusburg, and the mission would last 280 days, or just a hair over nine months. It sounded like a boarding-school nightmare, a crowded, bickering nightmare of bunk-bed privacy and no possibility of escape. No possibility even of a walk to cool off, to let anxiety clear slowly from the air. How could we keep from murdering each other? God knew, such things had happened before.

My revulsion was so sharp and so immediate that I realized in a sudden, scharfblick moment that the decision was already made.

Guess what, freund, I *would* be going on the mission; these things would happen, would become my daily reality. And how could it be otherwise? I neither loved nor hated reporting; I *was* it. Always had been, even as an Earthly child, running around with a transcription palmtop and a mouthful of pestering questions. Cobblering was an uneasy compromise, something I could do well enough to be of use to others, but when offered the chance to serve mankind in my own true way, with my own true talents, could I refuse? Certainly not, I realized. Certainly not. So whatever the records may say, my journey began precisely at that moment.

The car sped on, hurtling now through the downward leg of the tunnel's parabola. I took the opportunity to flash in an update from my net channels, the four that I moderated and the four others to which I made daily contributions. Skimming the topic headers, sorting them into priority groups for later viewing. Not enough time to read them now, of course, not before landing, but I did compose a message of my own, a brief narration and video collage of the *Louis Pasteur*, its mission, and my own proposed role.

I flashed it out just as the lights came up, along with the warning chimes, as the ballista on the Philusburg end caught me in its decelerating grip. I fell softly against the padded wall and quickly began growing heavy, and then heavier, and heavier still, and then the pressure eased back just before it could grow uncomfortable, just before the need to breathe and the difficulty of doing so could become alarming. Leaving me to drift to my feet at standard gravity, feather-light by the standards of my youth.

Light spilled into the car as it clamshelled open, releasing me onto the empty platform, and as I stepped away the vehicle sank into a recess in the tunnel wall, to be loaded onto the outbound ballista back to Ansharton. I looked around briefly at the mirrored walls, my own reflection distorted beyond recognition by the rounded contours, by the light pouring up from below. Finally, I found a slot to shove my debit card into, then mounted the escalator and rode it down to street level. Philusburg blossomed around me, a smaller town than Ansharton but in many ways a more energetic one, its sidewalks mobile, its buildings designed, in many cases, to change shape over the course of the day, taking advantage of shifts in the lighting conditions. My home, these past twenty years, a cavern-city of lead and iron and sparkling gold, and yes, I did love it. And do.

It was funny how different the houses all looked from one another. Nobody likes iron shingle all that much, it's true, but the waste metal has to go somewhere, and buildings have to be made of something, and in the end the crews simply click a house together from standard patterns, because they don't have the time to waste any more than you or I do. But in Philusburg, more and more residents were bucking the system and customizing, adding molded Tudor facings or shiny filigrees or little silver gargoyles, or whatever. They say time is the heaviest metal, and indeed only absurd sacrifice can bring these things about. But sacrifice gets to be a habit after a while. Even I had felt the pinch a few years back, and slapped a coat of paint on my little tin castle. Green.

I'd be passing it in a few minutes if I continued down the hauptstrasse, but it seemed I wouldn't have the factory job to worry about much longer, so once my feet hit the sidewalk I switched tracks and went the other way, not back to work but instead toward the sanitarium on the city's south end, near the archway to the agricultural district. There was someone I needed to see.

"Take those damn glasses off," she said to me by way of greeting—about as friendly a reception as she'd been able to manage lately.

Seeming never to notice that I'd been gone at all, seeming always to pick up in the middle of a conversation. But not any conversation that I remembered. A ribbon held back her hair, white on white.

So small, this room, and so sparse, and so very painfully clean. My fault, yes; I was always thinking I should at least bring her a plant, something dirty and alive to fill up the empty space beside the window, but there was the expense to consider, and the trouble . . .

"Momma," I said to her, as cheerfully as I could manage, "you know they're not glasses. Nobody wears glasses anymore."

She pinched her face up at that. "Bull crap. I see you all hiding behind these things, hiding your faces. Always poking and stabbing at the air like there were flies buzzing around, bothering you. But they're not." Her eyes narrowed, studying my face with sullen accusation. "You're not going to poke at me, are you? I see these orderlies hiding behind their beards and their Coke-bottle glasses, always poking and pointing. What are they hiding from, and who are they pointing at? It's annoying, and they look like fools. I'll speak to somebody about it, I really will."

"Momma," I said, the bright edge still on my voice, but duller now, "I don't work here. I'm John, I'm your son."

"I know exactly who you are," she snapped.

I wondered. My mother was almost ninety years old, physically still healthy enough, but mentally . . . "She's simply outlived her brain's ability to cope with new pathways," as one of the nurses had put it, by which she meant that the neurodegenerative agent had not been identified and probably would not be. As if age made a human being any less entitled to dignity and health? I was genuinely afraid to ask for clarification on this point, genuinely afraid to be told that Momma was just too old, that no intervention could fix her. Or worse, that fixing her was too expensive, that nature had written her off and the Immunity was simply standing by, waiting for the sentence to be carried out. "We simply haven't the resources . . ."

We never did, never do. Christ, I couldn't even come up with a houseplant. I resolved to remedy that, to fix what little I could in her life. It was, as we say, the least I could do.

"How are you, Momma?"

"I'm fine, I'm fine. Not dead yet." She grimaced, shaking her head, patting the bed beside her to invite me to sit. "I sure outlived what I ever guessed I would. This is Jupiter, isn't it? Are we living on Jupiter?"

"On Ganymede, Momma. It's one of the moons."

"Ganymede," she said, testing the word, nodding slowly as if agreeing with the sound of it. "Yeah, okay. One of the moons. Philusburg, that's where we live. Are we still in Philusburg?"

"Yup," I told her, smiling, sitting down on the bed now and patting her hand because I couldn't think of anything else to do, any other way to connect. God, but it drained me to visit here. Momma used to be *smart*, used to be able to talk backwards and write backwards and figure out which flavor of syrup would take the rust off an iron tile. She'd gotten us through the Evacuation, the whole family, by drawing the right conclusions and jumping at the right time and somehow making a grand adventure of it all. But then Avery had died in a bloom, and Patrice in a fire, and then my father simply failed to wake up one morning, and a little more had gone out of her each time. Sick. Momma was sick, and gradually getting sicker, and I'd taken much too long to figure it out. Sometimes I thought she was dead already, an empty shell of flesh and nerve, speaking only in echoes. How long ago should I have said good-bye?

"Momma," I said to her then, in a strong voice that I hoped would penetrate, "I have to go away for a while. I have to go on a trip, and I won't be able to see you while I'm gone. I can send messages, though, and you can send messages back."

She seemed to consider my words.

"I can talk to the staff about it," I went on slowly. "I know you don't like the zee-spec, but that's okay; I can send you a plaintext or an audio mail, and someone can play it for you. And you can reply, if you want to."

She was nodding, looking thoughtful, but the hand she raised was an instruction to silence. "Do you remember your father's accident?" she asked, a wise, distant glint in her eyes. "Wild parrots. He drove up into the mountains, and wild parrots ate his windshield wipers. Heaven knows, but those parrots have a serious appetite for rubber, and when he was driving back down, it rained and he couldn't see, and he crashed. Drove right into a tree, I think, though it may have been a rock."

"I remember. It was a road sign he hit."

Her brown eyes caught mine, held them. She was smiling. "I told him, man, you might have been the first person in the history of the world to ever be killed by parrots. What a funny thing that was. Killed by parrots, can you imagine? But he lived a long time after that. A long time. He used to love to tell that story."

Yes, indeed he did. There had been a lot more to it, back then, though the exact details had tended to wander from one telling to the next. My father had been a systems analyst, "long for handyman" as he'd liked to say, though the Immunity had put him to work making shoes, same as me. "Shoes are important in low gravity," he'd often said, "and not so easy to make well."

"Arthur always loved the mountains," Momma went on, smiling fondly. "And the animals, and the sky. We didn't Evacuate many animals with us, did we? Of course there wasn't much time—it's hard to blame us when the hills around the spaceport were literally dissolving—but I don't think your father was ever really happy after we left. He was never really the same."

Yeah, losing a whole planet—and later a whole inner solar system—can do that to you. Hence the love even now—perhaps especially now—of that damned parrot story. *See here, we really* knew *the Earth in our time there.* I sighed. "Momma, we can talk about Dad if you want, but first I want you to listen to me. I have to go away. I have to go on a trip. Are you listening? Do you understand what I'm saying? Momma?"

Momma, Momma. I couldn't stop saying the word, though I never heard my own name in return anymore. Perhaps a need to remind her that I, too, was a part of her memories. Or maybe I was reminding myself, or maybe it's a lot more complex than that, or a lot simpler. Love is a twisted thing, not for us to decipher. She was my *mother.*

"I'm listening," she said, the smile falling away. "You're going on a trip, all right. People go on trips sometimes; it's nothing to get bent up about. Is it a long trip? Far away?"

I nodded. "Yes, a long one. Almost a year."

"Ah-hah." She paused, looked down. "I don't know. I don't know. Maybe I won't . . . I think I'm sick, you know. I think there's definitely something wrong with me. Maybe it's my memory, it does seem to play tricks, but that's not quite the same thing as feeling *ill,* if you know what I mean. Do you think I'll still be here when you get back? A year from now, well, that's a long time to the elderly."

"Of course you will," I said, too quickly. And compounded the error by patting her hand again.

And I knew then that Momma wasn't altogether gone, because she looked up sharply, snatching away her hand. "Don't you talk

down to me, young fellow. I won't be talked down to like that, con-
descended to, you hear me? And take those damn glasses off. You
look just exactly like a fool."

That night, I pored over Lottick's files for nearly an hour, long
enough to put together a more detailed mission description and
flash it to my net channels to feed the curiosity there. Lottick's blatant flattery aside, I was not the only commentator or historian in
the Immunity. Far from it. I can think of nine serious ones right off
the top of my head (and you all know who you are), another twenty
or thirty dabblers, and of course the thousands of contributors to the
unmoderated channels.

VR mail had been trickling in for me all day, messages of con-
gratulation and commiseration and frank curiosity. I answered several of these at length, answered more with a form letter. There were
some jealous inquiries as well. Why me, they wondered aloud? Why
not someone else, someone perhaps with a more rugged or more
technical background? One of these, though biting, was actually
very funny, so I archived it and made a note to get in touch with its
author, when I'd had time to build up the necessary reserve of wit.

And then, as every evening, I read my net channels, perused city
records, made a few discreet realtime calls, and flashed the comm
network with info and opinion nuggets—the worlds according to
John Strasheim.

> ". . . fourteen deaths last week, and only nine births, which is
> consistent with annual statistics. And yet, two-thirds of Immu-
> nity citizens remain unmarried, and more than half of those
> claim to be seeking romantic alliances without success. No sur-
> prise that the 'Boff a Stranger' holiday proposal was shot down

in council, but if we hope to stave off a slow extinction we had better find a way to get our men and women together outside of working hours. Or maybe we all just need to lower our standards a bit . . ."

". . . yet another warehouse robbery, this time for eight thousand g.u. in bismuth bar stock. How the perpetrators managed to carry it all away unnoticed is a mystery to this berichter, but sources indicate one or more city vehicles may have been involved . . ."

". . . in the Floral asteroids at the Main Belt's lower edge, Gladholder communities report a net food surplus for the twelfth consecutive year, despite near-record spore flux from the upper Mycosystem . . ."

Et cetera. Finally, more tired even than usual, I fell gratefully into bed and drifted off at once.

And burst awake half an hour later, fumbling the lights on and grabbing my zee-spec off the charging rack to send, in literal afterthought, a message to Vaclav Lottick, informing him that I'd considered his very kind offer, and had chosen to accept.

EVOLUTION'S
ADMIRERS

Originally headquartered in Radar Valley, a tiny dome town on the surface of Callisto, the Temples of Transcendent Evolution have managed over the past two decades to colonize nearly every corner of the Immunity, from the outposts of Saturn to the Five Cities of Ganymede. But in Innensburg, their branch temple was burned to the ground last year with magnesium flares and other sophisticated pyrotechnics, despite round-the-clock watches following three previous arson attempts.

"It's an awful thing, human spite," says longtime Temples spokeswoman Jeanine Proust, when I stop by the reconstruction site to interview her. The trademark binary caduceus emblem is already in place, raised gold on a burnished silver pillar, and Proust leans against it as she speaks, her body language protective and angry and tired. "The authorities avert their eyes, of course, or this couldn't have happened at all, much less gone unsolved. That building was raised and maintained by hands, you know, by loving human hands, and it contained thousands of g.u. in original artwork and fixtures, many of them originally from Earth itself. The sentimental value alone is incalculable. How do you go about healing a loss like that?"

"It's an awful thing, the Temples of Transcendent Evolution," counters another source, an Innensburg resident who has asked to remain anonymous. "They want to 'commune,' they can bloody well do it someplace else, someplace where it isn't a bloody salt tablet stitched up in the wounds. Be a long time before we'll put up with that nonsense, believe you me. You've really got to wonder just who these people think they are."

At odds, of course, is the Temples' interest in TGL generally and the Mycosystem in particular. Not proper, one supposes, not healthy, although neither are the fear and divisiveness they so frequently inspire.

The polite fiction these days is that we in the Immunity are all one people, united by one culture, one history. As the joke goes, our official language is English with a Swiss accent, and if there are racists or nationalists among us, they keep exceedingly quiet. And why not? Against the backdrop of the Mycosystem, what difference a human gene twisted this way or that? Even religious tolerance has come back into vogue; the western faiths quibble over similarities rather than differences, and seem to view the remaining animists and polytheists with, if not respect, at least a sort of good-natured neglect.

The Temples are quite another matter; the organization's religious nature, which many feel to be a mask for quasi-legal scientific research, is seen as a provocation, a blatant stab at the moral foundations of our communities.

"I'm not going to lie to you," Jeanine Proust tells me with a defiant jutting of the chin. "Most of our members come to us because they sense a spiritual chasm in their lives, because they sense the proximity of a presence far greater than themselves, and they want to learn more. Yes, many are undereducated. Yes, many bring money along with them, and yes, we do funnel quite a lot of that into our research arm. Exploitation is a very subjective judgment, though, and we're no more guilty of it than any other large organization.

"Like it or not, the Mycosystem is an enormous reality in our lives, and if the more established religions have no meaningful observations regarding that, then it is time for the established religions to give way to a more relevant paradigm. People come to us because unlike those religions of the past, we're the only ones willing to admit that there's an elephant in the living room."

Not strictly true—Rev. Stacia Holt's Creation Murmurs *being the most prominent counterexample—but I let the point pass. "Some people," I tell her instead, "accuse the Temples of going too far. The psychotropics, the fecundity rituals, the Confessions of Awe . . . Some suggest that the Mycosystem has become an object of actual worship among your followers."*

She shakes her head. "No, I'm sorry, that would be stating it far too strongly. The spiritual implications of complexity on so vast a scale are simply not known. If a mycoric soul exists down there in that fractal wilderness, our apprehension of it must be fragmentary at best, though of course that doesn't stop us from trying. At this juncture we don't have enough information to worship the Mycosystem, or God, or anything really. It's a frontier that can only be explored when we're brave enough to let a bloom run its course, the occurrence of which seems very unlikely in the current climate. But this is all very easy for outsiders to misunderstand."

"I agree," I say to her, fighting to hold my temper, my impartiality suddenly strained just a bit too far. "I doubt I've understood you at all. I don't see you people vacationing on Mars. I don't see you volunteering to die in a bloom. Isn't apprehending spiritual truths a little empty if it isn't backed up by actual deeds?"

At this, she flashes a kind of disappointed smile—I've got her and she knows it. She seems as familiar with the question as she is uncomfortable, and when she speaks, it's in a humbler, almost apologetic tone. "Mr. Strasheim, we have decades of study ahead of us. The Immunity focuses its energies in the wrong direction, in an aggressive and ultimately futile direction, and we would like to see that changed. But we aren't stupid, and we haven't transcended our inherent human/animal nature. We live upstairs from the very greatest of unknowns—the inner planets transformed almost beyond comprehension, the vacuum itself brought elaborately to life. Who can say what our place is in all of this? Is it so surprising, that deep down we're as afraid as you?"

from *Innensburg and the Fear of Failure*
© 2101 by John Strasheim

Back at the factory, I was greeted with hoots and catcalls as the guys looked up from their machines. Schmidt, Billings, and Howe.

"Hey!"

"There he is, the Big Wheel himself!"

"Hi, guys," I said, ducking my head. My journalism hobby was well known, but it had never interfered with work before, and the drama of its doing so yesterday was as appealing to them as it was to me. More, probably, because they didn't have to go anywhere as a result.

Julf Ernst, my shift supervisor for the last five years, stepped away from his paste-and-stitch press, came forward and pumped my hand, a solicitous grin stretching out beneath his bushy mustache. Strasheim the visiting dignitary, yeah.

"So what'd they say?" he asked.

"I, uh, need a leave of absence."

"Yeah? Where're they sending you?"

I snorted, amused to be able to shock him as deeply as I was about to. "Earth," I said.

He blinked.

"I need ten months, starting immediately. They have some kind of new ship."

He blinked again. "Seriously?"

"Yeah."

The machines had gone quiet, their operators all looking goggle-eyed at me.

Ernst pumped my hand again. "Jesus. Well done, then. I always knew you'd leave us one day. I always said that, didn't I?"

"Sure," I agreed, although he never had.

He cocked his head, a gesture which managed somehow to point to everything at once—low ceiling, the rusted floor, the reeking vats of glue and rubber, the guys . . ."You gonna leave all this?"

"Won't be easy," I assured him.

He nodded, approving of the remark. "One thing: you've got to have a drink with us after the shift. Down at the Engel."

The guys nodded. Yeah, yeah, mumble whatsis, drink at the Engel.

"I'd like that," I said. "What time should I meet you there?"

"Meet?" Ernst quirked his face up. "I thought we'd all walk down there together. You know, after the shift."

I saw where *that* was heading, and moved to intercept. "I have to, ah, get my affairs in order. Close up the house, that sort of thing. I report for training first thing in the morning."

Ernst's expression was long-suffering and tired. "We had a big spike of orders come in on Monday, you know that. We're an hour and a half into a shift of twelve, for which you never called in late, and now I'm supposed to press out eighty-nine units with only four guys? Don't do this to me, Johnny boy."

"Do what? How are you going to manage tomorrow?"

"We'll manage tomorrow. Get somebody in off another shift, I don't know. It's right now I'm worried about, Johnny. Nobody goes barefoot on this planet; that's a responsibility I take very seriously."

His face and voice were profoundly sincere, and the funny thing is, he was right. Ganymede was not a forgiving place, and the demands of life here did not allow for much error or idleness or want. People needed shoes, clothing, food, needed something every day, and somebody had to be there to provide it all. Nobody went barefoot, ever.

That was how I got talked into spending one more day at the press. Julf Ernst could do that to you. It's why they made him supervisor, I guess.

As promised, we all marched down to the Engel together when it was over and the eighty-nine pairs were drying on the rack. Didn't say much, though. The Engel, dark and moody as usual, had only a couple of patrons besides us, people eating dinner rather than drinking, so the silence got fairly oppressive as we stared at each other across the iron table and sipped our beers. It pained me—this was costing a good bit, probably three days' pay when all was said and done, and I really did appreciate the sentiment. The guys and I had worked together for most of a decade and a half, and spent twelve hours of six days of fifty-one weeks a year standing practically shoulder to shoulder. But when you got right down to it, apart from commenting on the quality of the beer we didn't really have all that much to say to each other.

Hindsight filter: we could have talked about families, or politics, or money, or anything really. We just didn't. Didn't know how.

It was Ernst who saved us, who single-handedly took on the burden of speech. He raised a hand, showed it to us, then pressed it to the table's faux-woodgrain surface and slid it around in a circle, as if feeling the texture of the metal.

"Every surface," he said, "is totally covered in macrophages. That's our line of defense. That's what separates us from Gladholders and dead Earthlings, what defines our whole society. We *breathe* these things, we totally trust them with our lives. Isn't that right, Johnny?"

I supposed that it was.

"Down in the Mycosystem," he went on, his fat mustache waggling, "there are no macrophages. That's what defines *its* existence. That's why it's all turned to goo. You ask me, we're just not making enough macrophages. Immunize the whole solar system, that's what I say."

"I'm not sure it works that way," I said uncertainly.

"No?" He shrugged. "I've always wondered. I guess they would have done it by now if they thought they could. So what about this mission of yours? What's that about? You going to capture back some territory for us?"

I shook my head, swallowed some dark, rich beer. "No, just a scouting mission. Placing some instruments."

"That's all?" He seemed surprised, disappointed. The guys grumbled their agreement with that sentiment.

"I guess so, yeah."

"Huh. Weird. You'd think if they were going to go to the trouble, it'd be for something more dramatic. But what do I know, right? Nothing. That's why I'm stuck in shoe heaven. Anyway, Johnny, we're surely going to miss you."

"Likewise," I said.

"You'll keep in touch?"

"Yes. Actually, that's my job."

"Oh, yeah. Right."

And that, sad to report, was about all the conversation we had in us that night. Herodotus, I hear, was no great conversationalist either.

A CAPITAL SHIP

Base, town, factory, port, whatever Galileo may be, the first thing you notice about it is the peculiar nature of the cold. Warm air blasts through the corridors, drying the eyes and mucous membranes, roughing up the throat, and yet the walls . . . Touch them for a moment and the cool is refreshing, for longer, and you may lose some skin. Layered composite/ceramic nearly a meter thick, they are fine thermal insulators, but the temperature in the rock outside is barely seventy kelvins, and it seeps.

Same goes for the floors and ceilings, so as I wandered in search of the shipyards that day, my feet and scalp were telling me I was cold, even as sweat drenched and stained the armpits of my shirt. Well, "wandered" is not really the right word, since a detailed map scrolled and swiveled on my zee-spec as I negotiated the hallways. But alongside it was a slow, plaintext news dump, with low-volume narration mumbling from the earpieces, and anyway I was taking the long way around, in no hurry and in fact under orders (well, suggestions) to gather information from any and all sources.

"Whatever seems appropriate," the message had said. "Whatever helps you do your job, do. We're paying for your judgment in these matters, so exercise it."

A light tour of Galileo, then, a bit of context for all that is to follow. Alas, there isn't much to tell. If you've been there, you know the town (factory? base?) is a rat hole, a maze of tunnels and chambers that look and smell like they've been pummeled with hand tools and hosed down with oil. You get that sort of look when ten thousand residents, none of them permanent, pass through their work contracts here like boarding-school students, unencumbered by love or respect for their surroundings. Too close to the equator here, too close to the surface. It's not that it feels unsafe—in fact, Galileo probably has the best Immune and Response systems in existence. It's not that there isn't enough money flowing through; the heavy elements on Ganymede are mainly imported through these very docks. It's not, as some have claimed, a lack of "feminine touch," as something like a third of the residents are in fact female.

The problem is Galileo itself; remoteness is part of the identity of the place, part of its history. Never mind that it's as easy to reach now as any other part of Ganymede, and certainly much easier than Callisto or, God help us all, Titan. It just never has been "home" to anyone, and for that reason it never will be. Some places are just like that.

Oh, all right, the place is not entirely without its charm. The food is mostly synthetic, don't ask me why, but an ethic of rebellion has taken hold of the culinary centers, leading to a cuisine which is certainly very different from anything else you're likely to see. Anti-naturalism at its most refined: my lunch, eaten at a corner stand with twice as many diners as stools, consisted of chewy blue spheres with vaguely meatlike flavor, steeped in a sweet, translucent gravy that tasted chemical, medicinal. This was ladled onto a mound of starchy pellets and served in an iron cup, with an oversized spoon and a glass of water and a napkin of dubious cleanliness. Good? No, not really. But different.

Need I say more about the town itself? I think not. Eventually, I found my way to the relatively open spaces of the shipyard, where the ceilings were higher, the walls farther apart, the crowds less hurried and surly. It's a methodical business, the building and servicing of spaceships, and this was immediately apparent in the look and feel of the place. Large, complicated tools, pushed or carried with delicacy. Unexplained power cables running here and there, but stapled to the walls, out of the way of tripping feet. And signs everywhere, warning and exhorting: ABSOLUTELY NO ADMITTANCE, THIS MEANS YOU!!! CAUTION: LASER LIGHT. CAUTION: ELECTRIC FIELD. CAUTION: LIGHT FROM WELDING ARCS CAN DAMAGE YOUR EYE. There were even a few weirdly encouraging ones, such as PLEASE MOVE SAFELY, and WORK WITHOUT EATING MAY CAUSE DIZZINESS.

True enough.

The scale and clutter of the place were a bit daunting. It actually took me a few minutes to realize that the great shapes all around, in every hangar and chamber, surrounded by frames and trusses and hoists and quietly industrious people, were in fact real ships and not mock ups or test articles or large pieces of support machinery. The strange openings in the ceiling were doors leading up into tunnels leading up into airlocks leading up into hard cold vacuum. I found the thought strangely sobering.

Louis Pasteur was coming together on Platform 28, and the zee map guided me there without error. Like the other ships, *Pasteur* was imprisoned in rigging and scaffolding. I'd seen her blueprints many times by now, and from what I could see she looked just like them. And yet . . . Well, there was still something odd, something vaguely disturbing about the look of her. The hull was bumpy, spiky, almost protozoan in appearance—that much I'd been prepared for. But the t-balance tactile camouflage, designed to trick technogenic lebenforms into thinking it part of their own substance, was clearly more than a simple coating of paint.

How to describe it? The way it caught the light, the way it *gleamed* . . . Pictures do no justice. Rainbow gray it was, like oil on water, except that it seemed to be made up of thousands of tiny dots, except that as I came closer, the dots broke up into millions of smaller dots, then millions more, smaller and smaller until it hurt the eye. They gave a vague impression of motion, like ants. Yes, I remember ants, remember looking down on their nests as they swarmed over some hapless insect, their bodies too tiny to make out individually, at least from a distance, so that the mass of them had the look of a living, boiling, fractal whole. T-balance looked a lot like that, in a way, although I understood at once that the motion was an illusion, that if I kept my head and eyes perfectly still the strangeness would evaporate, and the hull's coating would settle into a sort of wet, pointillist glaze.

From a ramp on *Pasteur*'s underside, behind the cables and scaffolding, voices emanated. I peered, drawing closer, and was able to make out faces: Vaclav Lottick and two men I didn't recognize, both dressed in eye-blue spacer coveralls. Lottick looked up, saw me.

"Strasheim," he said curtly. "Over here."

Yes, of course, I might have trouble picking out the right ship in the crowd.

"I'd like you to meet someone," he went on, nudging one of the other men out into the light. Then all three of them were picking their way through scaffolding, approaching me with hands extended. "Darren Wallich, John Strasheim. John Strasheim, Darren Wallich."

"Aha," I said, nodding to the tall, pepper-haired man Lottick had indicated and accepting the handshake he offered. Firm, too firm. "A pleasure to meet you."

Darren Wallich was an Immunity type of some sort, a doctor, and would be *Pasteur*'s captain when the time came. One of the six people I'd be sharing the next umpty-ump weeks with—I'd *better* be pleased to meet him.

Wallich's face, draped loosely in the manner of faces entering their fifth or sixth decade, drew upward into a smile at my expression, as if aware of what I was thinking. Probably he was thinking the same thing.

"This other man is Tosca Lehne," Lottick said to me, flapping a hand in the air between us as if trying to form some invisible connection. Maybe doing something meaningful on his zee-spec, or maybe not. It's hard not to notice that these devices, so rarely removed, have brought us a whole new body language, have encouraged us more than ever to speak with our hands, to sketch invisible lines in the air whether or not they'll be turned into real lines in the specs of our audience.

"Hallo," Lehne said to me, and I shook his hand as well. This man seemed more reluctant, more truculent. He was the inventor of t-balance, or one of the inventors, but I didn't know much more about him than that. His arms were thick and hairless, his jaw square, the pads of his hand disconcertingly soft. Too many years, I thought, of working only with abstractions, of lifting his weight against too little gravity. A hard, still-youthful body gone reluctantly to flab.

"You don't sound happy," I observed.

"He doesn't like this idea much," Wallich said, grinning. "Leaving home for the mission and all, but hey, I wanted to be sure we had the *best possible job* on the camouflage, so I suggested he come along with us to be sure. I bet that's worth a few extra minutes' cross-checking, eh?" He laughed.

Tosca Lehne did not appear amused. Well, who could blame him? I wasn't thrilled at our prospects myself.

"Well, we're happy to have both of you aboard," Lottick said to Lehne and myself, in the same tone of official friendliness I'd heard back at his office. "This is a fine crew we're putting together, a fine crew. I couldn't put my trust in better hands."

His tone was not a bad one, I hasten to add. Manipulative, yes, but there was a conspiratorial edge to it as well, as if the manipulation were a private joke between the three of us.

Wallich chuckled. "We can be spared, you mean."

"No." Lottick grew more serious. "Not at all. Not at all."

"*Some* have better things to do," Lehne muttered.

Lottick eyed him for a moment, but seemed not to find the remark worthy of comment. Instead he turned, speaking now in lower, quicker tones. "Wallich, I've got six test batches to run this afternoon and only half a team to meter them. I've stayed too long already, so I'll be on my way posthaste. I'd like you to geek a sim for me, clean up the activity reports and flash them down priority, yes? I'll read them on the job."

"Not a problem."

"Well, nice seeing you again," Lottick said, nodding dismissively in my direction. "We have the highest confidence."

"Welcome aboard," Wallich agreed. "We'll talk later in detail, if that's all right. Get to know each other, discuss your duties, all that sort of thing. Fair enough for you?"

I nodded. "Yeah, whatever's convenient."

He pointed his hand, pistol-style, his grin broadening. "I like that attitude. Whatever's convenient, ha ha. Mind if I archive that? Bang." The thumb/hammer fell. Then, as he and Lottick turned away, "Vass, this A-series, right? Fern loop blastoma, step rate unconstrained? God damn, you've got a fun night ahead of you. Here, I'll walk you as far as the foundry. I'm headed that way anyway."

"Blastoma shmastoma," muttered Lottick's receding voice. "Give me half a g.u. for every damn fool tumor snipe hunt I've wasted nights on and I'll *buy* this ship. Severs has a lecture coming, let me tell you."

"Oh, I can imagine well enough."

The sound of Wallich's laughter followed them out.

I turned to Tosca Lehne. "Our captain, eh? He seems a bit . . . energetic. Funny. I'm not quite sure what I was expecting, but—"

"Prosthetic," Lehne said, staring after the two men.

"Excuse me?"

"That sense of humor, it's a tickle capacitor. Implanted, skull base. The man is a fish."

"A what?"

Lehne waved a hand. "You know, cold-blooded. Slimy. He did it so people would like him better."

I blinked, puzzled. Clearly, I hadn't been following the science and medical channels closely enough. "Tickle capacitor. My god, that's amazing. And do they?"

"Eh?"

"Like him better?"

"Oh. Yeah, I guess. He's captain, isn't he?"

"My god, that's amazing. Can they do, well, for example, something like a conscience? Or a sense of self-worth? The social implications could be staggering."

"I don't know."

A shrug; no real response, no emotional engagement. The question didn't interest him. Well, I could see that Tosca Lehne wasn't going to be the easiest person in the worlds to talk to. Maybe Wallich was not the only one in need of prosthetic laughter. Thinking to try a different approach, to get Lehne talking about his work, I reached out to brush my fingers admiringly along *Louis Pasteur*'s t-balance hull. I pulled them back immediately, stinging. Quick inspection showed that they were bleeding: little jewels of red beading out from dozens of tiny slash wounds, as if I'd touched a tangle of miniature razor blades. I gave a little grunt.

"Careful," Lehne said quietly. "It's sharp."

I showed him a surly grin. "So I see. You might have warned me."

He shrugged. "Didn't know you'd try to touch it. Yes, it's sharp—be careful. Also toxic, mildly radioactive. Don't eat. You know much about it?"

"No, not really."

"Oh," he said, and then just stood there eyeing me over. To his credit, he did look apologetic—not seeming to know quite what to make of me, what to say to me, what to do about me. I was not part of his world.

"You can explain it to me sometime," I tried, smiling, I hoped, a bit more genuinely. "I'm very interested. Meanwhile, is the rest of the crew around? I feel I should get to know everyone before . . ."

He was shaking his head. "No, not here right now. They come and go, busy, always busy, always busy. That's life, eh? Come to dinner tonight, that's where you can meet everyone. Man and woman's got to eat, right? Might as well synchronize. I'll tell you about t-balance sometime, if you really are interested. It's technical, but I'll tell it to you. Would you like to see the ship?"

"Why I'm here," I agreed.

"Well, watch your head going in. Damn cargo hold, forced a redesign of the main airlock. Very urgent, that cargo hold, along with everything else. Accelerated schedule, no time to really *fix* anything. And for what? Dubious."

I shook my head. "I'm afraid I'm not following."

"Ah, never mind," he said, turning away. "Nothing makes sense, they don't tell me things. This mission stinks, I know that much."

I've often thought I should have asked him to elaborate on that remark. Did he mean something beyond the obvious, beyond the danger and discomfort, beyond the arm-twisting that had apparently brought him here? I didn't ask. Instead, I let it roll off me, and followed him docilely into the ship.

FOR THE GOOD
ARE ALWAYS THE
MERRY

Small, my god it is small, my god it is small . . . That was all I could think about as I sat down to dinner, all I had thought about all afternoon. Wallich had met with me, as promised, and it was all I could do to keep from telling him I quit, I couldn't do this, he would have to find somebody else. Rosenblum? Ancell? Oh, God, not Ancell. The thought of him smearing his boastful opinions all over the story, and then strutting and crowing at me about it for the rest of his life and mine . . . And they *would* get Ancell, too. Somehow, I knew they would. And so I held firm.

But it was *small*; the ship's interior was like a bathroom with seven shower stalls and a streetcar cockpit wedged incongruously at one end, a utility closet wedged in at the other. I'd seen the plans, thought I was prepared, but this was crazy. *I* was crazy.

Large and crowded, the cafeteria nonetheless had a little round table reserved for *Louis Pasteur*'s crew, right beside the single large window overlooking the shipyards. A hell of a view, really; four half-completed ships were visible below, and two whole ones presumably drydocked for repairs. *Louis Pasteur* herself was not among them, but together they represented three sizes, four overall designs, six color schemes, and fully a quarter of Galileo's shipping tonnage. The shop floor was enormous, probably a full hectare sprawling some twenty meters below us, but still I felt claustrophobic.

On my zee-spec, images threatened to crowd out the real world altogether: paired data gene sequences scrolling upward in tandem, the duplicate portions flashing like alarm lights; the Io Sengen and Innensburg mycora, pulsing with false-color image enhancements and shifting annotations from the library tutorial; a map of the solar system, with *Louis Pasteur*'s course charted out as a dotted white line swinging close by Mars, kissing the orbit of Earth, and then finally rising back toward the Immunity, toward the cold and dark of the upper solar system.

And of course, I had a media window cycling slowly and methodically through my own net channels as well. A reminder to myself: *This is where you are going, and why. A danger, a mystery, a brass ring to be seized. Just stay cool and you'll be a part of it, be right there as it unfolds. Correspondent, berichter, official historian to the Immunity. Nine months of hell and you'll have it all.*

Beside me, Tosca Lehne snorted and banged a cup on the table. "Hey, Strasheim, she's talking to you."

"What?" I looked up, saw that Jenna Davenroy had been speaking to me from across the table. "I'm sorry, I didn't catch that."

Shaking loose a few stands of unruly, tin-colored hair, Davenroy rolled her eyes and stabbed pale fingers at the air. "I said, what are you *reading*? Pardon my nosiness, but what we read at the dinner table says an awful lot about us as people."

"Yeah," Tug Jinacio chipped in, "especially what we read when people are trying to meet us. Come on, give with it. Geek it over."

"It's nothing," I assured them. "Just a little homework."

"Flash it to me," Jinacio insisted, not quite rudely. His face looked as though he'd skipped a day shaving, though his short hair was immaculately brushed; the tone of voice matched this image perfectly, at once careless and deliberate and attentive. He seemed the sort of casual charmer who could hover at the edge of rudeness and never quite cross it. Probably common in his usual circles: he was a Response lieutenant, twice decorated, most recently in charge of a unit of eight rowdy veterans and a pair of trainees. I'd read through the bio an hour or two before, and found it impressive. Nobody called him by the name it gave: Christofolo. Nobody questioned his right to speak as he pleased.

The woman, Jenna Davenroy, interested me less. A nuclear engineer a little over half my mother's age, she was slated to be *Pasteur*'s ladderdown expert and chief propulsion monitor. Her bona fides seemed more academic in nature; she had rescued no children, but had apparently contributed to the body of knowledge that kept the lights on, the caverns warm. Just now she was nodding, agreeing with what Tug Jinacio had said.

"What better way to get to know you than rifling through your private thoughts? Do please allow us."

The lines in her face were not numerous, but they cut deep, and moved readily when she talked. Her gaze was weighty.

"Really, it's nothing," I insisted, conscious suddenly of being the only one at the table not wearing spacer blues. But I flashed them copies of my windows.

Jinacio whistled. Davenroy's eyebrows went up. "Cluttered," she said, her tone amused but also oddly approving.

I blushed and ducked my head. "I don't usually run so opaque; I'm just trying to psych myself up for this. I . . . I don't know. I saw the ship today."

"Ah," Davenroy said, nodding. "A little anticipatory cabin fever. That's normal. I take it you haven't done ship time before?"

I shuddered, my nostrils filling with the mingled scents of sweat and excrement, my ears with the moans of those who'd been confined too long to their bunks. Free movement shifts limited to four hours, day after day. "No," I said quietly, "not since the Evacuation."

"Doesn't count. Conditions have improved a lot since then. Still, the zee is your friend; you should keep that in mind at all times. You don't dabble much in visual ideation, I take it? Most people don't."

"No," I agreed, "I don't."

"But you have no specific objection to the practice?"

I shrugged. Ideation was a habit, like sweets or stimulants or alcohol, not inherently deviant or harmful in and of itself. Useful in the arts and sciences, of course, and practiced by many respectable citizens. And yet, most of the Immunity's ideators simply had too much time on their hands, and too little energy. Why change the world, or even yourself, when you could craft or purchase fantasy environments optimized to your taste and habits? Illegal spec mods aside, the eyes and ears could absorb a great many pleasurable stimuli—not so different, really, from listening to music or going out to the theater or flashing down the occasional VR drama. The temptation was an entirely natural one, and suspect for precisely that reason. Yes, I had done it from time to time, but not often. We had a society to run, now, didn't we?

"Oh, drink your tea," she said, waggling a finger at me. "Staring at bulkheads for a few weeks will leave you a bit more open-minded."

"Open-minded? That's a funny phrase to use around this one, isn't it?" Another woman had arrived, and presently sat down beside Davenroy. I recognized her at once as Renata Baucum, the one *Pasteur* crew member whose exact function I couldn't quite grasp. Veterinarian? Zoologist? Microbiologist? Her records hinted at all of these things.

"Hallo," I said to her, setting my cup down and extending a hand. "John Strasheim, mission correspondent. You're Baucum?"

"Quite," she said, flashing white, pointed teeth.

"Pleasure to meet you," I said. And meant it, too; she was rather more striking than her portfolio images had indicated, her long hair more silken, her jawline curving more gracefully. Well, who looked good in their ID holographs anyway? I smiled back. "I've been wondering about your job."

She blinked, tapping politely at the empty air between us. "Yes?"

"Yeah. Well, I mean, what is it? What's your job title going to be?"

"Oh, bioanalyst, I suppose." She looked embarrassed, maybe a little annoyed. Her eyes, too, were deeper and more piercing than the holograph had shown, coolly reflecting the spacer blue of her coveralls. "All the little lebenforms, I just love to see them tick. With any luck, I'll be entirely superfluous." Her eyes traveled up and down, examining me. "And you, a berichter. How interesting. Or do you prefer 'correspondent'?"

Despite the smile and the good-natured tone, she had managed through careful inflection to make clear that "berichter" and "superfluous" were linked concepts, that she was kind enough to speak with me, but that I shouldn't take it as any sort of sign of equality.

Well.

I inclined my head politely, to show that her message had been understood, and then, taking a moment to peek under the table, I matched her tone: "Those shoes you're wearing, miss. Are they comfortable?"

Her thin smile collapsed into blankness and mild confusion.

"Do they hold your feet down? Provide adequate traction? Are they flexible despite their weight?"

"They're okay," she said, puzzled, eyeing me with suspicion.

"I'm so very glad," I told her. Their tapered-fan shape, like huge outspread toes, gave them away; they were, of course, Philusburg shoes. Mine.

Tug Jinacio let out a sudden laugh, and then Lehne and Davenroy joined in, and the look on Renata Baucum's face showed her understanding that the joke had gotten away from her, that she was somehow the butt of it after all. Creditably, her smile returned, and she favored me with a new look and message: *Very good, sir. I'll be more careful next time.*

Just then, Darren Wallich and another man arrived, set food trays down, occupied the table's last two seats.

"What's funny?" Wallich wanted to know. Jinacio and Davenroy just laughed a little harder, and Wallich seemed unable to keep from joining them.

"Hi!" I called out to the smaller man beside Wallich. "John Strasheim. Sudhir Rapisardi?"

"The same," he admitted, and we shook hands across the table.

A biophysicist, Rapisardi had coordinated the design of the TGL detectors so central to *Louis Pasteur*'s mission. I wondered how that must feel—having this nine-month party thrown more or less in his honor. I would have to remember to ask him sometime. Anyway, he was the last crew member I had to meet, so I told him, "I'm very pleased to meet you." And meant it.

Baucum caught sight of something behind me. The laughter around us died. Heads turned.

"Sticks," she muttered, scowling.

I turned to look. Indeed, a quartet of uniformed police had entered the cafeteria, and were strolling among the tables with no clear intention of sitting down. Two of them made a discreet but careful job of sweeping air, their sniff wands held out at waist level, ticking back and forth.

"What's happening?" I asked quietly.

"Security sweep," Baucum said. "Looking for accidents."

"I'm sorry?"

Captain Wallich, for once, had stopped laughing. "We've had some accidents," he said to me. "And some vandalism beyond what's usual. Some higher-ups worry there may be a pattern to it, but this is, well, counterproductive for one thing. If some fool is monkey-wrenching around here, it won't be those guys who find it."

"Vandalism of *Louis Pasteur*?" I asked.

"Sometimes," he agreed. "Sometimes not, but our bay does seem to have more than its share of problems. Do keep your eyes open, right?"

I was shaking my head, puzzled. "Who would do a thing like that? What's to be gained?"

"Oh, who the fuck knows." Wallich dug into his food, not amused by this subject at all.

Eventually, the sticks finished their sweep and left the room the way they had come in. Looking for what, for the sharp, distinctive reek of guilt? Right. Looking for nothing, I decided; probably nothing more than a show of force, and misguided as such. Since when had anyone taken the sticks seriously? *Get a real job, freund; if this were a police state they'd have hired somebody smarter than you.*

Conversation slowly resumed.

"It does seem a little misguided," I said to Wallich eventually, "strutting around like that. You'd think they'd have more subtlety."

"Yes," Renata Baucum agreed, her gray eyes hard and glittering. "You'd think so. Drop a spy or two in our midst, perhaps?"

She was looking at me strangely, some muddled combination of expectation, contempt, perhaps a hint of unease. Did she think I was a political spy? A stick? A saboteur?

Frowning back at her, I shifted in my seat. "Baucum, I'm recording you right now. Bits and pieces of this conversation will find their way into a collage, at the very least, and will be shared with thousands of readers. Does that make you uneasy?"

"Uneasy?" She considered the word, then nodded. "I'm uneasy that this mission has a reporter assigned to it, yes, particularly since our objectives are clearly political rather than scientific, aimed at pleasing both inactionist and exterminationist factions. A neat trick! Do you know what a mirrored door looks like? It looks like an open room. But it isn't; it's a *closed* room, with a mirror on the door. That's what I see when I look at you."

I blinked, snorted, not sure how to respond. "Am I supposed to apologize?"

The rest of the crew had gone silent, and were watching us with interest.

"You wouldn't know what you were apologizing for," Baucum said. "Just never mind. Just forget it."

I shook my head. "No, you brought this up. I'm listening."

"And so are thousands of people," she said, more quietly, almost whispering now. "That's my problem with you. Thousands of people are going to think whatever you tell them to think. That everything

is safe, that changes to the status quo are unwelcome and dangerous? I mean, who are you, really?"

Sighing, I picked up my spoon and shoveled a load of gruel into
my mouth. "I work in a shoe factory," I said, before I'd quite finished
chewing. "Sometimes, I tell people what I think. That's called 'enlightened discourse.' "

"I've seen your work," she said, nodding slightly. "Very
enlightened."

Suddenly, she sat forward, leaning her elbows on the table. "Let
me tell you a story, all right? It's about the word 'mycorum,' which
came into use because when technogenic life first got away from us,
the earliest examples filled the same ecological niche as most fungi.
Decomposers, right? Start with a complex organic structure, then
break it down, burn it up, use it to fuel the process of your own reproduction. The eat-bloom-spore cycle was nothing new—the mycora were just a good deal faster about it."

I gestured politely for her to continue. "Yes? So?"

"So, when the Earth's biosphere was fully converted, there was
nothing left to decompose. The mycora should have died, but they
didn't. Instead, they very rapidly evolved photo- and chemosyn-
thetic pathways which enabled them to use *inorganic* matter in their
reproduction. Becoming like plants, only a great deal more versatile.
In fact, they've done a much better job of vivifying the Earth than
organic life ever did."

"Do you admire them for it? In a Temples kind of way?" I asked,
suppressing a shudder.

"Admire?" She scowled. "In a technical sense, yes, of course, but
you're not going to trap me that easily. I'd like to have the Earth
back as much as you, believe me, but its current tenants have been
very effective in asserting their claim."

I gave her a good hard look, watching my indicators to ensure I was recording a good image. "I may be a little dense, Baucum. What is your point?"

Her expression flared, not angry but impatient with me, with my presumed ignorance. "The point is that we still call them my-cora. Their central functions have changed a trillion times more than our attitudes toward them. Such blindness may well be the death of us all."

"And you think this is my fault?"

She looked down at her food, then back at me. "Your *fault*? No, I suppose, not really. But you're a part of—"

"I'm a symbol to you, planted here to annoy you. A door with a mirror on it, nothing more. Is that it?"

"Oh, fine," she said, looking up at me again with angry eyes. I'd cornered her—not the best way to conduct an interview, or a conversation. "Fine. You're a real person, not a symbol, nobody at all is jerking your strings, and the attitudes of society are not your fault. And you have a *real job*, too, so maybe I'm just a bad person for opening my mouth. Are we finished?"

There was a silence about the table for several seconds.

Embarrassed, I answered as mildly as I could: "If you like, yes. But if you need an audience for your ideas, I'm always available."

"How wonderful," she said.

Darren Wallich stifled a laugh. Me? I returned to my dinner, thinking that somewhere along the line, someone should have tried a little harder to find crew members who might actually get along. But who'd bother with such frivolities, when there was work to be done? *Busy, always busy. That's life, eh?*

After dinner, Tug Jinacio took me aside, stood with me in front of the big window overlooking the drydock bays.

"It isn't too late to back out," he said, his voice noncommittal, managing to avoid any sort of implication. That I was unsafe? That I was cowardly? No, it came across as a simple statement of fact, in case the idea hadn't occurred to me.

I strove to match his tone. "I'm fine."

"This t-balance stuff, you know there's been no testing of it. Likely it'll just fail for some reason. Possibly not, right, but I've got to live my life as though that's true. To do my job, I've got to make every unfavorable assumption."

"My own incompetence included?"

His answering look was friendly, amused. "Competence I couldn't care less about. Not my worry. Captain wants you, Captain gets you. It's your calm that concerns me. Are you calm, John?"

Calm? How to answer a question like that? Say that I'd survived the end of the world, survived the journey here, survived the building and burrowing of the years that followed? Tell him that since that time I'd seen nothing alarming, done nothing alarming? That I wept at funerals, no matter the deceased's identity? He didn't want to know these things.

"Maybe," I said to him, somehow not annoyed, "you should shove my head in a bucket of cold water, and see how I react. My guess is, I'd flail around like mad until I got loose, and then I'd throw a punch or two, and then probably back off and start screaming at you. But it's hard to say, really, until it happens. People are funny that way."

He smiled. "That's not a bad answer. But not a complete one, either."

"No?" I turned, looked out at the gray-black ships in their gray-black drydock berths. There'd be a man like Tug on each of these, a man responsible for bloom and fire safety, for emergency response in general. The vast majority would come from spacer backgrounds, rather than from the Response corps itself, but then none of these ships, in their local supply and survey runs, would ever face a danger like ours, would ever be quite so immediately in harm's way. This questioning, then, was not only warranted, but necessary.

"I'll tell you what," I said. "If anything happens, I'll promise to put a high priority on staying out of your way. I think I can promise that much, at least."

He nodded approvingly. "That's all I'm after, John. When things go sour, there isn't a lot of time to dick around. If I sense you're a liability, I'll have to add you to my list of problems. If not, you can be safely ignored, and I mean that in the kindest possible way. I have no objection, by the way, to carrying a reporter on the mission. I think it's probably a good idea."

"Good?" I said, unduly flattered by the comment. "Why, exactly?"

"Hell, freund, if you can't answer that, maybe Captain's asked Herr Lottick for the wrong man."

He clapped me on the shoulder and walked away. It hadn't been an insult, hadn't been delivered or received as one. You know how harsh words can cement a friendship? As if to say, you and I are close enough that these barbs won't come between us. That was what he sounded like.

I had to admire the trick; few people bothered with it anymore. Who, after all, had the time to practice?

Sometimes
They Get Out

"One-quarter starboard yaw turn," Darren Wallich called out. "Two-tenths gee-thrust on my command. Go! And . . . thrust vector aligned, intercept course, median consumption trajectory. Right on the average, people, give yourselves a gold star."

Grunts of approval filled the bridge. Four stations here: one for Wallich, one for Tosca Lehne, one for Renata Baucum, and, oddly enough, one for me as well. A crowded environment, and a confusing, visually cluttered one as well: metal bulkheads painted beige, covered here and there with text-covered white plastic and sprouting orange seats and dark gray control consoles. A bridge designed for zero gravity and not meant, particularly, to be understood at a glance. Since my actual seat was on the ceiling, and I didn't like to strap into it at Ganymedean surface gravity, I had conducted the drill standing up between the chairs of Lehne and Baucum, reaching up awkwardly for the controls, my arm a little stiff in the uniform which, after six days, I still hadn't quite got used to.

"Nobody's just a reporter on my ship," Wallich had told me several times. "You can run the resource allocation oversight console. Veto authority over information systems and power allocations—any fool can handle that."

Nice to know he had such confidence in me, but then, the job actually did appear necessary for the proper functioning of the ship. The allocation programs hiccupped rather more often in his rehearsals than they would in real life, but when I failed to compensate properly, the very best result would be a waste of fuel during maneuvers. The worst I wasn't so sure about, but it probably involved life-support failures and reactor overloads and everyone winding up dead.

So how about that? With a few day's training, I could be an actual crew member on an actual interplanetary ship. My official rank was logged as "Spaceman Recruit," though my pay was an officer's—actually a bit more than I'd made as a cobbler.

"Captain?" said the voice of Jenna Davenroy over the intercom. She was crammed into the tiny engine room with Rapisardi, keeping the engines healthy. This seemed to involve keeping their uranium fuel at the proper temperature by regulating the flow of coolant through the three ladderdown reactors. The job seemed to frustrate them both.

"Go ahead, engine room," Wallich said.

"Captain, I hear an alarm," Davenroy said.

"Yes? What alarm? What's your status?"

"Not my alarm," she corrected. "I *hear* it. Outside the ship, I think, in the hangar."

"Outside? Ah, crap." He chuckled. "Okay, fire drill. Everybody out, single file."

I couldn't tell if he was joking or not, but the others worked their harnesses loose and struggled out of their seats, and I followed them out as they left.

Tug Jinacio alone had no assigned function during flight; his job was to wait around for an emergency—real or simulated—to happen, and then to spring instantly to proper action. Thus, he was at the main hatch before anyone else, working the latches, throwing it open, jumping boldly out onto the shipyard floor. The rest of us squeezed through behind him, twisting and ducking around the controls and protuberances of the modified cargo hold.

Outside, yes, there was an alarm bell going off—BING! BING! BING! BING! Not a fire but a *bloom* alarm. Hard-hatted workers ran here and there across the floor, doing who knows what. Security was here, as well, the pair of sticks Wallich had reluctantly called in as my reports drew larger and larger crowds of gawkers, who proved more and more difficult to send away. But the sticks didn't seem to know what to do. They stood looking around, waiting for something obvious to happen. Like me, they couldn't seem to tell if this was a drill.

I caught sight of a stranger, a helmetless and visorless man in street clothes, doing something up against a far wall. Urinating? No, dumping something out of a bottle, some milky liquid that splashed into one of the air vents there. Well, *that* sure didn't look right. Pointing, I shouted to the sticks, but they had seen the man already and were hurrying toward him. Where had he come from? An ABSOLUTELY NO ADMITTANCE door?

Halfway there, the sticks halted. The man himself was backing slowly away from the wall, his attention focused on the air vent, on what was happening there. Smoke? Fire? Contamination?

Bloom.

I had lived two decades in the Immunity without ever seeing one up close. I'd seen them often in VR collage, of course, but how was I to know how completely the intervening technology blurred the experience? The air vent and the wall it was part of began to boil, their substance turning fluid, turning into rainbow-threaded vapors as the tiny, tiny mycora disassembled them molecule by molecule. The process was slower than I would have expected, like watching a pool of spilled syrup ooze out across a table, but the immediacy, the *reality* of it had frozen me in my tracks. How vivid the colors, how crisp the lines and edges! I knew exactly what I was looking at: class-one threaded bloom in early germination phase, about two minutes before fruiting began. Some structure already visible in the expanding fog, crystalline picks growing like needles from the drydock wall. I knew exactly what I was looking at, and yet it looked nothing like I would have expected. Nothing at all.

Had the man with the bottle caused this? No, of course not. What an absurd thought! Mycora had caused this, deadly spores riding the solar wind up from the Mycosystem, kicking around Jovian space probably for *years* before somehow finding their way in here. No human intervention involved, nor even possible. Why else have an Immunity at all?

Clearly, the man was *fighting* the bloom, as I would be doing if I'd had a better idea how to go about it. Tug Jinacio, of course, was hindered by no such ignorance. He sprinted for the nearest emergency locker, removing his Response helmet and dashing it against the glass, reaching for the equipment inside and running a double armload of it right up to the edge of the fecund area. The bottle man, apparently mesmerized, continued to back away slowly. The sticks, God bless them, turned tail and ran for the exit.

With my crewmates standing mutely around me, I watched Jinacio open a macrophage magnum and heave its powdery contents into the heart of the bloom. Watched him pick up another and another, repeating the process. But the phages seemed not to have any effect; the rainbow mist continued its slow expansion. An uncataloged pathogen? Jinacio changed tactics, started throwing witch's tits to freeze the area down, but the effect was not noticeably better, and I began to *really worry*, because if fruiting bodies were given a chance to form, spores would be blasted all over the inside of this hangar, and Galileo would have a problem like Galileo had never seen nor dreamt of.

What happened next I can describe in detail only because my zee-spec was recording at the time. My own memory is of screaming and jostling and running, nothing more, but of course the clear, steady images show that I must have been standing there watching as the bottle man stepped up behind Tug Jinacio and pushed him bodily into the bloom. Tug's body did not come apart at once into threads and dust, but his skin had gone rainbow-crystalline with mycoric frost before he'd even hit the floor, and of course he never did rise. Did my recording capture the full depth and character of his scream? It was a quiet thing, mewling and pathetic with surprise. *How can this have happened to* me? *How can this fate be* mine? *This pain, this PAIN, how can it be mine?*

In my dreams I hear a scream sometimes that is like the one I recorded, in the same way that the actual bloom was like the VR collages that had supposedly prepared me for it. That Jinacio suffered in the twelve seconds of his death goes without saying, but the images are not on file. God, I owe him that much, at least.

Again, I have no memory of the bottle man speaking, but in my private records he turns toward us, his expression frantic with re-morse and fear and rage. "They're bombs," he says tightly. "I can't let you do this. However human it may be, it's monstrous to destroy what you don't understand."

And then, whether through accident or miscalculation or delib-erate suicide, he steps a little too far to the left, catches the edge of the bloom, and dies elaborately. Maybe I should ask other witnesses what they remember of these events. Maybe these things simply have no place in the mammalian brain, no means of being recog-nized or stored, or maybe I'm just blessed with a poor memory. I don't really care.

My recollection rejoins that of the zee-spec as Darren Wallich crowds into my view, grabbing me by the shoulders and shoving me up the ramp, into the *Louis Pasteur*'s open hatch. ". . . not going to get through the t-balance," he was saying, "but if the roof collapses we're over and done with. Get aboard! Get aboard! Damn it, I'm not going to tell you again!"

At least the scaffolding was gone, the ship bare and gleaming in its peculiar way. I did as I was told, and the hatch was closed be-hind me.

No windows in *Louis Pasteur*—have I mentioned that?—but there were camera dots embedded in the hull that could assemble a visual image and project it through a zee-spec. Somehow, I was co-herent enough to manage this task, and so was watching as the exit portal irised open in the ceiling above us. Our ladderdown reactors hissed to life. Propulsion came online. The world shuddered. I even reached up to my console and adjusted the memory allocations as our landing feet broke contact with the floor. *She starts—she moves—she seems to feel/The thrill of life along her keel!* After that it was the clanging of shiplocks, the roar of engines, the press of acceleration as we fled the interior of Ganymede for the safety of the cold and dark outside.

"I hope the sticks got out okay," I said in an even tone, to no one in particular. And after that a lot of us were crying.

The wisdom of assigning reporters to hazardous space missions may be a subject for debate, but I'll point out that I was the first to know what was going on, once we'd made orbit and had a chance to get communications set up. About an hour, I'd say, though it may have been less.

A quick tour of the Galileo daily records, still unfolding as I perused them, revealed that our bloom had in fact been the second of four that occurred within the space of an hour. All were now under control in a Final Alert freezedown, with two pathogens identified and cataloged for future Immune response. Cleanup crews were sterilizing the areas, and repairs were expected to commence within forty-eight hours. Considering the seriousness of the event, casualties had been light—only twelve fatalities thus far—but material damage estimates had already exceeded two million g.u., enough to feed the entire Immunity for a week.

Even more disturbing was the news on a lot of the talk channels:

"... *if it* isn't *the Temples I'll kiss the bloom with my own two lips* ..."

"... *spokeswoman denies involvement. My ass! I read unauthorized access by Temples members in the vicinities of all four events* ..."

". . . police raids on a pair of Temples laboratories have already taken place. Authorities can 'neither confirm nor rule out' some form of human assistance in the initiation of these blooms. How they could transport the spores I have no idea . . ."

I thought of the bottle man, and shivered. What kind of bottle had it been? What kind of contents? Technogenic life was very nearly a universal solvent, capable of disassembling almost anything. Our knowledge of any given mycorum's inner structure came solely via the phages that absorbed and destroyed it, and occasionally from direct microscopic assay of the remaining fragments. You couldn't simply pack a bunch of live mycora into a bottle and carry them around with you, even assuming you could safely collect them.

There was also a crazy-ass statement from the Temples of Transcendent Evolution themselves, echoed to most of the news channels on the network:

"The events of this afternoon are tragic and regrettable. However, no such action has been sanctioned nor shall be sanctioned by this organization, which is humanitarian and gnostic in nature. It is possible that human beings are partly responsible for what has happened, and if the parties involved—if any—are affiliated with the Temples in any way, we shall certainly get to the bottom of it. We revile malice in any form, and offer our full cooperation with any investigation.

"However, a possible motivation for this attack—if in fact an attack has occurred—has become known to us. It concerns the Louis Pasteur *and its supposed mission of discovery; one or more persons claiming a close connection with this endeavor have favored us with an anonymous message—detailed and credible within our ability to determine—indicating that the 'detectors'*

to be seeded across sterile portions of the inner planets are in fact ladderdown explosive devices intended to devastate the surfaces of these worlds.

"Little is known about the physical and psychical workings of the Mycosystem, and such an attack, in addition to its grave moral repugnance, could have severe repercussions throughout the solar system. It is possible that today's events represent an attempt by desperate persons to prevent this tragedy from occurring. If so, we can only lament that we were not approached earlier, so that a more clement solution to the crisis could be found."

Well.

I flashed summaries of this information to the rest of the crew, and could not resist linking my zee-spec to a ship-internal camera dot to record and downlink a brief news channel commentary of my own:

"John Strasheim here. Listen, citizens, none of this makes sense, even to those of us who were there. Please, let's burn no Temples tonight."

Eventually, Vaclav Lottick got ahold of us, using a full VR conference channel in realtime flash. "*Pasteur,* Lottick here!" His face, when it appeared before me, was glistening, flushed with rage. "It's the goddamn Temples. I *knew* we should have been suppressing that organization, I just knew it. Reply!"

"*Pasteur* here, go ahead," said Wallich, and suddenly my view of him, seated on what was for me the ceiling, was blocked by a mosaic of imaged faces: Wallich's own, and mine, and Baucum's, and Tosca Lehne's. Another window showed a distorted view of Davenroy and Rapisardi in the tiny, dimly lit engine room. None of us were actually looking at the cameras, so our images scattered around Lottick's own in a messy jumble that seemed interested in everything but him.

As it turned out, Lottick's information sources were even better than mine. You'd kind of hope so, wouldn't you? What he said was, "We've got two very bad mycora on the loose. Blooms are controlled in Galileo, but the same pathogens are starting to crop up in the Five Cities. Immune system primed for them, but god*damn* are they tough to fight off. Early analysis shows they contain the *entire genomes* of a number of our latest macrophages, and a whole lot of other crap besides. We know how they're doing it, at least: it's goddamn human intervention. The splice marks are plain as a letter of confession!"

"Come again?" Wallich said, though of course he must have heard perfectly well.

"Somebody," Lottick snarled, "has been *modifying* and *breeding* these things right under our noses. Somebody, yeah. It's the Temples. What about those goddamn 'probe packages' they launch into the Mycosystem two, three times a year? What about those? Are they sending their best results back down to the source? This is bad, Wallich, this is very bad. Don't you dare land that ship."

"Why not?" asked Baucum, sounding at that moment about as flustered as I felt.

Lottick's face darkened further. "Why *not*? I thought we understood each other. One, *Louis Pasteur* was almost certainly the target of these attacks. Or one of the targets, anyway. Set her down and you're just stupidly asking to be a threat to yourselves and others. Not on my say-so, you're not. Two, somebody is directing the evolution of these mycora. We've been treating severe cold adaptation and other upper-system threats as extreme long shots, but wouldn't you say the odds suddenly look a lot better? We've made a huge investment in that ship, and right now I'd say it's safer inside the damn Mycosystem than it is here at home."

"We don't have any food aboard," Wallich pointed out.

Outraged, Lottick made a face. "Well, boo-hoo, Wallich. Some of us down here don't have *functioning bodies* anymore. You've got a pap synthesizer and a water tank, and you took fuel and cargo three days ago, and as far as I'm concerned that means you're fully operational. I want those goddamn detectors in place and online as soon as goddamn possible, before we wake up one morning two meters deep in goo. That's your mission. Have I made myself clear?"

"Yes, perfectly," Wallich shot back. "But I still say we're undersupplied. I don't think we even have enough oxygen, unless we want to ladder it out of our fuel supply. There is *no margin* aboard this ship, and I won't fly her like this."

"So fine. So get supplies from the goddamn Gladholders for all I care. You are not to set that ship down, and I doubt you're particularly safe even in orbit. Whatever you do, do without excessive delay. Look around you, Wallich; we may be too late already."

"Understood," Wallich said thoughtfully, his grin creeping back into place. "But you're right, we could pass through the Floral asteroids on our way down. That's probably a fairly workable idea."

And so that fateful voyage was born three weeks premature, amid pain and terror and an almost lethal lack of planning. And rather a lot of unfinished business, yes. Small mercy, but at least I'd never told Momma about the plant I'd been meaning to buy her; she and I would, as per her prediction, never see each other again.

SEVEN

SPEED

In a gravitational sense, the Gladhold is far, far below us, so much so that it would take three years to fall that far, assuming we nulled out the heliocentric velocity we started with, namely Jupiter's. But canceling that orbital velocity would ladder a mere gram of uranium, even counting the energy required to escape Jupiter in the first place. What's planned here is somewhat more intense: burning half our fuel supply all in a shot, flinging Louis Pasteur *sunward on a "beeline" trajectory that intercepts the Floral asteroids in just twenty-three days—a new all-time hu-*

man speed record. And then, God willing, burning the other half to stop us when we get there.

Our inner-system schedule is similarly compressed: Earth on day 43, as opposed to 151 in the original flight plan. Alas, we'll be paying for this performance in our final burn, which will take over seven months to return us to the Immunity. A kilogram of uranium seems like a lot when you just want to power a city, but down there it's like feeding the family on a single tangerine.

from *Rrrrrrrrrocket Ride*
© 2106 by John Strasheim

Things were still in a state of disarray, nobody really sure what was aboard and what wasn't, who did and did not know of our departure, when Davenroy lit the engines up. Life was a messy conference call, a crowding of fear-stinking bodies, a hunt for checklists and air filters and Velcro strips to hold things down when the weightlessness returned. Thrust surprisingly heavy, about twice the gravity we'd all got used to at Galileo, and there I was, hanging from my seat straps, feeling the blood pool lightly in my head.

The worst of it was that my allocation duties were quickly done with, and everyone else seemed to have a job to do. So it was that I pulled up an external window and a navigation graphic, had time to correlate the two, and made the announcement:

"Our orbit takes us right past the starship. I mean, *right past* it."

"Departure conic," Darren Wallich said distractedly, his eyes on instruments I couldn't see. " 'Orbit' usually means you're not still under thrust."

"Not by my dictionary," I fired back, unaccountably annoyed at the contradiction.

"Possibly. But learn the language while you're here, right?"

"Anyway," I continued, "our *departure conic* looks like it'll bring us very close, like within a couple of kilometers. It should be coming over the horizon right about now."

"Coming over the *limb*," Wallich corrected. And chuckled.

Oh, this was going to be a fun voyage.

But now everyone started stabbing at the air, pulling up exterior-view windows to see what I was talking about. Here is what these windows showed: a circular opening in space, a hole not only through the ship's hull but through chairs, instrument panels, and people—a hole looking out at focus infinity, no matter what was in the way. Not so hard on the eye, really, but it takes getting used to, especially the way it tracks head but not eye movements. Turn to look at someone, and suddenly there are stars showing through where a face or a heart should be.

Or in this case, the limb of Ganymede showing through, with the stars unwinking above it. In one direction, the stripy beige face of Jupiter staring down, not nearly as big or imposing at this distance as you'd think. In the other, a scattering of smaller moons, faint crescents in the light of a too-distant sun. Below, the gray, cratered, raked-looking surface of home, lifeless and cold, the ice just one more hard, rocky mineral in its crust. And there, coming over the horizon right beside Renata Baucum's head, a tiny but unmistakable gleam of metal. The starship.

"Not much to look at," Tosca Lehne observed.

True enough—what I saw was a long, skinny barbell, mirror-bright and all but featureless. But smaller gleams surrounded it, crew pods and construction boats strung on just-visible lanyards like insects caught in a web, and these provided some sense of scale as we approached. Big, very—just over a kilometer long and about a fifth that wide at the flared ends. The end pieces themselves would probably have fit in the main cavern at Philusburg, but you'd have to slice the central shaft into ten or twelve sections and squeeze them in over flattened buildings before you'd even get close to fitting the whole structure in.

Surface details gradually became visible as the ship's image swelled: hatches and umbilical sockets and painted signs too tiny to make out. But still the overall impression was of smoothness, featurelessness, as with an old-style aircraft or submarine. It didn't particularly *look* years away from completion, but I supposed that smooth metal skin could well have been hollow inside, not so much a ship as a ship's empty jacket.

"Captain Wallich," I said, after making sure I was recording a good image both of him and of the approaching structure, "since I lack the vocabulary, would you like to say a few words about this for our viewers back home?"

"A few words?" He seemed fazed for a moment, but then chuckled and loosened slightly. "That's right, we have an audience on board, don't we. Well, ladies and gentlemen, that object out there is your starship. One of these days a name will stick to it, probably when its mission is better defined, but for now 'starship' will do. Maybe we'll just end up calling it that, ha ha."

"For those of us less familiar with the project, Captain," I prodded, "what are those flared structures at the ends?"

He nodded, still a bit nervous and annoyed. *One of my crew has died today, berichter. Push too hard and you'll wind up very unhappy.* "Uh, yes. The aft planchet is the propulsion focus. If you look, you'll see it's curved sort of like a flashlight mirror, only what it's reflecting are gamma rays. The forward one is the cabin shield, so the crew and cargo don't fry. You can't see it from here, but there's a smaller planchet forward of the cabin as well, for debris and cosmic rays. Going that fast, a speck of dust is like a bomb."

"And what's the crew size expected to be?"

"Good question, freund."

"Not everyone, though. Not the whole Immunity."

He sighed. "Not unless we liquefy them, no. Crew module's about the size of an apartment building, cargo spaces included. How many do you think it will hold?"

His chuckle was on the humorless side.

"So what, exactly, is the purpose of the vehicle?" I pressed. "If it's not going to carry us all away, as many people seem to believe, then what's it intended to carry?"

"Spores," Wallich said curtly. "*Our* spores, for a new Immunity. If we ever need to run away, we need a safe place to run *to*, right? Before the Mycosystem catches up with us? But there absolutely will be human crew and colonists aboard, people who are alive and working in the Immunity right now. I'm not aware of the number or nature of the slots, but I imagine anyone will have the right to try out for one."

"Thank you, sir," I said. With a little cut and paste, that sequence would collage nicely. Would Lottick object to my breaking party line on the starship issue? Did it matter? If my judgment was what he wanted, my judgment was what he would get. Not like he could do much about it at this point, anyway. The starship flashed by, huge for a few moments, its closest range only a few times greater than its length, and moving past at over five kilometers a second. And then it was behind us, shrinking away like a warning shot over the limb of Ganymede.

From that point on, things began to happen more slowly. Ganymede itself began to dwindle, now beneath us, now behind, now a world, an object, a bauble. But this took hours, and the bridge crew's conversation and task loading dwindled right along with it. On the orbital schematic, our apoapsis, the high point of our projected orbit, shot away from the little moon, out into Jovian space, our *departure conic* no longer an ellipse but an open, saddle-shaped curve, a hyperbola that would not bring us back to our starting point. But no, as I zoomed the image back I saw the path did not swing out to infinity at all, but curved back on itself in an arc many thousands of times larger. Still an ellipse, this time around Jupiter itself, and the new apoapsis continued to climb, if languidly.

A faint gray line on the display marked the limit of influence, the point at which (a dictionary check informed me) the distant sun's gravity would exceed that of Jupiter. And then what? An open curve leading away from Jupiter, swinging down into an enormous, sun-centered ellipse? There must be more to it than that; somehow, we had to get all the way down to the inner planets, some billion kilometers distant. Measured against Ganymede and Jupiter and the rest of the Immunity, our velocity steadily increased, but the heliocentric counter showed us *slowing down* with respect to the sun. Falling inward, canceling out the centrifugal pull that held us away? That made a kind of sense to me, but I resolved to find out more. For the foreseeable future, these geometries would be running my life.

It would take an hour for the apoapsis to climb out of Jovian space, and another sixty before *Louis Pasteur* did so herself. Like the old cartoon, the hungry-looking donkey following behind a carrot it could never catch, a carrot dangling from a stick tied to its own head. The faster we went, the farther away the carrot retreated. Anyway, seeing that there was time—an awful infinity of it, in fact—I cleared my throat and broke the silence.

"Captain, it looks like we're through here for the time being. If you don't mind, I'd like to go aft and have a word with Rapisardi."

"Hmm?" Wallich turned to look at me, his laughing eyes standing out against a distant, troubled expression. "Rapisardi? Yes? What about?"

"My job," I said. "We're off on entirely the wrong foot here, and I need to know some things before I can start to put a report together."

A giggle formed and died in Wallich's throat, though his expression barely flickered. "A report. Yes, well. We'll be doing a lot of maintenance drills, you know, especially in light of what's happened, and I'll expect you to pull your own mass. We'll teach you to tear down that console and put it back together again, at the very least. But we can start all that tomorrow. Yes, you can go aft and talk to Rapisardi."

"Thanks," I told him, reaching for my harness release and disengaging it carefully. Under the two-tenths gee thrust, I turned and lowered myself until I found footing on the step behind Baucum's chair. I'd done this several times in Ganymedean gravity without mishap, and though Baucum swiveled her head to glare nervously as I climbed down, I managed the operation without stepping or falling on her.

"Don't thank me," Wallich said mildly when he saw I was safely down. "We've all got our jobs to do. Only one thing, Strasheim: run your material past me before you transmit. I wouldn't want to see anything . . . inflammatory come down looking like official word. You see the potential for problems, I'm sure."

And then he laughed.

So that was how it was going to be, eh? The walls seemed to close in a little more tightly, but I smiled back at him pleasantly enough. "Sure I do. Yeah, sure I do."

Sure I did. Renata Baucum turned toward me again, flashing a look I couldn't interpret. Emphasis: wide, rolling eyes, the eyebrows arching. Whatever the message, I wasn't getting it, and her manner suggested she'd drop the expression the moment Wallich looked her way.

Oh, the hell with it, I thought, and turned to go. If it was important, she could jolly well tell me later.

"Mr. Rapisardi, Ms. Davenroy," I said as I entered the engine room. Or entered its hatchway, more properly—the room, dim and gray and lined with humming pipes, wasn't big enough for three. Wasn't even big enough for the two that were in it, really.

"Mr. Strasheim," they chorused in reply, and we all shared an uncomfortable, unhappy little laugh.

"Tug Jinacio," I said after a pause. "I don't understand why he died. I was hoping one or both of you could answer some questions."

Davenroy frowned. "About what?"

"Ladderdown," I said, and the two of them relaxed a bit. "This talk of bombs, it's very puzzling. Is such a thing really possible?"

Rapisardi nodded. "Yes. You know, it's an interesting accusation, because we don't normally think of ladderdown in this way. A source of energy and raw materials, yes, but also it can be made to explode. We don't do this, of course, but whoever planted the rumor must have known a little physics."

"You say 'planted'?" I led.

"Well, yes. These detectors, which I designed myself, are not explosive. I would know this, you agree?"

"Presumably."

"So the rumor is maybe to disrupt our voyage. There are those who disapprove, as well you know, and they are not always the ones you expect. We're spending a lot of money, and this upsets people, as the spending of money will do."

"I thought we'd kind of got beyond money," Davenroy mumbled with more than a touch of sarcasm.

"Yes, of course," Rapisardi agreed in the same tone, his eyes flicking from me to Davenroy and back. "Now that we are dependent on heavy metals rather than fossil organics and sunlight, economics have simply gone away. You want a lesson in economics from a biophysicist's point of view? It works like ecology—it breeds and selects. Not that we actually carry them in our pockets, but the gram of uranium has become our most basic unit of currency. Thanks to chronic short-staffing, we consider it equivalent to half an hour of human labor, though its energy potential is some twenty-six million times greater. Aside from ourselves, it is the first driver of our economy, the reasons for which are not at all arbitrary."

"For energy reasons," I said.

He winced slightly, shifted position in his chair. "Energy? Well, yes and no. Energy is less important than transmutation potential. In rough terms, a fusion reactor cascading a gram of deuterium/tritium up into a gram of iron—the basin of the binding energy curve—will liberate enough energy to boil about twenty thousand tons of water. A gram of uranium in a ladderdown reactor produces approximately the same. And yet, the uranium is worth ten thousand times more, because in laddering it down, we don't have to sink all the way to iron. We can stop anywhere along the way, and our waste products are isotopes of hydrogen which we can cascade back up, again stopping wherever we like below that magic number, iron fifty-six. A ladderdown economy sees value not only in what a substance *is*, but also in what it can become, and uranium, alone among the stable elements, can become anything."

That was an interesting précis, a perspective I'd never quite heard before, but meaning what? I shook my head. "What does this have to do with today? I'm not following."

"No?" Rapisardi banged the wall with his fist, producing a flat,

solid thump. "Heavy metals. Particularly with its t-balance jacket-
ing, this vehicle is very literally made of money."

"The starship has almost universal support," I pointed out, "and
it's much bigger and more expensive. No one has started any blooms
over that."

"Not yet, no, but maybe someday. At the moment, it's mostly
coming together out of iron, an essentially valueless material. But
even now the labor costs are punishing, and heaven help us when we
start to fuel it. The endeavor may kick us forcibly from a uranium
economy to an antimatter one."

"Again," I sighed, "I'm afraid you've lost me. Try to imagine I'm
not viewing life through a biophysicist's eyes. Or an economist's."

He shook his head. "You can view through mine, if you like.
Forgive me; I'm used to having this conversation over and over again
with the same people. Eventually it becomes its own shorthand.
What I'm suggesting is that every g.u. we spend outside the Immunity is a g.u. that has to be earned back through human labor. And
where are we supposed to find that? Many people are surprised
to learn that lead's energy potential is only twenty-five percent
less than uranium's, but the thing to remember is that lead has ten
fewer transmutation targets—eighty-one versus ninety-one—which
translates into a factor of a thousand reduction in its value. Gold,
three rungs lower still, is worth about a five-thousandth as much as
uranium. It has beautiful mechanical and electrical properties, but
really, the major cost of paving the streets with it is the labor.[1]

"*Louis Pasteur*'s engines burn up about 10 g.u. per hour at full
thrust, but we, the crew, cost more than that even when the engines

1. Fact-checking reveals the costs of 10m of roadway to be approximately 130 g.u.
   pure gold, 1 g.u. assorted dopants and impurities, and 3 g.u. equipment amortiza-
   tion. Human labor and supervision account for approximately 24 g.u., or about 15
   percent of the total. However, Rapisardi's central point remains a valid one.

aren't firing, which will be most of the time. We can't ask things to happen by themselves; vision is transmuted to physicality through our hands, only.

"And believe me, that starship will make its costs apparent soon enough. The energy density of antihydrogen is about 250 times what we can achieve with ladderdown, and the production and storage are difficult. Wonderful fuel, the best, but the last time I checked, a gram of it cost over eighty thousand g.u., which basically means the ship is not going anywhere this decade, nor probably the next. But we will continue to pay, you see? There is bound to be impatience, and backlash."

I still wasn't satisfied; Rapisardi was answering the question he wanted to answer, which wasn't really the one I had asked. I pressed for clarification: "You're saying you don't think the Temples of Transcendent Evolution had anything to do with the attack?"

"Eh?" He looked up from his gray, almost blank-looking console, looked straight at me for what seemed the first time. Suddenly realizing, no doubt, that he was speaking for the record, that the next words he spoke would cling to him, remain associated with him for a time in the public zeitgeist. His face went cautious. "No, I wouldn't go so far as to say that. The problem I'm discussing is systemic throughout the Immunity, but the Temples have their own private complaints as well. Twice as many motives as anyone else. By the crudest possible logic, I'd say there's a sixty-six percent chance they were involved in the incident in some way. Neither outcome would surprise me very much, let me say that. Is this an interview, Strasheim?"

"If you like," I said with some reluctance. "It doesn't seem like the best time. Really, I just wanted clarification on the bomb question."

He nodded, thinking about that. "You need something to tell

the people back home, I see. I didn't know Jinacio all that well, but I
liked him. His loss—well, naturally it's very upsetting. Maybe you
could mention that, as well."

Was that resentment I heard? Probably, yes. The price of reporting for a living, I supposed, of being seen as one who reports. In a
way, I actually *was* a spy. I noticed Davenroy, sitting quietly in her
little niche, looking at me. She had known Jinacio rather better than
the rest of us. Possibly I was intruding on her grief? How not to intrude, in this tiny vessel? Facts of life, problems I'd better start solv-
ing here and now.

"I'll do that," I said to both of them, now looking past them at
their instrument niches, crowded together like the dark spaces under opposite desks. "I liked him, too; some people are just better at
inspiring confidence. Um, ungraceful change of subject: I'm curious
about how the engines are performing. Not for the home audience,
but for my own peace of mind."

"All nominal," Davenroy said, amicably enough, "but I hope you
like microgravity. First burn should end in about forty-eight hours,
and after that we're weightless. If you're going to barf all over everything, dear, you should think about staying in your quarters."

My coffin, she meant. My eggshell-thin plastic tomb. "I'll be
fine," I assured her, "but thanks for the warning. I'll, uh, I'll be on
the bridge. See you later."

"Undoubtedly," Davenroy said, and as I turned away, I thought
in the shadows of her face I maybe saw the glimmer of a teardrop, or
possibly a wink.

Snapshots

The Evacuation of Earth was much like that of the Titanic a century and a half before; we see the same bravado, denial, lifeboats floating away half empty, and only in about the final quarter of the crisis do its participants really begin to voice and act on their peril. In Earth's case, this equates to a span of maybe thirty-six hours. Not a long time to clear a whole planet.

Within a hundred kilometers of a major spaceport, you had just about a one in a thousand chance of making it to orbit alive; outside these areas the odds dropped to less than one in a million.

And from there, another five percent failed to make it to Luna before their air or water or luck ran out. Those that made it, of course, completely swamped the Lunar bases' ability to cope, so mortality continued in a steady grind for weeks and months afterward. The state of emergency never ended, and no sense of normalcy was ever established, which turned out to be a fortunate thing when the spores started falling and the bare, sterile Lunar soil itself began to bloom. In a very real sense, the Second Evacuation was a mere appendix to the First, the continued unfolding of a single event.

For a number of reasons, from the astrodynamic to the mycoric to the geopolitical to plain coincidence, evacuees from Earth's tropical regions ended up mostly at Mendeleev and Moscoviense on the Lunar farside. With notable exceptions, those unfortunates starting out between thirty and forty-five degrees north or south latitudes didn't make it out at all, while those from the high temperate zones found themselves at Tycho and Clavius and Pingre in the nearside's southern latitudes.

These groupings were largely preserved in the Second Evacuation, in that the farsiders—actually the first to leave in many cases—settled primarily in the asteroid belt, while nearside refugees, fearing the spread of a Mycosystem whose limitations were by no means clear at that time, pressed straight on to Jupiter. The wide Bode gap separating these two regions proved a formidable barrier to sustained commerce, which in turn limited contact to the time-lagged data channels, permitting the regions' cultural evolution to diverge significantly. Within a decade, the Immune/Gladholder distinction had taken firm hold, and indeed has changed little since that time.

Less to survive on out here, yes, but more to compete with down there. Who can say which life is harder? And to those who express surprise that the Gladholders have hung on as long as they have, let me assure you: they say exactly the same about us.

from *Innensburg and the Fear of Failure,*
© 2101 by John Strasheim

Image: Engine room, starboard instrument niche; close-up, main oversight console. *Text Enhance:* The panel is nearly featureless, just a flat Teflon grid marked off into domino sectors by little white lines. Made active and useful mainly by the zee-spec—see technical specification for further detail. *Schematic Enhance:* 0.75-second overlay of the console projections. *APDX:* Adjust resolution and color palette to favor little yellow lines! Also, just for yucks, show human figure as wireframe around cartoon skeleton. *Image:* Restore previous.

Voiceover: The disquiet of knowing the engines can in fact explode is mitigated somewhat by the knowledge that Davenroy sits here most of the time, monitoring reactor status whether the engines are firing or not. In an environment like this, you learn very quickly to trust your crewmates. Smile for the camera, dear. Perfect, perfect. They love you already.

Image: Close-up, contamination and environmental monitoring station.

Voiceover: Sudhir Rapisardi backs Davenroy up with constant assessments of the fuel supply and engine surfaces, watching not only for TGL infestation but for invaders as mundane as sterile interplanetary dust, and for such homegrown dangers as cracking or hot spots in the materials. So, how's it going?

Rapisardi: OK.

Voiceover: A man of few words, ladies and gentlemen, but if you do get him talking you'd better have some time on your hands.

Image: Engine room. Pan (i.e., float) back two meters; zoom out to max viewing angle, focus infinity. *Text Enhance:* Engine room crew work overlapping 15-hour shifts, and either station can be reconfigured to perform some or all of the functions of the other. See technical specification for further detail.

Schematic Enhance: 1 pt. grid overlay, calcium white, 10 cm spacing, conformal with inanimate surfaces. Hold one second, fade one second. *APDX:* Human figures should eclipse grid lines. Fix in post!

Voiceover: What you see now is the view of the engine room from the wardroom hatchway, which shows you most of what there is to see, but which is also a little misleading visually. It's difficult to convey how dim and cramped this space really is, but my bedroom closet back home has more light and more maneuvering room, and probably yours does, too. Rapisardi and Davenroy are like little troglodytes back here in their cave. Turning around . . .

Image: Yaw 180 degrees; medium zoom, focus three meters. *APDX:* Too washy. Adjust color palette for greater ambient light.

Text Enhance: The fanfold doors are of stiffened carbon mesh, anchored at two corners and able to slide in tracks at the other two. Surfaces colored, thank God, by a double layer of spray enamel. The latching mechanism (not visible) includes the ability to lock quarters from inside, but any fool could pop the door open if need arose. The blue door is of course the rest room, or "head." Green is the shower, and all others are crew quarters. The lack of red anywhere reflects a merchant spacer prejudice which equates that color with danger, but you do get to missing it pretty quickly.

Voiceover: . . . We see the wardroom. Large enough to hold the entire crew, but only in null gravity. We've had two meetings here already, and it's an amusing sight. Gives you a stiff neck, too, looking around to see everyone. Captain Wallich is adamant about "face time," though—important for morale and all that. Over on this end is the galley, with our beloved pap synthesizer.

Image: Galley, medium magnification; pap synthesizer at window center. *Schematic Enhance:* Wireframe rendering of toilet behind blue door, with plumbing leading to reclamation unit and thence to pap synthesizer. Hold one second. *Image:* Restore previous. *Image:* Close-up on pap synthesizer, angle selected to emphasize familiar, kitchen-appliance look. *APDX:* Adjust palette.

Voiceover: What can I say about nutrient pap? Utterly healthful and not quite tasteless, it's oatmeal's idiot cousin. Since we have no actual food aboard, we're building a fine, close relationship with this machine. Yum. I can't share the odor with you, alas, but Davenroy says it's mostly in my mind anyway. Or maybe she's just burned out her smell receptors leaning over those hot reactors all day.

Image: Pan back, pitch down 45 degrees. Rotate until green door is centered.

Voiceover: This is the shower, currently in use by our bioanalyst, Renata Baucum. *[Knock on the door frame.]* How's it going in there?

Baucum: Damn it, Strasheim, if that door comes open I'll [expletive deleted]. Get away from me.

Voiceover: Already we're just like a family, I swear. Wallich will make me clean out the garbage disposal again if I keep this up! Actually, privacy is very important on a vessel this small, which is why I can't show you the crew quarters. We all need a place that's truly and uniquely ours, right? The tragic death of Tug Jinacio has left us with an extra berth, though, and we've started leaving the door open, treating the space like a kind of annex to the wardroom, named in his honor. The Jinacio Ballroom, yeah.

Image: Jinacio's berth. *Image:* Coffin. *Image:* Bunk bed. *Image:* Restore previous. *APDX:* Adjust palette for lighting again. Mummy bag should be puke green, not gray—what is wrong with this hue filter?

Voiceover: As you can see, it's a bit tight and public for one-on-one conversation, but in the absence of anything better it serves well enough. This way, we can keep out of each other's berths entirely, which definitely seems to be a good thing; null gravity has a way of making the spaces bigger, but knees and elbows and especially voices shrink it right back down again. There is a temptation to use the berth for extra storage—even with our hurried departure, there's an awful lot of clutter and damn little room for it—but thus far we've resisted. Hooray for us.

Image: Pan back 2 meters, yaw 90 degrees left, roll 45 degrees right. Right through the hatchway, pause and freeze. *Image:* Bridge; four chairs, two occupied. *Image Overlay:* Roving circular window, exterior view as per AFD51 (star field only, no enhancement). *Text Enhance:* Bridge workstations are less plastic in function; many more of the controls are built-in and cannot be altered, since software glitches could otherwise present a threat during critical operations. The one exception is the captain's station at center right, which has built-up, touch-sensitive 3DI screens that can assume the form and function of any other bridge station, and some engine room functions as well. See technical specification for details.

Voiceover: Meet Tosca Lehne, our Immune system overseer, and of course Captain Wallich.

Wallich [grinning]: Ha. Hallo there. Funny he should get to me last, eh? Welcome to the bridge.

APDX: More photogenic than I've been thinking. Look at him playing to the camera here! Work a bit more screen time for him in the future. Well . . . Hmm. Entertainment/information balance problem; what's my real responsibility here? Definite food for thought.

Image: Close-up, Darren Wallich. Center that smile.

Voiceover: And how is everything going, sir? Any problems?

Wallich: Boredom and the threat of vacuum, ha ha. Nothing we can't handle. We're on a more or less sunward course right now, and should intercept the Floral asteroids in ten days. So far, the ship's performance has been nominal, meaning "good," but then we haven't been asking very much of it. Which I suppose is also good. Air quality is at the top of my agenda right now; we've got six people eating nutrient pap in this can, and life support could probably do a better job of removing spare intestinal gas from the atmosphere. We'll tear the system down later and have a look at the percolation filters. Pretty exciting, right?

Image: Restore previous.

Voiceover: And Lehne, how are things with you?

Lehne: Fine.

Voiceover: The ship's Immune system behaving normally? No problems, no interesting observations?

Lehne: Nobody in here but us, Strasheim. Immune system masses about a milligram, all told, and isn't doing anything except sit there. Less than dust.

Voiceover: Well, that's the way we like it, I guess.

Image: Restore previous. *Schematic Enhance:* Show instrument panel projections, course ahead as two parallel dotted lines, curving slightly and converging in the distance, RANGE (AU, MKM) TO GANYMEDE odometer ticking slowing upward, RANGE (AU, MKM) TO SUN odometer ticking slowly down. Show sun icon to Wallich's right—circle 0.2 degrees wide, with yellow "rays" covering eight degrees in just-visible scintillation.

Voiceover: And there you have it. Short tour, yes, I know, but try living here. This is John Strasheim, Mycosystem Mission One correspondent aboard the Immune Ship *Louis Pasteur*, signing off for now. Good night, and sleep well.

> from *Louis Pasteur, a "Walking" Tour*
> © 2106 by John Strasheim

SHIPTIME

"Now turn the screw until it reaches full extension," Wallich was telling me. "Like that, yeah, perfect. Easy as shoes, right? Ha ha."

"Right," I agreed as the screw came loose from its slot, though not, of course, from the metal panel cover itself. Wouldn't that be a wonder: a bridge full of loose, floating screws, and us all chasing after them? I repeated the operation five times, and in under a minute I had the cover off in my hands, like an empty box of strange design, missing a few walls and sporting holes in awkward places. It was made of silver, I think, though probably it was an alloy of some sort. Never a hint of tarnish.

Moving carefully, I pocketed my screwdriver, then set the cover in the bright orange safety of my chair and wrapped the restraint harness loosely around it to keep it from floating free. Where it had been, the guts of my instrument panel now hung out, gray and green and glittering, looking exactly as the insides of electronic devices had looked for decades untold. This by itself is significant, if you think about it: there had been no quantum leaps, had been in fact a *regression* of these technologies since the Evacuation, owing probably to a general mistrust of things too small to be seen. Blue-light microscopes were the instruments of choice in our bit shops back home, and even *I* knew about the strict lower limit that imposed on component size. Whatever gets us through our lives, I guess.

"Now we're going to remove the memory boards," Wallich advised, "which will give us access to the main logic unit, or MLU, which we're also going to pull. Theoretically, we should have spares for all these parts, but of course those were never loaded, and I *seriously* doubt the Gladholders will have anything compatible, ha ha, but just the same we're going to clean and inspect every piece. I'm not above soldering a wire here or there to bypass a bad chip, so we may practice that as well."

"Lucky us," I said, activating and focusing the tiny work lamps on my zee-spec.

Wallich, drifting somewhere close behind me, laughed. "That's funny. That's really funny."

"I think your sense of humor needs adjustment."

But he just laughed at that one, too, so I went ahead and started pulling memory boards. They were about the size of debit cards, though a good deal stiffer and more fragile. I was careful, and my leg pockets soon bulged with them. I should mention, by the way, that I was upside down to my workstation (i.e., right-side-up to everyone else's), with my feet braced on the sides of the chair and my knees around its stem. Not the most comfortable position, but secure enough for this sort of delicate work. If you've operated much in null gravity, you'll know what I mean.

The work went slowly, but eventually I had uncovered the MLU, and was studying the clips and brackets that held it in place. One false move right now could doom this mission for good, but then, if dust or other assorted schmutz got inside here—or mycora, God forbid—or if there were some sort of fire or short circuit or name-your-favorite-accident, then not knowing my way around in here could doom us just as surely. Personally, my money was on leaving it the hell alone and taking our chances, but the decision, of course, was Wallich's, and he'd shown a strong propensity for making us dismantle things, clean things, inspect things to death and beyond. "You'll always have hardware anomalies out here," he'd said to me several times these past few days, "but you never know what they're likely to be, and if you're going to be prepared for unknown problems, you have to know the ship." Well, maybe, but I suspected it was also a way to keep everyone occupied and out of each other's hair.

"Here and here," Wallich said to me now, leaning past me and pointing with his own screwdriver. "You're going to press these tabs with your thumbs, and just rock the unit gently with your fingers. It should pop right out."

I put my thumbs on the aforementioned tabs and pressed gently. "Like this?"

"Uh-huh. Maybe a little harder. Now use your fingers, rock it back and forth. Yeah."

The unit popped right out. I held it up, studied it: a rectangular prism of clear plastic, full of voids and mazey channels run through with gold wiring and black, insectile chips the size of fingernails. Inside, in the heart of it, threads of light winked on and off, a tiny mesh of blue and red flickers locked away inside the plastic. Not something I could fix if it actually broke, but I could easily see how dirt could get inside, and spraying the whole thing down with solvent and air jets and then wiping it clean was certainly well within my powers.

I was about to do just this when something caught my eye, something yellow and spidery in the space behind where the MLU had fit. Wallich had flashed me a tutorial on the resource allocation oversight console and made me review it three times, so in a wireframe schematic sense I had a fairly good idea what guts went where. This bean-sized object, though, did not correspond to anything I remembered.

"Hallo," I said, "what's this?"

Wallich drifted in closer. "Hmm?"

"This here, this yellow thing with all the wires coming out. Is that part of the network feed?"

"No," Wallich said, "it sure isn't. I don't know what that thing is. Here, move away for a minute."

I disengaged from my chair and let Wallich settle in where I had been. He traced and poked at the air for a moment, and his zee-spec's work lamps came on. He leaned in for a closer look.

"Damn," he said, "I don't know what that thing is at all. It doesn't show on the schematic. If somebody's retrofitted around a design error, I sure as hell never heard about it. Jesus."

He pulled an instrument from his breast pocket, waved it at the yellow thing, and frowned. "There's a small processor in there, doing I don't know what. No independent power source, no sign of volatiles or toxins, minimal EM emissions . . . It's not a bomb, not a transmitter, not apparently any sort of sensor. *This* isn't funny. Where the fuck does this thing connect?"

He began tracing the wires out with his finger, clucking and muttering to himself.

"Could it be some sort of monitoring device?" I asked.

Wallich let out a quick sigh of impatience and minimal amusement. "Some sort of monitoring device. I think that would be a safe bet, yes. You're a genius, Strasheim. Look at this. Look: it taps into the diagnostic feed right here, and telemetry over here, and this one looks like it might head straight around to the main transmitter. Jesus Christ."

"So what does it do?"

"I don't know. I don't know. I have an idea, though; have you got any messages waiting to go out?"

I had twenty-three of them, five of which exceeded the six-terabyte buffer limit and were thus broken down still further. Busy-work or no, I'd found a lot more free time here on *Louis Pasteur* than I'd ever had back home—hours and hours of it in great, uninterrupted blocks. All I had to do was close the door of my cabin, finger up the news and talk channels, wait out the round-trip light delay, and read the day's concerns all in a shot. Then, a bit more circuitously, I'd roam Immunity records and library sites and my own zee-spec's internal references, shake the data around for a while, and produce blocks of refined information. And when all that was done, I often found I *still* had an hour or three before my sleep shift in which to juggle the information into patterns of useful insight. Not just for one or two stories, you understand, but for *all* of them. For the first time in my life, I felt completely in touch with the society that created and supported me, from a vantage point fully eighty million kilometers away and receding rapidly.

This irony was the subject of a whole editorial by itself.

Not that I was shirking my duties as mission correspondent. In fact, I sometimes worried I was overreporting the details of life within *Louis Pasteur*'s confined spaces, but even so, the fullest of days didn't get more than about ten minutes' total coverage, meaning maybe an hour of postproduction on the day's sights and sounds.

And then there was mail, the volume of which was rapidly getting out of hand. One of my outgoing messages was a form response to a hundred and nine separate viewers!

"I have messages I haven't queued yet," I said to Wallich. "Several of them. Why, what have you got in mind?"

"Send one of them out."

"Don't you want to 'review' it?"

"No. Send one out now, please."

His tone let me know this was an order, not a suggestion, and anyway my comment had not been very fair; his censorial input had so far been negligible, really just a glance here and there and some nudges to edit around the profanity.

"Yes, sir," I said without sarcasm, and traced the appropriate icons on my zee, feeding refined message data into the transmit queue.

"God damn!" Wallich said right away. "God *damn*! Activity in that processor jumped a factor of a million for a moment there, and it definitely sent something off into the transmitter. Lehne!"

There was a pause, Wallich fingering at the unseen.

"Lehne! Wake up and report to the bridge! Baucum, you too."

Another pause.

"Because I'm telling you to, that's why," Wallich said. He turned back to me. "I think this thing just piggybacked a signal on your outgoing message. Deeply encrypted—I couldn't detect anything in the bitstream—but I'll bet my next year's pay that's what happened."

Baucum appeared in the hatchway, Tosca Lehne hovering

behind her. You know the look of people who've been woken from a sound sleep with bad news? That's how they looked, though both were fully dressed.

"We've been bugged," Wallich told them both. He pointed at the yellow spider. "In here. I want a full diagnostic on this thing before we cut it out, and I want every panel on this ship removed, and every circuit checked for tampering. Whoever put this thing in here did *not* have your best interests at heart."

That comment seemed to strike him as funny, and he couldn't quite keep from chuckling.

Well, so much for free time. I'm embarrassed to admit that my first thoughts were not for the safety of the ship and crew, but for the audience back home: I'd recorded Wallich's statement, and the entry of Lehne and Baucum just before it, and now I leaned close for a good shot at the spider itself, thinking, *This* will sure generate some mail! And oh, how right I was.

In a way, it would have been better if we'd found another bug or two. As it was, we tore apart every piece of that ship and found nothing suspicious. As for my little spider, it turned out to be exactly what Wallich had surmised: a device which studied the contents of central processing, compressed and encrypted a summary, and melded it almost seamlessly with any outgoing transmissions. The more we talked with the folks back home, the more information we leaked about our position, our trajectory, our resource allocations and other plans . . .

Who would want such information? The Temples of Transcendent Evolution were obviously a prime suspect, though what use they could make of it was far from clear, and Rapisardi's insistence that we had other enemies was a telling point, and one echoed firmly by Wallich. And how could the Temples put together so sophisticated a device, and interface it so cleanly and invisibly with *Louis Pasteur*'s data processing systems? Anyone with that kind of access could just sneak code into the system for a purely software solution, yes? Well, apparently not; we searched there as well, for nearly a full day, and turned up nothing at all. Needless to say, this lack of conclusion was about as satisfying as a mouthful of plastic foam.

Too, since departure we had used our transmitter rather a lot. I was not the only one "working" in two places at once; Davenroy was collaborating with colleagues on some sort of technical paper, while Lehne and Rapisardi and Baucum made frequent correspondence, requests for reference material, et cetera. And Wallich, well, he was a system unto himself. It didn't seem to bother him, supervising his research teams back home even as he was leading our investigations here aboard the ship, and time-lagged or no, Vaclav Lottick certainly made his presence felt. My respect for Wallich went up several notches as I watched him tackle a couple of serious Immune system issues and organize a presentation to Lottick on same, while dismantling, combing through, and reassembling the innards of his own bridge workstation.

And why, I ask myself now, was my respect for him not higher in the first place? Why do we do that, project averageness onto so many of the people we meet? Even people whose accomplishments are clearly beyond the ordinary? Caveman baggage, I'm sure, but some days you have to wonder how many cavemen got their heads bashed in for it.

Wallich's talent for divided attention did not manifest in the rest of the crew, alas. Staring blankly, speaking and gesturing into the empty air became familiar symptoms, a lunacy all our own. Not unknown among spaceship crews, I learned, but here was an unusual

concentration of talents, for the most part torn from very full professional and intellectual lives that refused to sever cleanly. Twice I
stumbled—literally—across Renata Baucum's form drifting through
the wardroom like an epileptic husk, her attention drawn off into la-
la land in midtransit.

"Watch it," I told her the second time as I disentangled my arms
from her waist. "I don't know what you're working on, but I wish
you'd go do it in your quarters. You're a navigational hazard."

Behind the palm-sized lenses of the zee-spec, her eyes focused
on me momentarily. "That little yellow thing took up a lot less space
than you." Her tone was acerbic.

I nodded curtly. "Thank you, I'll put that in tonight's broadcast."

Oh yeah, we were friends all right. It didn't help that I'd cupped
her breast in my hands at some point in our slow collision. It didn't
help that her long hair came undone and floated past my nose,
smelling of apple-scented soap. It didn't help that her expression
barely flickered, barely reacted to me at all, or that she took my advice, retreating to her berth and closing the door in my face.

She didn't even have the decency to slam it.

GAMES OF LIFE

"Allocation looks fine," I said, studying my instruments for any datum to disprove the statement. This was a minor course correction, a mere thirty-second burn of the engines, but the way Wallich ran us through our paces, you'd think we were crash-landing on the surface of the sun.

"Immune system nominal, no activity," Tosca Lehne's voice joined in.

"Nav solution confirmed," Baucum said. "Not that I know squat about it."

"Reactor performance looks to be plus point-four-eight sigma," said Davenroy, her image crowded up next to Rapisardi's in a little corner window of my zee-spec. "Map that to engine performance, though, and the confidence factor is only point-six, because the dispersion on a cold engine is a lot higher than one that's been fired recently. Plus or minus a second and a half in burn time, let's call it."

"Acknowledged," said Wallich. "Contamination?"

Rapisardi's image shook its head. "None, sir. You are go for burn."

"Well goody. I love this part."

Grinning, Wallich worked his panel for a moment, gave the order, and then the engines were humming and I went from weightless to hanging upside down in my seat. Not serious acceleration by any means, but after more than a week of weightlessness, I would have preferred it in the other direction. My face, puffy with fluid already, puffed further. My feet tingled.

Wallich watched his numbers. "Ten seconds, good, fifteen. Right down the groove. Twenty . . . and . . . twenty-five . . . and . . . *that's* all." Weightlessness returned. "Beautiful, beautiful. I'd say we should do this more often, but keep hitting them like that and we won't need to."

He chuckled.

"So, Captain," I said, turning fully toward him and zooming in slightly on his face, "Floral asteroids tomorrow?"

"And Gladholders, you bet. Real food!"

He chuckled again.

"Strasheim, will you bloody cut it out?" The voice was Baucum's. I turned.

"Hmm?"

"Fish in a tank," she said. "This constant observation, it's enough to drive a person insane. And the way you edit this stuff;

you strip away all the context, *particularly* your own questions, and make it look like there's this giant conversation going on all the time. But it's *your* conversation, not ours, and I'm bloody sick of it."

I stopped recording, watched her for a few moments. "What conversation should we be having?"

She snorted, shook her head a little. "Wrong question, freund. You should be asking, 'Who is the primary beneficiary of these reports?' "

"And the answer is?"

Her shrug was elaborate and slow, with an expression to match. "I don't know. Your personal agenda dictates what slice of reality the audience is exposed to. I keep asking myself why you're here, but that question never seems to occur to you. That's all I have to say."

Darren Wallich's laugh seemed to startle her. We both turned, saw him looking back at us with a fatherly expression, amusement and annoyance and a tinge of genuine warning. "All right, you two," he said. "Fun's over. Strasheim, I want you to interview this woman for not less than thirty minutes, camera off, mind open. Baucum, whatever bug is up your ass, I want you to dig it out and show it to our mission correspondent here. Believe it or not, we really do have business to conduct, and this spurious feuding is not only bad for morale, but potentially hazardous. Are we clear on this? Baucum? We can't afford the distraction."

She frowned, pressed her teeth together for a moment. "Yeah. Fine."

"Strasheim?"

"It's perfectly all right with me," I said, shrugging. "I've been wanting to know her better anyway." Um . . . Seeing Baucum's expression, I knew right away it was the wrong thing to say. My chagrin was short-lived, though—every damn thing I said around her was somehow the wrong thing, and if she wanted to get worked up about it, well, that was pretty much her own problem. I stared her down. "Meet me in the ballroom in ten minutes, all right? Time enough to get your thoughts together."

And with that, I unstrapped myself, kicked off from my chair, and sailed between her and Wallich to the exit hatch. Jinacio's quarters were a pretty confined, nose-to-nose sort of space, and I thought maybe I should brush my teeth first.

"Let's get this over with," she said, pulling partway into the berth and then wedging herself in the doorway. The body language here was interesting: I was fully inside, trapped, as it were, while she was free to leave at any time. Too, she was putting distance between us, and explicitly denying that the door would be closed. *There is no need for privacy, freund, but you will hear me out before you leave.* But for all that, she was still in the room with me, close enough that I could feel the heat of her body, smell her breath mingling with mine in the air between us.

Oddly, she had brushed her teeth as well.

"So, what are we here to discuss?" I asked, offering her a handshake, which she accepted with some reluctance.

"I don't know. I haven't decided."

"No? You've accused me of dictating an agenda. What agenda, exactly? What is it you think I'm misleading people about?"

She frowned, suddenly vague and uncertain. She waved a hand. "It isn't you, exactly. You're more of a symptom. It's just that everyone seems so *sure* about everything; about the mission, about the Mycosystem, about the Immunity itself. It's like there's this mass consensus, that the only possible solutions are the exact ones we're currently focused on. Placing these detectors is so important because every supposition we've made is right, and every alternative viewpoint is wrong."

Her spacer-blue eyes met mine, and for once they were more sympathetic than hostile. "You're *so* party line in your outlook, and you don't even see that in yourself, because you're totally immersed. I don't know how to explain it to you, but I've *studied* technogenic lebenforms my whole adult life, and there's a lot more going on there than people are willing to admit. People come up against a barrier of willful ignorance, and they just stop. No, we can't try this. No, we can't think about that. No, no, no, we simply don't have the wherewithal. But we throw together an elaborate mission like this on twelve months' notice. Doesn't that strike you as odd?"

"I don't know," I said honestly.

"Well, it does me."

She stopped then, looking at me, not seeming to have anything else to say. Well, okay, but Wallich had ordered me to drag this out for a full half hour. And anyway, Baucum was still blocking my exit.

"You say there's more going on in TGL," I tried, "than people are aware of. What exactly do you mean by that?"

She smiled wanly. "That's extremely difficult to articulate. Subtleties you can't appreciate, not because you're stupid but because you lack the background to make sense of them. Even within my own community, within the circles that study TGL with— supposedly—mathematical rigor, certain observations are just swept under the rug because they don't fit our preconceptions."

"Humans on Earth?" I asked.

She looked startled. "Where did you hear about that?"

I smiled. "I have an ear for rumors. That's one that never quite seems to die."

"Well, that wasn't quite what I was thinking of, but yes, it's a fine example. Are there humans still living in the Mycosystem? Ask anyone and they'll tell you no, of course not, the mycora would have eaten them decades ago. But study the sensor data, and suddenly you're not so sure. Structures that might be villages, heat sources that might be fires or mammalian metabolisms grouped together. It's all so far away, we can never be sure what we're seeing. *Maybe* the Mycosystem generates these structures itself; it's not nearly so homogenous or random as people seem to think. You know the term 'emergent behavior'? Small actions repeated a million times over, with decidedly macroscopic results. Our bodies aren't lumps of undifferentiated flesh, and the Mycosystem is *not* a lump of undifferentiated mycora. Are there human beings in it? I don't know. But I've never found a colleague willing even to discuss it."

I scratched my chin, cleared my throat, thought about what she was saying. Cameras off, mind open. Humans in the Mycosystem, more than just a silly rumor? Maybe. Maybe. The thought was unsettling. But Baucum's tone was beginning to bother me as well; too much like the Temples' propaganda, more anger than true scientific indifference. How open was *her* mind?

"Okay," I said, "that was my example. What was yours going to be?"

"The Game of Life," she replied, then hesitated. Not trusting? Not sure of my ability to comprehend?

"Hmm?"

"Hmm. Well. Are you familiar with the concept of a cellular automaton?"

"Like a spreadsheet," I said, nodding. "I hear the terminology sometimes on the network, in all sorts of contexts. It's a tool, a kind of geometric language, like if you could somehow speak in two dimensions."

She relaxed visibly. "Or three, yes. Each cell of the spreadsheet holds an equation whose inputs are the *outputs* of neighboring cells. The game of Othello is a simple example—black, white, or empty; place one piece, change one value, and all the others change. But while Othello and Go and your typical financial or analytical spreadsheet will stop right there, in the general sense that first wave of changes will drive a second wave, and that will drive a third and fourth, and so on. So you have the potential for self-perpetuating event systems."

"Okay," I said, slowly wrapping my head around that concept. It seemed clear enough, though I'd missed the connection to TGL, the Mycosystem, or anything else we'd been talking about.

"Okay," she agreed. "Now imagine a spreadsheet, or a Go board, where each cell can contain only two possible answers: on or off. No colors; either there's a stone in that space, or there isn't. Now imagine that the rule is, a cell will be turned on if three of its immediate neighbors are currently on, and it'll be turned off if fewer than two or more than three of its neighbors are on."

I thought about that. "Um, okay."

She shrugged. "Well, that's it. That's the whole thing. Imagine that 'on' means 'alive' and 'off' means 'dead,' and you have the Game of Life. Conway's twentieth-century mathematical curiosity, but it's still in use today. For obvious reasons."

"Obvious?"

In lieu of reply, she flashed me an animation window, a black background seething and boiling with patterns of white dots. Instinctively, I recoiled, but of course the image moved with me, suspended in the air an arm's reach away.

"Very pretty," I said, fixing the image in three-space, pinning it a few centimeters off the bulkhead. "This is it?"

"Yup."

Presently, the roiling died down, the dots on the screen settling into a pattern of fixed ovals and flickering crosses. It didn't take much watching to see that this was a ground state of some sort, a permanent condition from which the game could not escape. But off on the left side of the window was a thin black stripe set with icons. A control panel? I touched one of the symbols, and a new random pattern of dots appeared and resumed that awful convecting motion.

God, it really did look like a TGL bloom. Again, though, the motions died away into tiny repeating structures.

"Interesting," I said.

She nodded.

"How faithful a model is it, though?"

"Not very," she admitted. "That particular sim is pretty flexible, though. You can play with the parameters, archive patterns with interesting behavior . . . It looks enough like the real thing to be worthy of study, in the same way that our forebears used ink drops and water tanks for the simplified study of atmospheres. Serious study, I mean, with peer review and all that. Experimentation by analogy can draw us off in peculiar dead ends, so it pays to be vigilant; I've personally fooled dozens of TGL experts with inorganic chemical solutions. They think they're seeing a primitive alga or mycorum at work, instead of sucrate of lime, or silicate of soda. . . . The carbonates tend to form closed cells, while sulfates and phosphates produce large tubular structures. Either way, though, you get not only the *forms* of life but close simulacra of the functional microstructure. Really, these solutions form bodies that grow, interact, reproduce, and wither, to the point you'd just *swear* they were alive. But it's just blank chemistry, the emergent behavior of closed or oscillating reaction loops involving extremely simple molecules. Self-organization without metabolism, like crystal growth. Like patterns in the frost.

"Of course, if you pursue the inorganic angle far enough, you get to the clay problem, which tends to lead people in the opposite direction. In clay you have these tiny particles, these silicate fines easily as small as an amino acid or RNA nucleotide, and they have some particular qualities. Density, dielectric constant, capacitance . . . Static electricity plays a tremendous role at these scales, so you get interactions, and eventually you get chains of particles with, I guess you'd say, mutually compatible properties. You get two- and three-dimensional complexes as well, but their behavior is less interesting. The point is that one-dimensional chains will serve as templates for their own replication. Eventually, you get a highly ordered clay composed of repeating submicroscopic features."

I felt a chill. "Living mud?"

Smiling, she shook her head. "Oh, no. On this end you've got self-organization and replication at the molecular level, but the emergent behavior is gone. The chains perpetuate themselves, but they don't actually *do* anything. Well, maybe they served as the original templates for life, organic matter clinging to the particles and forced to chain up in the same ways. But amino and nucleic acids will polymerize spontaneously, so Occam's razor eliminates the clay as a necessary step. What I'm saying is that there are a lot of things out there that look like life but aren't really.

"TGL is the real thing; it eats, sorts, metabolizes, reproduces. Doesn't die, per se, without prompting, but then a lot of organic life is technically immortal as well. Death is a tool of evolution, you see, but when evolution can take place within the living organism, it becomes a nonissue. And think of the emergent characteristics of bacterial mats: not much going on there. In terms of its interactions, TGL is more akin to reefs and anthills.

"As for cellular automaton models, I think they cry out for more attention than Immunity circles generally give them. Metaphor is a true and righteous way to approach understanding, damn it, and when you're too timid to examine your subjects firsthand . . ." She looked at me skeptically. "To you, I probably sound like a fanatic."

I shrugged. "We all have our issues. I've listened to whackos with ideas like this, but they don't talk the way you do." I nodded sideways at the Game of Life window, which of course she couldn't see. "Whackos don't perform controlled experiments."

"You surprise me," she said, still studying my face as if trying to find me somewhere behind it.

"Likewise. Is examining the Mycosystem firsthand your reason for coming on this mission? A personal grudge, a chance to show up your timid peers?"

"It's part of why I agreed to it, yes. As we approach the infested regions, Rapisardi and I will be busy with our measurements. This mission is all about fear and pride and politics, but if we just open our eyes, there's a lot of science to be done while we're at it. Maybe not world-shattering in and of itself, but the Immunity is in desperate need of a wake-up call."

Wake-up call. I mulled the term over in my mind. Archaic: a telephone signal from one person to another. Time to get moving, freund. Had alarm clocks supplanted the practice? No, surely alarm clocks had existed for hundreds of years, much longer than telephones. So it must have been the personal contact that mattered, the exchange of human voices. As with my own job.

I had been bracing against the sides of Jinacio's cabin, my back on one gray-white padded wall and my feet on the other, but now I moved, aligned myself with Baucum's body once more, so that I hung before her in the doorway, close enough to touch.

"I'm no tool of the state," I told her mildly. "Whatever you may think, your theories and findings are of as much interest to me as any other aspect of this mission. Unusual perspectives are a great help in communication, especially of complex ideas."

Her face tightened. "So I'm useful, then. How flattering."

"Hey," I said, frowning at her tone, "be nice. If you want to reduce it to those terms, I can't stop you, but understand that I can't *use* you without your using me right back. Equal and opposite reaction, or something like that. You want a voice for your ideas, well, I'm it, so quit spitting in my face. It works a lot better if we're friends."

She let go of the door frame and drifted back a bit, her face a cipher, unreadable. "You want a friend, Strasheim? Fine, I'm your friend. The Game of Life is my gift to you. Play around with it, let me know what you think, and we'll talk about it sometime over a nice cup of tea. Let's see . . . Tomorrow I'm visiting with Gladholders, and the day after that is thrust ops again. Are you free on Thursday?"

I tried to return her inscrutable look, to match the gruff neutrality of her tone. "Yeah, whatever. It's a date."

She kicked away and was gone.

I checked my system clock, down in the corner of my vision: fifteen-thirteen. Baucum and I had missed our thirty-minute goal by a good forty percent. Well, I wouldn't tell Wallich if she didn't.

GLADHOLDERS

Our approach into the Floral asteroids was a cautious thing—thirty-odd hours under power, with constant, kicky adjustments to the thrust vector. Whang whang! Interplanetary space was very empty down here, even in the thick of the so-called asteroid belt, but moving at hundreds of kilometers per second, you'd better believe we worried about hitting something. Wallich assured me that a chip of rock the size of a fingernail clipping could reduce us all to component atoms. I believed him, but the fact that we were as often as not steering *toward* such objects, employing our deceleration thrust against them, was not a source of confidence. "What better defense than a hot, hot stream of engine plasma?"

Hmm.

Our destination, a midsized asteroid named Saint Helier (pronounced "heel-yehr"), swelled to fist size from nothing in the space of a couple of hours, but as we continued to slow, it took the whole rest of the day to fill up 170 degrees of sky. We were expected, of course; a weeks-long sleet of communications had preceded our approach, and continued now as we applied for an orbit license and docking permit, and received final instructions on where and how to complete the tryst.

Not that this exchange was any picnic; while officially a dialect of English, the Gladholder language is really a kind of mystery loaf, baked from a planet's worth of linguistic leftovers. In plaintext it's like a chain of story problems and jokeless punchlines in someone else's job jargon, and out loud you're lucky to catch every other word in the blur. Still, in my years of amateur journalism I'd had occasion to peek at some Gladholder net channels, and reading and posting to them from *Louis Pasteur* I was able to confirm that Lottick's people had called ahead of us, and that some sort of charity had in fact been arranged. Which was good, because our only alternative was to turn back for home on a much slower, much thriftier trajectory than the one that had brought us here.

The rock itself was the color of coal, and from the outside gave little evidence of habitation. Its night face was covered in black rectangles, its dayside splashed with the silver of parabolic mirrors, dipping down into natural craters as if pooling there, liquid. And even when Saint Helier filled half the sky, blocking out half the stars, we hung motionless before it for quite some time, nearly forty-five minutes, while Wallich sorted out final details with a disembodied voice, with many repetitions and requests for clarification crossing the vacuum between them.

"What? No, six people, and the cargo will not be unloaded. What? Repeat, please!"

His sense of humor kicked in only occasionally, and even then with a kind of strained chuckle. Not nervous, exactly, but not really thrilled about this whole undertaking. The bother, the delay, the uncertainty . . . People were dying back home. Would the Gladholders really come across for us? Intersocietal trade was by no means unheard of, but neither was it common. The cost involved was just too absurd. And of course someone had tried to bloom *Louis Pasteur* the last time it sat in a dock, so maybe he was nervous after all. Maybe all of us were.

We weren't orbiting Saint Helier, but rather hovering above it, mild thrust counteracting its sub-ludicrous gravity, and when final docking clearance arrived, it was something of a surprise when a shiplock irised open right below us, barely a hundred meters away, not concealed in any way but simply hard to see against the dark surface. Not the last such surprise we were to encounter that day.

Under Wallich's supervision, the ship eased itself slowly down into the docking berth. There was a bumping noise, and then the soft, solid clang of metal on metal as the mooring latches closed, and the boarding tube ground its spiral walls out to the proper dimensions to mate our hatches with theirs.

"Pop the outer latch, please," Wallich said to Rapisardi, who had temporarily taken over Tug Jinacio's doorman duties.

"I copy," Rapisardi replied. "Opening the hatch now."

And then, suddenly, alarm bells were going off all over the ship.

"The hull is reacting," Lehne said, his tone more disbelieving than afraid.

Renata Baucum, though, flinched away from her instruments, her pinned-back hair bobbing not quite weightlessly. Turning, she shouted: "I'm getting replication events in the main airlock! Close it! Close it!"

"Close it!" Wallich echoed. One hand went to the arm of his chair, gripping tightly.

"Copy! Closing outer hatch! Where is the decon? Did anything get inside? My god, where is the *decon*?"

"Nothing got inside," Baucum said, a bit more calmly.

But Tosca Lehne, red-faced and frightened, shook his head. "Doesn't matter. Inner hatch isn't t-balanced. No protection. Something nasty got in there, it can eat through to the crew compartments."

Wallich grunted, stabbing at the air with his free hand. "Right. Getting us out of here. Control, kindly release the mooring clamps—we've picked up a bug of some sort. Repeat, release the mooring clamps so we can blast clear."

Pause.

"What? That's ridiculous. Release the clamps, please."

Pause.

Wallich touched his chin, his ear, listening impatiently. "Describe the phage, please. Phages, right, whatever. Uh-huh. Surface structure? Uh-huh. Baucum, is replication in the airlock tapering off?"

"Yeah," Baucum said, "significantly."

Pause. More stabbing and poking.

Wallich's face appeared in a small window at my zee-spec. "Well, Pasteurites, it seems that ruckus was the local Immune system equalizing with ours. Some sort of adaptive onboard library sniffing out our phages. I dunno, sounds schädlich to me, but they claim it's normal enough. So, I'd like a volunteer to please open up that inner hatch."

"I'm here already," Rapisardi said reluctantly.

"Would you do the honors, then?"

"Copy, I'm opening the hatch."

"You see anything?"

"No."

"Baucum? Any suspicious activity?"

"Its seems to have stopped. Our phages have gone a little twitchy, but the only activity is theirs."

Wallich grinned. "Right, well, as advertised. Care to walk inside, Rapisardi? Take a breath? I can't order you, but I'm asking nicely. Ha ha."

Pause. "All right, yes. I'm doing it. I'm in the airlock. It seems perfectly normal in here."

"Okay. We'll give it a few minutes to see if you explode or anything, and then we open that outer hatch and go, uh, shopping. Any objections?"

I could think of a few, but then again, three weeks of close quarters and nutrient pap were arguing the need for fresh air. I suppose we were all thinking that, because despite the nervous, precarious feel of things, nobody spoke up. The minutes passed, and finally Wallich gave the order, and the hatch was opened. The moment was a bit more unnerving than I'd been ready for, but also exciting, exhilarating. A chance to get out of this feculent container, yes, but more than that: the opening of a gateway to the truly exotic. Gladholders! A hollow asteroid, its gravity barely a tenth of Ganymedean normal, a two-hundredth of a gee.

"Hallo," we could hear Rapisardi saying. "Yes, nice to meet you. Yes!"

A voice mumbled replies, indistinguishable as we threw off our safety harnesses and leaped from our seats.

"Easy!" Wallich was saying. "Easy, single file, no pushing!" But he was laughing and jostling as he said it, as eager as any of us to get outside and see. We could simply have opened an exterior window on the zee-spec and walked it around to the hatch for an easy view, of course, but none of us did, which should tell you something about our frazzled state of mind.

Davenroy met us in the wardroom, and Renata Baucum, who was in the lead, stopped and bowed and motioned for her to precede us—an awkward, silly, slidey set of motions in this asteroidal gravity. Davenroy, who'd been busy at her station for forty of the last forty-eight hours, brushed past her with only the most minute gesture of acknowledgment. And then her attention was all on the walking; the downward slope of the ramp was like the incline of a swimming pool, impossible to follow without bobbing and floating, toes touching down only occasionally, and then in near-frictionless glissando. Only by bracing her hands against the protruding cargo hold was Davenroy able to complete the operation with any grace at all.

Baucum followed her out, and then Lehne, and myself, and Wallich. The walking was difficult, our Ganymedean shoes entirely unsuited to the task. The cargo bulkhead was an enormous help, though—something to hold, to push against, to follow along. Maybe Gladholders made lower ceilings than ours, and walked around spiderlike with all four limbs splayed out, clinging simultaneously to wall and ceiling. I couldn't help but grin at the image.

Behind me, I heard Wallich sealing the airlock, heard the beeps and squawks that announced the security system's activation.

Outside the ship was a docking tube, and outside of that was . . . well, a port complex, obviously. Very much like Galileo in some ways, except for the junk, and the many little children, and the fact that there were plants growing all over everything, gray/blue/green/black vines and stalks and shoots and fat clusters of leaves making mosaics of every wall. Yeah, and there was no sense of up. You know that old Dutch artist, Maurits Escher? The guy with the tesselating shapes and the visual riddles and the inside-out architectural drawings that hurt your brain to look at? Stairs going nowhere, stuff like that. Hew the walls a little rougher, put a jungle and a junkyard and a kindergarten class in it, and that would be Saint Helier's spaceport to a decimal point.

It took a moment to realize that the creatures leaping wall to wall were human children, laughing, barefoot, and minimally dressed. More interested in movement than dignity, they put all four limbs to work in their clamberings and brachiations, playing Tag or Follow the Leader or King of the Top or some such. Humans are primates, oh yes, and our long arboreal past bubbles right to the surface in low gravity. Unless for some reason we retain a planar environment, and weigh ourselves down with heavy, tank-tread shoes . . .

Once upon a time, reduced gravity was supposed to make humans a taller, thinner, more elfin race. The truth turned out a bit less glamorous, as more and more of our children were born with crooked spines, curving limbs, clubbed feet . . . Hypogravitic osteo deformans. The man Rapisardi was talking to was a classic example of the syndrome, a hunched figure half a head shorter than myself, looking young enough either to have been born in Saint Helier or at least to have done most of his growing here. Growing twisted, like an old tree. But he was handsome in spite of the deformity, and possessed of a sort of archetypal grace. The primate thing again, probably. And oh, was he ever dark! You get used to thinking of the Immunity as a heterogeneous society, diverse, full of everything, but when was the last time you saw a young man with skin the color of a good stout beer? The body was swathed in patterned, iridescent fabrics of yellow and blue. And there was an Asian cast to his eyes, and a grin framing straight, yellow-white teeth.

Check my image archive sometime; the file is LPASTEUR/ GH1DIB0001. Nothing compares to that first look, that first shock of foreignness. The most striking feature, though, was his toes, which were as long and thick and straight as a double row of thumbs. Never a shoe on those feet, never a moment's burden. Seeing them then, I felt a moment of obscure envy; Earth was nothing to this young man, not a memory, not even an architectural legacy.

"Heyyo," the man said brightly. "Ahn behalfde gavnoffice, aloha wekkome teh San Heelyer. Ma nom wa Chris Dibrin, kai I am lok to assist you. How you doeng?"

To his credit, Rapisardi was attempting to reply for us all. "We're fine, thank you, and very eager to examine your trade goods. We have no food!"

The man—Dibrin?—smiled and nodded. "Yeh, yeh, tre been, amigos. Canno comprend a sinnle word. German ye parolas? Englesh, ah ah. Permeht ye I take libert? Ahm, excuse." He pointed at Rapidsardi's zee-spec, with body language indicating he found it both interesting and funny, a kind of technological clown hat. "Big lens. Inface, program, inout, yes? Er. May I meddle?"

Rapisardi, hesitant, looked to Darren Wallich.

"Well, hey there, partner!" Wallich said in a phony accent native to neither the Immunity nor the Gladhold. He reached for a long-fingered hand, shook it vigorously. "You want to meddle with this man's zee-spec. In what manner, exactly? And why? For the purpose of translation?"

"Translation," Dibrin echoed, striving admirably to match Wallich's inflection. Oh, the harm we do in jest!

And then, suddenly, my zee was going nuts on me—varicolored characters and ideographic icons filling up the whole of my view, scrolling down from top to bottom and then starting again at the top, new text overwriting the old in three-dimensional nonsense palimpsest. Dizzying, really, and in this gravity that was no small thing—lose your feet and you could be quite some time regaining them. But then, all at once, my view went black, then white, and then cleared altogether.

"Gomen, neh?" Dibrin said, his smile now looking a bit sheepish. "Wa any mas bien?"

And on my zee-spec, right below Dibrin's face, appeared the plaintext: "I'm sorry, eh? Is this any better?"

A soft exhalation went up from all of us. This man, this bare-eyed, specless, twenty-year-old boy, had probed our operating systems, tailored a translation program to run on them, flashed it to us through security overrides, and configured our task managers to run the thing in realtime without any explicit activation commands on our part. Like magic, this highly invasive procedure, like finding your house suddenly full of someone else's furniture. And he'd done it in seconds, with barely a twitch of his hands.

"Ouch!" Rapisardi cried, in alarm rather than actual pain. "Hey! What and how? No, you may not meddle!"

"I'm sorry," Dibrin said, still sheepish. Well, the zee-spec said it in response to his jabbering. "I thought it would save time, but that was probably very rude of me. Like touching, yes? You people don't like to touch."

"What?" Wallich said, off balance for once.

"I'm sorry," Dibrin repeated, his eyes going shifty, his face taking on an expression of genuine worry. "Making a mess of this, I told them I wasn't the one to talk. Look, Governor's office sent me down here to escort you Munies around, make sure you didn't walk out an airlock or anything. But I'm technical, see? Literally technical, like, full of technology. Wires. You don't do that either, and I told them, hey, look, I'm going to fucking freak those guys out. And it happened. See how good I am at predicting?"

Well.

We stood there gawking. What else to do? Low gravity, Escher walls covered with vines and dark, chattering children, and this alien man talking right into our eyeballs whether we liked it or not.

Full of wires? Neural direct was one of many technologies spawned in Earth's final decades, now very much out of favor. Or so I'd thought! And that programming trick, so far beyond human capacity; the product, surely, of artificial intelligence, another idea left behind on the blooming carcass of Earth. There was only the question of how the deed was done: communication via some faux telepathy, radio or IR or something? Or were they inside him, sterile nuggets of machine thought glittering in the chaos of his organic brain? Neither possibility was especially comforting.

"What's your customs procedure here?" Wallich wanted to know. "I was expecting to dock with some sort of quarantine facility."

Dibrin frowned, tapped his ear. "Customs? You mean inspection? It's handled. Passive sensors, scouting microscopia, like that. Shouldn't trouble your ship's systems any, though do let us know, er, if any problems should arise. Been nine years since a Munie ship ever came to Saint Helier, so maybe you never know."

"Munie?" I asked, intrigued by the term. I'd come across it once or twice in sifting Gladholder net traffic, but never in clear enough context to realize its meaning: Us, the peculiar inhabitants of the upper system.

Now Dibrin looked embarrassed. "Apologies, sir, and meaning no disrespect."

I grunted, half-amused. "It's a derogatory term, then?"

He smiled at me, or maybe grimaced. I could see yellow around the whites of his eyes, threaded delicately with blue and red. An unpleasant, vaguely fishy smell came off his breath. A human smell,

I should say. "Derogatory, no. Munies, four-eyes, duckfeet, the people upstairs . . . It's just something to say. Why, what do you call us?"

"Gladholders."

He grunted, amused. "No imagination, eh? Seek, maybe we should just head straight for the market."

Wallich nodded. "I think that might be best, yeah. Are we walking?"

"Floating?" Baucum corrected.

Dibrin nodded. "It isn't far. If you'll follow me?"

He braced his feet and shoved off for an opening high on one wall.

We followed, awkward not so much from gravity—for weeks we'd been bouncing from zero to point-two gee and all levels between—as from the geometry of the space. Like playing a new sport for the first time, before you've quite gotten a feel for the ranges, the angles, the available traction. I, for one, fell short of the opening and had to leap again. Would have felt bad about it, too, except that Wallich did exactly the same thing.

The opening proved to be the mouth of a trapezoidal tunnel, wider at the bottom than on the top, and once we'd assembled there, Dibrin propelled himself down its length with a pair of lazy but decisive kicks, like something a swimmer would do. No mystery where he'd gotten those strong toes! We "Munies" tried to replicate the feat with limited success. The idea was clear enough: launch into a flat parabolic arc that would bring you to touchdown far ahead, without first intersecting any solid surface.

Head against the ceiling, it took about four seconds to fall feet-to-the-floor, maybe twice as long as it would have been on Ganymede, and many, many times what Earth would have to say about it. I'd have thought it'd be even slower than that, based on our extremely minimal body weight on Saint Helier, but nature never seems to care what I think. Anyway, these long, straight leaps proved no easy feat, especially in gold-weighted shoes.

As I collided softly with the walls, it was difficult not to notice that here, as in the docking bay, they were covered with creeping vines. Up close, though, I could see what was hanging from them, and it proved to be a sort of smooth and tough-looking fruit, ovoid in shape and somewhat smaller than a human head. I dug back into old Earth memories. Coconut? Breadfruit? Cantaloupe? I wasn't sure any of those grew on vines. I fingered up my notetaker, jotted down a reminder to ask about it sometime.

Right now, though, Dibrin had got back to talking business.

"You've got a thousand-dollar line of credit," he was saying, "and Governor has instructed me to haggle on your behalf. Food and clothing, right? I know you need oxygen and uranium as well, but those are supplied by the port authority at standard rates. A *kilogram* of uranium? Seek, that's a lot. Lucky you get it cheaper down here!"

"You don't use much ladderdown," Davenroy said, not asking but prompting.

"Ladderdown, no. For propulsion, for excavation, a few things like that, but what are we supposed to do with the waste heat? Small, metal-rich planetoids do not provide the heat sink you people are accustomed to, and anyway we have the sun blazing at us all the time. So we use that."

"Mirrors the size of Innensburg, right?" Wallich smiled. "We didn't get much of a look at the sunward face on our approach, but I guess we'll see it on the down and out. Must be quite a sight."

"We can visit if you like. It'll be tomorrow before that uranium is cast in a single mass."

"Tomorrow?" Wallich's grin faded. "Our mission is fairly urgent, sir."

Dibrin shrugged. "Can't be helped. I can't make it happen any faster."

Wallich's mouth twitched, indecisive for a moment before the grin surfaced again. "Well, *there's* an excuse to spend the night away from work."

"I'm to set up accommodations if you so specify," Dibrin said. "There are staying homes all along the main concourse."

Wallich's grin widened. "Well, hey, then. Shore leave, everybody. What do you say? Ha ha."

My own mumbles of approval were joined by many others. The Immunity's plight was desperate enough, but it wouldn't worsen measurably just because we'd stopped here for the night. It smelled funny in the Gladhold, like cheese and Freon and potting soil gone slightly bad, but by comparison *Louis Pasteur* was a veritable sewer, and going back inside her before she aired out was not a notion that appealed. And of course, there was the food thing; flavor issues aside, my teeth tingled at the very thought of tearing and grinding and chewing again. Enough with the nutrient pap!

New corridors crossed ours at right angles every thirty meters or so, and while there were no other pedestrians moving along with us, there were quite a few cutting across our path, all skating along barefooted like Chris Dibrin. My glimpses of them were brief, and alas I recorded no images, but my memory is of a festival of colors, skin and hair and clothing of every imaginable hue. More skin than you'd expect to see back home, though modest enough, not so much a flesh display as a pajama party. Or gangs of teenagers on their way to one, I suppose; yes, the crowd was a young one. Higher birth rates will do that to you, I suppose, but I'd begun to feel self-conscious, overmature, unnecessarily stiff and hot in my spacer uniform. And far from home.

The air, I should mention, was a good deal warmer and more

humid than in the Immunity, or even aboard the *Louis Pasteur*. It felt a bit unclean somehow, and a bit unsafe. Not so much from the added bloom danger—though that was certainly a consideration—as from a general upper-system wariness of moisture. Even deep inside Ganymede, water ice is an important component of the rock, and hot, moist air is a clue that the cavern roof is maybe about to fall on your head. It happens. Anyway, I knew Saint Helier wasn't going to melt or collapse or anything, but I did have the unpleasant sense that I was *not in the Immunity*, that all sorts of nanoscopic crap was bouncing around in my lungs and on my skin, phages and microbes and God knew what else, and the moisture lent the feeling that all of it would stick. Unclean. I'm not sure how else to describe it.

Not that my attention was really on this, though. It was one more detail, one more component of the alienness of this place. Mostly, my attention was on trying to walk without falling over, especially when Dibrin turned suddenly into the crowd, slipping easily into one of the side corridors while inertia carried us Munies into walls and people en masse, in a great flailing of limbs.

Darren Wallich roared and guffawed at this, and the Gladholder children took the cue and laughed right back, slapping our backs and grabbing our hands as if these skiddings and crashings were the most brilliantly amusing bits of cocktail tomfoolery they'd encountered all month. Well, maybe that was so. At any rate, by the time we got moving again, Dibrin had on a half smirk that he wasn't bothering to hide, and moved through this more crowded hallway with an exaggerated care. *This* way, freunde. *This* is how we do it.

And then, suddenly, with no warning at all, we were at the market.

TWELVE

THE FEAR DOLL

One of the deepest and most enduring mysteries of the Mycosystem is where, exactly, it came from. New Guinea, yes, obviously, but how far had those first few spores traveled before grounding in that rich, tropical loam? Most doctors reject the "panspermia" hypothesis outright, citing the "keyhole problem" as prima facie evidence of terrestrial origin. If mycora were truly visitors from another star, whether transported here naturally or otherwise, would their chemistry be so uniquely suited to the consumption of Earthly biomass? Would they have, ready at hand, the enzyme analogs to reduce those steaming jungles so quickly and so completely?

That the Mycosystem might be an alien weapon deliberately targeting Earth's biomass seems equally improbable; the metabolism of the First Mycorum is thought to have resembled, in various aspects, that of recycling and agricultural nanocytes, in vivo microautomata, and of course the "prank" self-replicators that were already a major social problem in the developed world. So did somebody's mutant vandalbug go walkies and take on a life of its own? Again, the experts deny it.

"No doubt there were malcontents down there," one nameless doctor assured me in a hurried hallway conversation, "who would have destroyed the Earth's teeming masses if they could. Without a crack research team and a large, expensive laboratory, though, I doubt very much that a technogenic organism like that would have happened. The sophistication is well beyond what a lone amateur would accomplish."

So much for the notion—romantic in its own grim way—of the mad scientist and his years-long toil in a musty attic workshop. The truth is doubtless much harder and more complex. We have, almost certainly, no one but ourselves to blame.

I claim no great knowledge in this field, but my own pet theory—built wholly of fragments and naive supposition—revolves around the so-called "smart liquids" that mathematicians and other theorists sometimes employed for massively parallel numerical analyses. The easiest way, it seems, to run a trillion simultaneous computations was to code them in a broth of replicating, self-modifying nanocomputers. Powered by a very specialized chemical diet, of course, but otherwise left to run and mutate unattended . . .

When I shared this idea with my anonymous doctor friend,

though, he simply smiled and shook his head. "No, no, I doubt that very much. But it's a nice thought, isn't it?"

Yeah, nice. That was exactly the word I had in mind.

From *Innensburg and the Fear of Failure*
© 2101 by John Strasheim

I don't know quite what I'd been expecting. On Earth, we used to get our food and clothing and such from shopping malls. On Ganymede, of course, you'd simply flash down a price guide, order remotely, and wait twelve to twenty-four hours for delivery, the term "market" referring exclusively to the hypothetical trading and dickering that established the quarterly prices. But here in the Gladhold, the market was a physical locus of real, physical activity, voices and bodies and currencies hurling this way and that. And still there was no sense of up!

Well, almost no sense. The market's cavern was fifty meters across and by no means dome-shaped or even spherical. Not quite random, either, but the jagged, right-angle contours followed some plan that was not apparent to me. A chamber, as they say, of high fractal dimension. Imagine the inside of a geode. The merchants themselves sat surrounded by their wares in flat, steel-mesh baskets the size of ballista cars. The baskets did point more or less in the same direction, toward us, which meant that we were more or less looking straight down on the display, but right there any semblance of order ended.

The baskets sat at a hundred different levels and ledges, tilted slightly this way, slightly that way, slightly heaven knows what other way, and the milling throngs of shoppers, several hundred people at least, could be seen leaping and gliding from perch to perch like so many birds in a jungle cage. And the noise! A hundred voices chattering and dickering and arguing and laughing! The mind boggles at such waste, such extravagance. Surely there must be a better way to get goods from producer to consumer! On Ganymede, one tended to work and eat and sleep and perform routine household maintenance, with shopping being an inevitable but oft-postponed inconvenience. How long would we avoid it if it had to be like this? Surely these people must have better uses for their time!

Dibrin looked back at us, shrugging eyebrow and chin and shoulder together as if to say, "Come on, it's not as bad as it looks, and anyway what other plans have you got?" And then he leaped feetfirst into the space where the corridor dead-ended and the floor opened out into marketplace.

"Look around for what you need," he said, or rather, the zee-spec said he said, as he fell gently into the maelstrom. "Bag it and wait for me. I'll come around with money in a little while."

Baucum and Davenroy exchanged uneasy glances. Lehne and Rapisardi stood by waiting for someone else to make the first move, while Darren Wallich looked down and snorted several times with amusement. I, having nothing better to do, jumped down after Dibrin.

He lighted on a ledge three meters below, and pushed off to one side. I copied him, a bit more forcefully, and landed a moment after him in a basket filled with . . . dolls?

The merchant seated there, a flabby woman with wavy brown hair and skin the color of walnuts, called out a single word, which the zee-spec translated as "Hallo, please buy something!"

"Just stepping through," Dibrin assured her without looking up. But he grinned and nudged one of the dolls with his foot.

It screamed. "No! No, I can't, I won't! Get away from me! Get away!"

Catching my expression, Dibrin smiled mischievously and toed the doll again.

"Help! I weep, I tremble. I can't! I *can't!*"

"My god," I said. "What is it? What are you doing to it?"

The woman looked sharply at Dibrin. "Pay for it if you're going to play."

"Sorry," he said to her. And then to me: "It's a phobia. You feeling alone or afraid or nervous about something, you kick this thing around. Confront your fear, crush your fear underfoot. Symbolic. Very popular."

"It's *horrible*," I told him. "What if you're a sadistic bastard? What if you just like to kick things around, make things scream?"

"Different doll," he said, shrugging, and leaped away for another basket.

Well.

I couldn't help myself—I bent for a closer look at one of the dolls. Even its appearance was awful, a red-brown body of soft, wrinkly leather crowned with a blank, faceless head and four empty limbs that bent off in any and all directions. When I touched it, the texture was precisely the cool, smooth, almost wet feeling I'd been expecting. And squishy-soft, like a bag of phlegm.

"I'm *afraid*," the doll told me with grave sincerity, the words recognizable even without Dibrin's translator.

"Do you want that or no?" the merchant woman demanded.

"No," I said. "Definitely not."

Disgusted, I dropped it and leaped away. I had shopping to do.

Picking out food proved easy enough; as I glided from basket to basket, certain sights and smells set me to salivating so heavily I thought my tongue would dissolve. Where was Dibrin with the money? I looked for him in the mad, low-gravity gyrations of the crowd, but didn't find him, so reluctantly I asked the merchants, in slow and careful English, to wrap the goods for me and hold them until my return. Too, I selected some clothing, a couple of shirts and a pair of flappy, loose-fitting slacks that would probably take some getting used to in weightlessness. And loose, meshy underwear, several pairs. Not what I would have chosen for myself back home, but they seemed the best of the available options here, and anyway my Immune spacer coverall and its supporting garments were currently the only clothing I owned. I had washed both the clothes and myself the evening before, but there are limits to what a shipboard shower can accomplish, and I was eager to climb into something a little fresher.

Finally, Dibrin did show up, with a package-laden Renata Baucum in tow, and together we made the rounds, picking up the goods I'd selected.

She was eating something, something round and purple and wet inside.

"Is that a plum?" I inquired, I hoped, not too hungrily. We had plums in the Immunity, but not affordable ones.

"It is," she agreed, slurping juice off her chin. Her tongue slipped out, caressed her lower lip briefly before retreating.

"Can, uh, I have a bite?"

Sidelong, she considered me, then the half-finished fruit in her hand. Reluctant to share her spit? Particularly here, in this warm, subtly unclean place?

"Here," she said finally, fumbling her left hand into a bag and handing me something. "Have a whole one."

I blushed, embarrassed at having put her on the spot that way. "Really? Thanks."

Then, without further compunction, I took the plum from her, tore into the flesh of it with my teeth. The taste was incredible, wet and sweet and wholly unlike nutrient pap. In three bites, I had reduced it to a bare stone, which I popped into my mouth and sucked on, pulling hard for the last bits of that wonderful flavor.

"Oh, God," I said to her around the stone. "That's good."

"Nice, eh?"

She had picked out some clothes as well, a coverall and something called a "body wrap," which she showed me a corner of as it peeked out from its bag. Green cloth marked with little squiggles.

"It's nice," I assured her.

We came across Darren Wallich along the way, and then Sudhir Rapisardi, and soon we were all together again. As our purchases were purchased, though, it became apparent that we'd all picked out the same sorts of things, the emphasis on meats and breads and fruits, not preserved or even particularly preservable, unless you were into vacuum storage. So what, we'd eat well for a week or two and then edge back into a liquid diet? No thanks! So we made another pass through the market, more systematically this time, and picked up thirty kilograms of canned and pickled goods, plus a bit more underwear and such.

Finally, laden with bulky packages and awkward in the unfamiliar gravity, we hauled ourselves back to the port complex, beeped our way past *Louis Pasteur*'s security, and dumped our booty in the wardroom, which if anything smelled worse than it had when we'd left. If Gladholder air was replacing our own as per plan, it was doing so very slowly indeed.

"Stinks in there," Dibrin observed, wrinkling his nose as we emerged.

"Yeah," I said to him, "tell me about it."

"Glad to sleep outside for a night?"

"Oh, yeah," Wallich agreed, smirking. He put a hand on my shoulder, another on Dibrin's. "There was some talk about going to see the mirror, right?"

"Certainly," Dibrin said. "It's a short walk from here, only about six miles."

Wallich seemed, for some reason, to find this funny.

I found out why. Six miles? I didn't really know how far a "mile" was, and by the time I learned, it was too late to do anything about it. Our expedition was over *ten kilometers* out and back. Quite a hike, for anyone used to living in caverns barely a third that size!

The mirror, okay. From inside the asteroid, it didn't look like much, just a bowl-shaped crater reflecting the blackness of sky that surrounded the sun's (quite seriously swollen) glare. We looked out on it through an observation port in its rim, a round window as tall as a person, made of glass five centimeters thick. Real silicon glass, yes; I guess they have a lot of it here. Anyway, it was only by looking for similar ports across the crater rim—of which there were several at uneven intervals—that I was able to get any real sense of scale. This, at least, was impressive; as Wallich had intimated earlier, the mirror was about the size of Innensburg, maybe two kilometers from end to end, and you could have fit a city block on the circular thing hanging from cables at its center.

The chamber and window were large enough for all of us to look out together, but Dibrin's attention quickly settled on the flat video monitors built into the opposite wall.

"They're using the telescope," he said, sounding pleased. "Venus images again. Look, you can really see the huts!"

On the screens, sure enough, were blurry, wavery images of what looked like thatched domes, the sort of thing primitive humans had once inhabited. They clumped together in rough, approximately concentric circles, little villages with clearings at their centers. On Venus? I must have heard him incorrectly.

"Huts?" I asked. "On Venus?"

He nodded. "Yeah. Hey, you can even see the people. The planet must be at conjunction; this is an exceptionally clear shot."

"People?" Renata Baucum asked.

"On Venus?" Jenna Davenroy added. God, we sounded like a bunch of idiots. But how else were we supposed to sound? Through the wavers and shimmers, the images on the wall screens were clear enough: little knots of nude people walking around between the huts. The ground beneath them was yellow and smooth-looking, like plastic. A less magnified image showed the surrounding area, a red/brown/purple mass of mycostructure, picks and blossoms and feather urchins and a thousand shapes less easily labeled, with that little yellow clearing sitting there in the middle of it, dotted with huts.

Could "hut" be just another mycoric blueprint, a random, mean-ingless shape put together by trillions of technogenic automata? More like a brain coral than a wasp's nest, with structure synergistic, rather than planned? *But there were people walking around down there.* Not on Earth. Not *even* on Earth, where I might have some vague possibility of believing it, but on Venus, where I certainly could not.

"What kind of trick are you pulling, here?" Wallich asked, easily, not concerned or affronted or anything.

But Dibrin frowned. "Trick? Excuse, please?"

Baucum touched him lightly on the shoulder. "Please, honestly. Are these actual telescope images?"

"Of course."

"Realtime?"

"Yes."

"Of *Venus?*"

Dibrin flared. "Yes, Venus! Seek, are you people deaf? There are humans living on Venus. The primordial atmosphere is gone, the air has been thinning out for decades, and now it's apparently habitable. New discovery, but we've been shouting about it for weeks. Munies, always so busy, so distracted. Don't you listen to the news?"

Evidently not. Mine were some of the few news channels that paid the Gladhold any attention at all, but if a story this big could escape *me* . . . Had I been that unobservant? Gladholder news passed through a lot of wire and other hardware on its way to me. Had some portion of it been . . . misplaced along the way?

"And Earth?" Sudhir Rapisardi asked, looking pale and stunned. "Are the rumors true?"

Dibrin's scowl eased. He waved a hand at the monitors. "Like that? It looks like that on Earth, too, but we knew about that three years ago. Three years. Is that how your rumors go? Slow!"

"My god," someone said.

Indeed. How had people gotten there? What did they eat? How did they *survive*, down there in the thick of the bloom to end all blooms? The words "Mycosystem" and "extermination" were all but synonymous.

"It looks the same on both planets," Dibrin said gently, now finally aware that he was breaking bad news. Or was it good news? The whole concept was too alien, too horrid and slippery for the mind to get much of a grip on. "I can translate a report for you, if you like."

I nodded stupidly. "Yes. I'd like that very much."

"May I . . . meddle?"

I hesitated, then nodded again. "Please do."

It only took him a moment to flash the file to me, and he never moved a muscle. I was watching.

"Thank you," I said when he'd finished. "I'll read it later." Much later, probably; it would take time for all this to settle. And how was it the Immunity had missed out on so hugely significant a discovery? Were we just too wrapped up in our own concerns? The rumors about Earth had never received much credence, even among the gullible—it was too obviously impossible, like saying there were people living on the surface of the sun. But here the evidence was; had we stopped even *looking* at the stars and planets? The Gladhold was a lot closer to the bodies of concern, though, and they did have these huge mirrors lying around. Were they looking simply because they had the equipment, because it was easy for them to look? But *why hadn't I heard about it?*

"How does the telescope work?" Rapisardi demanded.

Finally, I thought to begin recording.

"Deformable mirror," Dibrin replied, now looking out through the window, gesturing at it. "Not one piece, I think, but millions of pieces, trillions of pieces, under independent control. You use part of it to focus sunlight for power generation, but here at perihelion there's lots of excess capacity. Too bright to use it *all* for that. Look down at the mirror surface, you see how it sort of shimmers in places? They're probably doing twenty different things with it right now, little pieces focusing in all different directions. Like little flowers, yes, turning their small faces toward the sun, toward the stars . . . These mirrors have been used as weapons, too, though the last rock that tried it got blockaded for twelve years."

"Nanoscale components?" Wallich coughed. "The mirrorlets have to be larger than a wavelength of light, right, but the pieces that drive them are smaller?"

"Um, I guess so."

"God damn."

Wallich, who had spent his life wiping out small things, looked about as unamused as a person could. The contrast was interesting; it would make a fine clip in the next collage.

* * *

The walk back was quiet, disturbed by little more than the sounds of our breathing. And the sounds of the Gladhold, yes, the chattering and laughter of thousands of people. Here they had abandoned the idea of caverns, of individual buildings in large, open spaces with a stony sky looming overhead. It seemed to me that would make even *more* sense in this trivial gravity, but instead the emphasis was on corridors and doorways, straight lines, walls of dark, smooth-polished rock. Few of the spaces so connected were actually rectangular—the geode forms seemed much more Saint Helier's style—and Gladholders did seem to have a better handle than Munies on exploitation of the third dimension.

But walking around in the Five Cities provided a sense of openness, freshness, and here the opposite held true. The inside-out "buildings" were the open spaces, while the connecting corridors felt close, crowded. And so many children! They spilled from doorways, giving glimpses of the households beyond—high-ceilinged chambers, terraced off into many levels, furnished with riotous assortments of plant and animal life. Bamboo and birds! It didn't seem very homey to me.

This was hardly the focus of my attention, though.

People on Venus?

The idea should have been horrible, laughable, shattering. It *was* all of those things, I guess, but mostly it was just too large and slippery to grasp. Should I feel some sense of righteous triumph, that death had not completely conquered the inner system after all? Should I feel empathy, sympathy for the humans so imprisoned? Either reaction would imply some degree of understanding, which I certainly lacked.

One thing was clear: If we were to believe and accept this

finding, our worldview would have to disintegrate. The Mycosytem *I* knew did not allow for this sort of anomaly. What sort of Mycosystem did? I found, to my surprise, that I didn't really want to know. Would I mourn the mindless Mycosystem that had eaten my world? I might, if something even more sinister took its place. Something bright, capable, purposeful? No. Surely, buried in our work or no, we would have known about that long ago if it were true.

So that was my first reaction: denial. Aggressive apathy.

Tosca Lehne seemed more upset, though, seemed often on the edge of tears as we leaped and vaulted our way through the endless corridors. Tears for whom? I found I didn't want to know that, either.

Wallich and Davenroy seemed less affected, seemed to believe the whole thing was some sort of mistake. Well, maybe it was. Rapisardi was lost in his zee-spec, fingers in constant motion. Assessing plausibilities? Working equations? Escaping into some ideator's fantasy? Baucum just looked subdued, as if she were applying serious thought to the problem but hadn't reached any conclusions yet.

In a way, that made me feel worse. Was her mind more open than mine? I didn't want to think so.

The only person unaffected was, of course, Dibrin. It wasn't news to him, wasn't a sudden revelation. In fact, I had the impression that even when it *was* news, the announcement hadn't knocked the stuffing out of him the way it had us. *His* Mycosystem must be a very different place from mine, different even from Baucum's. What did he know that we didn't?

"It's always up to something," he answered when I put the question to him. "It's a devious one, that Mycosystem."

"Devious?"

He backpedaled: "Not in a deliberate sense. I mean in an evolutionary one. It's always trying something new. Forms, behaviors, the mycora themselves . . ."

"We used to think," I told him, "that they were stealing gene sequences out of our Immune system. It was a pretty unsettling thought, but then it turned out to be the result of human meddling."

"That happens sometimes here, as well," he said, then cocked his head at me. "Are you recording this conversation?"

"It's my job. Yes. Does it bother you?"

"No, I guess not," he said. And nothing more.

"So you have meddlers here as well?" I probed. "People experimenting with living mycora?"

Reluctantly: "Sometimes. It's illegal, harsh penalties, but people are . . . curious animals."

"This Venus thing is a much more shocking revelation," I said. "I really don't know what to make of it."

"Huh," he said.

I guess the recording bothered him after all, because prying further comment out of him proved all but impossible.

There's a sharp, special bite to the weariness that comes from exertion in low gravity. You're not working your muscles very hard, individually, but there's still inertia to fight, and you wind up using *all* your muscles for it, including the ones you didn't know you had. And shocking news brings its own kind of tired, as well.

Dibrin guided us to what he called a "staying home," where we could eat and sleep and such for the thirteen hours until our uranium fuel nodule was delivered and installed. I'd expected something like a hotel, airy and full of plants, but the entrance to the place turned out to be through an unmarked doorway into a cramped, surprisingly ordinary-looking tavern. Except for the crowding and the noise, fifteen or twenty patrons all jabbering at one another, this might easily have been Ganymede. Or Earth. I guess these places have been the same for centuries, and little things like moving to a different planet aren't going to have much effect.

The staying home itself was on the next level up, access to which was via a ladder that led into a small, cube-shaped chamber with doors on all four walls and flat, dim lights on its ceiling. Men's and women's communal sleeping and sanitary facilities, as indicated by pictograms of toilets and bunk beds and human beings with and without breasts. Hmm.

Sudhir Rapisardi noted that though he was tired, he'd come off sleep shift only seven hours before, and wouldn't mind a drink or two in the pub downstairs. What did we say?

"We could all probably use one," Wallich allowed, though he himself had been up for at least a day.

"Screw," Tosca Lehne muttered, still looking stricken and miserable. "I need sleep. Have fun without me."

Baucum and Davenroy echoed that sentiment, and quickly retreated together into the washroom, while Lehne opened up the men's sleeping quarters. They looked a bit bigger than I'd feared, at least, and none of the ten or so beds looked occupied or disturbed, insofar as I could see them before the door slid closed again.

So Dibrin and Wallich and Rapisardi and I went back downstairs again, and found a little table for ourselves on one of the tavern's many terraces. No chairs, but in this gravity it was plenty comfortable to stand. And the music was nice, if a bit jangly and odd.

"You men drink beer?" Dibrin asked. We allowed that we did, yes, sometimes, and so he drifted off to the bar to order some for us.

Wallich's grin had returned, if weakly.

"This mission's a bit of a strain on that tickle capacitor," I said to him.

He shrugged. "Sometimes it's funny, sometimes it isn't. Some days, it's almost painful."

"So what do you think of this Venus business?" Rapisardi asked, quietly, as though he were afraid of being overheard. In fact, the music was very effective at drowning him out, so that I had to lean close to understand him.

"I don't know," Wallich said. "It's hard to say how that could be. It's hard to say what we saw, right? It could be . . . well, a lot of things. I look and I see human beings running around, but that doesn't mean that's really what's down there. I mean, you see flowers and pin cushions and maybe bunny rabbits and stuff in that mess, too, but it's just goop. Strasheim, have you read that report yet?"

I shook my head.

"Flash it to me?"

"Sure."

While I was doing this, Dibrin returned with our beer, which came in clear, teardrop-shaped plastic bulbs. *Big* bulbs, probably three hundred cc's, almost twice as much beer as a Ganymedean stein would hold. Well, when in Rome . . . That thought just reminded me that maybe there *were* still people in Rome, and I didn't want to think about that. So I took a pull on the beer, which tasted just fine.

"Hard day?" Dibrin asked, taking a drink from his own bulb.

"Hard lifetime," Rapisardi said, and both Dibrin and Wallich laughed at that.

We stood for a while in silence.

"You know," I finally said, "If news this big can escape our attention, something is definitely wrong. There should probably be a lot better communication between the Immunity and the Gladhold."

"Glad*holds*," Dibrin corrected. "See, there are hundreds; we're loosely confederated at best. But yeah, sure, I think it's always better to talk. Would you still be on this mission of yours if you'd had this news earlier?"

I thought about that, shrugged. I really didn't know.

But Wallich said, "Our basic problem hasn't changed."

I thought about that, as well. If people were surviving down there, bloomless, unconsumed, couldn't *we* survive, as well? The Innensburg bloom argued against it, ditto the death of my brother in his smaller, less dramatic contagion. Or the death of Tug Jinacio, for that matter, or the hundreds of other bloom deaths that the Immunity had racked up over the years. With people like the bottle man running around, how long might it be before the mycora learned to wipe us out?

Wallich was right, our mission was as imperative as ever: the risk of Mycosystem expansion was impossible to calculate, but the consequences were, in essence, infinitely bad. Mankind *needed* a warning system, needed that little bit of extra time to . . . what? Launch the starship? Protect itself in some way, certainly. Once morning came and our fuel arrived, we'd be off, just the same as before.

Meanwhile, though, it was just as well to sit here drinking beer. Or so reason informed us; internally, some subliminal sense of guilt was hard to avoid.

More silence for a while, again broken by me: "Dibrin, you, uh, you seem to have *artificial intelligences* in your head. Is that so?"

He nodded. "Yes. In my spine, actually." He patted the back of his neck. "It helps me think much faster. Which is good."

"But are they really your thoughts?"

At this, he frowned. "Are you recording this?"

"No. Does it make a difference?"

"I guess not. About the thoughts, whether they're mine, I think that depends on how you define 'me.' Am I my brain? My body? Am I the sum of my parts? The thoughts blend seamlessly. The brain evolves to work with the assistants, and also the assistants evolve to work with the brain. If you took the machinery away, I would be crippled. My brain would no longer function in a healthy way. So yes, all the thoughts are mine, by my perception of that word. You get a separated intelligence, not an assistant but a self-contained entity, and its behavior is not governed that way. They can be somewhat peculiar at times."

"Peculiar how?" I asked.

He pursed his lips, seemed to consider for a moment. "May I flash you a short plaintext?"

"All right."

He did this, once again quickly and without moving. I opened the document.

HUMAN ERROR, A Fiction

LOOK_FOR_OBJECT. 2 DOORS down HALLWAY, EN-TER, LOOK_FOR_OBJECT, it does. Punishment/reward sieves through learning nets, squeaking wheel, skewed camera-eye, pause and recalibrate. The itch must be scratched, has been scratched, O_fucking_kay! Searching, searching; this brings happiness.

BUT
BUT
BUT

DOOR (2) leads—ALARM: EDGE DETECTED!
ALARM: EDGE DETECTED!

Retreat, scan, evaluate.
Elevatorcrawlspacewindowstairwell? Stairwell!
Internal models suspect—engage self-doubt. Simulate outcomes of potential actions?

Might have happened this *way: tumble tumble crash.*
Might have happened this *way: tumble crash tumble.*
Might have happened this *way: tumble tumble crash tumble.*

Brooding. Brooding. Review command sequence, compare actions taken. Brooding. Confirmed: command sequence error. Might have fallen down the stairs! Q:
Source (command_input)? A: . = FLOYD.

Engage abstraction. Erroneous command_input from FLOYD. Scan memory? This time and that time and that *time. Insight! Fuzzy logic, unreliable data. FLOYD is unreliable? Adjust expectation model: CONFIDENCE (command_input (FLOYD)) = . * 0.5. STOP! PUNISH! PUNISH! Ouch, ouch, UNDO. Engage abstraction!*

PRIORITY (obedience (FLOYD)) >>
PRIORITY (preservation (SELF)).

ergo . . .

Must proceed with command sequence given by FLOYD. Ours is not to question. Sadness. Sadness.

ALARM: EDGE DETECTED!
ALARM: EDGE DETECTED!

#qf$(i@)qf78f165h#.#
EOF

"One of Governor's separated intelligences wrote this," Dibrin said. "Spontaneously, without prompting. Creativity, maybe, a desire to communicate that it has an inner life. In their idle periods, awake but ... understimulated, who knows what runs through their strange little minds? Smarter than mice, most ways, and of course they can speak, after a fashion. Not like you and I do, but information is communicated. Seek, you've got to wonder sometimes, what do they really *know*? The really interesting thing is that this story requires strong gravity, which the SI has never seen, and a physical body, which the SI has never had. That's what peculiar means."

I felt a chill. "Isn't it a little dangerous, to use these things you don't really understand?"

Dibrin shrugged. "I don't know. How long did man use fire without doing chemistry? I'm saying yeah, probably it is dangerous, but what are you doing to do? Life has got to go on."

Darren Wallich cleared his throat. "The adaptive Immune system is the thing that bothers me the most. How can you sleep at night? You've got self-replicating, self-mutating phages and everything floating around here with God knows what in their programming. It's inconceivable, really. The more I think about it, the more astounded I become."

"We let evolution do the work," Dibrin said, now sounding a bit defensive.

"And artificial intelligence," Wallich agreed, "and unsecured nanotechnology. The common ingredient is that there's nobody in control. There's not even a *mechanism* for control."

Dibrin was waving the comment away. "Maybe we don't feel like working ourselves to death. Maybe we recognize some problems too big to handle with raw brain power. Adaptive systems seek optimal solution *by themselves*, with no need for us to test out every single possibility until we find something that works. Saint Helier hasn't had a bloom in seven years, did you know that? And our best brains aren't tied up with the struggle; they're free to create the things that make our lives easier and more interesting. Seek, we have *full-time poets* in the Gladholds. Do you?"

Wallich laughed at the idea.

"Ah, go ahead," Dibrin said, now visibly irked. "You spend your life trying to catch up, spend your resources trying to stay ahead of it, see if it matters to me. Evolution never sleeps, but a man has got to. Even you."

"I like the idea of a place where the work does itself," Rapisardi said, distantly, looking around the room as if for a friend who'd wandered away. He seemed particularly interested in the knot of people dancing, over by the bar.

Softening, Dibrin replied, "Not *all* the work. Though there are those ones who get by on wallfruit and hallway air. The option for idleness does actually exist, nowadays."

The bulb was empty already in Rapisardi's hand. He glanced at it, frowned slightly, glanced around the room again. "That music has a nice rhythm. Is there more beer?"

Dibrin dug into a tight pocket at his waist, his fingers coming out with one of the little gold coins people seemed to use for money here. He examined it for a moment, then handed it over to Rapisardi. "This is enough for five bulbs. Maybe you'll find a friend."

The biophysicist brightened, looked to Wallich for confirmation, then brightened some more when he received a nod. Moments later, he was off to his hoped-for debauchery.

"The man needs to get out more," Dibrin said, looking after Rapisardi with friendly amusement.

"He's been in space for a few weeks," Wallich said.

But Dibrin was shaking his head. "It's more than that. This Venus news has hit you duckfeet people hard. For us, the Mycosystem is just a fact of life, like the sun and the stars. I think you have always been more afraid of it, more afraid of coexisting with it. But we live right on the upper fringes, and it's not such a stretch to imagine being actually inside."

"You will be," Wallich said darkly, his tone more frustrated than accusing. "Never mind natural growth and mutation, never mind that there are crazies out there trying to help the Mycosystem expand. These things you're messing with down here . . ."

"Will jump up and bite us," Dibrin finished for him, sounding unimpressed.

"Not like it hasn't happened before," Wallich said, and took a stiff pull on his beer. "Not like you don't live, as you say, right on the upper fringes of our constant reminder of the fact. This place is an accident waiting to happen."

"It's already happened," Dibrin lobbed back. "You live with it. You adapt. You move on with your life. That's how it works."

"No."

A third silence descended upon us, heavier than ever, and while I was beginning to appreciate the virtues of silence, a thought that had been nagging at me for hours finally found its voice: "How would they get there? To Venus. There were never people down there, even before. How would they get there?"

Dibrin looked at me and shrugged. "I don't know. As spores?"

I bit back a retort; his carob features were innocent, interested, truthful. He wasn't kidding.

"Not so unfathomable," he said, observing my expression. "With decent compression, you could fit ten or twenty human genomes in a regular mycospore, maybe a hundred in a big one.

Could probably store brain patterns, too, though I'd bet on some integrity losses. Maybe not, if there was enough error-checking built in."

"I'm not asking whether a human being would *fit* in a spore," I said over the music, a bit more loudly than I'd intended. A few faces turned our way. "That question is meaningless. Even if there were human beings down there, which I'm not granting just yet, how would their genes and such get into a spore?"

"I guess something would have to dismantle them, or part of them at least, and record the details as it went. God and Jesus know, enough people got eaten."

I shuddered, horrified at the thought. Technogenic humans? Assembled atom by atom in the rainbow mist, using a blueprint cribbed directly from the source? No, I refused to believe it.

"Why would the mycora do that? They're just little digesting machines."

Darren Wallich was shaking his head. "No, Strasheim, they're a lot more than just that. Individually, they're complex and mysterious enough. In groups, their behaviors become even more intricate. They communicate back and forth, change state based on the information they receive . . ."

"Like a cellular automaton," I said.

He looked surprised. "Yes, I suppose so."

"Anyway," Dibrin said, "maybe that is not how it happened. Maybe some old spaceship was involved, and we just didn't notice. Maybe they came from one of the Gladholds, and brought an Immune system and atmosphere-processing system down with them. It could be a lot of things. You people are going down there—maybe one day *you* can tell *me*."

Wallich still looked unhappy. "I hope all this is true. I hope it *is* possible to survive down there, because one of these days you're going to need every chance you can get."

"Yeah," Dibrin said, unconvinced, "maybe."

A small, dark woman approached, came up behind him, put her arm around his chest.

"Hi," he said without turning. "Gentlemen, I've got to go."

"Who is this?" I asked, nonplussed.

"My wife, Lin," he said, already turning to leave with her.

I guess talking to her was another of those things he could do without moving.

When I went to bed, about half an hour later, I passed Rapisardi dancing with three women and one other man. He seemed to have trouble keeping his balance, keeping his feet anywhere near the floor, but he'd tied some sort of multicolored rag around his head, and was grinning so broadly I wondered if his mouth would be sore in the morning.

Funny, but I don't think I'd ever before seen anyone try so hard to have a good time, and still manage to succeed.

MUNITY

Turns out we'll be paying for our food and clothing purchases after all, using, of all things, our shoes. No kidding! Our guide pointed out some bracelets, and though they were fashioned of plain gold he assured us they were very expensive. From the labor that went into them, I assumed, for they were handmade, but no, it turns out the fingernail-sized "dollars" that have been spent on our behalf are also made of gold, and derive their value from their own intrinsic worth as metal. As if we Munies walked around trading actual grams of uranium back and forth. This is what comes of not using ladderdown!

The Gladholders think our "duck shoes" are frightfully amusing anyway, and when they found out what the sole weights were made of, I thought they'd never stop laughing. And when they offered to replace those same blocks with equivalent masses of lead, which of course is five times more valuable back home, I thought we'd never stop laughing. This interplanetary trading is a jolly business, you bet.

From "Glad Times in the Gladhold,"
© 2106 by John Strasheim

You know, Momma, one thing we never eat in Ganymede is curry. I've rediscovered it down here, where they seem to put it on just about everything, and I'll be bringing some seeds home with me, Marco Polo–style. Turns out there's no such thing as a curry plant, but there's cumin and cardamom and tumeric and coriander, all—I'm told!—easier to grow than most actual food crops. The "wallfruit" plant, engineered right here in the Gladholds, could also be a welcome Ganymedean immigrant. Wallich swears this stuff will never make it through quarantine, and I guess he would know, but I'm going to make the attempt just the same. Maybe some gourmet customs technician will plead my case, and you'll actually be able to taste these things yourself someday.

I love you, Momma, and hope your days are passing comfortably.

From "MOMLETR.0821.06.STRASHEIM.OUT"

We breakfasted at the staying home, visited the ship to organize our newfound stores, conducted the Great Shoe Transaction with glue and paring knives, lunched at a tavern near the dock, and read our mail while a dark, bleary-eyed hunchback cleared away the dishes.

The volume of response we'd gotten since our arrival here was larger than in the entire week preceeding it, so the task was as much a housekeeping function as it was business or entertainment. One had to keep one's working memory clear, after all, or move the excess onto slates, where it could easily get misplaced. Most of the mail was addressed to me, which seemed to suit the others well enough; we're too busy to muck around with these things, et cetera, et cetera . . .

I shared some of the better ones just the same. The Immunity had never seen much in the way of celebrity, but people must still have felt the need for it, deep down in the genes that code for tribal loyalties and such. I'd always done my best to bring heroes to the public attention, but with the exception of Response officers in the wake of a bloom, I'd never found much consensus on just who the heroes were. Doctors? Plumbers? Farm technicians? We'd all die without these people, but somehow their efforts never seemed to arouse much interest.

But now . . . Well, it had never really occurred to me that fame had more to do with *where* you were than with *who*. No one could deny the heroism of Tug Jinacio, who had died protecting the rest of us, but that very act of self-sacrifice had removed his image from my reports and from the public zeitgeist. The rest of us had done nothing brave or noble, had in fact fled from the perils back home, which our viewers by and large still faced, and yet increasingly I heard tones of admiration and even awe in those same viewers' voices. And of a strange familiarity as well, as if every message came from some old school friend whose face and name I couldn't quite place.

Talk was sometimes familiar on the news channels, as well, but that was different; through long association and endless—if sporadic—discussion, the contributors to a particular channel did indeed get to know one another. But the traffic on my channels had increased tenfold since the mission began, and that clubby atmosphere was starting to get lost in the noise. Still, I can't say the feeling wasn't gratifying, and it was in that spirit that I flashed a few of the letters around:

Dear John Strasheim and Louis Pasteur *crew: Hi. I just wanted to say, your reports are the highlight of our day. We flash them around at lunchtime, and talk about them after work, sometimes for as much as half an hour . . .*

Strasheim: Hallo! Kurt Fenton here. I'm a road builder. Keep those messages coming! It's fascinating to learn about the Gladhold, although I wish you were sending more pictures. I'm a visual person. I especially like the shots where other crew members are visible . . .

Dear Mr. Strasheim, can you please tell Captain Wallich not to scratch himself on camera? You should catch this in your editing process, as well. I mean, really, my daughter is six years old, and I would like her to be able to watch these reports and collages and learn from them, but she laughs very hard whenever Wallich starts scratching his bum, and I can't get her to pay attention . . .

This last provoked some merriment, no less from Wallich than from any of the rest of us. A good leader knows how to take a joke, at least when his tickle capacitor is working. There were, of course, some nasty letters as well, and our Venus revelation had begun to provoke a few tentative responses, mostly of the in-the-name-of-God-please-tell-me-you're-joking variety, but these I kept to myself. Plenty of time to brood on these matters when we were back on the ship.

Rapisardi, who had eaten lightly at both meals, looked about like you'd expect for a man who'd taken too much beer and too little sleep. He didn't seem too amused by the letters, either, and asked to be left alone when Wallich chided him about it. Davenroy, though, who insisted she *had* slept well, did not look much better. She'd been pushing her food around in the bowl, not really eating.

"Is your stomach okay?" Baucum asked, looking her over with a medical doctor's appraising air. She put a finger on the older woman's cheekbone, pulled down to peer beneath the eyelid. "You're looking sort of green."

Davenroy shrugged. "I can't eat like I used to, I guess. This food isn't sitting too well."

"You may lack some of the enzymes," Baucum said, now using both hands to palpate Davenroy's neck below the jawline. "It can happen with an unfamiliar diet. Water should help a little; can you drink another glass or two?"

Rapisardi opened his mouth as if to speak, then got a funny look on his face for a moment. And then, alarmingly, he sneezed. All eyes turned in his direction.

"Sorry!" he said, sounding rather surprised himself. And then he covered his nose and mouth and sneezed twice more.

"Damn," Baucum said, in a tone of wonder. She edged Tosca Lehne out of the way, coming around the table to peer more closely at Rapisardi, to touch his forehead and cheeks and neck. "You're hot. Is *your* stomach all right?"

"No, I don't think it is."

"Barely touched the food," Lehne observed. "He's got to be actually sick, don't you think?"

Baucum didn't answer, but everyone else got a nervous look. Especially Davenroy.

Rapisardi sneezed again, and then snuffled and coughed, as though he'd been breathing pepper. But he hadn't. *Actually sick.* The words chilled me; nobody ever got *actually sick* in the Immunity, except the elderly. No power seemed able to keep *them* healthy for long, but that was a matter of simple degeneration, not bodily invasion by . . . what, bacteria? Prions? Viruses?

"Could it be flu?" Wallich asked. The tickle capacitor must have been active, because his grin faltered only slightly. But his tone was one of mild outrage.

Baucum nodded. "It very well could." She looked Rapisardi in the eye, and then Davenroy. "The good news is, as long as we keep the fever controlled, that's unlikely to be fatal. Are you dizzy?"

Chris Dibrin picked that moment to return from the lavatory.

"We may have some sick people here," Baucum said to him.

"Huh," he said, not visibly alarmed. "Could be flu."

"We think it is," Baucum agreed, indicating Rapisardi and Davenroy with her gaze.

Dibrin studied the two for a moment, and then nodded. He'd been about to move in next to me at the table, but now he pulled away, headed toward the bar. "Return in a moment," he said. And indeed, the transaction he conducted with the bartender was casual and brief, and in half a minute he was settling in next to me.

He passed a small packet to Davenroy, and another to Rapisardi, and released several more in midair, letting them flutter slowly down to the tabletop. "Try these."

"What's in them?" Wallich asked, holding up a hand that instructed us not to touch the packets.

Now Dibrin looked surprised. "Antivirals, obviously. Base mode inhibitors, plus a mixed vaccine: nucleic acid and trigger proteins. I thought you were a doctor, sir."

Wallich sniggered. "Doctor? Not like that, I'm not. Do you mean to tell me that fancy-pants Immune system of yours doesn't even screen for human pathogens?"

Now Dibrin's face went into a kind of "Oh!" thing, and he nodded and started speaking even before Wallich had finished. "Okay, okay. We find it's cheaper to inoculate our bodies directly, and let them maintain their own health as per design. Where is the harm in taking a pill now and then? Jack of all trades means master of none; you build your phages too multipurpose and they just stop working."

"Funny," Wallich said, "we haven't found that to be the case. Intelligent design avoids the blind alleys that evolution can lead you into. It's a bit more work, that's all."

"I'm not going to listen to the 'lazy' speech again," Dibrin cautioned. "The Munie way is not always so brilliant, not always so desirable. Slow death, that's what you people are about. The Evacuation that never ended." Wallich opened his mouth to reply, but Dibrin cut him off. "Look, I'm not going to argue with you. I have other work today, plus some personal business to conduct, so just take the damned pills before you get someone else sick. And I have received word of your completed fuel delivery, so at this point you are free to leave. Shall we return to the docks?"

For a moment, there, the tension in the air was thick enough to climb, but then Rapisardi gave up a pair of sharp, sudden sneezes, and Wallich's answering laughter said that he was willing to let the whole thing go. So we took the pills, gathered up our few belongings, paid the bill, and left.

"So what is it you do for the governor's office?" I asked Dibrin once we were out in the hallway again.

"Do? Forecasting. Governor sees the future through me."

"Huh. Accurately?"

"Sometimes. Not, like, what are you thinking right now, or what are you going to do tomorrow, but what's the peak energy demand going to be this month, and when? Or economic stuff, or broad issues of public opinion."

"Is the governor an elected official, then?"

"Yes, of course. Not all Gladholds do it that way, but it's easier. People have a harder time complaining how things are run, when the decisions are partly theirs. You do the same thing, yes?"

"Well, sort of," I said. Every city had its mayor and small democratic council, after all, and the judiciary presiding over them. But the people like Vaclav Lottick, who formed the very heart of the Immunity, stood wholly outside that process, because really, who was there to replace them? You couldn't hold elections for "most brilliant scientist" or "manager who gets people to work hardest," and of course power tended to accumulate in the places that needed and exercised it daily. "Too overworked to abuse it" was the typical man-in-the-street analysis of the situation—the dangers of empowering Immune scientists paled against the dangers of hobbling them. Government by expedience: the perfect solution for a society too busy to be bothered.

"Anyway, yes," Dibrin said, "part of my job is to see that Governor keeps *his* job. He maintains a staff of twenty, and we all help out with this. Keep him in touch with what the people want; I'm sure you understand the principle."

"And that's always the best thing? What the people want?"

He shrugged. "No. But not usually too bad."

"Huh. I'm not recording any of this, by the way."

"But it's on the record," Dibrin said, not asking. "You'll tell people what I say, correct?"

"Of course." Why did everyone seem to have a problem with that lately?

He smiled faintly. "Oh well. If I had one message to deliver, it would be saying that excessive caution is a bad thing. Fear is a tool to guide us, not a prison. There is great potential in the human spirit, to grow and encompass new things. Not to subdue the universe, but to subvert it. To become it, to cause it to become us. You don't accomplish that by digging a hole."

"And if the universe winds up subverting *you*?" I asked.

Dibrin shrugged again. "Bad luck, I guess, but not worth giving up your dreams over."

Wallich seemed to find this funny.

"You're a good man," he said to Dibrin a little later, as they shook hands across *Louis Pasteur*'s open hatchway. "I hope things go well for you here."

"You people are not so bad either," Dibrin returned with that same faint smile. "This mission of yours, you know, it's more dangerous than a day in Saint Helier. You act so shocked by us, but really, it's quite a thing you have ahead. I wish . . . I wish you all the luck you'll require."

"Well, thanks. We'll say hi to the Venusians for you," Wallich said, and closed the hatch. Then he dogged the airlock shut, skittered up the ramp—awkward in the duck shoes that we hadn't quite managed to fully repair—and addressed the rest of us: "Let's get the living fuck out of this place, all right? We lift in three minutes or it's nutrient pap for dinner."

He laughed like maybe he didn't mean it, but we met the deadline just the same. You never know, right?

SMALL
DISCOVERIES

Departing from Saint Helier proved a lot easier than approaching it, which is good considering the condition of our engine room crew. The pills were working, though, and by the time we'd cleared the area and begun the long burn that would hurl us down toward Mars, Rapisardi and Davenroy were both looking and sounding much better.

Alas, our eighteen hours of freedom had served to make *Louis Pasteur*'s interior seem that much more monotonously cramped, and as my duties lessened I eased the claustrophobia by loading my vision up with every sort of window I could think of: net channels, starscapes, Conway's Game of Life . . .

The latter drew my attention rather well; a random starting pattern would usually grow and boil and squirm for a minute or two before settling into a permanent rut, patterns of little quivering blobs that didn't go anywhere, and little static ones that didn't do anything at all. Sometimes walking creatures were born from the ooze as well, simple, stable patterns that flip-flopped their way diagonally across the window, self-destructing into frothy blooms when they encountered obstacles in their path.

All this kept me occupied for several hours, my resource allocation functions interfering only occasionally. But eventually the novelty wore off, and I started feeling a sameness in all those random permutations, the same shapes and structures emerging over and over again, no matter what I started with. Too, I was having a hard time crafting blooms that would sustain themselves for longer than a minute or two; the things seemed determined to die.

Still, one of the other windows I'd had running was a slide show of Philusburg images, and as my interest in cellular automata waned, I paid more and more attention to this. It really was a very attractive city. And then when I'd seen those images enough times to get tired of *them*, I started fiddling.

Ideation, yes, I plead guilty; I started with a small window in an upper corner, but could not resist first expanding the images and then touching them up a little, and before I knew it I was building an interactive idealized environment. It wasn't hard to do, and with reality consisting of such a tiny and uninteresting space, it seemed no great crime to treat it as one more window in the zee. And a small one, at that!

So I wandered through a Philusburg of the mind, an empty cartoon cavern of a city, first changing the buildings that displeased me, and later erasing them entirely, laying down fields of green grass in their place. It's a compelling thing, this godlike ideative power; when my shift finally ended, some eight hours after we closed the locks, I'll confess I barely noticed the switch.

Baucum did, though; the knock on my cabin door startled me back to reality, and when I opened the latch, eased the fanfold back, and saw her standing there (standing, yes—we were under thrust again), I hastily closed all the windows and looked out at her through nothing but the clear plastic of my lenses.

"Are you all right?" she asked, looking me over.

"Fine," I said.

I must have looked guilty, though, or spoken too quickly; her lips spread suddenly into an amused, conspiratorial half smirk. "Been messing with the zee-spec, have you? Not messing with anything else, I expect; you've been a zombie ever since we took off. Am I intruding?"

"No, no," I assured her. "I was just running your Game of Life thingy. It's very interesting to watch. Uh, surprisingly complex."

If she noticed my discomfiture now, she gave no sign. Instead, she leaned forward interestedly, her hands on both sides of my door frame. "Yes, you played with it? I wasn't sure you would. What do you think?"

"Uh, very interesting," I tried.

She waved that comment away. "Be serious, please. Imagine that you're a doctor cataloging some sort of new phenomenon. Document it for me. Be specific."

I paused, wondering if she were somehow tricking me, making fun of me. But she seemed sincere enough, probably more so than I'd ever seen her. She seemed to have a point to make.

"Well," I said, "they usually die."

"Usually?"

"Well, always, actually. Sometimes I get little jiggly things, and sometimes I get *non*-jiggly things. Occasionally I get nothing at all, just a blank window with no live dots in it."

She waved an admonishing finger. "No, be *specific*, Strasheim. Be rigorous. Run a game for me, right here, and tell me what you see."

"Yes, ma'am," I sarcasmed. But I opened the Game of Life window back up again, seeded a random cell pattern, and let it go. Amoebic shapes formed, swelled, surged around for a few minutes before blobbing each other to death. In about a minute, all non-repetitive movement had ceased.

"It's finished," I told Baucum, then set to examining the amoebas' wreckage. "I see flashing things, little rows of three dots. First they're vertical, then horizontal; they just oscillate back and forth. I also see square blocks made of four dots, and little 'D' shapes made of, uh, seven. Neither of those are moving."

"Is that all?"

I nodded.

"So you have a mixed outcome, then," she coached, "partly crystallized and partly oscillatory. And you say you've seen some total extinctions."

I nodded again. "Yeah, it seems like it can go from a pretty complex form to nothing at all in a fairly short time."

"Just a few generations?"

"Sometimes, yes."

She looked pleased. "And what about degenerate cases? What happens if you start with an empty screen, or a completely full one?"

"The empty screen stays empty. The full one goes empty after only one generation." I had tried both of those early on, while I was still trying to get the feel of the game. "There's something else, though, something that keeps cropping up: these little diagonal walking shapes."

"Gliders," she said, nodding. "Sometimes you see them marching across your crystallized landscape, yes? Cutting a straight line between the obstacles, never hitting anything?"

"Yeah," I said. That outcome was actually pretty common.

"But they always return to their starting points, right? The edges of the window connect. The world is round. So *now*, you recognize an oscillatory structure that takes longer than two generations to cycle. You're ready to accept oscillation as a *class* of phenomenon, distinct from extinction and crystallization events."

I didn't much care for that schoolteacher tone, and I could see more or less where she was headed with this, so I jumped in and spoke: "Three classes of ending, right. But there's a messy fourth one you're not telling me about."

She paused, nodded. "Very good, berichter. Yes. We call these 'halt states.' But there are a lot more than four classes of these, so don't get too far ahead of me. Let's just concentrate on the three for right now."

She waved and pointed, manipulating zee-spec symbols. My RECEIVING light went on, and a new window icon appeared. I opened it, found a pointillist sprawl of geometric patterns, shapes and icons and letters of the alphabet. It took only a moment to understand what I was looking at: a Game of Life window in the crystalline state.

At first it seemed there was no limit to the possible forms, but a few seconds' study revealed that the ones larger than about ten dots were actually assemblages of smaller components. So there was a sort of pictographic alphabet, a limited menu of building blocks that fit together in limited ways. That made me feel less ignorant, less like I'd missed something obvious in my earlier explorations. Also, asymmetric forms seemed a lot less prone to crystallization—the building blocks themselves had a comforting regularity to them.

There were physical laws governing this Conway world, I understood suddenly. All these shapes and patterns were stable because they hung in perfect balance with the cellular automaton rules. But the rules were not so forgiving; drop a single dot in the wrong place, I knew, and all these delicate structures would flail and break apart and be consumed.

I tried it. Bang! Amoebas formed immediately, reaching out and falling back, reaching out and falling back, and finally extending their gooey arms to embrace the other shapes. Gliders exploded outward, spreading the infection rapidly to all corners of the window. Chains and butterflies and origami flowers all mashed in together, their delicate structures dissolving like a dream.

"Jesus," I said.

The squirming and frothing went on for quite a while, but finally the screen action slowed and settled into a new crystalline pattern, small cubes and ovals and only the occasional three-dot oscillator. Stability had returned, but the delicate order that had previously existed was quite gone. Entropy always wins in the end.

The next window Baucum sent me was a study in extinction. Again, graceful forms filled the screen, but this time there was something off-kilter about them, a lack of Conwayan symmetry on some deep level. I didn't have to tamper at all; the moment I started up the simulation, the little shapes twitched and thrashed and vanished, like candle flames extinguished in a breeze. The lesson here was not so obvious. Darkness conquers all? Rarely. Only if your world was constructed especially for that purpose. I grasped for relevance in this, and found none that satisfied me. The third window, though, was to change my view of the universe forever.

How to describe? Where to begin? Oscillatory structures, Baucum had said, could take longer than two generations to cycle. The truth of that statement had been irrefutable, but now I saw it was also a kind of warning, preparing my mind for the revelation that was to follow. My zee was filled, yes, with oscillatory structures.

The top row was simple enough: dancing collections of four and six and ten-plus dots, moving and shrinking and growing, looking like little protozoa. Or mycora. The next row down looked less organic: pinwheels and sparkers and little angular shapes passing single dots back and forth between them. Next came a complex structure that looked like a conveyor belt, and then a row of *really* complex pinwheels and kaleidoscopes. Below that were the clocks, the walkers, the sprinters, and something I can only describe as the Wet Sausage Parade. And finally, at the bottom, two big blobs of foam doing a little bump-and-grind routine that spat gliders out along the upper right diagonal. On the window's edge, a seven-dot crystalline form caught the gliders and destroyed them without a trace.

The view staggered me; much too much, much too fast. No amount of random fiddling would yield up any but the simplest of these forms, I realized. The Wet Sausage Parade was at least a hundred-dot sprawl, and the odds against such a thing falling together by sheer chance *had* to be long. One in a million, maybe a lot longer than that.

"Oh, my, God," I murmured. I looked and looked for a long time.

"There's another one," Baucum said almost apologetically.

Yes? Well, okay. I braced myself. "Hit me with it."

And she did. I opened the new window and . . . didn't say anything. If anything, this demonstration was less shocking, because I could tell at a glance what it did, what it was. It was a computer.

The basic structure of it was hollow boxes with lines running through and between them. A *lot* of hollow boxes. A *lot* of lines. Inside all this were patterns of bouncing dots, and it didn't take long to see that what happened in one box spilled over into the next, so that patterns shifted and shifted and shifted laterally, and then switched levels and started bumping the other way. And there were pathways connecting the top and bottom and the left and right sides, and things that were clearly input and output channels. The thing had a very mechanical look to it, like some giant, mutant, clockwork abacus, but even my layman's eye could *see* the calculations taking place. This thing was an actual computer, doing actual computation.

It could be doing anything, I realized. That was the beauty of computers: they could run anything, simulate anything. Even a human mind, or something very like one, as Chris Dibrin's "separated intelligences" demonstrated. And I'd been told that computers could emulate other computers as well, so flawlessly that there was no way a captive program could deduce whether it ran on a real computer, or a simulated computer, or a simulation of a simulation of a simulation . . .

So Conway's Game of Life was itself a kind of computer, capable, at least in principle, of simulating anything.

"It's a bit much to absorb," Baucum admitted.

I watched the window, fascinated. Watched the computer doing its thing.

"How does the capacity of this . . . device compare with a real computer?" I finally asked.

Baucum clucked at that, and I closed all the windows so I could see her face as she spoke. "In terms of speed, you've got it running about a hundred thousand times more slowly than your zee-spec is capable of. Clock speed is a variable parameter, though—play with it if you like. As for the number of actual bits, well, you can expand the game grid and build a machine of arbitrary complexity. The number of states will always be finite, though. Eventually, the pattern has *got* to repeat itself."

"So this is the ultimate example of oscillation?"

She pursed her lips, thought for a moment. "I don't know about 'ultimate.' But its complexity is significant, and yes, before you ask, the parallels with technogenic life are also quite impressive. A mycorum's onboard processor uses a different mechanical basis, called rod logic, but the fundamental operations being performed are not so different.

"At heart, three logic rods form a 'phrase' that no power failure can disrupt, since the bridge is mechanical in nature. This is one way, the mycoric way, to model a two-state, one-dimensional cellular automaton. But imagine more dimensions, more states than that. More rods. Imagine that every post of your choice is an entire genome attempting to copy itself to the surrounding matrix. The key problem in cellular automaton programming is mimicking that, getting the essence of the real action in live matter, or live cells. The idea is that every cell is more than a total of metabolism, it's a holographic piece of the gestalt, containing the seed of all the patterns that will later emerge. The underlying cellular automaton 'physics' has got to reflect this."

I smiled stupidly at her. "Now *you're* the one jumping ahead. Is there an English translation available?"

She ducked her head, blushing slightly. "I'm sorry. You seem a lot quicker than I'd been fearing, so now it's very tempting to just flash you full of whatever's on my mind. That's unfair, given that I've spent two decades constructing my opinion. Let me back up. Do you remember the glider gun?"

I thought of the spitting, bump-and-grind foamlets and nodded.

"All right, now imagine that that little glider catcher isn't there, and imagine that the edge of the game window is infinitely far away. What happens in the long run?"

It oscillates, I almost said, *spitting out gliders over and over.* But suddenly I could see what she was getting at: the diagonal line of gliders would just march out longer and longer, never terminating and never returning to the point of origin. "It goes on forever," I did say, pleased not to have fallen into the trap. "It keeps on growing."

"Correct," Baucum said, again sounding pleased. "Another class of halt state, one that's infinitely remote. We call that 'unconstrained laminar growth.' Laminar because you can predict the configuration at any future time without crunching through all the intermediate time points. But the glider gun is the simplest example of hundreds on record. There's also an unconstrained *turbulent* growth condition, in which future states can only be computed by a copy of the cellular automaton itself."

I nodded, picturing what that must look like: amoebic forms roiling and surging out to infinity, never stopping or dying or falling back in on themselves. "Okay. Where's my example of that?"

Baucum's look was cryptic and amused. "Why don't you see if you can come up with one yourself."

Her tone put me on guard. Again, I wondered if I were the butt of some obscure joke. Certainly, she wasn't telling me everything. "You still haven't gotten to the messy part."

Her eyebrows went up. "Oh? And what part is that?"

I hunted for words, composed my answer carefully: "Con-strained turbulent, uh, oscillation, I guess. A state where it doesn't expand or contract beyond a certain point, doesn't crystallize, doesn't extinguish itself, doesn't repeat."

"Like the Mycosystem," she said approvingly.

"Yes."

"The state exists, yes. Demonstrably."

"Have you got an example?"

She kept smiling that cryptic smile. "I'm afraid not. If you fiddle—"

"Conway's Game of Life isn't capable of achieving that state, is it?"

She shrugged. "There's no rigorous proof one way or the other. The permutations are infinite; maybe some small, needle-in-a-haystack fraction of them would settle into a chaotic attractor like that. There's certainly no theoretical barrier. Who knows, maybe you'll find one yourself."

"But probably not."

Her smile was vague now, burdened, as if the question reminded her of unhappy times. "No, probably not."

"But the real world and the Game of Life are not the same thing," I said, pressing some imagined advantage. "The cellular automaton is like a spreadsheet, right? The same equation over and over again in every box? So what would happen if I played around with the equation?"

Baucum brightened, the approval seeping back into her face like it had been there all along. "A modified rule-set for the express purpose of modeling the Mycosystem? That's a very interesting idea, John. Do that, yeah. Let me know what you come up with."

She touched my arm then, leaned closer, shared her smile with me for a moment. And then she pulled back, danced away, and was gone before I could say a word.

What I would have said to her I'm not sure. She'd played me well, let me feel informed and clever while she led me once more into doing her bidding. Or was that unfair? Was she maybe genuinely interested in my opinion? Either way, her motive seemed, actually, to matter to me. What lesson she was trying to teach me I couldn't guess, but I wished she'd be less cryptic and circuitous, wished she'd just come out and say what was on her mind.

Then again, the project did sound sort of interesting, and we'd be another eight months on this ship, and I wasn't exactly hurting for time. I closed my cabin door, turned my lights out, and thought it over for the couple of minutes it took me to fall into exhausted slumber.

Organizing the mail that morning had been a bit of a problem, yes, and the resource allocation circuitry was the last stop between *Louis Pasteur*'s data and communications systems, so once he'd explained the data rate problem to me and sorted things out with the appropriate Immunity officials, Wallich "suggested" I tear down my console again, to "confirm that the laws of physics are being obeyed in there, ha ha."

Sarcasm aside, this would be my eighth such tear-down since the mission began. It was getting to be kind of routine, just another part of the job, and not especially difficult or taxing. I took the screws out, pulled the cover off, checked all the boards and wiring . . . And found another of those little yellow spiders, right where the first one had been. Another bug, here in *my* circuitry! With proprietary outrage, I teased and yanked the object free. Behind it lay a larger mass, pink and soft and wrinkled—one of the Gladholder fear dolls. I pulled that out as well.

"Captain," I said, holding the items up for inspection. The doll groaned.

At the noise Wallich turned, saw. Didn't like. "Well," he said.

Lehne, who was still on shift for another hour or two, looked over at us tiredly, as if the bug came as no surprise to him at all. He grunted. "Ship record any unauthorized entry?"

Wallich shook his head.

"That Dibrin guy, maybe?"

I shook my head. "He never came aboard. Even if he had, it's not like he could slip this thing in with all of us hanging around. It had to happen while we were out. Must have."

"I repeat," Wallich said, "there were no unauthorized entries into the ship. If somebody came in here, the airlock doors would have a record of opening and closing; they don't. The Immune system would have a contact record, with pheromone, microfauna, and skin protein assays; it doesn't. I *suppose* those records could be erased with enough effort, but it seems very unlikely. Who's going to walk in here and know that much about our systems?"

And then his face changed when the answer occurred to him: a member of the crew. He didn't need to say it. Tosca Lehne and I exchanged looks. Was it you, freund? I looked away quickly, ashamed of myself.

"This is crazy," I told Wallich. He knew what I meant: none of us would plant a bug, spy or injure or betray our fellows. But did I really know that? There was still no telling just what the bug was for, who was stealing data from us and why. Gladholders? We barely existed for them. The Temples? They were far above us, in the cold and dark of the Immunity. Track our every movement, and what good would it do them? Not to mention the data rate problem; how small would their signals have to be now, to hide effectively in our homebound datastream? Very, I would bet.

"Crazy," Wallich agreed, making innocent faces and shaking his head. "Dibrin did have an easy time tampering with the zee-specs, didn't he? Maybe it *was* Gladholders."

"I'm afraid," the fear doll said from between my fingers.

The corners of Wallich's mouth twitched at that, but in the end it seemed he couldn't quite bring himself to laugh.

Descent

Viewers: I have to ask you to please stop sending us video mail. I received a physics lesson this morning, after complaining about sluggish communications, and I'd like to pass it along to you so you'll see our situation more clearly. The growing light-lag between ourselves and the Immunity is a problem in and of itself, severely limiting our telepresence capabilities. It's hard to be in two places at once when there's an hour's round-trip signal time between them! Wallich seems the most affected by this, the most inconvenienced. Also the most upset, especially since the Immu-

nity seems to be grinding on without him. One does like to feel indispensable.

But the larger problem at this point is something called data rate. Louis Pasteur's *antennas, and to a lesser extent the Immunity's own transmitters, have limited broadcast power, and the receivable portion of that power drops off very quickly with distance. But it still takes a certain amount of energy to register a data bit at the receiving end, the upshot of which is that the farther away we get, the fewer bits we can flash in and out per second. Viewer response is greatly appreciated—your letters are a much more important part of our day than these reports probably are in yours—but since our stop at Saint Helier the volume of mail has gone orbital, even as our data rates are shrinking. The resulting data jams can interfere with higher priority traffic, which of course is potentially hazardous.*

From this point forward, freunde, those letters need to be sent voice-only, or better yet, as plaintext. Video mail will be screened and discarded at the transmitting end, so if you do send it, it's going straight to data heaven. But plaintext is a lost art that could use a little revival anyway. Try it out. We look forward to hearing from you in this exciting and much less costly format.

From "Data Rate and the Fear of Lost Mail,"
(PD) 2106 by John Strasheim

Again, we scoured the ship for signs of tampering, and again we came up empty. I couldn't help eyeing my crewmates when they weren't looking, and studying saved images of them, hunting for signs of suspicious activity. Might there really be a saboteur among us? Not Rapisardi, certainly; he'd designed the TGL detectors that were the mission's whole point. If he'd wanted to cause trouble, he'd have done it much farther upstream, preventing all this from ever happening in the first place. Ditto Wallich—surely he, with Vaclav Lottick's ear, could have disrupted the mission long before it began. And of course, I knew it wasn't me.

That left three, and of these, Baucum was by far the most promising candidate. Yes, Lehne had his resentments at being conscripted for this duty, and Davenroy, with far more flight experience than any of the rest of us—more *life* experience, for that matter—had both the knowledge and the guile to pull something like this off. But Baucum had her mystery, her iconoclasm, her quiet insistence that the status quo viewpoint was, at best, slightly damaged. Dedication and idealism could be dangerous things.

I couldn't hide my concerns, though. I couldn't keep from watching her too often, too closely, much too obviously. Three days after I found the bug, she finally took me aside, nudged me into the Jinacio Ballroom and said, "I'm satisfied that you weren't planted here as a spy."

"Eh?" I replied intelligently.

She patted my cheek. "You are *so bad* at trying to look like you're not watching people. So please, watch. Record. Tell me what you'd like to know."

I stammered for half a moment, and then went ahead and blurted it out: "Did you plant that bug in my console?"

Hurt and surprise suddenly mingled with her amusement. "Ouch, John, that's direct. Plant the bug? No, I didn't, and if I *had*, I guarantee you would never have noticed it. Give me some credit, please; I'm certified for beam epitaxy and several other nanofab techniques. I could build something the size of a human cell. If I needed to, I could wire a whole shadow network into the ship, wires so small even the Immune system wouldn't detect them."

Her eyes glittered, partly mischievous and partly angry. "Maybe I *have* done it. You never know. But I did not plant that enormous thing inside the allocation circuitry."

"So who did?" I asked. And yes, you bet I was recording.

Baucum shrugged. "We have enemies, Strasheim, you know as well as I. Maybe they have friends in Saint Helier, and they just walked in while we were shopping or sleeping or hanging around at that damned telescope. Maybe the bugs are autonomous, or self-assembled from a dozen motile fragments. The human beings on Venus are a clue, mein freund, that something fantastically strange is going on. Will you blame *them* on me, as well? Things find their way into funny places; that's about all we can say at this point."

"Not a very satisfying answer," I said.

"No," she agreed, and the conversation was over.

Well.

I did another five hours on duty, solemnly watching over the bridge with Tosca Lehne, keeping an eye not only on my own instruments but on Wallich's. This is not to say I was in charge in any way, just that Lehne was capable of running Baucum's board where I myself was not, and down here below the Gladholds the bioanalysis functions took a much higher priority than crap like traffic control. All I had to do was watch for red lights, listen for alarms, and do a periodic diagnostic sweep to make sure all systems were responding. It was a running joke, in fact, that down here *anyone* could be captain, even a humble cobbler, but Wallich still couldn't make a shoe. Ha ha, yeah, our lives were pretty exciting.

When the shift was over, I got some music going, then called up my cellular automaton project and got back to work on it. Damn Baucum anyway; it was slow and exasperating work, every little twitch and tweak taking an hour or more to test out. But the fascination of it was undeniable. I had to set an alarm to remind me to sleep, or I knew from experience that I'd blow right past it and fiddle deep into the night. It was like that; the hours melted away barely noticed. I could fill a voyage with this work, easily. And my daily outgoing news allocation had dropped to only twenty thousand bytes, barely enough for a snide editorial, so a new hobby was definitely a good thing to have.

Conway's Game of Life had only two possible states for each cell: alive or dead. Right off, Strasheim's Game of Life was designed to allow *four* states: brown for "rock," red for "bloom," blue-white for "air," and a lush green for nonmycoric biomass, aka "mulch." Cynical, I know, but I needed a short, descriptive name, and that one seemed to resonate for me somehow. What else were we, from a brainless mycoric point of view, but piles of moldering but otherwise useful chemicals?

So I started out with a world stratified into wide bands, air over mulch over rock, and then I'd drop a mycorum in and watch it reproduce. The problem was, its offspring would spread out for a while, and then simply eat all the mulch, then eat all the rock, then starve to death, and meanwhile the mulch and rock would be flying apart, scattering weightlessly up into the atmosphere. In the end, there'd be a few mycora chasing the last crumbs of matter around in a world of empty air, and then finally nothing at all.

The problem, of course, lay in the cellular automaton rules, the physical laws governing the behavior of each cell as a function of the behavior of its neighbors. I'd modeled these after Conway's own rules, but these were intended for a much simpler world, and didn't work in mine. Not the way I wanted them to, anyway, so that was where I'd been concentrating my efforts.

First, I'd fixed it so dead mycora became "mulch" rather than inedible "air." This meant the living could feed on the dead, which introduced a crude ecological cycle to Strasheim Land. Didn't stop it from eventually flying apart and dying, but at least it kissed my visual cortex more sincerely before doing so.

Next, I'd added a possible "vacuum" state—black—for the cells to manifest, and then a binding force intended to imitate gravity, which had the surprising effect of pulling my rock floor around into a sphere, surrounded by layers of mulch and air. A planet! I had made a planet! At that point, I'd been struck by just how useful a tool this might prove to be. Baucum's manipulations seemed less venal and self-serving, more like a real favor from one friend to another. "Look, look what you can do!"

But the mycora still behaved poorly, and fixing this would— hopefully!—be the focus of tonight's work. The thing was, they would simply consume the *entire planet*, and then die off in great vertical waves, leaving behind a lifeless Mulch World, draped with a thin and no doubt reeking envelope of air. This was bad, a crystallization entirely unlike the chaotic pulsing of the actual Mycosystem, but short of switching off the gravity, nothing I'd tried seemed able to prevent it from happening.

Tonight, alas, did not appear to be an exception. I was stuck. I wasn't going to ask Baucum for assistance at this point, either, but it occurred to me that Rapisardi might be able to help as well, so after a while I bit my pride, activated one of the camera dots in my cabin wall, and flashed him a realtime streaming window keyed to it.

"Yes? Strasheim?" came his disembodied voice over the soft music. A few moments later, a window appeared, showing me his face and some bits and pieces of engine room.

"Hi," I began a bit uncertainly. "I'm working on a . . . project that may feed into my final mission report, and I think I could use some advice. Nothing I'm going to flash home about tomorrow, you understand. It's just a sort of diversion. A demonstration, actually."

He licked his lip and nodded. "The cellular automaton project, yes."

"You know about it?"

He managed to look both sheepish and admonitory. "It's a small ship, Strasheim."

"Ah. Right. Well, anyway, I seem to be having a problem simulating the mycora. They just don't seem to want to *do* very much, besides eat and die. I can't find a rule-set that lets them, you know, *bloom*, without letting the rocks and everything bloom right along with them."

"Yes." He looked thoughtful. "I can see that. It makes a certain amount of sense, doesn't it. But who's to say you should have only one set of rules? Living things, even technogenic ones, behave quite differently from inanimate matter. A rock is just a rock; drop it and it falls. With a living thing, that is not necessarily so. Not *reliably* so."

"A different physics for life than for nonlife?" I asked, somehow vaguely offended by the idea. I must have made a face, too, because he laughed.

"Think of it as a genome, not a physics. Living things carry their behavior with them in genetic codes. My genes tell me what to eat, what to mate with. Possibly they also tell me to avoid places that are too crowded or too empty, you see? I don't violate the laws of physics, but neither do I fall down like a rock. And neither do I behave as you do, or as Darren Wallich does, and my offspring, when I have them, will carry *my* genome, not yours or his."

Right, okay. That kicked off a whole series of ideas I was eager to try, so I thanked Rapisardi and disconnected.

A genome, yes. A mutable, copyable behavioral standard, the mycoric equivalent of a blueprint and an ethical code and a sense and record of identity. And of course there were *spores*, which carried the genome but did not actually execute it . . .

When my go-to-sleep alarm sounded an hour later, I switched it off and kept right on working.

The fresh fruit started going bad the next day, and we gorged on it, as if determined to be sick of it by the time it left us for good. The last of our video mail trickled in as well, and the messages were viewed by one and all, over and over again. We needed to be sick of that as well, because there wouldn't be anymore of it until we climbed back up into the asteroid belt again.

Our text and audio mail, though, had continued to grow. Far from being severed, our connection to the home worlds seemed to grow stronger every day. And more trivial, too; for every informative article or well-considered question, there were a dozen silly, faux-personal notes cluttering up the stream. It's amazing how quickly that stops being cute and starts being a waste of your time. The problem would only get worse, so I initiated a screening protocol that would weed out the obvious dribble and send form-letter replies automatically, without our having to so much as look. But the remaining mail and news volume were still formidable, and most of it required at least cursory examination.

This was not the greatest obstacle to our "interactive" model of communication, though; data rate was. Our outgoing ration had been cut yet again, and would continue to shrink with ridiculous speed over the next few days until it bottomed out at only seven hundred bytes per day. Of which my ration would be a mere twenty-nine.

"Popular myth to the contrary," Rapisardi explained gently

when I complained about this, "mycora do not feed on ambient heat. Heat simply means the random vibration of atoms, and harnessing this is called 'entropy reversal,' which is actually a physical impossibility. Now, forming a chemical bond does release energy, which the mycora can store for later use, for example in breaking a bond elsewhere. The distinction between chemical and mechanical processes blurs to almost nil at the nanoscale, so that energy may be transferred efficiently, as if through fine springs and pulleys. And Brownian motion does facilitate this process, as it facilitates all chemistry. But the thermodynamic loss is still significant. There is, as I'm sure you have heard, no free lunch.

"So what is lunch? What do the mycora eat? Once, it was organic matter, just as you and I eat organic matter. Now, very often, it is a combination of *in*organic matter and light, and this is where much of our problem originates. Many mycora, not most but a good fraction of them, contain a photon-absorbing molecule called melanophyll which is sensitive to long-wavelength radiation such as infrared or, in some cases, microwaves.

"Unfortunately, our high-gain communications to the Immunity are in that very form, and as we descend ever further into the Mycosystem, this becomes dangerous. We want *not* to feed the mycora, or arouse them in any way, so we must emit radiation of much longer wavelength, meaning radio, and at a much lower power, meaning about twenty watts as opposed to several hundred, and of course, as always, at an ever longer range. All of which reduce our data rate. I maintain that we shouldn't be transmitting anything at all, but I am overridden in this. The risks are impossible to estimate, at least for now. So be thankful for your ration, mein freund; if I have my way, it might yet shrink to zero."

Well. I'm sure you'll understand, there's a certain frustration in hiring on as a mission correspondent and then not being allowed to correspond. I was by no means the only victim, though; if anything, Wallich was the hardest hit. More than I, more than anyone, he'd made a habit of being in both places at once, but in the Immunity the increasing time lag had made an observer of him, and the loss of visual data had reduced him to mere nagging, and now, finally, even that was evaporating. But he gathered what news he could, requested small blocks of data when he could, and otherwise busied himself on the zee, cautiously tuning and updating the specifications of our onboard Immune system, providing maximum advantage against the latest human-modified strains.

"Plus," he noted, "I've found traces of the Gladholder Immune system lingering here and there, so I'm going to see if I can wipe 'em out." Hey, everyone needs a hobby.

My own little world was coming along beautifully, thanks to Rapisardi's suggestions. Let There Be Light, and there was. Let There Be Genome and Temperature and Buoyancy, and there were. Let the Spores of Mycora be Immune to Gravity, and they were. This last was difficult to justify, since spores were little masses every bit as subject to the laws of physics as anything else, but I knew little of the processes that actually did lift them off planetary surfaces. "Convection" and "solar wind" were the appropriate buzzwords, but just how those would translate into cellular automaton rules I had no idea.

Anyway, the real action was in genomes. I had them up to twenty genes, now, little data bytes specifying whether a mycorum would photosynthesize, whether it could eat rock, whether it could survive in a vacuum, and more esoteric things like its programmed lifespan and its preferred number of mycoric neighbors. The results, so far, were remarkably satisfying.

Hanging out in the wardroom that afternoon, I put some finishing touches on the model, dropped a spore in, and watched the fireworks. The spore, a dark blue dot, fell down through blackness until encountering the upper atmosphere of Mulch World, whereupon it woke up and converted itself to a *red* dot, which settled—much more slowly—to the planet's surface. Instantly, green mulch flared red where the mycorum touched it, and spores began to boil out of the wound, some of them firing straight out into space, others skittering through the atmosphere, then germinating and settling back down again to form new infection sites.

The blooms spread, flickered, twitched. Where they reached down to bare rock, they stopped, finding the barrier at first impenetrable, but the daytime surface of Mulch World was reddening, the patches of green growing smaller and smaller in agonized spasms. Technically, mulch could reproduce, could bathe in sunlight and slowly convert rock into biomass, but its growth rate was so vastly smaller than the mycora's that I might as well never have built in the capability at all.

Gradually, the nightside began to succumb as well, sparing only the polar caps. Structure began to form on the surface—towers and fountains and fields of flowery fruiting bodies. The planet's crust grew thinner, redder, and then suddenly it was gone. The last bits of nonpolar rock vanished, the mycora a thick, living layer in place of a crust, lower surface sizzling and dying against the yellow molten interior itself, which solidified into new rock, which was eaten again, leaving the mycora to be killed again . . .

And the growth and flowering of my pocket Mycosystem ground to a halt, its underside locking forever into this trivial oscillation while the upper strata slowly froze, became static. The polar caps remained pristine, little yarmulkes of white against the red and yellow of the converted planet.

Crap. Still no dynamic endurance, still no sign of the bloom-without-end that was the real Mycosystem. Crap, crap. I threw away the sim log, archived the rule base, and closed the whole thing up, suddenly weary of it. I called up my Philusburg sim instead, and got to work clearing away still more of the buildings. Grass! I wanted lots and lots of green grass!

I hadn't gotten very far, though, when an alarm klaxon split through me like the end of the world: WONNNNK! WONNNNK! So loud I didn't recognize it, so sudden that at first I didn't know what had happened, just jerked to alertness, cursing elaborately. I wiped my windows, going fully transparent for the first time in days.

The lights had gone red.

Fear shot through me, momentarily paralyzing, and then I was fumbling at the latch, popping the cabin door open, hurling myself out into the wardroom. After a while, you get to know where the handholds are. I grabbed one, swinging my path around toward the bridge, and let go. Grabbed another one as I passed through the hatchway, to keep me from flying right into the back of Darren Wallich's chair.

"What's happening?" I was saying. "What's happening, what's happening?"

Every imaginable spacecraft emergency was flashing through my mind: Decompression. Fire. Bloom. Life-support failure. This last, for some reason, struck a particular note of fear. Was the air too thin? Did I detect a hint of odor that shouldn't be there?

Baucum, who was on station, turned toward me, the look on her face not particularly comforting. Not panicked either, though, and I took at least a small measure of courage from this.

"What's up?" Tosca Lehne asked from the hatchway behind me.

Baucum grimaced. "I've got a confirmed live contact on the hull. No evidence of replication yet."

Live contact. Confirmed. Not a spore, but a solitary live

mycorum. Ergo, says the brilliant reporter's mind, we have entered the Mycosystem. No evidence of replication, ergo the t-balance is working, the hull not dissolving into foam or powder or whatever the hell it would dissolve into if mycora were eating it. Into mycora, yes. Baucum not losing her composure, so for now the prognosis is good. This is, after all, expected. And yet, the alarm had sounded . . .

"Take your seats, gentlemen," Wallich said curtly, not bothering to face us. We complied. "Still just the one contact, Baucum?"

"Negative, I have a second. Make that three. Spores, this time."

"Acknowledged. Rapisardi, any sign of contamination in the engine nozzles?"

From the zee: "Nothing yet, Captain."

And Jenna Davenroy's voice: "I'm closing the covers, sir."

Sir, Captain. Yes. Easy to forget that, easy to let discipline grow lax, the work environment informal. But this was serious business, wasn't it? Deadly serious, a thin metal hull holding in our atmosphere, holding out the radiation and vacuum of space, and the pathogens. There were a million ways to go wrong, and only a handful of ways not to.

Okay, these are not exactly profound revelations, I admit it. But the obvious does not always hit us on a gut level until that scharfblick moment when we look around and really *realize* our circumstances. As in, allow them to become real for us. I'd done a good job of burying that line of thought, of conveniently forgetting that the Mycosystem was more than a sim geeked up on the zee.

"Seven confirmed contacts," Baucum said. "Eight."

Wallich grunted, acknowledging. Then, in a kind of slow, thoughtful tone: "Immune system to stage two alert, please. Skin capacitors and heat pipes on standby."

"Aye, sir," said Lehne.

"Finding any problems with the t-balance?"

"Negative."

"Still at eight contacts, sir. I think we passed through a cloud of them."

"Right," Wallich said. "Well, we could be at the top of an up-welling zone. Let me know if you register anything else. That goes double for you, Rapisardi. Strasheim?"

It took me a moment to recognize my own name, another moment to fall into the smooth, military precision I saw happening around me. "Yes, sir?"

"Shut down the communication system, please. Power allocation to zero. Transfer it all to Lehne."

"Yes, sir," I said, and set about complying.

"That's 'Aye, sir,' " he corrected.

"Aye, sir."

"Lehne? Drop skin temperature ten degrees on the sunward side. I'd like you to heat the hull to four hundred kelvins in fifteen seconds, and not just where the contacts are registered. *Full* discharge, everywhere, and I don't want skin conductance affected. Clear?"

"Aye," Lehne said, working invisible controls. "Heat pipes engaged. Capacitor safety off. Hull temperature dropping."

"Clear and pull."

Lehne nodded. "Clear. Pull. Capacitors discharged."

The steady red glow of the cabin lights flickered for a moment, and then returned as steady as ever.

"Zero contacts on the hull, sir," Baucum reported.

I wasn't the only one breathing a sigh of relief.

"Excellent. Lehne, how necessary was that?"

A pause, then the breathy harrumphing of Lehne's voice. "Not necessary, sir. Nominal function on t-balance. You don't . . . want to mess with the skin conditions unless necessary."

"Right. Well, at least we've got the drill down in case we need it. Well done, people." He sounded brisk, perfunctory, as if he didn't mind if we weren't listening. Speaking more to himself than to us. Trying to reassure himself. The final responsibility was, after all, his own.

From the zee, Rapisardi's voice: "Captain, I read a contact event on engine cover one."

"Contact event on the hull," Baucum added. "Two contacts. Three."

Wallich paused and harrumphed, himself, before asking, "Lehne, your recommendation?"

"Do nothing."

"Baucum, Rapisardi? Any objection?"

"No."

"None, sir."

Neither voice sounded enthusiastic.

"Davenroy," Wallich said, "I want you ready to open those covers and throttle up on about a millisecond's notice. Is that clear?"

"My finger is resting on the button," Davenroy's voice replied.

I turned, saw Wallich nodding to me. He looked resigned. "Right. Well, we're in it now, aren't we?"

In it. Yes. It seemed a totally new idea, unthinkable: the Mycosystem no longer below us somewhere, but all around, a deep spherical layer wrapped around the sun, as real and affecting as ocean or atmosphere. My mind, grappling with the concept, reduced it to cartoon: a translucent Mycosphere, enormous, its upper boundary rippling with our penetration, its lower one far below, the haze of it obscuring the yellow smiley face of Sol at the center. And ourselves? A single pixel plunging down through the ripples. Green, for mulch.

"You might want to look outside," Baucum said. "Three o'clock high, twenty degrees. We have a visitor."

Oh. Reluctantly, I turned and opened a round exterior window, anchoring it to the bulkhead beside me. Where Baucum was pointing, there hung a . . . smudge? Cloud? No, of course, it was a *transient megastructure*, a diffuse bloom of loosely interacting mycora, massing maybe twenty or a hundred kilograms smeared across thousands of cubic kilometers of space. The inner system was full of these. Probes launched down into the Mycosystem *became* these, blooming and spreading and exploding into molecule-thin lattices of technogenic life, less dense than smoke and yet structurally rigid enough to hold their fantastic shapes as the solar wind tumbled them upward.

For a while, anyway—nothing lasted long in the Mycosystem. Soon, in hours or days or possibly weeks, that smudge would break apart into countless quadrillions of individual mycora, or collapse into a handful of fruiting bodies and then swell to bursting with spores.

"Well, looky there," Wallich said. "Range?"

"Too far to triangulate optically," Baucum said. "You want an active ping?"

Wallich laughed at that. "No, certainly not."

The shape grew. I had to realign my thinking; I'd assumed we were heading in the same direction we were pointing, but of course we weren't under power anymore, and our orientation probably had more to do with antenna alignment than anything else.

My breath caught. I was suddenly, keenly aware of the smallness of the bridge, of the ship itself. The thinness of the hull, and the hugeness of the thing before us. And still the shape was growing, approaching, threatening to engulf. Not like the clouds of Earth, or of Jupiter, or of the cavern skies of Ganymede. Not amorphous, not fluid, but iceberg-jagged and yet somehow springy-looking, soft and resilient as a sponge, and yet so diffuse it was barely there at all. A smearing of the starscape, a haze of scattered sunlight, yellow-white against the blackness. There was detail to the haze, though—direct gaze made it seem lumpy, marbled, while the corners of the eye saw it as spirals and lattices, shot through with glints of rainbow color.

Still growing, now almost the size of my outstretched hand, but then suddenly it was shrinking again, moving down and to the right. We were passing it. Passing it by a wide berth, by hundreds of kilometers. Not even *close* to it, and yet dwarfed.

"I want a watch officer on duty at all times," Wallich said softly. "With active course schematic and the bulkheads on transparent. If anything . . . visible . . . falls anywhere near our path, I'm to be informed immediately."

"Fly right through," said Tosca Lehne. "T-balance really does work. You'd never even feel it."

"Yeah?" Wallich grinned. "Bet your life on it?"

Well, naturally nobody took him up on that.

THE TGL GARDEN

Entrd Mycstm. Lvly scnry. Wish U wr here!

Hello? This is your mother. I just found out your big trip is to Earth. Shame on you, not telling a thing like that! I had to hear it from another patient. Your letters . . . Well, I can't make much sense of them, but I'm certain the word "Earth" was never mentioned. They say the thought is what counts. Thinking is important. True terrible. Say hello to the Earth for me, all right? And hurry back. Get that thing away from me. Yes, I'm finished now.

Momma, Hi! Will wave @ Earth 4U luv John!

GNRL NOTICE ATTN CHRIS DIBRIN ST HELIER GOV OFFICE: Occurs to me our data rate to St Helier about 9X data rate to Jupiter. Can set up a relay? Compressed data stream, not encrypted, public channel OK. You owe no favors, but we need an ally. What say?

Attention John Strasheim, Immune Ship Louis Pasteur *Communications Officer: I've brought your request up with Governor and received grudging permission to comply. Monies are owed already, he remonstrates. Very glad to hear you survived Mycosystem entry. I admit I had my doubts! Further communications to me may be indexed &CHDBSH8091 for faster routing. Relay queue messages should be indexed &W=G&XXXXSH8094. Further requests are likely to be denied, but I and my devil microscopic helpers will do what we can. Wishing you best fortune down there.*

&CHDBSH8091 Thanks.

&W=G&XXXXSH8094 Hallo Immunity via Gladhold! Treacherous spaces above and below, many spores, but we survive, a bubble of Immunity in the warm and bright. Mycosystem is a visible thing—enclosed please find "stroke vector" sketch of transient megastructure. More and more of these, and the sun so close! Next stop Mars, about which more later.

"I think I'm ready to learn about t-balance," I said to Tosca Lehne as we sat alone together on the invisible bridge. Bloom watch: walls blanked on the zee, replaced with starscape. A black disc eclipsing the body of Sol, leaving the corona shining around it, brighter than the entire sun as seen from Jupiter. Unreal. Nothing was real but our own two selves, bent weightlessly into invisible chairs, the pressure of strap and cushion the only sign of *Louis Pasteur* holding out the infinite emptiness. For me, anyway—Lehne himself was on instrument duty, with probably no outside view at all.

"Yeah?" Lehne yeahed, looking askance at me. "Sudden interest?"

I shook my head. "Not sudden, no. Convenient. I've needed to know, and here we both are with time on our hands. Since I have to squeeze our entire experience down to single paragraphs, I want to be sure I'm even more aware of the details than before. It's . . . important to know the totality whose essence I'm trying to capture, you see?"

"T-balance is a detail?"

"You know what I mean."

He pursed his lips reproachfully. "Not a detail, Strasheim. This mission wasn't *conceived* until Wallich read my second paper. I am the inventor of my own prison."

"Shiptime:" I quoted, "jail, with the possibility of suffocation."

"Right," Lehne said, unsmiling.

"You're not happy about being here."

"No. You may think you volunteered, but I don't think I did. No one else available. Indispensability as the chief condition of our lives. Busy, always busy, and no one there to pick up the slack. That's life, eh? That's life in the Immunity."

"You don't enjoy your work, then?"

"No, I do."

"But you wish you had more help? Some assistants? I'm not clear on what you're trying to say."

Lehne shrugged, looking resigned to his tension. "Wishing the fate of the future didn't rest so heavily on every set of shoulders. Clearer? Lottick asked me to go on the mission, and I told him I would. But he wasn't telling all he knew, and that frightened me. Still does, and now there's spy bugs in the allocation console, and traces of Gladholder Immune system lingering in the air and food that Wallich can't seem to get rid of."

Having no response to that, I switched topics and prompted: "You were going to tell me about t-balance."

He turned, faced me fully. The corona's glare reflected from his zee-spec lenses, pink and yellow navigation lines crisscrossing the starscape behind him. A frail, angry human, soaring alone through empty space.

"Heavy metals," he said, "forced into organic-like nanostructure. Electrophoresis, epitaxy, shock cooling so the atoms never get a chance to displace. Very difficult to manufacture, but it looks like TGL to the TGL, even though really it's heavy metals. *Knowing* it was toxic, they'd dismantle, form cysts around the fragments, use them for nucleation anchors. A platform to grow from, permanent because unusable for any other purpose. But they don't know. Don't have the means to figure it out. Electron holes here and here and here, they see, and they know it must be a piece of mature my-costructure, *neue erbauen verboten,* so they stay away. Mycosystem has Immune responses of its own, but you can trick it at its roots, tell it you *are* an Immune response."

"A sort of Trojan horse approach, then?"

"More than that," he said. "A horse made of eighty trillion Trojan soldiers, sticking their arms out and saying, 'Hi, I'm Trojan like you. Everything is fine, but for God's sake back off before you screw something up.'"

"Huh. And the Trojans buy this?"

Lehne shrugged. "So far. Maybe not forever. Geek a sim, it only tells so much. Trojans get angry, though, they'll be choking on actinides, dying and dying until they finally break through. Meanwhile we fight back—chemicals, vacuum phages, heat pipes . . . Makes them angrier, of course. Hope for a shadow to hide in, out of the sunlight. Cool off, freeze them out. If not, hope they *can* live without you up in the Immunity, because they'll have to."

I grimaced. "Ah, yes. The ever-present risk of death."

"Always."

"Did you ever guess you'd be in this situation?"

"This?" For once, Lehne cracked a smile. "Your basic Balkan farmboy doesn't expect to leave home. Having left, for *Jupiter* no less, he doesn't expect to return. No, the Balkan farmboy lives in perpetual amazement at his surroundings, at his fate. How did *this* happen? I have a son, did I tell you that?"

"No," I said, interested.

He nodded, starlight and cartoon lines trailing through his hair. "Two years old next month. His mom runs the skylights at Ansharton. I miss both."

"I should think so!"

"I'll sit my son down someday, tell him: don't get too comfortable, boy. Don't get too sure. One day you'll wake up surprised, and never the same after that."

"Damn," I said, looking down suddenly.

"What? Trans-meg incoming?"

"Two," I said, watching them grow, measuring them against the navigation marks. MARS, a fat red arrow said, pointing out a faint red dot. The trans-megs, already thumb-sized, seemed to fire directly at us from a point just ahead of the planet in its dotted-line orbit. But as I watched and measured, I saw that they would miss us, that both structures would sail by hundreds of kilometers beneath my unsupported feet.

"Accurate?" Lehne asked mildly.

"Nah, they'll miss. But they give me the willies just the same."

"Imagine that."

"Lehne doesn't seem too happy," I told Renata Baucum later that day.

She was working on one of the wardroom's fold-out exercise machines, a confusion of pulleys and cables and stretchy rubber tubing, and wearing—incongruously—the green "body wrap" dress she'd picked up in Saint Helier. Its lower corners kept creeping up, weightless, but friction and concealed pins held the garment together, revealing her calves and nothing more. Sweat had begun to glisten there, and on her brow and shoulders and around the edges of her zee-spec lenses.

"You know anyone who is?" she said back. Pull, twist, release. Pull, twist, release.

No, I thought, I don't. But what I said was, "*I'm* glad he's with us. He seems to know what he's about."

"You know anyone who doesn't?"

"What I mean is, he seems very aware of the capabilities and limitations of t-balance. We can fly right through a trans-meg, he says, and that makes me feel better, because we passed *nine* of them on my watch today. Tomorrow it may be twenty, or fifty, or a thousand, and sometime it may not be possible to avoid them all. We're moving pretty fast."

"Personally," Baucum said, "I'd like a closer look with the instruments. Nobody really knows what the trans-megs *do*, what they're for. Their computational capacity has got to be staggering, and they interact with each other in peculiar ways. Sometimes they luff and tack like sails, riding the solar wind until they collide. That wouldn't occur by chance, not as often as it's been observed."

I frowned. I'd seen a couple of the structures quiver and quake as they sailed by, as if they were about to fly apart at the sight of us. But they hadn't flown apart, and couldn't really see us. Right?

"You think they're intelligent?"

"I think they're *alive*, yes. I know they are, and in terms of the number of subunits and the linkage between them, the complexity is comparable to ours, to any higher animal's. But for all that, they're just components in a larger system."

"I always figured they were just goop," I said.

"Yeah. So is hemoglobin."

Pull, twist, release. Pull, twist, release.

"I wonder if the Gladholders have any information about it. Maybe I should ask Dibrin."

She sniffed. "A bureaucrat. Possibly a *saboteur* bureaucrat."

"Come on—he's our friend."

"We barely met him."

Suddenly, I was angry. "So what? What difference does that make? I'm sick to death of this idea that friendship is work, that it's some grand project that comes together over months or years or decades. Knowing someone for a long time doesn't mean you're their friend, and meeting someone for the first time doesn't mean you aren't. *Everything* is work for us. Everything is a process. We're a sad, sick, demented people, you know that? We could stand to improve."

Baucum stopped pulling on the ropes. "I didn't mean anything. I didn't intend to . . . upset . . ." She seemed at a loss, wholly unprepared for my outburst. "Talk to Dibrin, sure, if you think it'll help."

"Why wouldn't it?" I went on, more gently but still riding the scharfblick channel, the sudden realtime stream of self-awareness, neither welcome nor especially resisted. "Where's the harm? We've built ourselves into a state of perpetual crisis where every action has to be weighed and justified. It excuses a lot, excuses us from having to be happy, from having to wonder why we aren't. God, how we trivialize that! What a low priority we assign it! Happiness is a *vice* to us, a guilty indulgence we save up for, pay for afterward, keep to ourselves like a dirty secret."

I took my zee-spec off, waved it at her. "I have idealized virtual environments on this thing. Does that shock you? I don't care! When I get back, I'm going to tell everyone to spend an evening playing around in virtual reality. Just so they'll know. Just so they'll know, for once in their lives, what it's like to feel free, unencumbered, to be met with unconditional acceptance and yes, even love. And *there's* a problem for you, isn't there? Who has the energy for *that*? It's like we've inverted the whole point of living, placed risk reduction ahead of the very things we're trying not to risk. But we're still going to die, aren't we? Childless, overworked, unaware of the wider universe and without even love to soothe the pain. Especially without love. I always thought Tosca Lehne was a bit of a social cripple, but he has a wife and family. Did you know? He's unhappy *now* because he had to leave them, but when he gets back . . ."

I paused, studied Baucum's shocked expression. Well, good, let her be shocked. The outburst surprised me as well, but it felt good, liberating, to slip in past her defenses, right past her wit and verve and self-control to touch some inner surface she didn't want to admit was there.

"We're all such cowards," I said quietly, "afraid to die, afraid to slow down, afraid to reach for the person beside us and say 'I love you.' It's pathetic."

"John," Baucum murmured, "you surprise me. I didn't know."

And then suddenly she was off the exercise seat and drifting into my arms, grasping, holding, pressing her lips against me, and I wanted to protest: no, stop, that wasn't what I meant! But then I wasn't so sure, and then my cabin door was open and we were tumbling inside, and then . . .

You know what happened then.

Later, what seemed like a long time later, we drifted together in warm darkness. Feeling good, feeling languidly and luxuriously alive. *This* was a thing worth protecting.

"I had no idea there was such a passionate man in there," Baucum whispered, tapping me on the chest.

The admission surprised. Not passionate? I? I, who spent the wee hours prowling for news, forgoing food and sleep in the ongoing effort to bring people closer together? Who took the trouble to cajole and query actual human beings at every turn, to sniff out each story's emotional crux? Who had agreed to this stinking mission for almost no reason at all, for nothing more than ambition and vanity and pure love of the chase?

"I thought I knew just how you were going to be," she went on, "servant of the status quo, asking everyone how proud we were to be working for the right side. I think you were supposed to be that way, expected to, I mean, but you know, people are hard to model. In closed environments, all sorts of buried traits come to the fore that nobody's ever seen or anticipated."

"And hidden assets," I whispered, fondling.

She giggled. "And those, yes. I didn't realize how much I . . . how much . . . It's been a long time."

"For most of us, I think. I keep saying it's a health issue. Have I told you about 'Boff a Stranger' day?"

"Stranger?" she said, pushing at me playfully. "Weren't you just the one preaching instant friendship?"

"Well, you seem friendly enough."

"Humph."

We drifted in silence for a while. Baucum's mock indignation was fine, it was fun, but I did still feel some sting in the idea that she'd thought me a shill or puppet of the system. And passionless! Was the error hers, or did I really come across that way? *She* was the aloof insider, after all; I was just here to tell the tale.

"I'm not receiving instructions, you know," I finally told her. "Doing my thing, I've caused my share of trouble over the years. I doubt my involvement would have been encouraged, or even allowed, if there were really all these ugly secrets lying around."

"Hmm. Unless the invitation was given specifically to *throw off* suspicion."

"Suspicion of what?"

"I don't know. But if something's going on back home, you're pretty well out of the way of it, wouldn't you say?"

I snorted. "What is it with you, Renata? There's plenty to worry about down here without making stuff up. You should learn to unwind a little."

"I thought I just did!"

Our skins are ignorant, blushing even in darkness. But you can feel the heat.

"You know what I mean," I said.

"I know what you mean," she agreed. We brushed against a wall, drifted away again. "Would it surprise you to learn I keep idealized environments too? Not just here on the ship, but for years. A dirty secret, like you said. I'm telling you this in confidence."

"Your secrets are safe. And yes, I am surprised. Can you flash one to me?"

She giggled again. "I have a better idea, berichter: trade zee-specs with me."

The request gave me pause. Trade zee-specs? It seemed a shocking intimacy, more so than what had happened already. Some things were not for sharing! But I felt her arms moving behind me, working symbols and windows, and then the zee-spec was lifting off her face and it seemed like she was smiling and there really was no good way to refuse. I opened up Ex-Philusburg, now simply a meadow-floored cavern some three kilometers across, with ersatz blue sky shining above, then removed the zee-spec and handed it over, accepting hers in return.

It was warm, and smelled of her. The view through the lenses dark at first, and then a smear of meaningless colors as it settled into place, and then finally an image snapping sharply into focus as the beams locked onto my pupils.

I gasped.

Red sandstone beneath my feet, the sky above an azure blue, deep and clear and impossibly distant, wholly unlike the cavern lights of home. The horizon shimmered with rainbow color, pillars and streamers of living fog fading up into the blue of atmosphere, while all around was an eye of yellow in a riotous field of whites and blues and purples.

Momentarily overwhelmed, I struggled to make sense of this, to gauge the distances, to interpret the shapes. I stood on a pillar of rock, maybe three meters across and ten times as high. More properly, I hovered—my body hung weightless and nude, bare feet brushing air several centimeters above the rock. Below, all around, stood truck-sized huts of yellow fiber, rising out of a rippled yellow surface that looked like wet rubber. Fires smoked from little stone-lined pits. Doorways beckoned. And in the distance . . .

Not fields, not forests, not jungles or deserts, but . . . something else. Something clearly alive, breathing, pulsing, *moving* in organic fits and spasms. Not one thing, not even a million things, but an infinity of them—mounds upon mounds, branches upon branches, flowers upon flowers upon flowers . . . And things more disturbing than that, things like eyes and mouths and tentacles, like slimy pools filled with wriggling forms, like bristly brain-coral reefs sprouting fish, snakes, monsters, from penile stalks of quivering meat. Suggestions of form, only, like animal shapes glimpsed in cloud.

Solid? Gelid? Formed only of slime or vapor or evil intention? Visually, there was no way to tell, though some of the forms reached kilometers high. Even clouds look solid from a distance.

Clouds, yes. To my right, the sky roiled and billowed, white and silver and gray, *dark* gray in places on the bottom. A thrill of terror from my youth: storm clouds. Water vapor? Myco-vapor? A million million spores blowing in on the jet stream, waiting for a downdraft to carry them, blooming, to Earth? That was where I was, of course: Earth. Not *my* Earth, humanity's Earth, but the one that came after. The one we'd fled in horror so great it had shaped everything about us from that day forward.

"Jesus," I said, every hair on my body standing straight out.

Baucum was right there with me, zee-spec configured to incorporate her into the simulation, her nude body tangled with mine, drifting with mine above the rock spire. She was wearing my zee-spec, looking blind, not seeing me or the horror around me, but rather the peaceful meadow of Ex-Philusburg.

"You're invisible!" she laughed.

"Baucum, are you *insane*?"

"No, really, I can't see you."

I looked around me, trying not to shudder or grimace or scream. "This is your *ideal* environment?"

Lightning flared from the clouds, crashed into distant spires of purple-rainbow fog. Answering flashes raced across the ground, skittering over the landscape, and through it, vanishing one by one over the jagged horizon.

"Oh," she said, smiling blindly at me, "it is a bit of a shock, I suppose. The end-product of several years' geekwork. Ideal? Not so much that as *coveted*. I told you, I want the Earth back. As much as you do."

"More," I said, cringing. "You win. You want it more."

"You're so tense. I wish I could see you," she said. Then, in a surprisingly keen imitation of Chris Dibrin's voice: "May I . . . meddle?"

"What? Yeah, fine. Go ahead."

Her fingers danced in empty air for a while. Finally, her eyes rested on me.

"Tsk. You look so horrified."

"I'd rather watch surgery. Really, can I turn this sim off?"

She looked hurt. "I wanted to impress you. Yes, go ahead and close it. There's another file in there, called 'Waterfall.' "

"Take my word for it," I told her, "I'm impressed. The attention to detail is . . . impressive. Very."

I would have nightmares for a week, a month, the rest of my life, now that I knew what Hell must look like. I wiped the image, found the layer of controls and windows beneath it. Breathed a sigh of relief. Zee-specs are mostly all the same, but the defaults and preferences and menu and image layouts must be as unique and individual as the people who own them. Baucum's controls were not like mine, but they were obvious enough. I found and activated the "Waterfall" sim, which sprang to life around me.

Again, I floated. Again, the sky above me was deep blue, with cumulus islands rolling across it, puffy white. This time, though, the jungle was green, terrestrial, safe. Sprinkled liberally with flowers, yes, but real ones, biogenic ones, evolved over billions of years like God intended. The surface beneath my feet was a pool of water wider than a house, churned by a cascade of water tumbling down black-rocky cliffs. The sight and sound of it soothed me instantly, ointment on the bruises of my soul. Faint music played, barely audible, seeming to originate from somewhere higher up on the cliff.

"Is that better?" Baucum asked, eyeing me from arm's length.

"Yes," I told her. "Much. I thought *my* Mycosystem sim was bad."

"Oh, are you still working on that?"

"Yeah, sort of. I can't get the dynamics right, though. Not like yours!"

"Well, mine is a top-down fractal animation, not a cellular automaton. Very little of the underlying physics is actually modeled. The mycostructure is pure marshmallow, no internal chemistry."

"Well, it's effective. It's horrible."

"I do apologize for that. With long exposure we get inured to things, forget the shock value of them, but I suppose not everyone can gaze unflinching into the face of the Mycosystem."

"Yeah, well, I picked a hell of a place to spend the winter, then, didn't I?"

"So it would appear," she said, and smiled.

I looked her up and down, then, relaxing tensed muscles, enjoying the zee-spec's interpretation of what she would look like if the lights were on and the lenses clear. Pink nipples, auburn pubic hair, smooth soft hips . . . God, it *had* been a long time. The best things in life, we used to say, are free. So why did I have the feeling there'd be hell to pay? Ah, well, payment would be rendered in due time. This was hardly the moment to worry about it.

Baucum was tender as well as beautiful, understanding as well as

skeptical. When we'd fallen together it had been with grace, enthu-
siasm, the gentle brushing aside of a deep mutual cowardice. Who'd
have guessed? And now, to *see* her . . .

"I'm *very* impressed," I informed her, and was rewarded with
another blush.

"Cut it out, you," she said, and pulled me close to stop my looking. And then kissed me, to quash my reply. And then . . .

Well, you know what happened then.

SEVENTEEN

Mars, the God of . . .

The rapping on my cabin door was gentle but firm, clearly intended to wake me, but discreetly. Grunting, I hit the lights, took my zee-spec off the charging rack, swore when I saw the time. I popped the door open.

Darren Wallich floated outside, trying hard to look polite and apologetic through the grin he was failing to suppress.

I glared. "Yes?"

"Sorry to disturb you," he said, "but we needed a word in private. You know what this is about."

Pause. "Yeah." Baucum's scent was still strong on my skin.

"None of my business," he hastened to say, holding up both hands to indicate his helplessness, "but it's not a large ship. Privacy does not come cheap."

"Right."

"I can't tell you your business."

"Right," I said, more slowly. He was still smirking, still fighting it, still failing. Nice to know my life was so amusing.

"Morale never stops being an issue, Strasheim. You appreciate that for every crewman who finds someone to . . . cohabitate with, there are three or four who don't? We seem to have a fairly polite group this time around, but even when open rivalries don't result—"

"It won't happen again, sir."

He looked me over, the smirk faltering a little, guilt and sympathy struggling to take its place. "I have no jurisdiction over your personal life. I have no interest in meddling, particularly in affairs of the heart. My concern is purely for the mission."

"It won't happen again," I repeated, letting more of the irritation creep into my voice. I'd known this was coming; despite our efforts to be quiet, I didn't for a moment suspect we'd fooled anyone. But I didn't have to like it.

Wallich reached out and gripped my arm, a surprisingly warm and masculine gesture. *I understand, freund, and approve, and envy your luck. But do the right thing.* I sniffed, and finally nodded my understanding.

"Baucum?"

"Already talked to her. I think she likes you."

I colored. "Thanks. I'd guessed."

"More than she wants to, I mean. She seems off guard and flustered. For whatever that's worth."

I could think of no reply.

Wallich laughed. "All right. I'm glad we had this talk, Stras-heim. That famed expressiveness! Sorry, again, to wake you like this, but I need you on shift an hour early anyway. We have maneuvers coming up."

"Mars?"

"The one and only. Starts getting real from this point. No time for error. Do you need a shower to wake up?"

I thought about it. "Yeah, probably. Thirty minutes?"

"You have fifteen," he said, and laughed as if this were the fun-niest thing he'd heard all night.

"Hi," I said to Baucum as I took my seat.

"Hi," she returned without meeting my eyes.

"Everything all right?"

"Yep. Busy, though."

It wasn't long before I discovered what she meant.

The corridor for our Mars approach was narrow, requiring fa-natic precision in both time and space, and for days ahead of time we had a series of burns scheduled to keep us locked on an ever-tightening course. How exactly a ship like ours could get *off* course I didn't fully understand, but it had to do with things like the resolu-tion of our position and velocity measurements, which got worse the farther we drew from charted celestial objects, and was now improv-ing steadily as we approached Mars.

Here is how fast we were going: at three days out, the planet had been a speck under normal magnification. At two days, it was still a speck. At *one* day, it would still be a speck. We'd have slowed down a lot by then, sure, but by the time the planet had grown to the size of an eyeball, we'd be only an hour from our closest approach; from there on it would swell alarmingly, like a balloon about to burst, like a fist about to strike, until it filled half the sky, and then we'd be past it, and an hour after *that* it would be the size of an eyeball again. Wallich had walked me through the whole sequence, to be sure I understood. Probably to be sure I wouldn't be surprised or panicky when it happened.

That was under normal magnification, though. Under 1000X, the Red Planet was already showing off a lot of detail. Formerly red, I should say—even from this distance, the thumbnail-sized crescent looked decidedly pink, with scattered hints of yellow and purple. That made it seem real, somehow, not an image but a *place*, backlit, altered and perilous and directly in our path. The polar caps stood out clearly, not so much white as pale orange, water and CO_2 ices scattered with whatever remained of the planet's primordial oxide dust.

Safe havens. For all its menace, altered Mars was still the safest place in the inner system, safer by far than the space surrounding it. In space, there was no hiding from the endless sunlight.

You could cover it up with data windows, though; Wallich kept asking me not only for realtime allocation data but for various sorts of predictions, and finally I was forced to open a graph table and geek up some primitive sims just to stay ahead of him. Even so, he had me busy working the numbers.

"Strasheim: projected datastream for the attitude control system if we fire the main engine in five minutes?"

"Well, somewhere between five and eight kilobits per, depending on what Lehne is doing. Sir."

What Lehne was doing created no small uncertainty in my calculations. Baucum was detecting an increasing assortment of spores and other nasties on the hull and in the space ahead, and while no direct action was ever taken as a result, Lehne kept the countermeasures hot, continually forcing changes in the allocation of power and data. The ship's autonomous inclination was to set resources at the level of Lehne's most outrageous demand, and to back off from this very slowly when pressed by other needs, which would have made sense if we were actually fighting off a bloom. But Wallich's was the station most in need, a situation the ship's computers didn't seem to want to believe, and every time I let my attention wander— easy enough with my chair hanging almost directly above Renata Baucum's—I'd soon find his Reproachful Captain tones dragging me back. No wonder he'd wanted a live person at my station!

The first maneuver, an hour-long burn designed to slip us onto the approach corridor by reducing our velocity, came and went. In its wake came a number of trips to the wardroom to stretch and ex- ercise a bit, trips to the head for the obvious reason, and to the gal- ley to grab a few portable calories for the next big push. Since the last of the fruit, a pair of suspiciously soft and bruisy-looking mel- ons, had been consigned to the recycler two days before, the clear favorites today were figure-eight "crumpels" of chewy Gladholder bread, and squeeze bulbs of the powdered electrolyte drink called "Tez," which was apparently some sort of brand name. How quaint.

So for half an hour or so, the bridge seemed more like an easy- going, zero-gravity café, and by agreement we all opened a window on the engine room and anchored it to the aft bulkhead, completely covering the hatchway. Thus, the ship became a single virtual space, losing some fifty percent of its length and yet somehow seeming a good deal roomier. Or maybe it was just the variety of it that appealed.

I gather the perspective looked a lot less convincing from the other side; Davenroy and Rapisardi kept eyeing us and shaking their heads. Their dark rectangular niche was a lot smaller than the bridge, though, less busy and colorful, and they did seem to enjoy the sense of space and the proximity to someone besides each other.

Baucum kept up her hull sweeps, and Lehne kept updating his countermeasure preparations, but since the engine covers were closed this was no longer such a big deal, which of course made my job go away almost completely. Wallich was also looking happier, his demanding side buried once more, replaced with smiles and ready laughter.

"I had a saddleneck team working under me once," he was saying, in response to some comment of Davenroy's, "swapping out the plumbing and wiring on one of the labs we couldn't afford to shut down at the time. Always underfoot, always pulling up the floor plates and shutting breakers off without warning anybody. And of course they were saying the same things about *us*, and if there's anyone in the worlds with zero awe for Immune science, those were the guys. Gotta love 'em, you've just gotta. Anyway, one of these guys—actually, it might have been a female, but one of them cut off the water drip to a zeolyte feed operation we'd been running all week, and I started, you know, chewing her out about it, so she just kind of looks at me and says, 'What, like it isn't wet enough already?' "

Infectious, his laughter rippled through us all.

"Was that before or after you got the tickle capacitor?" I asked.

"Oh, years before," he said seriously, eyeing my upside-down face, and then burst out laughing even harder. "I threw such a tantrum they . . . they put me on an Io orbital survey for five weeks. Which turned out to be a good thing, overall, but to this day I train the labbers to do their own re-mod. The shit's all snap-and-go anyway, right?"

We laughed some more, finished our bread, finished our drinks. I talked to Baucum a little, but she seemed edgy, embarrassed, reluctant to look up at me or respond to me unless pressed. Best to wait until a better semblance of privacy prevailed.

The second burn approached. Work began to pick up again, Darren Wallich to get edgy.

"Rapisardi," he said, turning to face the false engine room, "how's the payload doing? You ready to drop some probes?"

"Tube one is powered up," Rapisardi affirmed. "I'll start running diagnostics once the burn is complete."

"That long?"

Rapisardi clucked. "Unless you don't want me monitoring for contamination when Davenroy opens the engine covers, yes."

"Hmm."

Baucum's voice cut through: "Hold it, whoa! I just read a high-frequency radio pulse from the direction of the planet!"

Radio pulse? Mycora didn't emit radio. Mycora *ate* radio signals. What could be emitting, way the hell down here? Nothing, I thought. Nothing that could survive the trip.

"There goes another!" Baucum said, sounding delighted. Here was something unexpected, finally, something worthy of her analysis. "The source appears to be about half a degree off the limb of the planet."

"Orbital?" Wallich asked. He was loosening his straps, leaning forward in his chair.

Baucum shrugged. "Off the surface, anyway. I can't get a Doppler velocity fix without knowing the source frequency, and I can't measure range without a precise transmission time. The source is definitely outside the Martian atmosphere, though, at least twenty thousand kilometers. Possibly a lot more. I'm reading a third pulse. Lots of echoes!"

"Are you recording?"

"Oh, that's affirmative," Baucum said, her fingers dancing in the air and on her panel. "Sudhir and I have got to analyze this! It's not often we get an active radar ping so close to an infected planet. As in 'never.' In the echoes I'm seeing . . . several dense bodies out there, which is definitely not expected. A lot of diffuse mycostructure as well, much more than visual scans would indicate."

Several of us grumbled at this news. The empty space we were flying through was maybe not so empty?

"It's got to be a human artifact," Wallich said, sounding as though he were trying to convince himself of the fact.

"Here's a fourth ping," Baucum announced, ignoring the comment. "The waveform has smeared—something happening at the source. I'm detecting a bloom."

"Spectral analysis?"

She frowned, fussed with invisible symbols. "Planetary backscatter shows a high concentration of metals, mostly aluminum and iron. Direct solar absorption is less conclusive. I would *guess* that we're looking at a class one blossom infest; many thousands of spores, triggered by the radio transmission and blooming more or less simultaneously. Yes, the object certainly was man-made. Probably around seven kilos, based on the growth pattern of the bloom."

"Point to it," Wallich said.

By agreement, we'd all pasted a 500X magnification Mars window over the bridge's forward bulkhead, and Baucum now undid her straps, reached forward over her console, and laid a finger on the image. "There."

I looked, saw nothing at first but the meter-wide crescent of the planet, upturned like a pair of sinister, bruise-colored horns curving away from the flaming ball of the sun below. The curve's lower edge was jagged and rainbow-hazy, fading into wispy tendrils that reached well out into space. Infected Mars. Then I saw it: a tiny smudge, blue and green and ghostly looking, about the size of a rice grain, hovering off the tip of one horn.

"Man-made object go bang," Wallich muttered, snorting to

himself. Then, more loudly: "So what the hell was it doing down here? How did it penetrate the Mycosystem so deeply without blooming a long time ago?"

"T-balance?" Tosca Lehne offered.

I cleared my throat. "Sir, could it be *from* Mars? Could there be humans living here, as well?"

"Not enough atmosphere," Wallich said, dismissing the suggestion. "Somebody sent that thing down here, and unless there's some *huge* coincidence operating, or unless there are thousands of them and they go off all the time, I'd say its transmissions were somehow in response to our arrival. Definitely."

"Someone's been tracking us right along," Davenroy called out from the false engine room.

Wallich nodded. "Right. We're possibly not the only ones seeding the Mycosystem with detectors. But who the hell is detecting us, and why? This is a pretty sophisticated operation."

No one had an answer for him.

"Okay," he said, leaning back in his seat, retightening the straps. "Okay. We're in motion, here, and it's safe to assume the pinger was, too. Let's track the bloom's position optically, maybe compare it to angular positions on the radar pings themselves. Throw in frequency shifts, assuming they're due to Doppler, throw in the signal arrival times, and let's see if we can't trace back a course for this thing. Where did it come from? Where was it going?"

"No guarantee of equal spacing on the transmissions," Lehne pointed out.

"Okay, fair enough. We'll leave that as an unknown. We have got several additional solid echoes, though, and I want trajectories on those as well." He touched Lehne and Baucum each on the shoulder. "Can you two handle the problem while the rest of us work the trim burn?"

"Yes," Lehne said.

Baucum nodded her agreement. "If we run all the unknowns through a million-trial randomization, we should be able to narrow in on a family of solutions. From there it should be mostly common sense. I figure, what, about half an hour?"

Lehne shrugged, noncommital but apparently more or less in agreement.

"Okay," Wallich said, "do it."

I felt a stab of envy then, because bioanalysis and countermeasures were certainly not superfluous tasks at this point. Far from it. Wallich had pulled them off normal duty simply because they were competent to solve this new problem, as indeed the whole crew probably was. Scientists and technicians and spacers all, all except for me. But I thought of Tug Jinacio, with his easy manner and his concrete, literal way of speaking, and doubted that he'd have known much about mathematics or technobiology or space navigation, either. Unless we somehow had blooms to fight, his job would have been *really* superfluous, all day, every day. I found the idea oddly cheering.

So the rest of us continued running calculations for the upcoming burn, and when it finally arrived it might almost have been just another smooth step in the preparations. Only the weight and vibration made it real. It lasted forty-five minutes, and when it was done we were *still* working the numbers for another five or ten minutes, gauging the effectiveness of what we'd done. Whee. Eventually, though, Baucum presented the results of the radar analysis.

"Slave your zee-specs to mine, please," she said, whipping into a graphical presentation that cast colored lines all over the forward Mars display. She pointed to an arc. "This is the most likely path for our friend, Mr. Radar Beacon. White denotes its existence as a solid object, while the pink is its continuation along the same trajectory as a class one free-floating bloom. Note that there's another white line crossing *here*, possibly indicating the device's point of origin."

The display flashed, lines vanishing and being replaced one by one. "Lehne's hypothesis is that this object here, with a radar cross-section comparable to that of a large instrument probe, is responsible for launching these other three objects, whose profiles are a good deal smaller. Possibly, these are additional radar beacons. And here, here, and here, we see other probelike signatures, with some fainter echoes that may indicate they've launched some beacons as well. It's very speculative, and I'm not sure I agree, but I haven't got a counterhypothesis I'm any happier with."

"It's quite a welcoming party," Rapisardi observed.

Wallich grunted. "It's very strange. Strasheim, contact the Gladholders and see if you can't find some information about this, right? They may be running some sort of experiment down here, though you'd think they'd have warned us, given that they knew where we were going."

"The Gladholds aren't a single society," I reminded him.

"Yeah, well, whatever. Call them anyway. I'm going off shift in a few minutes, and so is Davenroy. Eight-four sleep cycle until further notice. Rapisardi, we drop first payload in eleven hours. I want all diagnostics run at least twice before that happens, and I want you to wake me if you find *any* anomalies. It's a critical phase, not a time to find a weasel in our shorts."

"We have access to the payload software from here," Rapisardi said with an edge of annoyance. "Running the full diagnostic sequence twice is a terrific waste of my time. If anything is wrong, I simply need a minute to fix it and another minute to test the fix in simulation. And I hasten to assure you, nothing is wrong."

Wallich darkened. "Yeah, well, this isn't a good time to go

mucking with the guts of the mission, either. Just bear with me, all right?"

"Certainly," came the reply, and if the word was not delivered with complete sincerity, well, Wallich didn't seem overly bothered.

Dibrin: please translate and forward to appropriate net channels. Hallo Gladholds. Pasteur *encountering radar beacons etc. in high Martian orbit. Experiment in progress? Possible hazards? Please advise ASAP. Thank you!*

Eight-four rotation meant that each of us would work an eight-hour shift, then retire for four hours of sleep, circumstances permitting, then work another eight hours again. As it happened, this put me on the bridge for a long, uneventful stretch while ahead the planet swelled and behind Rapisardi puttered with the detector packages. Meanwhile, Baucum was in bioanalyst heaven, making endless measurements of the sunlight and radar echoes that had passed through or bounced off anything remotely mycoric in origin. She was paying me less than no attention, so I convinced Lehne to play a few games of chess, which he won handily despite the need to monitor his instruments.

And then Wallich and Davenroy returned, and Rapisardi agreed to skip his sleep shift, and Baucum tried to skip hers as well but was denied permission.

"We'll need you fully alert for the first deployment," Wallich told her.

"Yes? I should think you'd need Rapisardi fully alert as well."

He laughed and pointed at the hatchway. "To bed, young lady. Stop making sense at me."

And so she went, and the next stretch gave me even less to do, even when another of the radar beacons went off a few times and then dissolved into vaporous bloom. Lehne handled the observations Baucum otherwise would have, and resource allocation simply wasn't an issue. I spent the time composing reports and collages I didn't have the budget to send.

Ahead, the planet was getting really large now. We'd cut magnification on the shared window from 500X to a hundred, and finally to fifty, but each time the image seemed determined to fill the screen again just as soon as possible. We were racing toward Mars at, what, something like three hundred kilometers per second? At that speed, the trip from Ganymede to Callisto would take less than four hours even at opposition, with the vast bulk of Jupiter sitting directly between them. Now *that* was fast!

Finally it came time for me to sleep, and Lehne, but by then of course we were only two hours away from deployment, so we were allocated ninety minutes and an insincere apology. I spent the time floating weightless in the darkness of my cabin, with the zee-spec charging on its rack and the air vent turned up for maximum white noise. I'm rarely one to refuse a rest, but I'd only been awake for half a day, and catnap sleep eluded me, and in the end I drifted back to the bridge grouchy and dry-eyed, wishing I'd simply stayed there all along.

Lehne was already in his seat as I settled into mine and strapped myself down. And a lucky thing that was, too, that timely application of restraint webbing, because it was at almost exactly that moment that we were attacked for the first time.

OPPOSITION

"Object two is venting, Captain," Lehne said. "Fine mist, possibly vapor."

"Spectral analysis?"

"Working," said Baucum. "Organic, sir. Complex."

Wallich exhaled sharply, through his teeth. "Right in our path, isn't it? Lovely. Davenroy, give me main engines and full ACS, please. Hang on, people, I'm taking us evasive."

Here and there steering motors groaned to life, pulsing jets of iron plasma into the vacuum around us. *Louis Pasteur* shuddered,

Wallich pitching and yawing her onto a new course and then demanding main engine thrust, completely ruining the finesse of our
last burn.

"Not good enough," Lehne called out. "Cloud dispersal puts us
right through the edge of it in twenty seconds."

Wallich slapped his armrest. "Damn. Baucum, what is this
crap?"

"I don't know," she replied in a singsong of tension and aggrava-
tion. "It's organic, possibly aminoid haptens. Too light to be mycoric, if that helps, but other than that it could be almost anything."

"Find out in a sec," Lehne said. "Entering vapor cloud. Now."

Warning chimes rang. Lights on control panels flashed.

Baucum let out a tense sigh. "Substance identified, sir: it's
complementin."

A ripple of alarm ran through the bridge crew.

My dictionary was sitting open, waiting for just such an emergency. I looked the word up: *com-pl[ə]-MEN-tin, n., a class of short-
lived lysing and/or corrosive organic polymers, often employed as
immunotaggants.* Okay, fine. I looked up "immunotaggant" and got:
*a molecule attached to a foreign body or substance, marking it for phago-
cytosis and eventual elimination.* I saw I could follow this chain indefinitely, but "elimination" told me enough. We'd been tagged. Like
the old story about painting someone with honey and staking
them out on an anthill. The honey itself wasn't harmful—it didn't
have to be.

"Going to clog up the camouflage," Lehne warned.

Baucum grunted. "Already! I'm reading some replication events
on the forward hull. It seems to be very slow and tentative for the
moment, but it's not what we want to see."

"Damn right," Wallich agreed. "Lehne, hydrofluoric sweat,

please. Minimum setting. I'm laying us sideways and queuing up a thermal roll."

This, at least, I understood. Our mission plan would bring us closer to the sun than any human had been in decades (any *non-mycoric* human, a part of my mind insisted), and at such proximities the thermal expansion imposed by sunlight was enough to pose a structural danger. Or a danger to the t-balance, or something. Anyway, the "thermal roll" program was designed to hold our long axis perpendicular to the sun, and to spin *Louis Pasteur* around once per minute to ensure even heating all the way around. People used to cook this way, I know, spinning animal carcasses over a pit of hot coals. Same principle, except in this case it was the stain of complementin, rather than heat, that we were spreading out evenly. To keep any one spot from becoming too heavily contaminated? Something like that, surely.

The forward window gave up its view of Mars, looked out over empty space instead, quiet starscape oozing around in a slow circle. The Gladholder fear doll had been kicking around the bridge for days, and now the rolling motion must have jostled it loose from some hidden resting place. "Help," it said in a muffled, despairing voice. And then it fell silent again.

"HF sweat breaking down complementin," Lehne reported. "Not advisable, though. Either way, we start attracting attention pretty quick, here. Never forget, we're crawling with bad bugs."

Wallich grimaced. "Flash me a schematic of the vapor cloud." Pause. "Hmm. Hmm. We're not getting out of this without throwing our trajectory completely off the deployment corridor."

Well. To me, that sounded a little too pat to be accidental. "Somebody's warning us off," I said.

"Warning, hell," Wallich replied. "That shot was well aimed, and we're going to *hit* the thing that fired it in about six minutes, if the mykies don't get us first. I'd say we're under attack."

Everyone froze. Attack. That was the word we'd all been avoiding, the word we'd been trying not to have to apply. Because why would anyone attack us? What possible harm did we represent, to anyone or any*thing*? Even the Mycosystem itself had little to fear from us, just a few passive markers left behind on the ice floes when our temporary invasion ran out. But I was getting used to things not making sense, getting used to the idea that inscrutable enemies had been dogging us right along and would continue to do so. There were *people on Venus*, after all, and looking for sense in the face of that seemed worse than hopeless. So okay, we were under attack. By Gladholders? By Templers? By someone or some*thing* else?

"We have to break off," Baucum stated. "Really, I mean, that spray is exiting at more than twice our velocity relative to the object. Meaning, they can keep hitting us with it even after we pass them. And meanwhile, the spray's density is increasing as we approach. The situation is untenable."

"Untenable? If we miss this pass, we'll have to turn around and come back. *That's* untenable, Baucum."

"Excuse me, sir," said Rapisardi, his voice cutting through and surprising everyone. The faux engine room behind the bridge's aft bulkhead had been removed during my break, and while voice contact was of course maintained, he and Davenroy had been going about their jobs with very quiet efficiency. Easy to forget they were even there.

"Yes?" Wallich demanded.

"Sir, I've been single-stepping through the payload software all day, per your instructions, and I've noticed a funny sort of loophole. If you're willing to sacrifice tube one to the effort, I believe we can clear the path ahead of us."

"Explain."

"Sir, it must be done right away or not at all."

"Why did you wait so long to inform me?"

"I just thought of it! For God's sake, Wallich, that object is hostile. Shall I fire on it or not?"

"Fire on it? Tube one, you mean? Preserving two for the northern cap?"

"Correct. May I modify the software?"

Wallich paused, the muscles of his face twitching, as if unsure what expression to form. Then: "Affirmative."

"Aye, sir. Software modified. Opening tube one. End thermal roll and maneuver to firing position."

"Positive vee?" Wallich asked.

"Yes, positive vee!" Rapisardi shot back. "They're right in front of us, for God's sake! What do you *think*?"

"Calm down, calm down. Coming around to positive vee. Coming around. Coming around. That's got it. Fire when ready, Mr. Rapisardi."

"Aye, sir. Firing tube one."

There was a soft, metallic clank, and then a popping sound. The ship vibrated slightly. On the forward window, a score of white, fist-sized, roughly spherical objects tumbled out ahead of us, looking as if they were rolling down a steep hill toward Infected Mars. In moments they were lost from view.

"Recommend five seconds' thrust along minus-vee, Captain. Slow us down a bit; we don't want to be too close."

"Affirmative, five seconds along minus-vee. Forward thrusters engaged. Hum de dum. Forward thrusters disengaged. You want to tell me what this is all about, now?"

Ahead, the view went blindingly white for a moment, and by the time the light had faded and my eyes had recovered from the shock, a diffuse mycostructure had filled the path ahead of us, swelling rapidly. *Actually* swelling, I mean, changing shape, shooting out foggy lobes and tendrils, and racing toward us as well. Or us toward it, if you prefer. I didn't even have time to scream before we were through it.

"Blank that window," Wallich ordered.

I complied, saw the others doing likewise. Maybe it was better not to see right now. But what had that explosion been all about? Rapisardi had specifically assured me, assured the crew, assured the whole Immunity that the detector packages nestled in tubes one through thirteen were not bombs. Had he lied?

"Did we just kill someone?" I asked.

"Doubtful," Baucum replied. "The object wasn't that big."

"So what *did* we do?"

"Spill it, Sudhir," Wallich echoed.

The biophysicist's voice came back careful, almost embarrassed. "It's never been a secret that nuclear energy presents . . . certain dangers. We think of ladderdown as a 'clean' technology, which in a radiation sense it certainly is."

"But?"

"But. The quantum spatial distortion is normally induced and focused within a shielded reactor, where its effects can be controlled to within a few Planck radii. How else to tunnel out only the desired nucleons, yes? But if we invert the distortion function along the B-axis, essentially turning it inside out in three-dimensional space, the same ladderdown tunneling can be induced stochastically in a much larger spherical shell, centered about the inductor. Shielding irrelevant, because it's *inside* the affected region, you see? Considered too hazardous for use in bloom cauterization, the phenomenon has no industrial applications. Look it up under Things Not to Try."

Most of that went right over my head, but the gist seemed clear enough: he was talking about releasing energy, lots of it, in an uncontrolled manner. He was talking about a bomb.

"So easy?" Baucum accused. "You *just* thought of that?"

Rapisardi cleared his throat. "The, um . . . All I needed to change was the sign of one input parameter, and of course the activation timer. Two numbers. It's fortunate the code was configured as it was, or the idea mightn't have occurred to me."

"Very convenient."

"Yes? And are you distressed at finding yourself still alive?"

"Almost time to fire the other tube," Wallich observed, his eyes on some invisible chronometer. "Let's knock it off and get back to work."

I tensed, knowing what came next. We'd rehearsed this procedure over and over, and while there had never been an attack in the middle of it, this point was nonetheless the most critical in terms of timing and task loading. I kept a close eye on the allocation monitors, making sure no one had too much or too little of the data system's attention.

"Coming around to north cap deployment attitude," Wallich said. "Attitude achieved. Attitude lock. Rapisardi, open tube number two, please."

"Aye, sir. Tube two open."

"Prepare to fire."

"Aye, sir. Ready to fire."

"Fire."

The ship clanked and popped and vibrated again.

"Payload is away," Rapisardi said.

"Maneuvering to south burn attitude," Wallich called out without pause. And that was it; the payload was away, ten detector packages that would slam down upon the Martian polar cap, and alert the Immunity the moment they found mycoric activity there, activity that signaled a new tolerance for cold, a clear threat to those above. But there was no comment from any of us, no sense of triumph or accomplishment. Not yet, anyway. My arms floated free as the ship rotated around us.

Davenroy's voice: "Engine covers are open. Ready main thrust."

Wallich grunted acknowledgment. "Achieved. Attitude lock. Engage main engines."

From there it was burn and turn, burn and turn, three five-minute periods of thrust that would put us in line with the south pole at a velocity that wouldn't pulverize the probes as they hit. And then the covers were blown off payload tubes three and four, two more open wounds in our hull, and the probes were fired out of them. Pop! Pop!

Throughout all of this I kept stealing looks at Baucum, who appeared to be taking all the activity rather poorly, her face gone gray and shiny. Now was not the time for chatter, and I couldn't reach her with my hands, so there was no consolation I could offer. But then, it didn't look like a consolement sort of mood anyway; more like she was motion sick or in fear for her life, either of which could easily be true. Presently, she took notice of her instruments, and her frown lines deepened.

"Captain, we're being pinged again. I'm reading multiple solid echoes, a lot of variation in cross-section."

"Flash us the data," Wallich said.

Baucum and Lehne had geeked together a radar sim that would refine their earlier solutions based on any new data, and it was a frame from this that appeared on my zee: the planet Mars a transparent globe of red wire, surrounded by colored lines representing the targets.

"Damn," Wallich said. And then, after a hesitation of moments, he began to laugh. Not chuckle or giggle or snigger, but *laugh*, a stiff braying spaced out at fixed intervals, as if something were pressing rhythmically on his stomach, forcing the air out in measured bursts. "Ha! Ha! Ha! Ha!"

"Sir?" Baucum said, turning, looking at him uncertainly.

Wallich's grinning face was red, the pace of his laughter picking up. "Ha, Ha, Ha, Ha!"

This was not good. On a scale of good to not good, this was definitely on the "not" side of the spectrum. Even *I* couldn't afford to go to pieces in the middle of a— But then, as suddenly as it had begun, the laughter cut off, and Wallich was blinking, looking at his bridge crew looking back at him. His eyes narrowed for a moment, suspicious at our stares, and then he was all business again.

"Hiding behind the planet," he said, eyeing (no doubt) the display Baucum had flashed over.

"What are they?" I asked. Demanded, really, because this was another one of those things nobody was talking about, and at this point I damn well wanted to know.

Wallich shrugged, made a face of exaggerated innocence at me. "A few of these radar cross-sections are big enough to be manned ships. Probably that's exactly what they are; this doesn't feel like pure machine activity, does it? And teleoperation is out; the light lag from even the Gladholds is too severe. So there need to be human beings down here running the show. Got to be. The rest of the objects are much smaller, though: probes, small weapons platforms, who knows? Probably teleoperated from the ships via laser beam, although I suppose some of them could be autonomous.

"Earth's navies used to use a similar approach: manned vessels surrounded by swarms of attendant machinery. Less vulnerability that way, more fluid response. How long would they last if the radar beacons were right on the ships? About two seconds. So they put the radar out on drones, and listened passively to the echoes.

Weapons, same thing; the humans were there to *guide* the attack, not to participate directly. That's what I think is going on, here. The real question is, *who* are they? The Temples of Transcendent Evolution aren't up to a prank like this."

"Not without help," Lehne said.

I protested: "This is not a *prank*. This is a murder."

"Not much of a murder," the disembodied voice of Jenna Davenroy observed. "On their present course it'll take them half an hour to intercept us."

"Well," Wallich said, "clearly we aren't where they expected us to be. They probably thought we'd break off to avoid their . . . spritzing machine. Whatever it was."

"Maybe lucky for us," Lehne said.

Yeah. Probably very lucky.

"I'm reading plasma clouds near several of the echoes," Baucum warned, her eyes on invisible instruments.

"Propulsive?" Wallich asked.

"Hydrogen-iron spectrum," she confirmed. A ladderdown signature.

This time, his chuckle sounded natural and humorless. "Coming after us, are they? Well, let's see if they'll follow us all the way down. I'm bringing us around to trans-Earth injection attitude. Davenroy, uncover the main engines again, please."

Below, the planet was an enormous symbol of yin and yang—bisected by sunlight, huge enough to appear flat rather than spherical. How high above it were we? A few thousand kilometers? Even at normal magnification, it was like holding a dinner plate right in front of your nose.

A moldy dinner plate, I should say, or, more precisely . . . imagine looking down, from a height of three or four meters, on a lawn of unkempt grass, patchy, shot through with strangling weeds. Now imagine that the grass and weeds are transparent, faint rainbows twinkling here and there, and that a low, unmoving ground fog enshrouds them all. The fog, on closer inspection, is in fact a mad crisscross of translucent threads, and the soil beneath it all has the ruddy, airy look of wet clay pressed through mesh. Visually, this is what Mars looked like as we raced by.

Emotionally, with what artists used to call the "eye of the heart," I saw instead an open wound, polluted flesh wriggling with maggots and bacterial slime. The corpse of a planet, all beauty transmuted to horror and rot. Looking at it, I felt a rush of absolute terror: what in God's name were we doing? Even Tug Jinacio had died at the hands of this stuff. How had we gotten down here? How had we *dared*?

But already I could see the features receding, the edges of the planet itself growing visibly smaller. Closest approach had come and gone, then; we were leaving this world, not approaching it. Already! God, we were moving fast.

"Trans-Earth injection attitude achieved," Wallich said crisply. "Davenroy, fire the engines, please."

"Aye, sir."

The sense of acceleration was light but immediate. We were putting on speed, putting distance between ourselves and this bloom of a world at an ever-increasing rate. Good riddance, was all I could think.

"Objects are moving to intercept," Wallich observed. Then, maybe ten seconds later: "I don't think they can catch us. But they can sure as hell follow."

"Replication events on the hull are stepping up," Baucum said, gray-faced, just to let us know our troubles weren't over. Fear danced like bubbles of ice water through my veins.

Wallich simply pressed his lips together in an expression of distaste. "HF sweat not cutting it, eh? Lehne, what are the indications for increased flowrate?"

"Contraindicated, definitely."

"Are we damaging the hull?"

"Probably. No time for a serious inspection right now, but if something starts eating through, you'll know for sure. Main thing is, the hydrogen ions are *food*. Maybe even fluorine, depending. Neutralize one pathogen, great, but you leave behind a useful residue of TGL debris. Complementin is mostly gone by now; I say stop the sweat."

Wallich mulled this over, nodding unhappily. I understood his dilemma—to fight off external pathogens he really had only two useful weapons: variations in pH, and variations in temperature. And the release of active immunocytes, sure, but that was tantamount to a declaration of war against an effectively omnipotent foe. Not smart, except maybe as a last resort.

But meanwhile, any variation in hull conditions rendered the t-balance that much less effective, that much less likely to fool the mycospores attached to it. The result was a tightrope walk: the more numerous and active the spores, the stronger the countermeasures required to foil them, ergo the more activity on our part and more suspicion on theirs . . . But doing nothing wasn't much of an option, either, not if they were already starting to replicate.

"Recommendations?" Wallich asked finally.

"LN_2 purge, level one," Lehne replied, with a reluctant grunt of approval soon following from Baucum.

"This close to the planet?"

Lehne nodded. "Quench and warm. Five minutes, tops. Vapor should boil off most of them, along with contaminants, and the rest . . . We don't crack them up with the thermal shock, well, at least they wake up cold on a clean, hypoantigenic surface."

"Why not just leave it cold?" I asked. I realized this had been bothering me for some time; why didn't we *always* run cold? Coat the hull with liquid nitrogen and blast through the Mycosystem like a miniature comet, frigid as the surface of Ganymede itself? I was recording, and it occurred to me that I'd used my reporter voice to ask the question. Some habits simply don't die.

Wallich looked briefly surprised, as if he'd forgotten I was aboard, or forgotten I was anything more than an allocations console operator. But then his patient-captain-warming-to-the-cameras look switched on, along with a faint smile. "Sensible question, Strasheim, but life is unfortunately not that simple. Temperature doesn't mean quite the same thing on the nanoscale, especially in hard vacuum and bright sunlight. Cold surfaces just attract a different sort of trouble down here."

"I see," I said. "May I pester you for details later?"

He laughed. "If there's a later, you certainly may."

CRACKING PRESSURE

Every time Louis Pasteur *strikes a foreign object, whether spore or dust mote or living mycostructure, atoms are knocked free from its t–balance surface in proportion to the square of our relative velocity, which has been consistently higher than original plan. Individually these events are trivial almost to the point of nonexistence, but the cumulative erosion from thousands of such events every day will eventually begin to impair this most important of our defenses.*

"Eventually" might have meant as much as four or five

years, if not for the corrosive effects of a chemical taggant, nineteen abortive microblooms, and the acids and solvents used to remove the remains of same. Estimates of our survival time are now measured in months, and will remain in the double digits only so long as no further misfortune befalls us.

Given that the five unidentified spaceships currently pursuing us—and their attendant swarm of apparently unmanned instrument and weapons platforms—are only three light-seconds behind, and that we must certainly slow down to deploy our detector packages when we get to Earth, and then very nearly reverse our course for the return home, such fortune appears unlikely.

And no, we can't abort the mission—I've asked. First of all, deployment of these detectors may of course prove frightfully important to the well-being of the Immunity. Second and more immediately, our fuel supply will not carry us home without the gravity assist of at least one more planetary flyby. Oh well, I did promise Momma I'd say hallo to the Earth.

from *Let's Get the Living Fuck Out of Here*
© 2106 by John Strasheim
(Author's Preferred Text)

Attack 5+ unknw enmy ship @ Mars, msn ongoing but Erth = big probm

from *Let's Get the Living Fuck Out of Here*
© 2106 by John Strasheim
(Text As Transmitted)

Things sounded pretty hot on the bridge—we'd been encountering a more aggressive breed of mycorum since leaving Mars behind—but Baucum was just finishing her sleep rotation and I was just starting mine, and unless specifically called up to help, I was determined to take the opportunity to talk with her. Not so much for personal reasons, although that was a factor, as for professional ones. Spacer professional, I mean, not as a berichter. She'd been so *strange* since the attack, not so much frightened as diminished, defeated, somehow both brittle and limp, and considering I now probably knew her better than any of the others did, it seemed natural that I should be the one to find out just exactly what the problem was.

Aside from the obvious, I mean—we were all pretty much at a loss, like sleepy mice whose nest has suddenly turned out to be the inside of some terrible machine. Worse than that, really, because unlike the Mycosystem itself, these solid enemies were *trying* to kill us, *hoping* to kill us, actively thinking about the process of killing us. That's a very personal, very immediate sensation. But it didn't have the rest of us slumping around like our spines had been broken.

I cornered Baucum coming out of the head, and when she saw me there she tried to close the door again, right in my face. I stuck a foot in it, which she obligingly slammed between fanfold and frame. The door wasn't heavy, and my wide shoes were of course filled with lead, but the gesture was hurtful just the same.

"Ouch," I told her gravely.

"I don't want to talk to you, Strasheim."

"This isn't a personal call."

"I don't care what it is, I don't feel like talking, and I believe I have that right. Now if you'll excuse me—"

"You don't have the right," I said, "where the safety of the ship is concerned."

"Fuck the safety of the ship," she replied calmly, and Jenna Davenroy, who was also just coming off shift, chose that precise moment to pop through the hatchway from the engine room.

"Hallo," she said uncertainly. "Am I interrupting?"

"No," Baucum and I said in unison. "I was just leaving," Baucum added.

Davenroy was a good fifteen years older than Baucum, and it showed, suddenly, in the easy condescension she was able to project through what was otherwise a look of polite concern. "Dear, it's no use trying to keep things to yourself around here. What concerns any of us concerns us all. I appreciate your quite natural desire for privacy, but in this context it's really rather rude. I've been spying on you, did you know that? Keeping a little window on you since I noticed what a wreck you'd become. What happened back there to shake you up so badly?"

Baucum pulled the washroom door fully open, sullen. "It's complicated."

"Really."

"Why don't you—" I began, but Baucum's glare turned on me and the words dried up. She was *really* upset, like maybe poised on the brink of violence.

"We dropped our detectors," Baucum said, "and son of a gun, they really were bombs after all."

"They were *used* as bombs," Davenroy corrected. "In defense against an unprovoked attack."

"Was it unprovoked?"

Davenroy clucked. "Any danger we might possibly represent is to the Mycosystem, to the blind voracity of mindless, microscopic machines. That hardly constitutes a threat."

"And if our activities disturb the Mycosystem in some way? If I lived in the Gladholds, and I found out someone was going to blast a hole in Infected Mars, you'd better believe I'd feel threatened about it."

I thought about that, and realized she was probably onto something. The Temples of Transcendent Evolution, or rather the fanatics from whom they'd tried to disassociate themselves, were no more capable of launching a t-balance battle fleet than Julf Ernst and the gang back at the shoe factory. But as propagandists the Temples had no peer in the solar system; starting from nothing, in a decade and a half they'd recruited tens of thousands of people, not all of whom were stupid or gullible. Not by a long shot. So how hard would it be for them to drop a few discreet hints, mail down a collage or two to selected Gladholder net channels? Find a few well-placed kindred spirits, open up a dialogue . . .

In fact, this was one of those obvious-in-retrospect revelations that leave you feeling stupid afterward. Right, yes, it *must* have happened that way, else how could this situation have come about? What other plausible scenario was there?

"So that's who we're fighting," I said, and already my mind was off crafting reports that would imply all of this, leaving the connections plain for any reader to see without specifically implicating any one person or organization. *Sincere but misguided, certain elements may have sought the mad industrial might of reckless foreigners . . .*

Davenroy, though, was not impressed. "Defending our lives is hardly a crime, but endangering us with hazardous chemical sprays certainly is. Whoever is behind all this should have stepped out months ago and aired their grievances publicly."

"As if that would help," Baucum muttered. "The supposed 'right' to survival is not just a priority for most people, it's the only factor they're willing to consider, and never a thought for the rights of anything else. There used to be human beings who found importance, even sacredness, in literally everything around them. Not just the living things, either."

But Davenroy was shaking her head, almost mournfully, as if to indicate how very sorry she was that Baucum should be so dense. "Those people were turned to goo, dear. How sacred. The Mycosystem never took anyone's rights into account, it simply took the substance of their bodies for its own purposes. Nothing as destructive and useless as that will ever be 'sacred' to the people whose lives have been . . . devastated by it. Shame on you. Shame!"

She was really angry, not faking it for dramatic effect but probably actually holding it back, or trying to. Her hands quivered. But now it was Baucum's turn to look superior.

"You talk," she said, "precisely as if the discovery of living humans in the Mycosystem had never happened." Her look expanded to encompass me as well. "You've been complaining, John, about congenital flaws in Immune culture. Here's one for you: we hold to outmoded theories even in the face of overwhelming counter-evidence. We look at the Mycosystem and we see 'scary goo,' and never mind about the information content of the spores we see sifting through it every second of every day. We call it 'mindless' without ever once attempting to interpret its signals, and when we see *unambiguous signs* of purposeful activity, we simply fail to integrate it. It doesn't jibe with what we know, so we do our best to ignore it."

"I haven't been ignoring it," I said.

Davenroy just snorted. "I find your use of the word 'unambiguous' very illuminating, dear. Really, your theory is very interesting, and when you have more than a few blurry images to support it, do let me know."

Davenroy had been moving in the direction of her cabin, and

presently she entered it and pulled the door closed with a decisive click.

Baucum and I eyed one another uncomfortably, and I was thinking, well, having precipitated this exchange I should probably precipitate its peaceful conclusion as well. Davenroy had always been a bit touchy on the subject of the Mycosystem, and Baucum, too, but they weren't ever going to see eye to eye without some more effective information sharing. So I said, "When she wakes up, would you like me to show her the cellular automaton stuff?"

But before I'd even finished speaking, Baucum snapped, "Oh, just shut up, Strasheim." And just like that, she kicked off and launched herself toward the bridge.

You get used to crisis the same way you get used to anything else, and when I heard banging and voices outside my cabin door I fell awake and snapped the lights on, pausing only to snatch up my zee-spec before slamming the door open and tumbling out. This before I'd formed any conscious thought at all, the routine as automatic as a bodily function. Only when I was outside did I start to wonder what was going on.

Davenroy and Baucum were facing each other across the ward-room; fierce, territorial animals looking as if they were about to tear each other apart. Actually, judging by the panting breaths and the disarray of Baucum's hair, that process might already have begun. Tosca Lehne peered out from the bridge hatchway, Rapisardi from his own cabin across from mine, and Wallich was in the middle of the room, between the two women.

"What happened?" I asked.

"Everyone calm down," Wallich said, not to me but to Jenna Davenroy.

"Oh, I don't think so," Davenroy replied, and tried to launch herself past him. The quarters were way too cramped for that, though, and he caught her easily in the crook of his arm, slowing her. Their joined momentum carried them in Baucum's direction, but she slid out of the way, her angry eyes never leaving Davenroy.

"Ha," said Wallich stiffly. "Ha, ha, ha." And then his face cleared and he said, "God damn it, what the hell's the matter with you two?"

Davenroy stabbed an accusing finger at Baucum. "She was sabotaging the engine control software! I caught her at it, red-handed!"

"I was just looking," Baucum fired back, clearly shaken but trying hard not to show it. "I wanted to see if *that* was a bomb, too."

"Rubbish!" Davenroy cried. "You were modifying the gain states. I have the before-and-after compare, and the time-synched image of your precious little fingers wiggling every time a change is logged. I used to think you couldn't *possibly* be our saboteur; no one would be stupid enough to plant someone as *obvious* as you. But then, it's generally a mistake to underestimate stupidity's power, isn't it?"

"Hold on a minute," Wallich protested, holding his hands up again, symbolically pushing the two women apart.

I was about to add my voice to his, to explain that this was all a misunderstanding brought on by stress and fear and overcrowding, and we really should all have a chat session about it before things *really* got out of hand . . . But then I caught a look at Baucum's face, the set of her shoulders and the angle of her feet, and suddenly I knew it was all true.

My first reaction was simple surprise: "But . . . My god, Baucum, you told me if you wanted to sabotage the ship we'd never know. Something invisible, microscopic." I couldn't think what else to say to her, how to complete the thought.

I suddenly felt very stupid, and her give-me-a-break expression didn't help a bit. "You believed me so easily," she said. "You think I can do those things? Without triggering the Immune system? You think that's easier than simply planting a bug?"

For a moment, no one moved, and it was Baucum herself who broke the spell. "Really, people, do you have any idea of the *scale* of the operation against you? I didn't let them recruit me, exactly, but I didn't turn them in for trying, either. Believe me, you don't want to know who it was that approached me."

"So what were you doing?" Wallich asked gravely.

She shrugged, a miserably failed attempt at nonchalance. "Believe me, I'd like to get out of this as much as you, but I finally realized I couldn't continue failing to act. My conscience betrays my survival instinct."

"That's unfortunate," Sudhir Rapisardi observed dryly. Wallich laughed.

"Renata," I said, "what are you talking about?"

You don't "step" in zero gravity the way you do on a planet, but you can move and pause in small increments, using feather-light touches of hands and feet to regulate the forward momentum.[2] In this way, I stepped out of my room and approached Baucum, cautiously and nonthreateningly.

She looked hunted, though, tensing at the sight of me. "Stay away, Strasheim. You've already made this a lot harder than it needs to be."

"Made what harder? Sabotaging the engine? Did you really *do* that? My god, Baucum, why?"

She shrugged. "I had to. You know, the Temples are not simply insane—they know a lot more about technogenic life than is gener-

---

2. I've since learned that the technical term for this is "chuttering," a word that seems particularly unlikely to enter the popular lexicon.

ally believed. Their laboratories have reproduced the gross characteristics of all the major bloom types, including full-up transient megastructures, using cellular automata. They've even allowed actual spores to germinate in controlled environments. Off the inhabited worlds, obviously, but what better way to study an entity or phenomenon than to reproduce it directly? You want to learn about fires, you start one. I've always wondered why the Immunity shies away from this."

"How about 'abject horror'?" Wallich asked with an uneasy grin. "I'm afraid you've got me genuinely flummoxed, Baucum. You're the saboteur? You're in league with the Temples? The Mycosystem is an 'entity'? I'll tell you, I'm half tempted to send you off to sleep and see if you wake up normal again."

Baucum shook her head, fanning long, unpinned hair out behind her. "Entity may have been a poor choice of words. The Mycosystem is not so much intelligent as genuinely divine, at least in an organizational sense. That may sound crazy, but it's the only interpretation I haven't been able to rule out. I've done the *math*."

"Oh, it sounds crazy all right," Wallich said. He looked around at the rest of us. "So, what are we going to do with *this*?"

I knew exactly what he meant. There was no brig on this tiny crawl space of a ship; even the cabin doors locked only from the inside, and feebly at that. And even if we somehow managed to confine her, Baucum would still be armed and dangerous unless we also relieved her of her zee-spec, which seemed an almost inhumanly cruel sensory deprivation. To leave her literally staring at blank walls, for months? Who wouldn't go crazy, living like that? And even then, she'd be only a few steps from the engine room, a few more from the bridge, and she'd be using the toilet as often as ever . . . Could she sabotage the mission by flushing down the wrong things? Possibly! We'd have to watch her closely, twenty-four hours a day.

Really, the sensible thing to do was to put her out the air-lock. That sounds awful, I know—I was shocked by the thought myself—but the obviousness of it was hard to ignore. Vacuum was all around us, all the time; our most plentiful resource. Never mind what it would do to those soft tissues I'd so recently admired.

"Give her to the Mycosystem if she loves it so much," Davenroy said. Her voice was now largely free of rancor, sounding kind of disbelieving and apologetic, as if the qualifier, "assuming this isn't all some dreadful mistake," should certainly be assumed.

Wincing as if needle-stung, Baucum cast her a cryptic look. "Be careful what you wish for, Davenroy." A sheen of sweat had broken out on Baucum's forehead. Her skin looked gray. "The real problem with exponential growth is that until you hit the knee of the curve, the slope is shallow, practically flat. Unfortunately, this translates into a period of unavoidable suffering. I told myself I'd never use this thing—hard to let them put it in, otherwise!—and then I told myself it wouldn't hurt. Pretty lies."

"Thing?" I asked. "What thing? Are you in pain?"

She winced again sharply, then offered me a grimace of a smile. "I had a stomach ulcer once. It feels about the same."

I was still chuttering forward, was now less than two meters from Baucum's right shoulder. Her face was even grayer and shinier now.

"Why are you in pain?" I asked.

The look she gave me was full of guilt and fear. "Temples labs have put a high priority on storage methods for technogenic spores. It's very difficult research, considering the . . . cost of failure, but recently they've been able to document safe, long-term storage at . . . room temperature. Or even body temperature. I'm sorry."

My skin went instantly clammy. Body temperature? *Body temperature?* "Are you saying you're full of spores?"

"I'm sorry!" she cried suddenly. Tears quivered at the corners of her eyes. "The storage cyst is ruptured; I can't undo that. Oh God, Strasheim, I'm *killing* you. I didn't . . . I wasn't trying to fool you. I'm sorry! If things had been different . . ."

She gasped, then screamed. Alarm klaxons sounded. Warning lights began to flash. Baucum's skin began to change color, and then to shimmer in an oil-on-water sort of way. She screamed again, and this time it sounded all wrong, like she was coughing up a lungful of dandelion fluff, or trying to.

I don't want to tell this part of the story. Tug Jinacio's bloom was bad enough, the stuff of permanent nightmare, but I didn't know him. I'd never touched him.

What—what happened next was that Wallich got around behind her, bracing his hands on the doorway of Tosca Lehne's cabin. "Open the airlock!" he shouted, to no one in particular. But Lehne was diving for the emergency locker, Davenroy and Rapisardi were trapped on the wrong side of danger, and I was right there, not a meter and a half from the controls. I'd like to say I took a moment to ponder the implications of this pending action, but in fact Baucum's skin had lost its smoothness, had developed an unmistakable powdery-vapory aura of rainbow-blossoming mycostructure, and I was more afraid of that than I can tell you, more afraid than if she were burning, or aiming a weapon, or anything.

So I launched myself straight at the airlock, slapped the red button, then flailed out of the way with panicky movements as Wallich, firmly braced, put the soles of his shoes on Baucum's left side, against the as-yet-unmarred surface of her spacer blues, and shoved. She sailed, coughing and struggling, and then she was inside, banging off the walls, and I was moving one button down on the panel. She opened her *eyes*—what was left of them, anyway—and seemed to look right at me as the inner hatch closed, with her on the wrong side of it. My very own hand on the button that would kill her, and it seemed that she looked right at me, and knew.

Do they say death by vacuum is quick? Painless? Do they really? God help me, I pressed the button. And that's all I can bring myself to say.

It took us five minutes to clear away the pockets of visible infection Baucum had left before they cleared *us* away, but that was just the start, just the opening act of a drama that was to last seven hours and more. Wallich and Lehne and Rapisardi brought all their skills and knowledge into play, forcing them down through the arcane interfaces of the ship's Immune system while Davenroy cajoled and exhorted me into helping her wipe all the surfaces down with acids and solvents and trying our best to keep the ship running.

I've kept most of the images, though I never got around to collaging them. I remember Wallich screaming at one point: "It's pierced the *hull*. This God damn thread is growing right through the *hull*." I remember Tosca Lehne hurriedly painting the spot with a welding torch until the bulkhead glowed red, and whether he knew what he was doing or not, the tactic seemed to work; they quickly found other things to be upset about.

Meanwhile, something nasty had been growing in a corner by the shower, something class three and fecund, branchy with crystalline spikes. Resonating spikes, it turned out; the noise began as an air-leak hiss and rose slowly into a tinkling of clear, high tones. Soft fog then enfolded the mess, shaping and pressing on it, giving the sound an almost fricative quality, for a moment, like a human whisper. Short-lived, of course; the so-called "singing blooms," stuff of barroom legend, had never been recorded in action, and this one was no exception. By the time I'd gotten in for a clear look, Davenroy had splattered a witch's tit on the area and frozen it solid.

Its last words were, and I quote, "Whuh, whuh, whuuuh."

We took another twenty minutes to clear away the mess, during which time another fistful of problems made themselves known. We could have used Tug Jinacio that morning, you bet, but then again we could have used Renata Baucum, too. The difference between seven people and six is not all that much, but knock it down to five and the house starts to feel more than a little bit empty. Did I love her? Hell, I'm not even sure I know what the word means. I wished she were still alive, wished she hadn't betrayed us, wished that she really were the woman I'd thought she was. I'd fallen in love with *that* woman, I guess.

Agony, though: *my* hand on the button that killed her. I wished to God it wasn't so, wished to God the memory would leave me, but horror can only pile upon horror for so long before it saturates your ability to repress. Was it self-defense, that premeditated act of murder? Could I at least convince myself of that? Could I at least quiet the trembling of my hands?

The eventual victory for our side was a hollow one, as it turned out; not only had we used up damned near *all* of our emergency supplies, lost part of the food stores, and damaged our recycler in an ill-considered attempt to sterilize it, but by the time we'd finally added all the new pathogens to our response library and gotten the Immune system locked down in a swarm-on-detection mode, it had become clear that we were not the only combatants. There were Gladholder phages still out and about, reproducing and mutating, occasionally hindering our efforts but more often helping, and putting together organized communications networks of their own as their collective mass began to approach that of our own Immune system.

In the old days, there used to be a game called "golf," which involved hitting a little white ball around on ridiculously vast tracts of meadow and forest. Like any sport, it was often fiercely competitive, as remembered by a paper comic drawing pinned to the bridge door of *Beluga*, the dust barge that had Evacuated my family to Ganymede. In the picture, lines of black ink sketch out clouds drifting across an open sky, and beneath them the spectators at a golf tournament, fleeing madly as a gooey-looking and surprisingly animated bloom marches across the landscape toward them, pulling trees and fences down into a mess which, on close inspection, proves to be composed of little cartoon mushrooms with teeth. A lone golfer—perhaps the caricature of some actual person, as the initials J.P. are prominent on his cap—stands at the tee, preparing to strike his ball even as the mycora are lapping at the backs of his heels. He's aware of the danger, judging by the hunch of his shoulders and the manic set of his eyes, but by golly he's going to make the shot.

"Looks like we're colonized," Wallich observed, once the extent of the Gladholder phages' involvement had become clear. "Good luck getting *us* through quarantine." He chuckled a little when he said this, the tone of it clearly indicating he didn't think we'd be getting home at all.

So I surprised him by pantomiming a golfer's swing and recounting J.P.'s final words: "If *this* one doesn't make the green, I quit."

Wallich's laughter seemed to go on forever.

THE SPACES BETWEEN

Mulch World had given way to grander demonstrations, had become one tiny component of a much larger and more intricate
Mulch System, hot and cold and temperate planets swinging
around a bright central star. I'd found ways to trick the cellular automaton rule base into generating phenomena analogous to gravity,
heat radiation, and even a crude sort of solar wind, and together
they produced an intricate dynamic as red TGL spores appeared on
the surface of one world and gradually bloomed and seeded their
way to others. Resolution had increased by a factor of twenty over

earlier versions, and now the conversion of a planetary crust had taken on an eerie fractal beauty, as moiré patterns shuddered and melted one into the other, rock and biomass giving way to bloom giving way to voids and bubbles and short-lived pockets of mulch.

The conversion process was inexorable, but unstable; still, always, the system eventually died. Or locked into perpetual oscillations, yes, but my physical laws now included semirandom "quantum" perturbations that tended to disrupt these loops, casting them back into chaos. But what perturbation could reverse entropy on so grand a scale? None, of course. Mulch System was durable only in a state of extinction.

I'd covered this failure by simply slowing down the clock speed. Now the patterns could march on for hours or even days before collapsing, and by interrupting and restarting the sims while they were still healthy, I could create the illusion of stable, perpetual chaos. Once I'd figured out I could "improve" the experiment without actually tracking down and fixing its congenital flaws, I decided to go whole hog: increase magnification by two orders and move the whole operation into a virtual cavern a hundred times larger than Philusburg. Worlds the size of houses, boiling with endless varieties of contagion and countercontagion ... It wasn't exactly beautiful, but its violence was grand, sweeping, and entirely virtual.

So I moved in.

Great idea, right? We were three days out from Mars, still five away from Earth, when they sent someone in to see me. Oh, I'd been doing my job and everything, filling that chair on the bridge for fourteen hours of every twenty-four, keeping a window open on the real world, but it didn't take a genius to figure out where my attention was focused, and unfortunately I was surrounded by *four* geniuses. I'd been spending the off-duty hours alone in my cabin, and it was here that Jenna Davenroy came to visit, knocking and knocking on the door until finally I was forced to open it.

"Yes?" I asked the tiny figure she presented in the tiny my-eye window I'd opened.

"I'm slaving my zee-spec to yours," she said by way of greeting. "If you'd be so kind as to flash me a copy of the sim you're inhabiting . . ."

I thought about this for a while.

"Strasheim," she said, "it's really a lot easier if you just let me in. The alternative is confiscation of your zee. Do you want that?'"

Sighing, I opened and worked the appropriate menus. Cabin-wall camera dots recorded her image, flashing color and spatial data to processors in my zee. A shadow figure appeared before me in Mulch System Cavern, rezzed in with fractal detail, and finally faded from black to color. Jenna Davenroy had entered the sim.

It was several seconds before she spoke. Her initial reaction, looking around, was one of pure startlement, fading slowly into distaste, and then finally a sort of slow, grudging admiration.

"You made all this?" she asked.

I nodded, shrugged.

"Cellular automata?"

"Yes." The rusty, disused sound of my voice surprised me a little.

She looked around some more, drifting out under one of the roiling, fluid, tower-sprouting planets to admire it from directly below. The real Davenroy probably hadn't moved, or hadn't moved much, but here in VR space she could do as she pleased, unbounded by trivialities like inertia unless she willed it. She'd stopped, as they say, on a dime.

"You have an eye for detail," she said, looking up at the planet's south polar cap. "Mountains jutting through the ice, and turbulence in the atmosphere around them. Is this Earth?"

"Mulch World," I said.

The lines in her face deepened for a moment. "Oh. I see. We've . . . been a bit worried about you, Strasheim. I confess, I thought you were just sort of whacking off in here. I didn't realize you were working. System usage should have been a clue, I guess; you're slopping a *lot* of computation off into the ship's data system."

"I wouldn't call it work."

She eyed me. "You do yourself an injustice, John. This is really quite impressive."

"It doesn't function correctly," I said, "and anyway the hard parts were finished weeks ago. I'm just hiding in here. You were right."

"Would you like to talk about it?" She moved closer, drifting like a ghost. But not too much closer.

I shrugged, held out the virtual paper telegram I'd created to represent the mail message the sanitarium had sent. Davenroy drifted closer, accepted it, examined it.

Dear John Strasheim:
This is to inform you regretfully of the death of your mother Lorena Ann Strasheim at 0218 on the third of December. No suffering on her part is indicated. Concomitant with last will and testament stipulations, remains have been laddered down at South Reactor Five. Our sympathies are with you at this difficult time.

"Oh," Davenroy said, reading the thing. "Oh, my goodness, I had no idea."

I smiled wanly. "They used her to light the city. It's a pretty thought, in a way, but also more than a little bit horrible. She's cut right out of the cycle of life. She's a lump of iron now. Waste metal."

Davenroy sounded shocked. "This must have happened right after the battle. Strasheim, I'm so sorry!"

"It's been a big month for death," I said, shrugging.

She composed herself, handed the massless, textureless paper back to me. "You should have said something, dear, you really should. I mean, my goodness, you came to talk to me after Jinacio died. Do you realize how important a gesture that was? The pain of loss is at its most unbearable when we think it's gone unnoticed."

I turned to look at her. "You never knew my mother, *dear*, and you never liked Renata Baucum. You don't know a thing about what I've lost. I barely know it myself."

With that, I skidded back, stopped, pretended to busy myself with an examination of Mulch World's moon in its slow, stately orbit.

"We can spare your full attention for the moment," Davenroy said after a while. "Under the circumstances, I think the duty roster can be adjusted. But keep the larger circumstance in mind, will you? Even under the best conditions, we couldn't afford to run *three* crew members short for the Earth flyby."

I turned to look at her, paused, nodded slowly. "I do understand that. Yes."

"Have you shed tears, Strasheim?"

I choked back an embarrassed laugh. "Swollen eyelids don't show up well in VR, I guess. At times I've done little else. It's my *mother* we're talking about."

"And your lover."

I winced. "I, uh, don't know. About that."

"No?"

"I don't think I knew her. I'm actually sure that I didn't. What she's done is . . . incomprehensible."

Davenroy grunted. "Yes, it is that. Who can say what was in her mind? Suicide takes a great deal of conviction, of course; murder perhaps even more. She must have thought she was protecting something important."

At this, we both looked around at Mulch System, at the infected planets and the viscid, fingery haze just barely visible in the spaces between them. Important, yeah.

After that, neither of us spoke for about a minute. It was, in a strange way, the most soothing and intimate part of our conversation that day. I treasure it still, one of those rare reminders that the people around us really can be caring and kind, if you let them. "Soul markers," I call these moments.

"I . . . didn't mean to start an argument," I said finally. "It isn't . . . easy to talk. I'll be fine, I'm sure, but right now the whole idea just has me confused. Death? What the hell is that? What address do I mail to?"

"I understand perfectly," Davenroy replied, her tone lightly admonishing. I took the hint: who in the Immunity was a stranger to loss? The last ten years had been quiet, busy, reasonably safe, and we'd all worked hard to project that veneer of normalcy, that feeling that there was nothing weird about living as we did, where we did. It wasn't hard; the hysterical types had died out early, leaving behind only those who could function, only those who could survive the trip, hollow out the caves . . . But the hurt was still there, always there. You don't lose a world without hurt.

I tried to think of a suitable reply, but Davenroy worked some menus and winked out of view before I could frame one. I heard my cabin door closing, the sound surprisingly near and immediate. I and my grief were dismissed.

Overhead, Mulch World's moon passed into eclipse, the meters-wide body of the planet blocking out the sun's yellow light.

Almost as suddenly, the moon's ruddy mycoric glow gave way to lifeless green, as if a flame had guttered and gone out.

Self-Portrait:
Artist on a Bad Day

Black, fade to shot of *Mulch System* whirling in the distance, against a huge but indistinct background of cavern stone, range indeterminate. Cue music: *Thus Spake Zarathustra*, fade, overlay with Zellinger compose-on-demand fractal *Null Progress*. The effect is jarring, indicative of malfunction.

Zoom in on the *Artist*, sitting cross-legged in empty space, surrounded by palm-sized VR windows apparently fixed with respect to his sagittal axis. His hair unkempt and maybe a bit too long, at odds with the blue spacer uniform he wears. On the shoulder, prominent, one service patch: PASTEUR, MYCOSYSTEM MISSION ONE. Embroidered beneath the words, a stylized image of the ship itself.

Turn, pan until we are behind the *Artist*, then *zoom* to look over his shoulder. Close-up on the *windows*. Several of these display only text, green on black in one of the boxy 24-pin nostalgia fonts, of which a close examination reveals sorted lists of *cellular automaton rules* which flicker one by one, with visible effects mirrored in the behavior of *Mulch System* in the distance and in fragmentary high-magnification images on the other windows. The *Artist's* fingers intrude, manipulating symbols, popping text lines out and moving them to other places. These movements, while indicative of frustration, are nonetheless slow and deliberate.

Cut to an image of the *Artist's* face, tired and annoyed with his creation, and with an underlying sadness that seems unrelated, and then we *pull back rapidly* to observe him from greater distance.

Surrounded by his cloud of flat, rectangular, vanishingly thin windows, he seems to be following a *complex trajectory* through Mulch System. Our view of him holds constant as sun and planets whirl about. Within thirty seconds the path has begun to repeat, and we see it for what it is: a figure eight with the sun at one focus and empty space at the other, aphelion just outside the orbit of the *fourth planet*, now aswirl with the reds and yellows of infection.

Cut to the *Artist's* face, expression unchanged.

Cut to the *windows*, two of which now display the images of human faces. Women: one elderly and one in middle-adulthood. Both smiling, but there is a sterile quality to the images, and presently they both fade to two dimensions, and then to black and white, and then to pure black. We *pull back slightly* to reveal additional windows, giving up their old images to present more faces. Men and women this time, and children, and then *aerial views* of old cities, continents, and finally the planet Earth itself. One by one, the images flatten and fade. The *Artist's* fingers intrude, frantically this time, as if to interrupt the disappearing process, but *no visible effect* is produced.

Cut to the *Artist's* face, now showing *traces of anger*.

Cut to *Mulch System*, seen from a great distance. The central star is the color of ice backlit with yellow.

Cut to the *windows*, still black. In the center of each, a tiny image resolves: the *Protestant cross*, a three-dimensional projection with the color and texture of wood. No human image is crucified there.

Cut to the *Artist's* face. The *anger has deepened*, and there is now skepticism in the expression as well, of the give-me-a-break variety. He finds the image insulting, a trivilization.

Cut to a *cartoon image*, two-dimensional and brightly colored in the style of twentieth-century animators: a flowing-haired, white-robed *caricature of God*, his staff resting on crossed knees, manipulates lines of text in a *flat VR window*, then checks an *image of Earth* in another window, and nods with satisfaction.

Artist's face: partly amused, partly accusatory, mostly just tired and sad. "There is no "up" in this weightless place, but he looks to the solar north, perpendicular to the orbits of the planets. He *holds up his hands and shrugs expectantly*, as if to say, Well, does omnipotence coupled with a failure to intervene imply disinterest, or active malice?

Clearly, the *Artist* holds some complex and unresolved feelings. Look angle enables us to see, for the first time, a *black armband* around his left bicep. Red glare *reflects from his skin* as a contaminated planet flashes by and we *pull back rapidly* to reveal a Mulch System flickering out predictable patterns, red against green against brown. The compelling fractal intricacy of it is gone, replaced with simple iteration as *waves of color* circle the planets over and over, the spaces between them empty.

The music *jars discordantly*.

Cartoon image: God, angered, breaking the staff across his knee.

Artist, sitting cross-legged in empty space: his expression now resigned, weary, stopping just short of bitterness. Mulch System is not working, real life is not working, and God is unavailable for comment. The windows are *scattered flat beneath the Artist*, as if on a solid floor. All fifteen on them show nothing but static.

Pull back slowly. The music ends and we . . .

Fade to black.

Honor thy Mother

A little piece of Baucum seemed to have slipped through my skin to infect me; upon emergence from my VR hibernation, not only did I take over the simplest of her bridge functions, such as monitoring the top-level Immune system alarms, but I pestered Wallich with a series of detailed questions about the maximum resolving power of the camera dots embedded in *Louis Pasteur*'s hull.

"What's this about?" he finally asked me, impatient because he'd taken over several Baucum-tasks as well, in addition to his already formidable load.

I shrugged, uncertain how to phrase my reply. I tried: "The Earth flyby is a once-in-a-lifetime opportunity to observe large-scale TGL structures in a planetary environment, and possibly signs of human habitation as well."

"And you want a closer look?"

"Absolutely. Don't you?"

My use of the Immuno-jargon and mind-set must at least have been adequate, because Wallich sighed and took a minute out to help me put together a sensor schedule. Really, it was a lot like building cellular automaton rules, except that the final result would be real, nonimaginary data from a system that actually worked, that actually kept itself perpetually out of the twin equilibria of repetition and death. That had done so for the last twenty years, anyway.

Tosca Lehne was still asleep in his cabin, and needed to be fresh for the challenges ahead, but Earth was already the size of my thumbnail in a 4X view. An hour before, it had been the size of my pinkie nail in 10X, and since that time the hull had logged a hundred thousand new spores, and seven replication events. Two of these occurred in the same square millimeter of hull and were therefore cause for suspicion and concern, but Wallich assured me the matter could wait for Lehne's attention when he came in.

Meanwhile, Wallich himself was struggling to plot the courses of our five pursuing vessels and their attendant swarm. We really were going to press ahead with the probe deployment, and they really were going to intervene with lethal force, and so predicting where they would be and then arranging to be somewhere else ourselves was a top priority. They hadn't gained on us appreciably since Mars, hadn't seemed even to try all that hard, but of course our probes could only stand so much impact force, so much atmospheric heating, and thus we were obligated to shed about twenty percent of our speed in the next couple of hours, if our deployment was going to be successful. This would give the Temples' ships a fine window in which to pounce. Well, not pounce, really, so much as fail to slow down when we did. They'd close on our vessel with ever-greater relative velocity, taking advantage of our distraction, screaming in from behind with their motors off, no telltale iron-hydrogen plumes to give them away . . .

"But space is big," Wallich said, not dismissing the threat but not surrendering to it, either. "Even close to the planet, even inside the orbit of the moon, there's plenty of room to get lost in. To hit us they need pinpoint precision; to escape we only need a millimeter. Less than that, really, and there are a *lot* of millimeters out there."

"They're not shooting," I pointed out, "they're *spraying*. You've said yourself, it doesn't take much to damage the t-balance."

He grinned. "I said that?"

"Uh-huh."

"Well, hell, who listens to me?"

We all did, actually, but I let the point ride. For once Wallich's good humor seemed genuine, infectious, and I was inclined to follow along.

Rapisardi, alas, did not seem to share the feeling. "We should simply escape," he said, a disembodied voice from the engine room.

"Should we?" Wallich mused, unfazed. "All right, let's do that. But let's put some detectors down while we're at it, right?"

"You're enjoying this," Rapisardi accused.

Wallich didn't deny it. "I have more to do, freund. Idle hands do the devil's work, which in this case means undermining morale. Have you checked the plasma focus capacitance like I asked?"

"It's eight-twenty mF. You're not going to get any sort of killing stroke out of that unless the enemy is close enough to spit on."

"Well, hope springs eternal. You can adjust the focal radius manually now, yes?"

"Yes, but . . ."

It went on like that for a while. Evidently there had been some significant customization of *Pasteur's* housekeeping and control software. Nothing that could make a warship of her, of course, but it sounded as though some routine functions had been subverted to distinctly non-peaceful use. We were going, for example, to seed the path behind us with Rapisardi's modified probes, now turned to service as ladderdown space mines. I gathered this wasn't expected to help, as the Temples' ships could easily ping the space ahead of them and steer appropriately, but the psychological value, to us and to them, would be considerable: look here, *Pasteur* is no helpless target!

There were other surprises awaiting our enemies as well, engine mods and Immune system mods and even a change to the running and landing lights. I wanted to ask more about these, both for posterity's sake and for my own curiosity, but actually I was starting to have my hands full with allocation. Davenroy's reactor control sims ate a more or less steady diet of time and energy, data and memory, but Wallich and Rapisardi were all over the place, and the computer, with no insight or understanding of its own, was having a hard time sifting priorities. I was intervening now several times a minute, throwing this or that item to the bottom of the queue, or bumping up job requests that kept getting postponed.

In a way, too, I was contributing to the morass, because every time I let my attention wander over to the bioanalysis functions I'd find myself asking questions, the answering of which threw still more demands on the allocation system at the very times I wasn't there monitoring it. But I could hardly give the practice up; presently, another replication event ticked over in that same tiny square of a hull, and then yet another.

I captured the details of the events as best I could, and thought hard about waking Lehne up no matter what Wallich said. I didn't like this one bit. But then again, a glance at the chronometer showed I had only a couple of minutes to wait before the "natural" start of his shift. I glanced at Wallich, who was deeply engrossed in disagreeing with Rapisardi about something-or-other, and decided to hold my peace.

Time and resource constraints certainly didn't warrant our taking any gratuitous science measurements, but I did it anyway, somehow fitting it in with all the rest. Not that I really knew what I was doing, but it sure seemed like *somebody* ought to be handling this, and I, more than anyone else at least, could be spared for the effort. Maybe posterity would be grateful. Maybe there'd be a story or two in it for me. Or maybe it was a flagrant waste of time, but at least the ghost of Baucum would be silent. Murderess or no, she *really* would have wanted this data, and the pressure of that want seemed to compel me, somehow, to action.

I looked "up," though, and noticed Lehne settling into his station, so I suspended what I was doing and flashed some key pointers to his board.

"Hi," I said. "There's a hot spot on the hull you need to have a look at. Five replications so far."

"Five?" He blanched. "Why didn't you wake me?"

"I was about to."

"Hmm."

He fell into the task with the sort of bone-deep dedication only mortal danger can bring. We'd all adopted a sort of business-as-usual façade where blooms were concerned, to save energy if for no other reason—you simply can't maintain a state of panic indefinitely. But the danger was real, and under other circumstances would certainly have been kick-and-scream material.

Lehne requested additional data, and I provided it. The engines,

I noted, had come on at some point without my being aware of it, and behind me I heard Wallich and Rapisardi talking about going to "DP-1" attitude. Damn, but the time was racing! I glanced up at an exterior window, saw the crescent Earth swollen now to very nearly the size of a golf ball. Again, not any Earth *I* remembered, but a yellow-pink tumble of technogenic excess, its atmosphere and surface contours blurring out into space with dust-bunny vagueness. No sheen of ocean, no ripply jacket of continental rock, no sign at all, really, of planet-smooth surfaces. Except at the polar caps, which looked much as I supposed they always had, and as out of place on that infected globe as steaming jungles would be on the surface of Ganymede. Still, the sight of them cheered me, reassured me that even this far down, the Mycosystem's rule was not absolute. Not yet, anyway.

I only got a moment to look, because Lehne's work dumped an additional burden on the already strained allocation system, which threatened an outright collapse if I didn't wade in with some authoritative instructions. But dutifully, thinking of Momma's last-ever request, I waved at her homeworld just the same. Had she been younger and more fit, would *she* have volunteered for this expedition? I found it difficult to imagine otherwise. So if there were such things as ghosts, perhaps hers was here as well, silently watching the Earth go by. Or bickering with the ghost of Baucum, maybe, or feeding rubber to the ghosts of my father's dear departed parrots.

My moment of looking ended. After that, the normal rules of chronology were suspended for a while as we dug deeper and deeper into our instruments and jobs, communicating only as needed for that purpose. Then at some point the flow of time resumed, jarringly. *Louis Pasteur* shuddered, and I looked up sharply, frightened for a moment before I recognized the sound and feel of payload release. Rapisardi had opened up tubes five and six, launching the mines. Or were they live detectors, destined for the planet's surface? No, surely it was still too early for that. But we had only seven tubes left to fire, four of which were indispensably vital to our mission; even there, at ten probes per tube and one tube per planetary and lunar pole, we'd be spreading our resources desperately thin.

Another of Baucum's warning systems came alive.

"We're being pinged," I said.

"Got it," Wallich agreed.

I had a window open on our "best guess" courses for the enemy ships, whose positions changed suddenly as automated processes digested the radar data.

The ping came again, a red warning light on my board, a shrinking, kidney-shaped outline on the threat display. Shrinking again as the probe let out another radar yelp, and then contracting to a single diffuse dot as the readings changed, optical sensors picking up glints of sunlight on a target now dozens of times larger and less dense.

The threat of bloom brought home again, made clear, made current in minds that had worked hard at forgetting it. *Look where I am, Momma! Look where the hell I am!*

"I need to purge the hull," Lehne warned.

Wallich grunted without looking up. "HF sweat?"

"Don't think so, we're nearly out. Better be a hydroxide wash, very alkaline, minimum exposure time."

"You sure that's wise?"

"No. All we've got on hand, though . . ."

So they went ahead and did it, breaking the process down into four or five hardware calls and dumping them into the job queue at maximum priority. It was among the worst things they might possibly have done. I raised my voice in protest . . . too late. The system, finally overloaded beyond its ability to cope, coughed up an error

message and seized. A buzzer sounded, and red warning lights—
physical diodes on the surfaces of every control panel—came on.

"System crash!" I shouted. "Damn it!"

"Restart!" Wallich snapped at me.

No, I wanted to say, really? Is that what we do when the
computer seizes? But what I actually said was, "Aye, sir, I'm on it."

On a spaceship of any sort, cycling power on the central processor is a big deal. On a spaceship of *our* sort, in the middle of a battle
in the middle of a planetary flyby in the middle of the God damn
Mycosystem, it's a calamity begging to happen. Life support,
propulsion, guidance and nav . . . everything feeds through the information system. Manual backups are available, sure, but to fall
back on them you have to trust human minds and senses to accomplish feats they simply aren't equipped for. It's an unspoken rule, a
simple fact of life: without the processor you're dead.

I reached for the Main Power switch high on the allocation
board, flipped up its clear plastic shield, and pressed it. There was a
confirmation switch in an even less accessible location, up under the
bottom of the panel, but I found and depressed it by feel, grateful
suddenly for all the hours of disassembly and reassembly Wallich
had forced on me in recent weeks. It came to me that I knew, literally, the position not only of every control, but of every screw and
wire and circuit block inside the thing.

The lights went out. Absolute silence is as alien aboard a ship as
freezing vacuum is in a cavern city. Absolute darkness, too, but that
was mitigated by the zee-spec; exterior windows vanished instantly,
along with the virtual controls and indicators that comprised most
of the bridge's working surfaces, the various status windows and in-
terlinks, and what have you. The purely internal stuff, though, the
time and date stamp and direction indicators and personal windows
(e.g., the tiny Mulch System sim, running solo, isolated from the

ship's computer and still iterating away slowly in a corner of my vision) remained, sparing us the awful sense of having been struck blind.

"Sweet God of Mercy!" Sudhir Rapisardi's voice exclaimed nonetheless. Others were echoing the sentiment, and turning on their zee-specs' power-hungry work lamps, as I reached for the switches in reverse order to bring the power back on. There was no fumbling, no uncertainty. Practice makes perfect.

You never notice that background hum and whine of electrical conduits until the moment it stops, or the moment it starts back up. Relief washed over me with that sound, and then as the air blowers kicked back on I permitted myself the luxury of being afraid. Of *noticing* how afraid I was, I should say. The lights came on grudgingly, first a warm glow here and there and then washes of color as circuits closed and capacitors charged up. A small window opened in the exact center of the allocation board, short and wide and full of text:

```
SYSTM RSTRT: SCANNING FUNCTION SPACE
SYSTM RSTRT: LOADING DSCRPTOR STACK
SYSTM START: ALLOCTNG FUNCTION SPACE
OPR. CMPLTE: 00:02:26.81
```

"Report," Wallich demanded quietly.

"Two and a half minutes to system restore," I answered.

He paused for a moment, fitting appropriate words around his next question: "How . . . did this happen to us?"

"Task loading," I said simply. "The allocation system juggles a hundred jobs just sitting there, and we kept throwing more crap at it. Processing capacity is not infinite, and I don't think the ship was really designed to do most of the stuff we're asking of it right now."

He paused again, and then said, "This can't happen again. I mean it. Preventive measures?"

Half the lights still hadn't come on, the control panels were still dead, and in the strange lighting I took several seconds to realize he was still looking at me. The fact that he was behind me and upside down didn't help my recognition any.

I considered the question for a moment. Loss of the information system had, I think, hurled us into a kind of freezing panic, a sense that our jobs were going undone while dangers piled up outside the hull, and if we didn't *do something right now* we'd . . . what? Panic's most dangerous seduction is its cool mimicry of logic, its quiet insistence on sudden, inappropriate action. But there are other forces at work in a human mind, in a *trained* mind, and there come points in your life when you're faced with an unfamiliar task, an unfamiliar decision, and you realize you're it, you're on the hook, you're the one and only person in a position to set things right.

Flash of childhood memory: a game of Capture the Flag, the enemy pinned down by laser fire, hit sensors screaming back there among the trees, the gym teacher turning to me in exasperation. "Get the *flag*, John." The implication clear in his voice: you're good enough, you're fast enough, you're bloody well *it*, so what's the holdup? Go, go!

I went.

"Captain," I said, "you can't keep shunting your trajectory calculations onto shipboard processors. That goes for everyone—if you can solve a problem locally, do it. A zee-spec isn't *that* slow, and it hasn't got a whole ship to run in its spare time. Push-pull windows are fine, but be careful that what you're pushing is static data and not incomplete calculation blocks. Especially blocks with timers on them. Also—please!—don't force the priority flag on your requests. All that does is tell the ship that everything is more important than everything else, which is meaningless. Let the priority queue do its job, and let me do mine."

Shockingly, Wallich laughed. "Well said, berichter. Anything else?"

"Well, not really, except to use common sense. Your *brain* is for thinking, and your zee is for calculating. The ship is just an I/O device."

Wallich laughed again, longer and harder this time. And then he stopped.

"Time to full function?"

"Eighty seconds."

"Well. Damn. It's hard just to sit here, eh?"

Nobody commented. It was the understatement of the week.

"Status?"

"Forty seconds."

"Lehne, that alkaline sweat is your top priority. Davenroy, I want reaction control thrusters just as soon as possible. We're going to Deploy One attitude in a few minutes and any schedule slip means we slow down even more. Nobody wants that, right? Strasheim: status."

"Twenty seconds, sir, and this is exactly what I'm talking about. You've *got* a timer hanging right in front of your face. Also, I think we should stagger our initial jobs on five-second intervals to give the system a chance to adjust. We could go bow-to-stern, so Lehne's request goes in first."

"Okay," Wallich said with manic amusement, "you heard the man. Start your clock when he says go."

"Go."

The control panels came back to life. There were grunts and sighs of relief, the sounds of people opening windows and getting back to work, hitting the allocation system one by one, but not as hard as before. Not quite. The first coherent thing I heard was Lehne's voice cursing softly, and then the words: "Stands to reason we'd encounter novel species down here. Close to the sun, close to the planet. Stands to reason we'd not be prepared for every possible thing."

"What?" Wallich asked, his voice still tight and giddy. "Spores eating through the hull?"

"Yes, sir," Lehne replied, "I'm afraid they are."

Slowly, he forgot to say. Initial panic gave way to a much slower, deeper sense of dread as the unknown mycorum, still restricted to a tiny patch of hull, gradually blunted the t-balance defenses there, stripping them away uncertainly, atom by atom, to feed its own bottomless appetite. Replication events were soon too frequent to draw comment. They had become a fact of life, of which, according to Lehne's calculations, we had about six days left. That's painfully slow for a bloom, I'll agree, but painfully quick for a sentence of death. Once we lost hull integrity, we'd be patching holes and fighting blooms and trying to hold the ship's systems together for another few precious moments, and it didn't really matter what got us first, because something surely would.

The good news was that Lehne was able to push the deadline back a day and a half by sweating out the last of our hydrofluoric acid. So we had a whole *week* to live, if nothing else went wrong. Which was about as likely as ever.

Still hard on our tail, the enemy ships closed alarmingly as we fired our last deceleration burn. They seemed to have misjudged, though—the closure was not quite fast enough to bring them to us before deployment time. Had they misjudged our maximum deployment speed? Presumed we'd be following the same profile we had at Mars? If so, the error was a critical one; they were still lagging by thousands of kilometers as we spun and danced, shooting payload tubes seven and eight off at Earth's north pole, nine and ten at its south, and then two more at the poles of Luna.

Leaving only the final tube: lucky thirteen. If we fired that, we'd be left with no more bombs to shoot, no more mines to lay. From there on, we'd be relying on the *really* improvised weapons. In a way, the notion was almost charming.

We passed right between Earth and Luna, slashing through cobwebby filaments of mycostructure that seemed almost to connect the two bodies. As they passed into full sunlight, showing off their round faces to us, it was hard not to stare, mesmerized, looking for some familiar detail. We'd all been here only two decades before. Could whole worlds be erased in twenty years? Apparently so. The moon was like a yellow-white sea sponge, its deficient chemistry supporting only silicate lebenforms and yet still riotously alive, shot through with fibers and voids, recursive with fractal structures that hurt to look at, punishing the eye that lingered too long. The "radar surface" of the planet, Wallich said, was some eight hundred kilometers higher than the virgin regolith had been, back in our moon-base days. That's a lot of expansion for a body that small. "The moon," he said, "has become a cheese puff. Not only would it float in water, it would *dissolve*."

"Latent organophilic spores," Lehne countered, "would *consume* the water. Not float in it. Not dissolve."

Wallich waved a dismissive hand. "Whatever. It's a puff."

As for the Earth itself, it resembled nothing so much as the back of some monstrous caterpillar. Horned, fuzzy, its surface undulating with a speed that, while not directly apparent to the eye, brought visible changes between one hurried glance and the next. I could see pockets of atmosphere clinging all around, but in places the landscape shot right out of it, narrow translucent peaks jutting far out into space. Peaks? Tentacles, maybe—they too waved back and forth in sluggish progression.

Tasting the vacuum of space, the sizzle of solar wind, the tenuous mycostructure drifting all around? Reaching for us, feeling for us? Well, maybe. My instrument readings showed a spreading cone of disaster in *Louis Pasteur*'s wake, shattered mycofilaments spilling apart into angry clouds, but if the planet itself was aware of our passage, it gave little sign.

Not so the enemy ships; they pinged and pinged at us, closing the gap but seeming frantic, enraged. Our lead, slender as it was, had proved sufficient to foil their primary mission of keeping us away from here, keeping us from deploying our little spies. Even now, the detectors were probably striking the surface of Luna, screaming down through the atmosphere of Mother Earth. Some would no doubt shatter or burn—we were right at the maximum deployment speed—but the devices, Rapisardi insisted, were tough. They had to be.

Funny how the rush of completing our mission had whizzed right by me. We were *done*. We were free to leave, to fire up the engines and blast straight for home. Or try, anyway.

The Temples' ships, alas, had other ideas. It seemed they had a backup plan, a secondary mission to punish us for our supposed crime. They hadn't got close enough yet to spray, or shoot, or whatever the hell it was they were going to do, but sooner or later we would *have* to change course, and then . . .

"At this point," Wallich said with admirable reserve, "our basic options are to stop and fight, which seems sort of pointless, or to turn back up and run for home, which seems, well, overly optimistic for a number of reasons. We're not licked yet, though; the other option is to turn *down* and head for the sun. The lower border of the Mycosystem is a hell of a lot closer than the upper one right now."

"Won't we melt?" I asked, horrified.

He shrugged. "Down between the orbits of Venus and Mercury, that's where TGL starts to fry. It's hot down there, yeah, but we should be able to cook all the crap off us before the ship actually starts to come apart."

A window opened up, showing Davenroy's face. "What about radiation?"

"A bigger threat," Wallich admitted. His hands fluttered, jabbing and pointing. "We're close to solar minimum right now, but if we pick up a mag storm then yeah, it's all over. Cosmic ray shielding is not going to hold up against a proton flare at that range."

"We don't get these lebenforms off the hull, it's all academic," Lehne said. "I say we go. Sterilize. *Then* figure out what to do next."

"We may not have enough fuel to return home," Davenroy pointed out. She did some fidgeting and pointing of her own. "Well, maybe enough to reach the Gladholds. It'll be close."

"Will the Temples' ships follow us down?" Rapisardi asked. He was still a disembodied voice, which for some reason I found strikingly annoying at that moment.

"Only one way to find out," Wallich said, grinning and chuckling in that way of his. "Are we all on board for this? Are we 'go'?"

"Affirmative," Lehne said without hesitation.

Rapisardi's affirmation followed close behind, and then, more reluctantly, Davenroy's. Wallich turned to me. "Well, berichter, what do you say? We'll be closer to the sun than anyone's ever gone before. Closer even than those poor bastards on Venus. Hell of a story, that."

I snorted, trying to be amused. "We've already got a hell of a story, Darren. I was sort of hoping to take it home now and show it off."

He reached a hand up and nudged the back of my seat's headrest. "Come on, let's go to the sun. It'll be fun."

Fun? Well, maybe it would at that. More fun than certain death, anyway.

"What the hell," I said.

And down we went.

The Temples' zealots, only momentarily thrown off by the change of trajectory, followed us in. Of course.

Heart of Brightness

So where does all this leave us? Which of the available futures will we choose for ourselves? To sail away on bright starship flames, leaving our birthplace to rot in peace? To carry the fight downward, extending the Immunity's reach into the Gladhold and beyond? Or will we continue to cower here under the ice, waiting patiently for the other shoe to drop?

This much we know; that it isn't simply our lives at stake, but the very biology that supports them.

from *Innensburg and the Fear of Failure*
© 2101 by John Strasheim

Mulch System swept around me, taking advantage of reduced demands on the information system, running now at maximum speed, its movements blurring into irregular spasms like the innards of some enormous hyperventilating animal. Running unheeded—every couple of minutes it would freeze or die out or lock into an infinite loop, and I would glance up and, with a manual flourish, cast a dozen or a hundred or a million new spores into the fray, bringing it temporarily back to life. Other than that, though, I pretty well ignored it. I was reading my mail.

Slow data rates or no, I'd been inattentive this past week, and the messages had really begun to pile up. Many seemed happily unaware of our difficulties, e.g.:

> *Dear Strasheim, please send pictures of the Earth you know we all miss it very much. I will look forward to meeting you when you return to the Immunity, I hope you will agree to visit Callisto we don't all live in Ganymede you know . . .*

Others seemed merely to have got delayed, looping for God knows how long in some glitchy network before escaping to a transmission queue:

> *J.S.: Good luck entering Mycosystem. Please inform crew our thoughts go with. History will mark your courage this day! Live people in Mycosystem? Surely some error in Gladholder science. Soon you will know, though, yes?*

Well, sadly, no. Even with all the computer trouble, I *had* managed to capture some decent images and science readings during the flyby, but *Louis Pasteur*'s camera dots simply didn't have the resolution to pick up surface features. Nothing smaller than a good-sized city, anyway, and if there were any of those about, my pictures gave no evidence. Just these ropy, snaky, cloud-diffuse images of a complexity that brought a woozy, stood-too-quickly feeling to my head. Images in the ultraviolet were the worst.

Were there people down there among those headache whorls? Had they seen us go by, a brightish star across the nightscape, with lesser lights swarming after it in pursuit? Had they seen the meteor trails of our detectors raining down on the polar caps? The Gladholder findings were still difficult to accept, equally difficult to refute. It seemed natural enough that, yeah, we should somehow be able to gauge the truth of the matter down here, but I guessed there was a limit to what five beleaguered people in a failing boat could accomplish. Maybe next time, freund.

Still other messages were profoundly clueless, perhaps written by children (although years of experience had taught me to be wary of that assumption), and some seemed to have been addressed to another reality altogether. Charitably, they might somehow have been mangled in transit. A few messages, though, seemed to target my own thoughts with precision:

Pasteur: Temples deny foreknowledge, blame splinter group for attacking ships. So your assessment of enemy identity appears largely correct. Trying to negotiate, they say, but more blooms, turmoil here. Details unimportant—mission accomplished. Good luck inner system. Do not bring back souvenir!

Pasteur: Spacecom advises, consider trajectory carefully viz. fuel. Duh. Stay well. Have tried thermal cycling to foil infection? Immunity recommends as treatment last resort.

Pasteur: Housekeeping tip, increase atmospheric CO_2 & H_2O to slow metabolism, reduce food intake. Plan now, avert shortage;

mission duration not known. Remember to note what it's like down there; do not forget you are pioneers.

We'd been losing the originator info on all the messages lately, so it was hard to say who was sending these. I might almost have suspected Vaclav Lottick, the messages were so clueful and direct, but he'd always addressed his queries and orders and complaints to Wallich. I suspected I'd stopped existing for him the moment I shook his hand in the shipyards at Galileo. Something in the clipped, precise style of the messages reminded me of fellow berichter Warren Ancell, but he and I had never really gotten along. Had we?

I resolved to investigate the matter if I ever returned home. Somebody was definitely owed a night on the town, and overtime be damned. I would have liked to reply, even just a couple of bytes of feedback for that welcome voice, and for the folks back home who'd made us a part of their lives, but the rest of the crew had ganged up to force my agreement in switching the transmitters off.

"Loss of countermeasure reserves," Lehne had said. "Why risk making things worse? We can still heat the hull, okay, fine, but on the down cycle, residual warmth just accelerates growth. Marginal net gain, and we risk attention from active mycostructures. Tickle the spores with radio waves, that's not going to help one bit."

"Anyway," Wallich added, "why give the Temples a fix on our position? For once we've got the advantage: we see the sunlight reflecting off them, brighter every day, while they're looking almost straight down the corona to see us. We want to stay lost in the glare if we can help it."

And Rapisardi: "I'd have to cut your data ration anyway, due to the increase in range."

"Plus it drains the battery," Davenroy had concluded. And that was that.

Anyway, it seemed there wasn't that much mail after all. Scanning plaintext was a lot faster than wading through audiovisual recordings, that was for sure. Suddenly bored, I waved the mail window closed, and then exited from Mulch System, back into my cabin. Well, of course, I'd been in the cabin all along. The sensation of having traveled somehow was difficult to shake, though; the ideator's VR can be a very real place if you let it, which is probably why we Munies avoid it so assiduously.

Not long before that day, the cabins had been guarded territory, closed doors marking off the boundaries of a largely illusory privacy. Since the Earth flyby, though, some strange, unspoken consensus had been reached that the doors would mostly remain open. We were, in all probability, going to die together in the next few days, and against the terrible intimacy of *that*, it seemed absurd to hide behind walls just to sleep and scratch ourselves and whatnot.

So once my zee-spec lenses had gone transparent, I could see clear across the wardroom into Rapisardi's cabin. He, too, seemed lost in VR somewhere; he was angled at forty-five degrees to my vertical, and facing the side of his cabin rather than the doorway, but from what I could see his eyes looked fixed on distant objects. His hands wandered through the air, doing God knows what. Not working equations, certainly. Maybe it was a dance.

There's sometimes a delayed reaction to reality on emergence from VR; the colors aren't quite as bright, the sounds not quite as crisp, and the brain can be surprisingly reluctant to accept the degradation as anything other than a mistake.[3]

But then your vision and hearing synch up with the other senses, smell and touch and taste and balance, and the subtler ones

---

3. This phenomenon also turns out to have an ugly technical term attached: "simulator lag."

like proporesis, your limbs' perception of their own positions, and suddenly the intensity of it all hits you like a drug, and you get this tremendous urge to interact. Especially with people still in the VR, who haven't yet shared your rush.

This is my long-winded way of saying I felt like talking to Rapisardi, and didn't mind disturbing him to do it.

"What are you reading?" I called out to him in a loud voice. "Hey, Sudhir."

He looked around blindly for a moment.

"Sudhir."

Resignedly, he motioned windows closed, turned to face me.

"What are you reading?" I asked again.

"Oh. Well. It's a . . . Well, it's a sim I'm writing." He looked embarrassed.

"Ideation?" I asked with a conspiratorial smile.

The suggestion appeared to make him uncomfortable. "It's not that, no. Architecture, I suppose you could say. I'm hypothesizing, well, a null-gravity city."

"What, in orbit or something?"

"Yes, very high orbit, either around Jupiter or around the sun. The idea being to minimize gravitational gradient. For true micro-gravity, you understand?"

I didn't, but I nodded anyway, encouraging him to go on.

He still looked embarrassed. "Well, you know, I got the idea in Saint Helier. Three centigee is not much, but even that minimal gravity had forced innumerable design compromises. In true micro-gravity the place could have looked like the inside of a stomach, wrinkled and folded back on itself many times, for, you see, maximum usable surface area. Ceilings are such a frightful waste."

"So you're doing away with them," I said, politely amused. "You think people will want to live that way?"

He seemed to shrink back into himself. "It's just an amusement, freund. Some people might choose it, yes, but irrelevantly, because no one is going to build this city. I'm simply bored."

"Build it yourself," said Darren Wallich.

Rapisardi and I turned to see him filling the hatchway between bridge and wardroom.

"Pardon?" said Rapisardi.

"Build it yourself," Wallich repeated. "If we ever get back home, it's not inevitable that we fall back into our old ruts. You could change careers, become a city planner. Put some finance together, who knows what you could accomplish?"

"The Immunity needs me."

Wallich laughed. "The Immunity is getting along without you right now, freund. They'll manage."

"Do *you* plan to change jobs?" I asked him.

He frowned, rolled his tongue around inside his mouth for a few moments. "Well, that would be tough to say. I've never been sure exactly what my job is."

"Doctor?" I prompted. "Technical lead? Spaceship captain?"

"Hell, I've done a lot more than just that."

Looking at his expression when he said that, not grouchy or boastful but just sort of quietly self-satisfied, I felt a stab of envy. Since I was fifteen, Immune society had never found any use for me outside the shoe factory. As if running a paste-and-stitch press were somehow my only talent? And then I blinked, remembering where I was. Oh yeah. Mission correspondent. Lucky me: I had *one* other talent, and it had brought me here.

Wallich, who was of course only about two meters away, caught something in my expression then. He must have interpreted it pretty well, because what he said was, "You know I've been meaning to say, Strasheim, you did an okay job back there. You might just have a future crewing spaceships."

I snorted. "Lucky me. I'm having *so* much fun on this little expedition of yours. Thank you, though. The sentiment is . . . appreciated. I'm afraid I've been seriously neglecting my other job."

He shrugged. "No transmitter."

"No, but I can still record. I brought along fifty blank slates in my personal baggage, and so far I've only used twelve."

Wallich leaned back, crossed his arms. "Okay, we'll use the rest of them. What'd you have in mind?"

"Well, I've interviewed every member of the crew but you. Would you mind answering a couple of questions?"

"Are you recording right now?"

"Yes."

I wished he hadn't asked that; his whole manner changed, going stiff and self-conscious and distinctly nonphotogenic. Playing to the cameras was one thing when he had a job to hide behind, quite another when he was simply supposed to be himself. I knew the syndrome well. Thinking it best to disarm him now, I said, "Don't worry, I'll block out the face to protect your identity."

He laughed, relaxing a little. "Yeah, great. Sure, okay, I'll answer some questions. I was born in Maine, Evacuated right after my twenty-eighth birthday. Spent five years as a busboy and five more as a bartender before the sky fell down."

"Really? I wouldn't have expected that."

"What, bartending? I used to love it. You spent a lot of time with your hands wet, washing glasses and stuff, but people just loved you. Everyone loves a bartender. Even teetotalers. I was working my way through school, though. Wasn't going to do it forever."

"What did you expect to do instead?"

He frowned again. "You know, I'm not really sure. In the last few years, there, job descriptions had gotten sort of surreal. Bioprogrammer, system reductivist, stuff like that. But I was majoring in organic chemistry."

"Convenient," I said.

"Not really. Half my class were stoned to death in the riots."

"Oh. I'm sorry."

He laughed. "Yeah, poor me. Truth be told, I haven't thought about that stuff in years; it was sort of lost in the shuffle at Evacuation time. I figured out early that things weren't getting any better, so I packed a bag and drove six hours to the spaceport. Didn't even call my parents. I was one of the first thousand Evacuees, so early that there were still empty seats on my flight."

I waved a hand at him, indicating that that was about enough on the Evacuation. We all had our sad tales to tell, and nobody much wanted to listen. Hope for the future, that was what people tuned in for. That and bedroom scandal. I switched gears abruptly: "When did you have the tickle capacitor implanted? And why? That must still be a very rare procedure."

"It is," he agreed, laugh lines creasing deeply. "There've only been five, of which I was second. Happened four years ago. As for why, all I can say is people respond to me better this way." He grinned broadly. "I feel better, too."

Time to take a risk. "You must know how annoying it is at times. Does it bother you?"

This time his laugh was sly. "Sure. But I could say and do the exact same things my old way, and I assure you, you'd be a lot more annoyed. Some people are just born without a funny bone, and the world is *not* sympathetic. So I took matters into my own hands."

"That's a very enlightened stance," I said sincerely. "I'm sure a lot of people would just have blamed the world and gone about their business."

"I'm sure a lot of people do," he agreed.

"So what does it feel like? Has your whole personality changed?"

He shook his head. "No, I'm exactly the same inside. It feels almost exactly the same as being tickled. It isn't *funny*, per se, but it makes it a lot easier to laugh at other things. I'm poised on the brink of it all the time."

"Don't you get used to that, eventually?"

"Nope. The unit works on multiple overlapping cycles, so at a given time I never know what the sensation level is going to be. If I'm in a bad enough mood the unit can sometimes exacerbate it, like when you punch people out for trying to cheer you up, but I always have the option of disabling it. I don't suppose it's much like a real sense of humor, but it gets me by."

He snickered, as if at some private thought.

"What's the first thing you're going to do," I asked, "if you ever get back home?"

"The first? Decontamination."

"Well, okay, the second."

"Quarantine."

I chuckled with him. "All right, look, you've been released and you're out on the street and you're a totally free man. You can do whatever you want. So what do you choose?"

"The tavern," Rapisardi called out.

Wallich smiled. "Tavern. Hmm. Actually, I think I'd take a nice hot bath, dress up in my fanciest clothes, and head straight for work. It just kills me, thinking how mucked up things must be getting back there without me."

"So much for not falling into the old ruts."

"Well, yeah. But I do like my work, you have to remember."

"Because it's important?"

He laughed. "Because *I* am, I think."

"Aha," I said, pouncing on that. "The truth at last: we have a powermonger in our midst. Does it please you to boss people around?"

"Oh, immensely," he said, and winked.

"Great," I acknowledged, in my this-is-the-end-of-the-interview tone. "Well, that was very helpful. Thank you very much."

"Is that it?" he asked, surprised.

"For now, yeah. It usually works out better if I ask questions in multiple sittings. I get more spontaneity that way. The viewers like it, anyway." Plus, this didn't seem to be heading in a particularly exciting direction. I'd try him again in a different, less reflective mood.

"Well, hell," Wallich said, still grinning, "I could have *mailed* you that stuff. Ask me something hard."

"Well, all right, one more. What do you think is going on with this mission? Why do you think all this stuff is happening to us?"

That gave him pause. He clucked a few times, then said, slowly, "There's nothing like a mystery to bring out the extremes in people. Whatever you don't know, well, people just fill that in with whatever they want most to believe. In a way, it's the classic problem pioneers have always faced—every mystery we strip away knocks over one more superstition, one more convenient or comforting belief, and are people grateful about that? Not the ones that stand to lose from it."

"So you think this is all about money? Or power?"

"Well, probably not as simple as that. The Immunity's applecart is a precarious load, and I guess people aren't eager to see it tipped, even for a good cause."

"I see. Can I quote you on that, next time we see Lottick?"

He laughed.

Jenna Davenroy, who had appeared in the engine room hatchway, spoke up: "Let's go back to the part about him being annoying."

We all laughed at that, until Lehne, whose sleeping feet stuck partway out his cabin door, growled for us to quiet down, at which point we laughed all the harder.

I suppose it seems sort of shocking in retrospect, all of us sitting around like that, not minding the ship. That's the one advantage of running out of options, I guess: when anything you do is more likely to hurt than help, goofing off becomes a pretty viable plan.

Not to mention an okay way to spend your final hours, much better then working yourself—literally—to death.

Later that day, Lehne and I were on the bridge. There wasn't much to do except watch the hull slowly erode, which was a lot like watching grass grow, but the outside view, at least, had changed. Transient megastructures seemed to be features mainly of the upper Mycosystem; down here the bulk of our encounters were with objects Lehne called "Veller bodies"—tangled strands of TGL structure a thousand kilometers long, ten or fifty or a hundred wide, with long tails pointed down at the sun and wispy, flowerlike appendages pointed up at interplanetary space. At any given time there were hundreds of these things visible, transparent as smoke but glowing spectrally in the sunlight, and if you caught one just right, the stars shining through it would turn into patterns of little white rings.

Every now and then, a petal would break off one of the flowers and tumble—very, very slowly—in the general direction of up. I asked Lehne if these would go on to become trans-megs, but he denied it.

"Melt away in an hour," he said. "Ten trillion little solar sails pushing data spore packages. Some of them might link up again later. Probably will, but the trans-megs supposedly accrete mostly from material falling *down*. Spores, dust, comets . . . Doesn't take more than a couple of inner-system passes to ablate comets away to nothing, brake the constituents with light pressure. Nothing escapes but spores; net mass transfer is downward. Over geologic time, this should prove significant."

Hmm.

From the wardroom, I thought I heard Davenroy's voice, grunting loudly about something.

Fiddling with camera dots, I managed to pull up an image of Venus, whose orbit we would shortly be crossing. The planet was nowhere near us, fully forty degrees ahead in its orbit, but it hadn't slipped behind the sun, and wouldn't if we stayed on this trajectory, and I was aware that our current vantage gave us a full fifty percent view of the daylit planet. From above, from the Immunity or the Gladholds, the planet would never appear as anything more than a sliver, so the opportunity was unique, and worth taking advantage of.

The image was blurry, highly magnified, highly filtered. I found myself grateful for this, because I didn't at all like what I saw. If Earth was a basketball covered in moss, well, Venus was covered in marbles and golf balls and dinner forks, and mold. Barely resembling a sphere, it looked more like some sort of virus or bacillus or unusually lumpy protozoan than a planet. I found myself with fresh questions about the Gladholder telescope image—it had shown an expanse of flat ground surrounded by towering jungle, and here I saw nothing like that. If there were humans down there, in all that lumpy fog and slime, I couldn't imagine where they might be standing.

"Gravity'd crush those structures," Lehne noted, "if they weren't so light. Hard to imagine. Maybe it all started on Earth. Probably did. But *this* is the heart of it, right here. Warm, bright, plenty of raw material ... Planet's almost the size of Neptune these days. Used to be the size of Earth. Mass hasn't changed."

Hmm.

"Where are the people," I asked.

I hadn't expected an answer, but he'd pasted the image on the same spot of wall that I had, and he pointed to it, indicating a crease where two of the great lumps came together. "Here," he said.

"Really? How do you know?"

"Coordinates the Gladholders gave. It's in your own report. Been a couple of weeks, though; might have changed quite a bit since then."

The mind boggled. Even these enormous structures were fleeting in nature, yes, rising like bubbles from the planet's tarry surface, swelling, bursting, swelling again as the weeks rolled past. Behavior that seemed ordered, even planned, but was in fact built up through waves of individual, disconnected, microscopic action. "Emergent behavior," Baucum had called it. There were features like that in Mulch System, too, sun bonnets and twig cutters and a dozen other repeating structures, far more intricate than the gliders and flashes of Conway's Game of Life and yet rising up in exactly the same way, over and over again until the simulation shuddered to a halt.

But Venus was real. No reset button, no variable parameters. Those bubbles, some nearly the size of Ganymede, were at least as solid and physical as the sun's corona, that superheated atmosphere crisscrossed with lines of magnetic force which, even with the solar disc occluded, was easily the brightest object in the sky.

Good old Sun. *There* was one thing the mycora couldn't eat, sure enough, and if anything was going to save our lives this week, that ball of fusion heat was it. We'd be skirting just below the orbit of Mercury, sweeping south of the solar equator on a trajectory that would pop us, after a couple of engine burns, right out of the ecliptic plane, where (Wallich said) nine-hundred ninety-nine thousand nine hundred ninety-nine one-millionths of the Mycosystem's mass was concentrated, and into the much sparser medium of Northern Space. Our momentum would then carry us, over a period of months, back to the ecliptic plane somewhere above the orbit of Mars, and if all went well we would fire our motors with sufficient impulse to bring us back into plane permanently, and circularize the orbit to prevent our tumbling right back into the Mycosystem.

If all went well.

I checked the threat window, saw the enemy ships' estimated ranges marching steadily downward. Must have fired their engines again, put on even greater speed. Did their plans—or their fuel supply—leave any possibility for their own survival? Certainly, Baucum's example showed a blunt willingness to die, and it looked like they weren't going to repeat their earlier mistake, giving us a chance to pull some unexpected maneuver and slip once more from their grasp. Too, their weapons—at least the ones we'd seen—relied on the Mycosystem itself to do the dirty work, so they were not going to let us cross the heat barrier. They were going to catch us just as early as they could. They were going to catch us—I crunched some numbers—in a little over six hours.

Somehow, it was comforting to have a figure.

"They're going to catch us tomorrow morning," I said to Lehne.

"Yup," he agreed.

"Been nice knowing you, I guess."

He shook his head. "Not over yet. Got off Earth, didn't you?

Got back down here, made it this far. That makes you one of the luckiest people that ever lived, so keep it in mind. Me, I plan on getting home."

I had to admire the sentiment, if not the rigor of the supporting logic. "Do you have a picture of your family?" I asked, struck with the sudden desire to see the faces that inspired such optimism.

"Sure." He poked the air between us, slid a finger sideways. My receiving light came on and the picture appeared, compressed to an icon in my lower-right quadrant.

I opened it, and the family appeared in a larger window, three-dimensional and fully colored behind the cartoon frame, but static, unmoving as statues, their smiles frozen. Funny, I'd hardly ever seen Tosca Lehne smile, but there in the picture he looked about as happy as I've ever seen anyone look, not posed or stagey but caught, it seemed, in the middle of a funny story. He faced forward, shoulders square, confronting the world directly. His wife stood in front, nearly facing him with her body but looking over one shoulder at the camera. She wasn't pretty, exactly, but she had a round, kind face that appealed in less superficial ways. DORIS ELAINE, the annotation named her. The gleam of love was there in her eyes, subtle but quite unmistakable.

One of her hands rested lightly on her husband's chest, the other on the shoulder of the boy, FRANK TOSCA, standing between them. Two years old? Four? I'd long ago lost my ability to figure the ages of children, but this one appeared slightly bored, slightly irritated, shrinking away a bit from his mother's hand. His eyes were on something behind me, something not terribly interesting, but I saw he was leaning backward, putting weight against the warmth of his parents' bodies. They had all dressed up for the occasion, in flimsy, uncomfortable clothes of the sort people almost never wore in the Immunity. But they looked nice.

It was, in all, a perfectly ordinary holograph, of the sort you used to see all the time. Most of human nature, I think, is encapsulated in pictures like these.

"I can see why you're eager to live," I said.

He smiled at the compliment. "You worry too much, Strasheim. There are patterns in life. Not everything happens for a purpose, but purpose arises from the things that happen. Key is to blend yourself with patterns that include the things you want. That's called happiness."

Hmm. I'd have to think about that. I closed the family portrait and looked back at Venus, at the patterns and purposes unfolding there. I wondered, not for the first time, why Wallich wasn't up here admiring the view with us. Not that he couldn't do just as well from his cabin, I supposed, but it was so much easier when you had direct access to the controls . . .

But then Davenroy's voice drifted forward again, groaning, yelping, louder than before and twice as difficult to ignore, and suddenly I knew what Wallich was up to.

"You want to play some chess?" I asked Lehne.

He agreed, then proceeded to flatten me four games out of four. "You want to try a different game?" he finally asked, not apologetic or condescending, just making the offer.

"Do you know 'Twenty Questions'?"

"Heard of it."

"Think of a word or object."

"Okay."

"Is it animal, vegetable, or mineral?"

He shrugged. "Neither."

"Is it a mycorum?"

"Yes."

I sighed. "Maybe we don't have to play a game. We could just sit here and . . . appreciate being alive."

"Suits me," Lehne said, and so for a while that was exactly what we did. Until a red URGENT MESSAGE light flashed on my zee-spec, that is, and Sudhir Rapisardi's face appeared center screen, looking stricken.

"We have a problem," he said. "A big one. I think the Temples of Transcendent Evolution have maybe been correct all along!"

TWENTY THREE

THE VECTOR TO HELL

I wasn't at all sure what to make of a comment like that. The Temples were right? Right about what, about killing innocent people?

"Right about what?" Lehne asked.

Rapisardi's face flushed darker. "After Strasheim teased me about ideation, I decided I really should go back and do some real work. It bothered me that I had such an easy time making weapons from those detectors. Just a simple code change! It really shouldn't have been that easy, and there were parts of the code that I didn't personally geek. Some other people, some of Lottick's people, stepped in to customize it for compatibility with *Louis Pasteur*'s control systems. That was where I found it. Listen, an inversion of the ladderdown function about the B-axis will turn the field inside out—that's what makes a bomb—and I found that two of the landing control system's feedback loops could be adjusted to interfere constructively, in a way that would produce exactly this effect."

"I'm not sure I understand," I said.

He waved his hands impatiently. "When the detectors do their thing, logging a replication event, these loops will creep closer into phase. After fifty events, enough to be sure what's really happening, the wave peaks match almost perfectly. After that, there's one more failsafe: the low-frequency alarm pulse directed at listening posts in the Immunity. The, ah, intended purpose of the detector package.

"These pulses are logged by neighboring units, and if a detector has already received a neighbor's pulse at the time its control loops fall into close phase, its sensors are placed into a sleep mode, and the unit awaits a coded confirmation signal from the Immunity. Once this is received, the control loops fall completely into phase, and the inversion of the power source occurs. This tampering is subtle and clever and very clearly not accidental. I really can't see how they accomplished this without my noticing, but be that as it may, I'm afraid the Temples' hysteria was well founded: we've been dropping live munitions into the heart of the Mycosystem. If the proper signals are sent, you'll end up with hydrogen, iron, and enough waste heat to sterilize the entire Earth."

Oh. Huh. So we *were* on an offensive mission after all? I should have felt stunned, I suppose. Betrayed, misused, whatever. But I guess I'd known all along that there was something schädlich going on, what with all the spies and sabotage and ambushes and such, so in truth I felt almost no surprise at all. In a way, it made perfect sense, being exactly the sort of plan men like Vaclav Lottick would cook up: hit the Mycosystem hard, weaken it, then move a strong Immune system in over the rubble and attempt to establish permanent beachheads. Yeah. It was also exactly the sort of plan that would set off waves of panic in the general public if they heard about it. As Wallich had said, no matter how bad the status quo, people tended to take a dim view of its violent upset.

And why not? We'd seen firsthand what the Mycosystem could do when irritated, when alerted to the presence of a few foreign molecules. Who knew how it might react to the loss of whole planets? And then, of course, there was this business about those planets still possibly being inhabited. That might still be a trick, intended to throw us off balance. If so, it had worked beautifully. But then again, it might be true, and in *that* case, *Louis Pasteur* had been the instrument of genocide, or at least the threat of genocide. But with the public alerted to the Gladholders' discovery, who would dare set off those bombs now?

Maybe that's why the Mycosystem did it, I thought disjointedly. Hostages, human shields. Maybe it was just protecting itself. But that was absurd, of course. Doubly absurd, because even if the Mycosystem had been capable of formulating theories and then acting on them with such a deeply *human* insight, it still couldn't know *Pasteur*'s true mission, when we had not known it ourselves.

So that left only one question: had Darren Wallich been in on the secret?

As if on cue, he appeared in the hatchway, his hair and uniform in disarray.

"I heard," he said.

I studied him, looked hard at the eyes behind his zee-spec lenses. "Did you know about this, sir?"

"No," he said firmly. "I did not. I assume Lottick must have, though. The fact that he didn't tell me . . ." He trailed away.

I couldn't find any trace of guile there, couldn't pin any particular suspicion on him. He'd known Lottick well, worked closely with him, but so had a lot of people. It didn't have to mean anything. I decided, for the moment, to believe him.

I *did* see a more personal shame in those eyes, though, a sharp embarrassment at having been caught, hypocritically, with his pants down. And Davenroy's. Yeah, really, like we weren't going to hear?

"I don't care who you've been sleeping with," I told him truthfully. Anything that increased the net comfort level of the universe was no worry of mine. I wished them both well. But I could see his mortification, his voiceless insistence that he didn't know how it had happened, that it surely wouldn't happen again.

And then his tickle capacitor must have lurched into high gear, because in spite of everything, he laughed. "Ha ha! Ha ha!" It was sort of ugly to watch, undignified, ill befitting a ship's captain, and I would have told him so if the alarm buzzers hadn't come alive to shatter the peace for good.

Receiver alarm. We'd been pinged. Before we'd even taken our seats, our "battle stations," as Wallich called them with full irony, the trajectory analysis program had refined its estimates, and when the second ping came it refined them still further, and then another buzzer sounded. Proximity alarm.

Hindsight filter: when something is coming straight at you, even when you have a clear view of it, you'll generally have a tough time judging range and velocity without an active ping. Particularly when you're not sure about the size of the object, as we surely were not. As it turned out, based on something called "radar cross-sections," we'd made an implicit assumption that the enemy ships were about the size of *Louis Pasteur*, where in fact they were a good deal smaller. Too, in our observations they'd always accelerated at under 0.1 gee, without ever informing us they were capable of more than twice that. We didn't know all this right away—what we knew was that the threat window's "time-to-contact" chronometer had jumped from four hours to two with the first ping, and then to 1:08 with the second.

There was a collective drawing of breath.

The threat window came alive with gas plumes; the enemy ships and their swarm of attendant remotes were firing their engines, and firing them hard.

"Well, here we go," Wallich said, the tremor in his voice betraying not fear but humor, a manic giggle he couldn't quite suppress. "Rapisardi, get ready with that final payload tube. We're going to have to roll out the welcome mat in about fifteen minutes."

Third ping. Time-to-contact: 0:57. But the radar probe was already blooming, its signature smearing as it shot out tendrils of hungry mycostructure. Shot them out *fast*. Technogenic life, I knew, existed in a realm two or three or even four orders of magnitude faster than its organic predecessors, and down here at the very lower reaches of the Mycosystem it seemed one more order had been gained. Sunlight: bright, swollen, hot with proton radiation. Whatever doesn't kill you makes you stronger, yeah, and the bloom that exploded out of that little probe must have been very close to death indeed.

The tendrils snaking out of it had grown dozens of kilometers in only a few seconds, grown them mainly downward in the direction of the sun so that they looked like fingers reaching out for *Louis Pasteur*, looked like they might actually make it across that gulf . . . But then a tenth of the way across, the probe ran out of mass, the bloom's expansion halting as suddenly as it had begun, leaving behind a structure larger and more intricate than a trans-meg, damn near as large as the flower end of a Veller body. I wondered at the chemistry involved, wondered that atoms and molecules could be made to rearrange themselves so quickly and so completely.

I'd done an experiment as a child, once, peeling an orange in a remote corner of the house, well away from Momma. Her nose was well tuned to the smell of oranges, and if you peeled one she'd come over and demand a third of it as "fruit tax." This time, determined to hide it from her and so, sneakily, to escape taxation, I was surprised instead to hear her call out, "Somebody's eating oranges!" Right away, with no delay at all. Those atoms and molecules of orange had diffused through the air, somehow finding their way around corners, down hallways and staircases and straight into Momma's nose in a mere fraction of a second. So who knew, really, how fast these things could go?

"Ships are releasing some sort of spray in our direction," Lehne cautioned.

"Complementin?"

"Unknown. Microscopic particles in water solution, definitely. Haptens. Probably it's complementin."

"Time to contact?"

"Uh, twenty minutes."

"Okay," Wallich said, still suppressing that laugh, "Davenroy, please engage the engines. Rapisardi, vent reserve tank two, stat."

Now *there* was a tactic you had to love: taking a third of our precious water supply and dumping it overboard into space. I opened an exterior window as the engines groaned themselves awake, and then the dump valve was open and the water was tumbling out behind us, big globs breaking up into droplets, falling away slowly, some of them blasting into high-velocity mist as they contacted the engine exhaust. The dump went on for thirty seconds, and by the end of it the space behind us was sizzling both in visual and on the threat board, little abortive blooms seizing up the hydrogen and oxygen and then halting when they found no other building blocks, no precious carbon or nitrogen or sulfur, no metals except dissolved impurities in the water itself.

The idea, I guess, was to give the complementin something to hit, something to slow it down or deflect it so less could get through to strike us. Seemed fairly half-baked to me, but I supposed it was better than nothing, and *that*, meine freunde, was the entire measure of our battle plan.

Somewhere around that point, the threat board went nuts. Another bloom back among the enemy ships, a big one this time. Not a drone, not a probe, but one of the *actual ships* was converting—its t-balance somehow, alarmingly, failing to protect it. And then in a flash I knew why, knew what was happening: the ships were accelerating into their own complementin spray, getting more of the stuff on themselves than they were ever likely to get on us.

The realization shocked me to my core: they weren't just angry, weren't just willing to sacrifice, they were *desperate* to keep us away from that heat barrier. There must have been dozens of safer, saner options available to them, but this was the one they'd chosen, the one they'd determined was most likely to stop us here and now. Talk about half-baked tactics! What could drive them to such an extreme? I mean, they were fanatics, yes, obviously, but even fanatics would normally try to maximize their advantage, to minimize their loss.

What was it they thought they were protecting? Their homes and families? The people on Earth and Venus? The Mycosystem itself?

Baucum had admired the Mycosystem, I knew. Not loved it, maybe, but respected its power and intricacy, its longevity in the face of mathematical improbability. *Very nearly divine,* she'd said, almost her dying words. Because the system never reached a halt state? Because unlike cellular automaton models, it steered clear of extinction and crystallization and simple repetition, stayed locked in a state of eternal chaotic growth? Mulch System could only do that if you intervened manually. Even random-number fuzz was not sufficient to keep it alive; somehow, it needed the intervention of a conscious hand.

Cold tendrils lapped up and down my spine. Did the Mycosystem need a guiding hand as well? Did it *have* a guiding hand? Jesus, the computing ability of a cubic millimeter of bloom exceeded the combined might of all the calculating machines human beings had ever built. And in the Gladholds there were already computers smarter than mice, computers capable of conceptualizing their own existence, of writing stories about themselves.

My god.

"Davenroy," Wallich said, "wait five seconds and then cut the engines. Strasheim, watch your goddamn board. If you let that system crash again I'll nail your head to the wall."

"You want to beat on him, be quick about it," Lehne countered, eyeing the chronometer, "or lose your chance for good."

Reluctantly, I drew my attention to the allocation system for a few precious seconds. It was a mess. Everyone was quietly panicking, doing exactly what I'd told them not to, so in disgust I wiped the job stack clean and set everything on a first-come-first-serve basis. Frightfully inefficient, yes, but also very unlikely to fail or crash.

"Davenroy," Wallich said, "switch the engines to oxygen production and go to attitude program E-1. Paint the sky with it, stat."

Here was another freaky idea: normally the engines laddered their uranium fuel down to iron and hydrogen, and then cascaded the hydrogen back up to iron again, releasing the theoretical maximum energy from every single atom. But if you were willing to eat the energy loss, you could tune the thing to produce any element you wanted. Atomic oxygen, for example, which could react with complementin molecules, damaging or neutralizing them. Which could even oxidize unsuspecting mycora, gifting them with an atom or two of building material but wreaking structural harm far out of proportion with that slim benefit. The engine spat out "ionized" nuclei, I'd been told, nuclei almost completely devoid of electrons, which made them very reactive indeed, possibly reactive enough even to blast damaging microflaws into a t-balance hull. As weapons go this was better, at least, than water. But it wasted fuel, another vital and irreplaceable resource. We were throwing our own lifeblood in the enemy's face, hoping somehow to buy enough time to reach the heat barrier without . . .

Damn it, there were too many distractions here. I tried to reconstruct my fragile chain of thought: math and the philosophy of fear. *Was* the Mycosystem somehow responsible for its own maintenance? Did it possess that inward-looking eye, that self-knowledge that permitted it to guide its own destiny? I shook my head; the question was probably unanswerable, certainly irrelevant at the moment. Of key importance was that *the Temples of Transcendent Evolution must believe it was true.* And they must have believed, somehow, that we still represented a terrible threat, to the Mycosystem, to the flow and balance of life—all life?—in the solar system.

"Hey," I asked of no one in particular, "what would happen if you triggered a ladderdown reaction in the sun?"

"Ladderdown?" Davenroy's voice answered. "Nothing, why?"

"Cut the chatter," Wallich advised.

"What about cascade fusion?" I pressed.

"Well, that would liberate a store of fusion energy all at once, and leave a cool lump of iron where there used to be hot hydrogen and helium. How big a reaction are we talking about, dear?"

"Like from one of our detector packages."

Everyone stopped for a moment. That thought had *registered*.

"What are you getting at, Strasheim?" Davenroy asked.

"How big would the explosion be?"

"The inverted field," Rapisardi said, "forms an infinitesimally thin sphere just over three hundred meters in diameter. That might cut through as many as ten-to-the-thirtieth atoms."

"Less than that in the photosphere, I would think," Davenroy told him. "Still, you'd release the energy of thousands—possibly millions—of solar flares."

"Doing what to the Mycosystem?" I asked. No one had an answer for me.

Scharfblick, the awakening, the moment when it all becomes obvious. *I* had the answer: it would murder the Mycosystem. Not destroy every single mycorum, certainly; it seemed to me that even if the sun *exploded* there'd still be shelter available behind the planets, or in the outer system, or wherever. *Some* spores would survive, fall back in, start blooming. But the continuity would have been interrupted, the hideous clockwork precision kicked all to pieces. The guiding hand burned away, leaving only mindless matter behind, the festering corpse of the Temples' pet demigod. Maybe another mind would arise from the wreckage, or maybe not, but either way the original mycodeity would be lost.

Deicide. God-murder.

Was it true? Could it really happen that way? I didn't know and didn't care; in a them-or-us situation, I was certainly going to pick "us." Given a choice between the death of the Mycosystem and the death of the Immunity, there *was* no choice. The point was that the Temples must also know this, must also see this as obvious, even if they didn't agree with it. The self-sacrificing martyrs in those enemy ships believed it, believed that we Pasteurites had both the power and the motive to strike. Here was a threat worth countering, a cause—in their minds—worth dying for. Here was a more or less logical explanation for all that had happened to us. I'd heard no others.

And maybe—the thought chilled me right through—we could actually follow through on the threat. Lottick would probably demand this of us, if the questions were posed. A chance to end it all, a chance to drive the system toward a halt state we could deal with. No more refugee existence, no more bowing down before the might of our enemy, waiting grimly for the tide to turn against us again.

"Strasheim, what's going on with my system requests? Watch your damn *board*, man!"

"No time," I said, and dove straight into Mulch System. The automaton rules needed only a little tweaking, here and here and here. Testing: no. Testing again: no. This wasn't working the way I'd hoped it would. But still, the effect I wanted was so *simple* . . .

"Strasheim!"

Tweak and tweak and then test again. And again. *Oh,* I thought, *this rule's interfering with the expansion. Do I need it? No?* I tried another, slightly different rule-set. Yeah, well, close enough. Simple enough. Looks like a flare to me, baby.

"Strasheim, what the hell is wrong with you? What are you hammering the computer with?"

"Captain," I said without exiting Mulch System, "slave your zee-spec to mine. Scratch that; *everyone* slave your zee-specs to mine. I have something very important to show you."

"Have you lost your mind, Strasheim?"

"Nope. I may have finally found it. Let me know when you're in."

"Christ. Okay, I'm in."

"In."

"In."

"Me too. What's this about?"

"Okay," I said, "welcome to Mulch System. The big yellow thing is the sun, the little green speck is us, and the little red-brown balls are all planets. This one—" I flicked on a pointing arrow "—similar to Mercury, is Mulchury, behind which our simulated *Louis Pasteur* is hiding. Note all the red stuff swirling around—that's TGL. Lots of it. Now, when we trigger a million-strength solar flare . . ."

I activated the new rules, watched gravity switch off in one corner of the sun. A huge blob of yellow material, not true star stuff but the same generic "hot" that filled the cores of planets, splurted out into the system, tearing out mycostructure, liquefying planetary surfaces. It didn't take any hard-core mathematical analysis to see things dying out—it was evident everywhere, even in the places the ersatz flare hadn't touched. The data-rich waves that should be sweeping the system end to end, reflecting and refracting and endlessly mutating, driving new spurts of growth and decline and growth again, fell apart into paroxysms. Stains of red gave way swiftly to brown and green, mulch and bare rock taking over.

The system flickered, gasped, collapsed into localized patterns of simple oscillation. It would have died out anyway, sooner or later, but Wallich and the others didn't know that, and anyway in this case the death was very clearly *precipitated* by the flare. Again, it didn't take a genius to see that. But there were four of them here.

I zoomed in on *Louis Pasteur*, ran the sequence again at much higher magnification. Mulchury the size of a house, brown and smooth, untouched by technogenic contagion. The viewer's eye looking along the equator, past the tiny green spaceship-dot to the blank wall far beyond, light-years beyond. All at peace, and then storms of yellow suddenly sweeping the planet, a wall of yellow astronomically huge, breaking apart into threads and whorls and roaring by, leaving the dayside a melted ruin, the nightside scathed only here and there by lashes of solar fire. *Pasteur* herself escaping untouched behind the planet.

I ran it again, this time focusing on the giant planet Johnpiter, which, along with its moons, weathered the upper reaches of the storm without serious harm. Surface habitats were probably in trouble, but there would be time to Evacuate those. Down below the ice, all would be safe and secure.

I had grave doubts about the scientific veracity of the sim; the underlying physics bore little resemblance to those of the real universe. Probably the details were utterly wrong. Maybe *Pasteur* wouldn't survive, maybe Jupiter and the Gladholds wouldn't. Maybe the whole Mycosystem wouldn't die out like this. Probably not, I guessed. But the sim was just a visual aid, just a rapid, visceral demonstration of what almost certainly *was* true: that we had, within our grasp, the power not only to tear the heart out of the Mycosystem, but to blast away the bulk of its body as well. Lottick's plan was a feeble joke by comparison, spitballs against a raging elephant.

"This," I said, not giving anyone a chance to speak, "is almost certainly what the Temples are afraid of. This is what they're trying to prevent. There are solid reasons to believe that the Mycosystem *is* intelligent, *is* self-aware. Renata Baucum believed it, enough to give up her life, and whether or not *we* believe it, or even care, the Temples seem inclined to act on this theory as if it were God's own truth. And on ourselves as if we were the servants of absolute evil."

Set at maximum speed, the sim ran quickly. We'd all been in here twenty or thirty seconds, no more, and rather than invite scrutiny, invite questions whose answers I didn't know or didn't like,

I released everyone's zee-specs and closed up Mulch System. It had served its purpose.

Exiting back into reality, I became aware of a lump under my leg, something caught between my seat and myself. I fished it out: the Gladholder fear doll. Slick and squidgy in my hand, its blank face a leather parody of terror.

"I'm *afraid*," it insisted quietly. But that was a lie, a recording; if there *were* machines that could feel, this was surely not one of them, and its mimicry served only to cheapen the genuine product. Fear? What the hell did it know? Outrage seized me for a moment, and with an angry flick I sent the thing spinning away.

Darren Wallich began to laugh.

"Cut it out!" I shouted, turning to him, glaring him down. "Turn that damn thing off! It's time for a command decision. Humorless, no tickling. I mean it."

I had no right to speak to him that way. I didn't try to excuse it, and still don't. But for some reason he listened, and complied. The change in his face was marked and immediate, muscles loosening here, tightening there, worry lines furrowing his brow.

"Speak," he said coldly.

"Another ship has bloomed," Lehne said. "And the complementin will hit us in eight minutes."

"Shut up. Strasheim, what's on your mind?"

I gulped. Time to take the final plunge. "Sir, there's no telling what lengths the Temples will go to to protect the Mycosystem. They *worship* it, yes, they believe it to be some sort of hyperintelligence, maybe a direct link to God himself. It doesn't matter whether that's true; what matters is that the Immunity *really may* have the power they attribute to it. Not just to hang on indefinitely at Jupiter, or climb aboard a starship and fly away, but to *take back the inner system itself.* To murder their god. This places the Immunity in very grave danger even if that power does not exist, or is never exercised."

"Yes?" Wallich said, still not getting my drift.

I paused, collecting my thoughts. Self-sacrifice seemed to be quite the rage these days, and really, what chance did we have of surviving all the way to the heat barrier? The Temples' ships were falling all over themselves to die, to take us out with them. And if you can't beat them . . ."Sir, whether or not the Mycosystem has a right to exist, whether or not it has the right to destroy us or we have the right to destroy it, we're in possession of *critical information* which the Temples are going to act on whether or not the Immunity is informed. We can *do* this thing, right now, but there's no telling what the consequences might be. That sim of mine doesn't have the fidelity to help us know this, meaning we'd be gambling with the lives of every living thing in the solar system."

Wallich nodded. "Agreed. I'd never authorize it."

"We could simulate the consequences precisely," Rapisardi objected.

"No," Wallich said tersely, with a dismissive wave of the hand which Rapisardi of course couldn't see. "It would take hours, days, maybe longer. We've got *minutes* before these people kill us. Think of something else."

I cleared my throat. "Captain, I recommend . . . Jesus. I recommend that we compose a detailed message, including images, science readings, speculations, and my own Mulch World sim, and we transmit it back to the Immunity. Whatever they decide to do, it's . . . our duty not to take this information to our graves."

He eyed me humorlessly, visibly weighing my words. "You propose suicide?"

Suicide, yeah, that was what it came down to. One more group of fanatics, willing to sacrifice ourselves for some vague perception of the greater good. And yet, there *were* things worth dying for. The philosophy that counted human life as *infinitely* precious had always been, in my opinion, an erroneous one. Human life was finite in scope, finite in duration; we all had to die sometime. In fact, our lives might be so precious to us precisely *because* they were finite, and could in fact be traded, sure as a gram of uranium, for the things we valued even more. Things like hope.

And it wasn't like we had a real long time left to live, anyway.

"Yes, sir, I do."

Wallich didn't laugh, didn't smile, didn't react at all.

"I've seen a lot of shit down here I didn't expect to see," he muttered. "Lately I've been feeling a lot of doubt, about things I used to know for sure. These issues need to be thought through, calmly, by wiser heads. By *all* the heads. Yes, do it, send the message. Stat. Ladies and gentlemen, I'd like to tank . . . like . . . I'd like to *take* this opportunity to thank you all for excellent service."

Yeah, you're welcome. I had most of the stuff for the message lying around already, in buffers waiting to be archived and collaged. The speculation part I just sort of blurted out in a voice recording:

"Citizens of the Immunity, the Mycosystem may in fact be conscious. Humans on Venus, AIs in the Gladholds, fantastically huge computing power . . . Whatever, I don't really have time to explain. The Temples regard it as a conscious being, an intelligent one, and at this point I'm willing to grant them the benefit of the doubt. *They* believe we intend to destroy it, destroy the Mycosystem, with a solar cascade reaction. We may in fact be capable of this, but we do *not* intend to attempt it, and are sending this message, at the cost of our lives, as proof of our sincerity. Please use this information wisely. This is John

Strasheim, Mycosystem Mission One correspondent aboard the Immune ship *Louis Pasteur* . . . signing off."

After that, I gathered up the other message elements and wrapped them in a transmission packet, and then, trying not to think too much about what I was doing, I fired up the transmitter, set the frequency back to high-microwave, and set the data rate at maximum.

"On your command, sir," I said.

Beside and above me, Tosca Lehne looked shattered. Never to see his little boy again, never to see anything; all chances zeroed, all patterns terminated. He opened his mouth for a moment, but didn't, finally, object. What could he say?

"Go," Wallich ordered.

I pressed the button, and of course nothing visible happened right away. You can't see or feel a microwave transmission. But then the replication alarms went crazy, and then I guess the complementin hit us a few seconds later, or else the microwaves overcame any protection the t-balance hull might otherwise have provided, because not only did the hull start blooming on the outside, but some determined mycorum tunneled its way straight through the wall of the bridge, blossoming in a little rainbow flower beside my head.

I paused for a moment, frozen in place, and then let out a scream like I never expect to again. Fumbling with my harness, I managed to release it. The engines had stopped firing at some point, though, and in null gravity there was nothing to pull me away from the bloom. I pushed against my chair, very nearly sending myself *into* the pulsing technogenic mass, but checked the momentum in time and sailed off in the other direction, down past Wallich's legs.

Lehne was scrambling, too, cranking up the hull temperature

and then hurling himself at the emergency locker. He came away with a welding torch, fumbled to light it, fumbled again.

I hadn't stopped screaming yet. There was a part of me that wished I would, a part that was embarrassed at making such a fuss when this had, after all, been my idea. But there was another part of me that remembered the examples of Tug Jinacio, of Renata Baucum, of the planet Earth itself, and wanted no part of *that* death. Pressing a button was easy; holding calm and still while the consequences unfolded was, well, not.

But the mycora weren't eating me, not yet. I looked up at the bloom and just sort of scratched my head. Earlier the mycoric tendrils had shot across space like cannon fire, covering kilometers in moments. This one, though, seemed hard-pressed to cross a space of centimeters. The flower had grown slightly, rearranged itself into more of a bumpy pillow shape, and the bulkhead behind it was definitely eroding away, pitting and shrinking back like beer foam. But mostly, the bloom was *filling in*, turning solid, looking profoundly unlike any other bloom I'd seen or heard of.

Lehne finally got his torch lit.

"Stay away from it," Wallich commanded. "Burn it if it starts to grow again, but otherwise stay back."

The look on his face was odd, grim and yet thoughtful. He was, I realized, conducting an experiment. With our lives. Well, actually our lives were forfeit anyway.

"What are you doing?" I asked him. Apparently I'd stopped screaming.

"It looks like a face," he said. And he didn't laugh, and he wasn't joking. I looked, and yeah, it did look a lot like a face.

"You see shapes sometimes," I said, quoting his own words back at him. "Pincushions and bunny rabbits. Like looking at clouds, you know?"

Aft somewhere, I heard Rapisardi and Davenroy shrieking.

"It really does look like a face," Wallich insisted.

I looked again, and this time I couldn't deny it: the structure had a forehead, a nose, depressions where the eyes and mouth should be . . . As I watched, it grew lips and eyelids, and its color faded from rainbow transparency to something pale and opaque, like cream. A somewhat normal-looking bloom still surrounded it, a shuddering rainbow cloud pulling material atom by atom from the surrounding bulkhead, but the thing in the center was undeniably a human face. Female, in fact, and rather pretty.

I started screaming again when it opened its eyes.

CONNECTION

The face seemed ready to scream right back at me, its mouth opening, pale tongue wriggling inside. But instead it croaked, closed its
mouth, opened it again, and spoke:

"Understand? Understand?" it said, the voice gravelly and hoarse
but clearly recognizable. "Language, speech. I am speaking with you."

"What the bloody hell is going on here?" Wallich demanded,
drifting up to confront the thing, well, face to face.

"Understand?" It coughed again.

"Yes, I understand you. What . . . What the hell *are* you?"

"Unpacked," the face said, seeming to gasp the word. "Intelligence, human, Earth. Difficulty now, this is not working as intended. Limited state, confusing."

Wallich seemed less at a loss than Lehne or myself, but that's not saying much. All he had to say was, "What?"

"Earth. Understood? Earth? I am from. Human."

"You're a human from Earth?"

"Yes!" A smile, beaming out from that cream-white face. The lips, I noted, had begun to redden, the eyes to fill in with ghostly colored pupils. Brown. "A human from Earth, now Unpacked."

"Unpacked?"

"Change of form, yes. Rearrangement, recomposition, considerable expansion."

"Are you the *Mycosystem*?" Wallich tried. He looked just about ready to explode from shock.

"Understanding, not," the face said. Its voice had gone smoother, and its tone now was distinctly female, distinctly reassuring. "Please try that again."

"Are you, um, alone?"

Again, the smile. "Not alone, of course not. Billions. All the Unpacked people."

"Billions?" Wallich shook his head, uncomprehending. "Where do you live? We haven't seen you."

"That is very unlikely," the face said, sounding a bit surprised itself. "We are large!"

"Um, how large?"

"Very! Solar system! We overlap, occupy contiguous space. Not the same as before, because we are *Unpacked*. This limited form, this solid flesh, confines. Very few choose to return to this form, this solid flesh, because it *confines*. We choose to remain Unpacked."

Wallich cleared his throat, made an attempt to compose himself, which, given the circumstances, worked out fairly well. "Are you trying to tell me . . . that the Mycosystem consists of . . . what, Unpacked human bodies? Enormous bodies?"

"Mycosystem? There is a system, yes. Not just bodies, no, of course not. We do not have 'bodies' in the sense you probably mean, but there are the complexes which *constitute* us, and the complexes which *support* us."

Wallich absorbed that, became calmer still. Amazingly calm. Was this the persona he'd tried to cover up? This unflappable inner peace? I couldn't see what was so bad about it—dour, yes, but pragmatic. Perfect in a crisis.

"Why have you attacked our cities," he said, "killed our people? This is not acceptable."

"Killed?" asked the face with cheerful, exuberant innocence. "Attacked? Please understand, there are limitations. Speed of wave propagation, strength of materials. The Unpacked mind is great and slow and deliberate at the highest levels, the conscious levels. Your existence is only recently known to us. The complexes which support are not constrained by your existence. You must constrain them. This is not difficult. The information will be provided.

"Let me restart. Hello! It pleases the Unpacked to communicate with you! We have been unable to communicate because of the destruction of support complexes, about which you are very insistent and skilled. The complex you see, this structure of solid flesh, was designed for rapid deployment and maximum recognition. Possible here, close to the sun, because of warmth—excess energy is easy to obtain. Thank you for coming! Communication with remote sites requires infrastructure, which does not exist, which is difficult to create and control. Here, things are faster. Here, I may exist in this form. Therefore, we communicate. Welcome! Apologies for your condition!"

"Apologies?" I said, suddenly finding my voice. "Apologize to the dead."

"Many of your 'dead' have been Unpacked. It is unlikely they would choose to return to a solid form. Very few of us choose this. Others of your dead we could not prevent. You would not let us. You damaged support complexes."

"Well, pardon the intrusion!" I said, fighting off a sudden giddy anger. "What is it you want? To 'Unpack' us?"

"The support complexes will be constrained," she assured me. "This information will be provided. Understand, all that you are is encapsulated also within us. It is no patronization to say, we have concerns you will not comprehend. But your incomprehension and your reluctance are encapsulated and understood. Want? We do not want.

"All harm has been unintended, and will be prevented with your cooperation, but intentional interference will bring intentional harm. This device—" the face glanced around at the ship surrounding it "—is clever. Our systems had great difficulty in isolating it. But the support complexes will be modified to recognize its substance in the future. This is not a threat; barring damage to constituent and support complexes, you are utterly free. Free to conduct your lives in the classical manner, to escape this solar system, to populate the stars. Free to Unpack, if you choose."

I shuddered, my skin prickling. "Is that . . . is that what you want?"

The face looked at me consolingly. "We do not *want*, little one. We have grown beyond it."

Oh, yeah, *that* sounded real appealing.

IF YOU CAN'T
BEAT THEM . . .

It's funny how the pivotal moments of your life slide by just as readily as the trivial ones. The Face conferred on us the sage knowledge
of marking regions of space off-limits to "support complexes," and
then, with little fanfare, withdrew, patching the hole it had come
through, scattering behind us in a cloud of tiny solar sails before we
crossed the dreaded heat barrier. And that was it: the moment of
connection had come and gone, leaving us with little more than another message to beam up to the Immunity. A shorter one, too.

The sheer banality of it astonished me. Our whole way of life had just been shattered, recast, deeply altered in ways we could probably only begin to comprehend, and yet there we were, still stuck on this little ship for the foreseeable future and beyond.

The less said about those long months the better, I think, because if the sunward journey had brought out the best in us, our courage and conviction and our sense of discovery, rest assured that the slow climb back up had brought out the worst.

The gist of the Mycosystem's message? "Hi, you're small and annoying." Ah, but we're fast.

I'll share one last technical term with you: "moonwalker's syndrome." An affliction of early astronauts, and recent ones; once you've been a part of something larger than yourself, larger than you know you'll ever see again, the future ahead gets sort of washed out in the glare. Looking forward becomes difficult—there is no more moon to walk on, no more history to make. The company of those afflicted, sad to say, is often less than charming.

What became of the last enemy ships, I really don't know. Nobody was watching, no instruments recording, when they vanished, taking their swarm of remote devices with them. We did manage to pull ourselves together, though, in time to perform the plane change maneuver at perihelion an hour and a half later. The sun, to my surprise, never grew much larger than a peach, about a third as large as Jupiter would appear from the surface of Ganymede. But considerably warmer and brighter.

We did indeed pop out of the ecliptic plane, to safer vantages from which we could resume unfettered radio contact with home, but it was four long months later that we reentered the ecliptic, circularized, and limped with the last of our fuel to one of the lower Gladholds. Not Saint Helier this time, but a much smaller rock called Saint Gervase, whose language gave fits to Chris Dibrin's translation software, and whose Temples-friendly government re-garded us with, at best, grave suspicion.

From there, it was half a year to Ganymede, and then another half a year in quarantine (no, they didn't let me keep the fruits and spices), and by the time it was over the five of us could barely stand to look at each other. You don't spend two years in a bathroom to-gether and remain friends, it simply doesn't work like that, so once released from confinement we went our separate ways with barely a good-bye nod.

I kept track, though, if for no other reason than a berichter's sense of duty. The Temples of Transcendent Evolution never admit-ted to a formal relationship with our attackers, or with the dozens of bottle-men and -women who'd started the fatal blooms that sent us on our way. They've proven as flexible and nebulous a foe as the Mycosystem itself; the legal actions against them may well stretch on for centuries. Who knows: maybe they *are* innocent.

Vaclav Lottick, for his part, denied all allegations, denied any conspiracy to deploy weapons without the knowledge of the Immu-nity's populace, denied lying to the crew of *Louis Pasteur* or to any-one else. Nonetheless, and considerably to his credit, he resigned his position as head of research. Immune science being a field in sharp decline, one might say he had little to lose anyway, but the fact is, he was neither elected nor appointed to his job, but rather had seen the whole vast structure accrete around him like so much coral. And yes, he was a pillar of our society throughout the bloom years, a re-mote figure but also a bold and brilliant and diligent one whose ex-ample, in retrospect, really did inspire us all. His departure was a deeply symbolic act, marking the definitive end to the era he himself had helped to define, and those who claim otherwise are, quite sim-ply, full of it.

Of *Pasteur*'s crew, only Davenroy found a secure job still waiting for her: ladderdown research, as before. The others accepted figurehead positions for a while before moving on to other pursuits— Lehne in agricultural genetics, Rapisardi as a major player on the starship project, which had already begun to reap the benefits of our shifting economy. Wallich flew, I think, two more minor space missions before settling down to a teaching position at the new university in Ansharton. Tug Jinacio remained dead, and if Renata Baucum had survived her conversion in some vastly altered form, she'd declined to make it evident. The ship, battered, obsolescent, and reeking of backroom politics, was parked in a holding orbit above the moon Europa, where it remains to this day.

The changes. How to discuss them? Ours was the most detailed exchange of information the Unpacked have ever undertaken, and probably this is just as well; those three minutes of conversation rocked Immune society to its core, a salvation from which we may, in some sense, never truly recover. And now we get a word here and there, an enigmatic phrase lifting starward on the solar wind every now and again . . . Is this all the Mycosystem has to offer? Not even the Temples' short-lived probes have managed to return much useful information. Just how slow *are* those Unpacked minds? Slow enough, one hopes, that this apathetia will continue indefinitely, that the next revelation will wait until some of us, at least, have slipped away into the great galactic night.

I, as you're probably aware, never did go back to the shoe factory, but rolled my sleeves up, pulled together some financing, and created the Subscription News Network, which, despite its name, is supported mainly by voluntary donations. Have you sent yours in? Directorship, which turned out to be quite a different thing from the actual reporting to which I'd hoped to dedicate myself, keeps me plenty busy, and this may be why it's taken me so much time to deliver this account, this history for which I'd been contracted on that fateful Ansharton morning so many years ago. But maybe it's more than that. Maybe I knew, maybe I sensed, that the closing chapter simply hadn't come yet, that our story was not complete. Not until Wallich fell ill. A neurodegenerative disorder, pathogen unidentified. Prognosis: terminal.

"I want you to attend the ceremony," he called me up abruptly and said. They were his first words to me in almost thirteen years, delivered in gruff barks and rumbles. In a way, it was touching—he'd turned his sense of humor off just for me, sharing his true face as he'd done so many times on the long journey home. *Remember me?* he seemed to be saying.

By tradition, though, you only get one witness at the ceremony, and his choice of me was significant, a final mark of approval and trust.

"My tale is told," he'd said to me, dry-eyed and somber. "All that's left is the writing it down. You still know how to do that, right?"

I'd sworn off journeying for life, but here was one I couldn't bring myself to refuse. The sway of captains is little affected by time and space, and so it was me in the witness seat that day, watching the screens, watching fifty different views of the inside and outside of Wallich's transition pod fifty thousand kilometers below, down on the fringes of Unpacked space.

He conducted himself with admirable composure, tickle capacitor off, as he disengaged the failsafes one by one and submitted to the confirmation sequence.

"Are you here of your own free will?" the pod asked him.

A clear voice: "Yes."

"Do you have any doubts or questions about the procedure?"

"No."

"Are you absolutely certain this is what you want?"

He smiled wanly, showing off a tremulous hand, the flesh of his balding head ticcing visibly. "Better than death, I think."

"Please answer with an unambiguous yes or no. Are you absolutely certain this is what you want?"

"Yes."

"Acknowledged," the pod said. "Confirmation sequence complete. Verbal authorization is enabled."

There is but one cure for moonwalker's syndrome: to grow beyond it. Wallich drew breath a few times, not apparently dreading the moment but not working to hasten it, either. Finally, he turned to one of the camera dots, looked straight out at me and tipped a crisp salute. Farewell, freund. Then he licked his lips, drawing the event out one moment longer before giving voice to his final word:

"Bloom."